D1228697

THE MAID

THE MAID

Kimberly Cutter

WINDSOR
PARAGON

First published 2010
by Bloomsbury Publishing
This Large Print edition published 2011
by AudioGO Ltd
by arrangement with
Bloomsbury Publishing

Hardcover ISBN: 978 1 445 85752 7
Softcover   ISBN: 978 1 445 85753 4

British Library Cataloguing in Publication Data available

Printed and bound in Great Britain by
MPG Books Group Limited

For Piki, who kept the faith

They promised to lead me to Paradise,
for that was what I asked of them.

—JOAN OF ARC

PRELUDE

In the dream, death is as far off as the mountains. It's a cold, blue winter morning, and she is riding her horse very fast over a field of snow toward a high pine forest, still dim with shadow. Her armor glints in the early light, the steel giant's hands flashing on either side of her horse's mane, but the metal is strangely weightless in the dream. She does not feel it. What she feels instead is the still and brilliant morning, the snow and the speed and the cold air on her cheeks, and inside of her a violent, holy joy that makes her eyes very bright and propels her wildly over the fields toward the enemy forest, snow spraying and glittering beneath her horse's hooves.

Behind the girl rides her army of ten thousand men, all of them eager as she is, united by the same strange and feverish joy as they crash across the winter fields, across a black icy river that winds, shining like a ribbon, through the white land and toward the shadowed stillness of the pines. She can hear them thundering behind her, and hearing them, she knows that they are riding together toward a mad and glorious victory. And she knows too that they are riding toward death. But there is no fear in her this morning. She is seventeen, a peasant, unschooled, simple as a thumb. Fear has no place in her heart yet, though soon enough it will. Soon enough she will be caged, tortured, branded a witch, a whore, a limb of Satan. But on this morning she is simply God's arrow, shot across the winterland, brilliant and savage and divine. Unstoppable.

PART 1

CHAPTER ONE

She awakes in darkness, curled on the cold stone floor of the tower. The stink of urine and rotted straw burning her nostrils. Iron cuffs biting at the sores on her wrists. Quickly she grabs at the receding dream, hoping to pull it back, to wrap herself up once more in its fierce joy. But no, it's too late. The last tendrils slip through her fingers, and she is left in the dark with her guards—three of them inside the cell with her, two out in the hall.

They are all asleep now, in this dim, lonesome hour. Propped in the shadows like dolls with their heads fallen forward and their mouths open, snoring. But soon enough, she knows, they'll be awake. Soon enough the big one, the one they call Berwoit, will grin with his square blue teeth and start in with his taunts. 'Lift up your skirts for us, witch. Show us what you got under there. Is it a cock or is it a pussy?'

It's clear that she'll die soon. She sees this too in her dreams. The enormous, crackling yellow fire in the square, the grinning Bishop, the appalled, delighted crowds. The priest Massieu says it's not true. 'You're safe now,' he whispers. Now that she's repented, she's safe.

Soon, he says, they'll transfer her to a church prison, and there will be no more beatings and no more trial, and eventually, the Goddons will forget about her. The war will end, and she'll be set free. 'Be patient, child,' he says. 'Give them time to forget.'

She feels sorry for Massieu. Knows he's half in

3

love with her. Even with her shaved head and the rough burlap dress the Bishop makes her wear, even with her ribs jutting out like a starved dog's, he looks at her with shining eyes, sneaks her bits of bread and extra cups of water, brings her wormwood salve for her bruises. She'd like to believe him, but she knows it isn't true. They hate her too much, the English. They will not be happy until they dance on her bones.

*   *   *

Often in the night, when she can't sleep, Massieu comes and sits with her. He waits until the guards are snoring, then drags his low wooden stool over to her cell and sits beside her in the darkness. Holds the bars with his big pink hands, gazes at her. Sometimes he reads from the Bible. Other times he sings, jokes, tries to make her laugh. Occasionally he grows daring, asks questions: 'Is it true what they say? Are you a saint?'

CHAPTER TWO

She was twelve the first time she heard the voices. It was in the garden in Domrémy, behind her parents' house. A summer day. Hot and green. A great wind rolling in the air, the country a riot of shaking leaves. She was picking beetles off the cucumber plants, collecting them in an old corked jug. Her father said, 'You just like it because you can sit there and daydream,' but it wasn't true. She liked hunting under the big, rough leaves for the

4

dark little beetles with their black helmets and their scratchy hooked legs. The strange purple and green lights in their armor. Cockroaches disgusted her, but not beetles. Beetles seemed clean and somehow noble, like tiny polished knights.

As she worked, she thought of Catherine, her saint. Catherine whom her mother told about—the bravest one of all. She pictured Catherine tall and slim and very fair, with long heavy gold hair and a pale, secretive spoon-shaped face. She loved Catherine, idolized her, but she was jealous of her too. Jealous of her miracles. Jealous that she had died for her love of God. She thought of all the Romans that Catherine had taught to love God. The Emperor's thousands of soldiers kneeling down suddenly, bowing their heads in prayer, their hearts thrown open like shutters on the first warm day of spring. Even the Empress herself kneeling, even the Empress seized by this sudden love of Christ. She thought of how the Emperor Maxentius had hated Catherine for her power, and of all the ways he'd tried to have her killed: the spiked wooden torture wheel that broke apart when the guards tried to tie her to it . . . the river from which she kept rising up like a cork, no matter how long they held her under . . . the fire that raged around her but left no mark, left her skin cool and white as lilies. At last they had to cut Catherine's head off with an ax to kill her. Jehanne saw the great blade flashing, the pale, shocked face spinning through air, and she wished she could be that brave. That pure.

It was like a fever in her, her love for God. Not mild, not polite. Consuming. Every evening in Domrémy, the bells rang out in the church tower

5

for Compline, and she ran downhill through the wheat fields to be with Him, her feet flying over the grass and dirt, her heart pounding like a hot red drum. He was all she could think about. All she wanted.

'Where does God live?' she'd asked her mother once.

'God lives in Heaven.'

'What's Heaven?'

Her mother had looked sad then. Finally she pointed up to the clouds and said, 'Heaven is God's beautiful paradise in the sky. If we are very good, we'll go there to live with Him after we die.' As her mother spoke, her eyes looked so hungry that Jehanne's heart swelled up like a sail.

'Can't we go there now?'

'No,' her mother said. 'We can't go there now.'

She doesn't know when it first took root inside her, that hunger for God. Perhaps it was always there. She remembers knowing that He was the one who made the trees. And the wind in the trees. And the clear, icy green river with the round white stones on the bottom. And the red harvest moon. And the little black starlings that dipped and soared over her head at sunset, thousands of them rising and tilting and soaring, flashing their black wings against the flushed pink sky.

She remembers knowing this, and the awe she felt knowing it—gratitude rising in her like music, so strong it brought her to her knees, made her weep. *Please*, she would think. *How can I thank you? How can I show you?*

But she wasn't thinking about it when it happened. She'd forgotten. She was just sitting in the garden with her face turned up to the sun, listening to the wind shaking the trees, when a voice came suddenly, very loud. A man's voice and a great spangle of light to the right of her. A warmth like sunlight on her cheek, down her neck, along her spine. *Jehanne*, it said. The voice very deep, masculine, enormous. Setting her blood on fire. *Jehanne, my virgin, Maid of France.*

She was terrified at first, weeping, clutching at the grass as if she expected to be ripped away from the earth. Terrified and overjoyed. *Who are you?* she asked. The light had blinded her. She could not see her house.

You know who I am.

No, I don't.

Yes, Jehanne, you do.

She did know. In her bones, she knew. It was the thing she'd prayed for. The only thing she'd ever wanted. Slowly the light began to spread inside her, through her belly, her hips, her breasts, her mouth, her thighs, rinsing through her like sunlight, warm and radiant, filling her up, releasing her . . . a bird in flight.

*   *   *

She doesn't know how long it lasted. It felt like a long time, but she doesn't know. What she knows is that afterward, when the voice and the light were gone, it was terrible. All the world gray and cold, like a tomb. Gray trees, gray sky, black sun. Black leaves scuttling down the hillside. Everything cold, shriveled, bereft. She lay curled on the ground, sobbing. *Come back, please. Come back.* Wanting nothing but to die, sleep. Return.

When she awoke, the shadow had passed.

7

Amazement took its place. She turned over on her back and looked up at the sky through the puzzle of leaves. Everything was heightened, buzzing with life. Singing. The sky perfectly clear, blue and dazzling. The trees bending and waving in the breeze. Smell of onion weed and sweet clover in her nostrils. Cows lowing in the distance. Her mother inside, grinding flour, her father in the pasture, screaming at the cows.

It's all perfect, all as it must be, she sees. Even the worst things. Even the boy Volo, in his cage in Madame de Pois' barn, with his gray cauliflower head and his tiny slanted eyes. Or mad King Charles, running naked through the palace in Paris, throwing his own shit against the windows. The Goddons and Burgundians thundering through the hills, setting whole villages on fire, tearing apart the women and children, stealing land, cows, sheep, gold, stealing their entire country out from under them. It's all all right now. All of it necessary, part of His plan. Just as she, Jehanne, lying in the garden, is part of His plan, though she knows not how yet, or why. She knows simply that He has pulled back life's curtain for an instant and shown her His miraculous fire, lit her up with His miraculous fire. And she knows that she will do anything to feel that fire again.

*   *   *

She did not tell anyone. She knew they would laugh, call her crazy, a fool, a liar. She kept it inside her, secret, burning like a small fierce sun. Waiting.

8

CHAPTER THREE

There were seven of them in her family. Her mother, her father, and five children. The three oldest were boys: Jacquemin, Jean, and Pierrelot. Cowards, the father called them. Wastrels. And so they were. Sullen and slump-shouldered, sleeping late, kicking the dog. Next came Jehanne's sister, Catherine, the beauty, named after the saint. Catherine with the bright plum mouth and the thick blond waterfall of hair. Hair that everyone stared at in church. She, Jehanne, was the youngest. A tomboy. Dark and watchful, with short, sturdy legs like a donkey.

They lived in the rolling green hill country of northern France, far away from Paris. Far away from everything. Theirs was a land of wide, slow rivers and tall ancient oaks. In summer the fields filled up with poppies, their red upflung skirts glowing in the sun. In winter their forest was silent as a church.

They were common people, unschooled, sunburned. Their hands and feet were calloused. The new lambs and goats slept with them inside the house during the spring frosts, huddled and snuffing in the red glow of the hearth. Jehanne and Catherine wrapped rags around their feet to keep warm, waited until summer to wash themselves in the river. But they were respected in their village. Because their father owned his land, they were respected.

They believed in one God. They were Christians. Jehanne and her mother and Catherine went to church every evening for Compline, knelt together on the dark packed-earth floor, their hands knotted in prayer. The whole family went on Sunday mornings. Jehanne's mother prayed for God's help and forgiveness. Her father begged God to smite down the Goddons the way He once smote down the Ethiopians. *Send them all to Hell.*

They disapproved of the old forest gods, the pagan superstitions. Thought them shameful, blasphemous, stupid. Jehanne's mother tucked in her lips and shook her head when their neighbor Mariette hitched herself naked to the plow each April and dragged it through the muddy fields on her hands and knees, singing and praying to the old gods for a bountiful harvest, the fat bells of her breasts and belly swinging back and forth, slick with gray mud. Jehanne's father did not keep a mandrake under his bed.

They lived in a stone house near the river with four rooms and two small, but finely made, glass windows. Those windows were her father's great delight. 'See how fine the mullion work is,' he'd say to visitors. 'Even Lord Bourlémont doesn't have better windows.'

A proud man, her father. He saw himself as a kind of country king. He worked tirelessly, at a run all day, plowing the fields, planting wheat and rye, taking the cream and hen's eggs to market, collecting taxes, organizing men for the village watch. The family sat in the front pew at church on Sunday. After services were finished, he went around shaking hands, smiling, clapping shoulders. Her father, King of the Peasants.

As a child, Jehanne had adored him. On summer afternoons, he'd take her along with him

10

to bring the cows down from the high pasture near the old oak forest, the *bois chênu*. She can remember his enormous hand, rough and warm around hers, his long dark shadow going ahead of hers on the road. His hand making her safe. At the top of the hill, he'd take her to where the little *fraises du bois* grew in the green and white sunlight at the edge of the forest. Small ruby-red berries, cone-shaped and so sweet. Intoxicating. They ate handfuls of them as they walked. When they finished, their palms were wet and sticky, stained red. Her father held his up and laughed. 'Guilty,' he said. 'Guilty, guilty.'

Jehanne didn't know what the word meant then, but she sensed it meant something bad. A cold snake of warning slid through her stomach.

When he began to go mad, no one outside the family knew it. He confined his rages to the house. The red-eyed beast that reared up only occasionally in Jehanne's earliest memories began to appear more and more, circling the house with his long teeth bared, striking out at anyone who got in his way. 'Who do you think you are?' he would scream at her suddenly, for no reason. 'Who the hell do you think you are?'

Her mother blamed it on the war. 'It kills him to see all his hard work destroyed,' she said, squeezing one hand very tightly with the other, as if to keep it from flying away. Or later she'd say, 'It's because of Catherine. He was never like this when Catherine was here.' Her mother, pious and loving, but a coward too, hiding in her prayers, her dreams of Jesus.

CHAPTER FOUR

It made me very tall, my secret. It made me very tall, and it made everyone around me very small. Like dollhouse people. Little dollhouse people with little muddy problems. Cattle, pigs, taxes, harvests. My problems were huge, vast as the universe. God. War. The King. France. And I knew I was worthy of them. I knew when the time was right, God would pour His courage into me, and I'd stride across the country like a giant, stepping over forests and villages, rivers and mountains, leaving my enormous footprints behind me. Footprints the world would remember forever.

CHAPTER FIVE

They'd been at war with the English for as long as anyone could remember. So long that most of northern France had gone over to the English side. No longer just the Goddons to worry about. Now the Burgundians too. 'Bloody traitors,' her father called them. 'Spineless pigs.'

Sixty or seventy years, her father said. For sixty or seventy years the Goddons and Burgundians had been ravaging the countryside, stealing their land, slaying them in their beds as they slept, destroying their crops, feasting on their shanks. They all knew about the slaughter at Agincourt, the terrible siege at Rouen. 'Poor souls eating their dogs, babies sucking at the blue breasts of their dead mothers.' But it wasn't until Jehanne was ten or eleven that the war came close to her—that she began to understand what it meant.

One hot September night she awoke to the smell of smoke. Red light was pulsing on the walls. She sat up in bed and looked out the window and saw the wheat fields burning. A sea of fire. The air black and rolling, thick with smoke. Their harvest destroyed. Her mother sank to the bed, moaning, 'Oh my God.' Her father shouted at her mother to take the children up and hide in the hayloft. Then there came a great thundering of hooves past the house. Loud, ugly laughter with it. Her father ran out the door naked with an ax, screaming. But the men just laughed at him. Twenty or thirty of them on horseback, *les écorcheurs*. Not even soldiers that time. No flags or banners, no embroidered tunics. Just Goddon mercenaries in old rusted mail, bandits riding down out of the hills, tearing apart the villages and setting them on fire, taking whatever they wanted because who would stop them? 'You going to take us, old man? Eh? You and your shriveled little prick?' Laughing as they loaded all of her father's sheep into a wagon and rode off into the night.

CHAPTER SIX

For a time her father and the other men had tried to protect the village. They got together whatever money they had and went to Lord Bourlémont, begged him to rent them the old ruined chateau on the island in the river. A big roofless place with a crumbling turret, home now only to foxes and

13

some robins that had nested up in the old murder holes, the walls streaked white and pale green with long stalactites of shit. But they were still good, the main walls, still high and thick and strong. Their plan was to hide the entire village inside during the next raid. 'Now let them try and steal our livestock,' Jehanne's father said, wiping his mouth with the back of his hand.

He and the other men began taking turns up on the rooftops at the edge of the village, standing watch through the night, pacing and slapping their cheeks to stay awake. But in the end it did no good. They couldn't get the animals out of their pens and across the river to the island fast enough. When the bandits came through again, they trotted right up to the villagers who were sliding around on the muddy riverbanks, trying to push the frightened calves into the dark water. Knives drawn, laughing, their faces like carved wooden masks in the torchlight. 'Thank you so much for your help.'

After they left, her father tore their house apart. Hurled everything across the room, chairs, tables, bowls, pots, candlesticks, pitchers, plates. Insane with rage, he tore the door clear off the hinges. Jehanne had never seen him so angry. Her mother stood in the corner, cowering and sobbing. 'Please, Jacques, in the name of God.' Sobbing until he punched her too.

CHAPTER SEVEN

Jehanne began to spend more time in the forest. It had become a wild place by then. 'The forests

14

came back with the English,' her mother said. In their terror, people abandoned their farms, their villages, ran to hide from the Goddons and live in the woods. They ate roots, grass, sometimes their own children, it was said. They slept in caves, curled up in the roots of old trees. And the woods themselves grew monstrous, spread out over the fields and old roads and abandoned villages, reclaiming the country. Trees growing up inside of burned-out churches and houses, creeper vines curling out of the chimneys, leaves twisting up into the sky like smoke.

People said the woods were dangerous, full of starving animals, wolves and bears, wild boar, but that didn't scare Jehanne. She'd seen a wolf once in the road right outside her house after a raid. She came out in the morning and saw her cousin Hemet lying very still in a ditch. The wolf was lying beside him, calmly chewing on the shiny pink ropes of his intestines. Jehanne stared, mesmerized by the splendid color, thinking, *We have those inside of us?* Then her mother ran at the wolf with a shovel, screaming, 'Get away, get away from him!' The wolf just looked at her, flat yellow eyes like the Devil's. Then it went back to eating. No, the woods were better. She liked it there in the shadows, hidden, silent. Safe.

Often she prayed there, in an old fallen-down shrine to the Virgin Mary she'd found deep in the trees. She'd kneel in front of the wooden statue and press her cheek against the hem of the Virgin's robe, kiss her little wooden feet. *Help us*, she would say. *Please help us.*

She said real prayers too sometimes. Prayers her mother had taught her. 'Whenever you are afraid, pray to God and He will help you,' she said. *Our Father, who art in Heaven, hallowed be thy name . . . Thy kingdom come, thy will be done, on earth as it is in Heaven . . .*

It amazed her, that prayer. It was like a secret room inside of her that she could run to whenever she wanted. A place where she could feel safe any time, any hour of the day. All she had to do was close her eyes and say the words, and there it was, safety, the enormous hand of God on her chest, soothing her heart.

Soon she began to pray everywhere. In church, at home, in the fields. Three times each day the church bells rang out, and each time she thought, *Yes, now. Now.* She went down on her knees and lifted her face to the sky. She entered the secret room.

CHAPTER EIGHT

After the day in the garden, there were three of them who came to her. Three saints, standing in the air above her like planets. Shining. The first one stern, enormous, king-like. His hands like antlers. His voice lighting up her bones as if they were candles. He was their leader. She knew as soon as he spoke. The deep lion's voice thundering through her, clasping her between her legs, making her want to drop to her knees, to bow her head, call him Sire.

He never had to say his name. She knew who he was immediately. Knew he was Michael, the Archangel. He who is like God. His face filled up

16

the sky. *Oh Lord*, she said, shaking, feeling as if she would break apart with joy. *Jehanne*, he said. Just one word and it was clear. She'd do anything for him.

He'd be the one to deliver the bad news.

Then came the two virgins. Glowing like dandelions. Motherly, consoling. Saint Catherine with the sad spoon face, the hands like carved ivory. Wise, beautiful Catherine who had broken the spiked torture wheel. Her voice a flute of cool water, so clear it made Jehanne feel as if she understood everything in the world, could count every stone in the bottom of the river. And Saint Margaret. Plump, brazen Margaret with the faint brown mustache and wildfires blazing in her eyes. Margaret who had fought her way out of the belly of Satan's dragon with her sword. *Don't be afraid, cabbage*, said Margaret. *We'll be with you all the way.*

What do you mean, all the way?

Nothing, love, said Catherine, embracing her. *Lay down your worries and rest now, darling. Rest your head in my arms.*

CHAPTER NINE

They made fun of her in the village. The other children. They mocked her for giving alms to the begging friars, for taking her *choyne* bread out to Volo in his cage. They said she was pious, a righteous little prig. Once they'd tried to destroy her. She'd been playing in the field by the Fairies' Tree with some other girls from the village.

17

Hauviette, Mengette, Valerie. They were making poppy garlands to hang up for the May festival. It had started out a sunny morning, but suddenly a cloud slid over the sun. A large purple cloud, heavy with rain. Everything grew darker, cooler, like evening. The grass looked angry and sharp. Jehanne's heart crawled backward in her chest. She walked a little way off into the field, to where she thought they couldn't see her anymore, and went down on her knees. She began to pray.

When she opened her eyes, they were all standing around her, staring down at her. Big faces, leering. Valerie with a wicked look in her eyes. 'Look at little Saintie Pie,' she said, coming closer. 'Think you're awfully high and mighty don't you, Saintie Pie?' Jehanne stood up. Her hands had begun to sweat. Valerie took another step closer. She was taller than Jehanne, perhaps a year or two older. A big, sturdy girl with a coarse, pale face, large breasts, and small black eyes. Odd little marks like sparrow tracks on her cheeks. Her clothes were always tattered. Everyone knew her father was a drunk. Everyone knew she'd go into the hayloft with any boy who asked. 'What's the matter, Saintie Pie, you scared?' Valerie and the other girls crowded in, with ugly fixed looks on their faces.

She wanted to run then. Or collapse, fall on her knees and beg. 'Please, no, don't hurt me.' But as she looked up at the older girl, that pale blunt face, she thought, *Who is she? Why should she scare me?* A wild fighting spirit rose up inside her. 'Better than you,' she said. 'Dirty slut.' The other girls stared at each other with their mouths open. Everyone except Valerie. She stepped forward and slapped Jehanne's cheek very hard. 'Little bitch,' she said as Jehanne stumbled backward. 'How dare you speak to me like that?'

The world became a red, rippling place then. Everything happening very slowly, as if she were underwater, and somehow also very fast. Jehanne walked over and punched the older girl in the stomach. 'I do what I want,' she said. The older girl sat down on the ground, her mouth hanging open, round as an O. The other girls burst out laughing. 'Jesus!' Valerie cried at last. Then she scrambled to her feet and ran away.

CHAPTER TEN

Later Jehanne walked down the dirt road toward the church. She was sorry for what she'd done. Her heart felt heavy, like something chained to the bottom of a well. 'Forgive me, Father, I have sinned,' she said as she sat in the confessional box. She loved sitting there in the darkness, looking at the honeycomb screen carved from wood. Loved trying to see Père Guillaume's wrinkled apple face through the holes, catching only his strange spiced breath in the darkness. 'Tell me your sins, Jehanne,' he said. She put her fingertips against the screen as she spoke, traced along the rough edges of the cutouts. She thought of what she'd done, the unexpected doughlike softness of Valerie's stomach, Valerie's stunned face as she sat down on the ground. She whispered to the priest. 'I got so angry,' she said, her ears hot with shame, tears prickling her eyes. But with every word she spoke, she grew lighter, cleaner, the rage pouring out of her, the light pouring in. 'God forgives you, my child,' he said at last. 'You are forgiven.'

And the feeling then! *Forgiven*. It washed over her like the ocean. Wave upon wave. Eventually the priest coughed, shuffled his boots against the rough stone floor, and said, 'All right, dear, you can go now.'

But she didn't want to leave the church yet, didn't want to leave the feeling. She walked out into the pale, still nave and stood for a while in the great stone silence, feeling it on her skin, the coolness, the peace. She looked up at her saints in the stained-glass windows, Saint Catherine, Saint Margaret, Saint Clare . . . those tall, sad, lovely women illuminated by the sun. She thought of their enormous love for God, their heroic lives, their miracles. How they'd found a way to be bigger, better, to do good, fight evil, escape the mud, the smallness of life. She thought they were the luckiest people in the world.

CHAPTER ELEVEN

She never considered telling the priest about her voices. She knew he would hate her for it. Would not be able to help hating her for it. He was a gentle man, Père Guillaume, a decent man even, but fearful too. Scared, trembling beneath his holy robes. You could see it in his face. The thin purple lips, the dry, papery white hands, the cold, silent judgments . . . She knew if she told him, he would see to it that she suffered. He would not inflict the

20

suffering himself, that was not his way, but he would tell someone who would be sure to inflict it. 'I'm concerned about Jehannette . . .' he'd say, and then it would be all over. They'd beat her until she broke and apologized, begged for forgiveness, swore it was all a lie, a fantasy. Madness. Beat her until she promised to behave, be silent. Repent.

The only person she wanted to tell was Durand. Her cousin's husband who lived in Burey-le-Petit. Durand of the tall black boots and the deep windy laugh. The one Jehanne called Uncle. Every year at Christmastime they visited him at the big cracked house in Burey. He kept a little pet fawn that slept in a basket by the hearth and would come right up to you and press its face against your thighs like a dog. Eat oats right out of your hand. Durand's wife, Marie, was sour—a cold, frowning woman who shouted and slapped your hand if you went for a second slice of meat at supper—but Durand was different. Durand, Jehanne thought, was so kind it was as if he had two hearts pounding in his chest. When she was a child, he was always pulling her up onto his lap and telling her stories about the saints. Of Saint Bernard of Clairvaux who ate only boiled beech leaves. And Saint Anthony who was tortured by demons in the Outer Mountain near Pispir. Saint Anthony who said, 'I fear the demon no more than I fear a fly, and with the sign of the cross I can at once put him to flight.'

Durand loved God as she did: hot and fierce. He had traveled all over France on pilgrimages to visit the holy places. He'd seen the Black Madonna at Le Puy and the golden statue of Saint Foy in Conques. Stood in line all day to see the chin bone of the Virgin or a lock of Saint Peter's hair. The

21

little girl in Rodez who bore the stigmata—the wounds of Christ. 'They say she was seized one day by a vision of the crucifixion,' he told Jehanne during one of her visits, 'and afterward, holes opened up in her wrists and feet and blood poured out, as if nails had been driven straight through them. The day I saw her, the poor child was sitting there in the church with blood all over her, weeping and wailing one minute, then laughing the next, the whole time with this fixed look in her eyes, as if there were people in the room that only she could see.' He looked at Jehanne, his eyes shining. 'It was real. God was there, inside her.'

How she'd wanted to tell him then! To pull him in close and say, 'I know. He visits me too.' But she did not dare. Even with Durand, she did not dare. It was too precious, too fragile a thing to put out into the world yet. It needed to be protected, like the rosebush her mother covered with hay in the early spring. It needed time to grow safely, silently, in the dark.

CHAPTER TWELVE

From Durand and her mother she knew about the saints. Everything else she knew of the world came from Claude, the pedlar. Her father's friend. Once every few weeks he came over the hill, his big wagon lurching behind him, piled high with wonders and junk—old pots and kettles, glass jars, dice, kitchen knives, mirrors, spices, oils, candles. Once he had shown her a coconut all the way from Majorca. 'Got it off a sailor in Le Havre,' he said.

A brown hairy thing, ugly as a monkey. He hacked it open with his big rust-spotted knife and gave Jehanne a piece of the crisp white flesh inside. A delicious taste. Creamy and sweet, slightly nutty. She remembers how neatly it had broken apart in her hands. 'That's what the islands taste like.'

Her father loved Claude. After he finished making his rounds in the village, he'd come and spend the night at their house. A small, grizzled man, smelling of cloves, with big, sparkling, rich blue eyes that reminded Jehanne of the sky in autumn. After dinner, when she was supposed to be asleep, Claude and her father would drag their chairs up close to the hearth and drink late into the night, their profiles gleaming like coin heads in the firelight. Jehanne crept up into the hayloft and hid there in the straw, listening.

The King's madness was Claude's favorite topic. 'Not just spells anymore; Old Charlie's completely loo-loo now,' he said. He told how Charles had gone out into the forest hunting with his four best knights and murdered all but one of them. Why? 'Who knows?' said Claude. It was said that a noise had startled him—a twig snapped or a little animal moved in the bushes—and suddenly he went berserk. Jehanne saw it in her mind's eye, the King's wild red face, the King screaming that they were all out to get him. 'To murder me and steal my crown!' Then he drew his sword and hacked away at his men until they lay like broken china dolls on the forest floor. All the birch trees around them spackled in blood. All three heads hacked clean off, their frozen eyes staring at the sky.

'Jesus,' her father said.

'They say he's still wild from it,' said the pedlar.

23

'Won't let anyone near him. Tells people he's made of glass. If anyone touches him, he'll shatter like an icicle.'

*   *   *

Sometimes Claude spoke of the Queen too. Isabeau. The Whore Queen, he called her. She'd caught fire with her own brand of madness and was running wild through the kingdom like an animal in heat. 'Opens her legs to anyone who so much as blinks at her. The King's best friends, his family, anyone she can get her hands on.' Claude knew. His sister worked in the palace kitchens. She'd watched Isabeau's gentlewoman mix up a face cream of crocodile glands, wolf's blood, and boar brains to keep the Queen's skin looking young. Watched Isabeau's maids lug buckets of ass's milk upstairs for the royal bath. 'She puts belladonna in her eyes at night and smiles at the poor fools in the candlelight, lets her hand brush their cocks under the table.' Isabeau's current favorite, Claude said, was the King's brother, Louis. She'd been seen with her fat white legs locked around his waist one night on a dim stone staircase, pulling his hair, grunting like a sow.

The whole country, Claude said, was rotting from the inside like an old wedding cake. All the nobles knew it, but nobody would do anything about it. They'd either been swept along into the madness themselves, dining on roasted swans and peacocks at their banquets, drinking and sobbing into their champagne cups as their country toppled down around them, screwing each other silly, or else they watched from the shadows and plotted to seize the crown for themselves. 'Louis, Burgundy, Henry, they're all circling the throne like wolves,' Claude said. 'All three of them screwing Isabeau, each one taking his turn, lying there with her in the dark, stroking her breasts, and telling her how rich he'll make her if she'll just convince poor Charlie to sign over the Regency to him.'

'My God, she'll be the end of us,' Jehanne's father would say, his face going dark, ugly with hate. 'She'll be the end of us all.'

Jehanne hadn't believed this at first. She thought: *It's all so far away. It will never come here.* But by the time the raids on Domrémy began, poor mad Charles was dead, and Isabeau had done exactly what Claude said she would. Sold their country off to the English—married her daughter to their King, Henry V, and denounced her own son, Charles VII, the true heir to the throne, as illegitimate, a bastard. Unfit to rule. Henry became King of France, the monster Duke of Burgundy was put in charge of governing Paris, and the Dauphin, Charles VII, had barely escaped with his life. 'Now young Charlie hides in his castle down there in the Loire, poor as a squirrel, afraid of his own shadow,' Claude said. 'And the Goddons win more territory every day.'

The south of France, they knew, was still loyal to the crown, but the English and their Burgundian allies had snatched up almost all of the northern part of the country. Jehanne's little village of Domrémy was one of the last pockets in the north that still held out. But it was clear they couldn't for much longer. Every month more villages were burned, more horses and cows were stolen, more towns occupied, more peasants slaughtered in

25

their beds. There was no one to help them. No law. No sheriff. They were abandoned, marooned, easy targets for Goddons, Burgundians, bandits.

'Doesn't she see what this is doing to the country?' her father would shout as Jehanne watched from the hayloft—her jaw knotted, her fists clenched tight.

'Does she not care that the finest vineyards in France are burning? All the great farms and castles of Lorraine being looted, destroyed?'

'Isabeau can barely hold on to her own chateaux,' Claude said. 'You think she gives a damn about us?'

*   *   *

Once, when they were drunk, very late at night, Jehanne's father had looked up from where he'd been staring into the fire, his eyes desperate like a drowning man's. 'Is there no hope at all?' he said. 'Are we doomed to become slaves of the English, no country at all, just a million broken-down wretches for them to rob and rape and murder whenever they please?'

Claude was leaning back in his chair, his long, skinny, blue-stockinged legs stretched out in front of the hearth, the curled tips of his shoes silhouetted in the firelight. He took a deep drink of his wine, then swirled his cup, gazing into it as if it held a vision of the future. 'Well, you know the prophecy la Gasque d'Avignon made, don't you?'

Her father flapped his hand, rolled his eyes. 'Spare me the wives' tales.'

Up in the hayloft, Jehanne leaned in closer to listen.

26

Claude grinned, told the story in a singsong voice. 'France will be ruined by a woman and restored by a virgin from the forests of Lorraine.'

A snort of laughter from Jacques. 'Not bloody likely, given the ones around here.'

'You asked if there was any hope,' said Claude.

'Hope, sure. Not a fairy tale.'

CHAPTER THIRTEEN

La Belle. That was what they called Jehanne's older sister in the village. The Beauty. She was named after Saint Catherine, Jehanne's favorite saint, her mother's favorite saint too. Her laugh was deep and silvery and musical, and her eyes were clear pale green, like freshly sliced cucumbers. The only unbeautiful things about her were her feet, which were short and bulbous and yellowish in color, and which she was careful to hide under her skirt. *La Belle*. Catherine *La Belle*. 'Who am I?' Jehanne would ask her mother. 'You're the brave one,' the mother said. 'The strong one.'

Catherine was the only one their father never screamed at. Even when she stole a fistful of butter from the cellar and gobbled it up right in front of him, laughing. He was helpless, gazing at her as if he could hardly believe he'd made something so lovely. When it rained on Sundays, their father would pick her up and carry her in his arms all the way from church back to the house so she wouldn't spoil the hem of her good pink dress in the mud. 'Jehanne, run open the door for us quick,' he'd say.

'There's a good girl.'

Jehanne hated her sister in these moments, but it never lasted long. It was impossible to stay angry with Catherine. Impossible not to love her. Living with Catherine was like living with Durand's fawn. The room turned magical whenever she walked into it.

The night before she married the mayor's son, Colin, Catherine and Jehanne had sat up together in their room, talking late into the night. Catherine had combed all the snarls and tangles out of Jehanne's impossible hair and braided it with red satin ribbons for the next day, her fingers strong and firm, her nails raking deliciously over Jehanne's scalp. At one point Jehanne felt so close to her sister that she grew bold. 'Have you seen it yet?' she asked. Catherine's eyes flew open. 'Jehanne!' she said. But later she said, 'I did see it once for a minute.' She wrinkled her nose. 'It was so ugly.' Then she laughed. That lovely musical laugh. Deep and gurgling like a baby's laugh. 'But kind of beautiful too. Like a big blue mushroom.'

Jehanne had lain awake in bed that night for hours, picturing the big blue mushroom and trying to think of something she could say the next day to make her sister laugh that way again.

They never knew for sure what happened to her. Two years after she married Colin, she disappeared. Jehanne was fourteen when it happened. Catherine was very pregnant. Colin had seen her out by the road, picking daffodils before sunset. When she didn't come in for supper, he went looking for her there, but she was gone.

A week later, Jehanne's brother, Jean, found Catherine's body under a pile of leaves in the forest. He carried it as far as the front yard and then stopped there, frozen, unable to take another step. They'd taken her hair—the golden waterfall—and hacked it off at the nape. Taken her dress and shoes too. Pierrelot told her this later, in secret, for the adults would not let Jehanne see her sister's body. 'Nothing for a child to see,' they said. They told her that Catherine had died of a blow to the head, but later, Jehanne heard her father say it was the shame that killed her first. 'Shame at what the Goddons had done to her. Oh my darling little girl.'

That was the end of him, her father. He walked the fields for days, screaming, sobbing at the sky. Hurling himself against the trees. Pounding his fists against the earth. Later he came home and lay down on his bed. He stayed there for a year, staring at the wall. Jean and Pierrelot took over the farming, proved good workers without the father there to scream at them. Eventually Jacques got up. He resumed his place in village life, became good old Jacques d'Arc again, smiling, collecting taxes, clapping shoulders. But at home the mask came off; he beat Pierrelot for dropping an egg on the floor. Beat Jehanne for giving him a haughty look. Beat her so savagely she could not walk for a week.

*   *   *

It made the father clairvoyant, the madness. Allowed him to see Jehanne's future in his dreams. And what he saw there appalled him. His child, his youngest, galloping across the fields, dressed in a gleaming suit of armor, followed by a howling sea

29

of soldiers, her jaw set, her eyes wild, the men thundering and screaming behind her, all of them riding, running toward war.

He woke in the night, screaming. Grabbed his wife by the throat and pressed his thumb against her windpipe. 'She'll be the ruin of us,' he gasped. 'She'll be the ruin of this family.' It was beyond him. His mind couldn't do anything with the images but think that his child was doomed to run off and become an army whore, a camp prostitute, bedding down with any man who would pay. And it killed him, the thought of it, the ruin of his good family name. His hard-earned reputation. The thought that this girl, this child, could destroy his life.

In the wan early morning sunlight he studied her, sullen and slump-shouldered, eating her bread by the hearth. A small, sturdy girl, dark hair, big black eyes, round and wet like a seal's, pink-brown cheeks, a country loveliness to her. Also a fury. A righteous, carefully bottled fury that terrified him.

Later, drunk on wine, he announced that she had to be watched. 'Watch her or she'll run off the first chance she gets,' he said. 'Become a filthy army slut.' He told her brothers that if they caught her trying to run off, they must take her and drown her in the river. 'If you don't, I'll do it myself, you hear me?' he shouted at her. 'So help me God, you will not shame this family. You will not drag our good name through the mud.'

Jehanne looked at him, her eyes lidded, unreadable. 'I'm not going anywhere,' she said.

CHAPTER FOURTEEN

But watch her now as she moves through the blond wheat fields behind the little hunchbacked house by the river. Watch her walk uphill, this small, intent figure in a rough red dress, moving through the fields beneath the summer sky, a fire, a kind of possession growing in her eyes as she goes, running her palms over the velvet tops of the wheat tassels, whistling lightly through her teeth. At the brow of the hill stands the high, rustling oak forest. She approaches it slowly, with reverence, pushing carefully through the branches into the green cathedral of leaves, the twigs reaching out, tugging at her dress, her braids, as she moves, pulled forward through the sun-dappled world until she comes to the old stone altar deep in the trees.

A small collapsed ruin, roofless and forsaken. Open to starlight, thunderstorms, lightning. The walls are half fallen down, saplings have sprouted here and there, and at one end of the space stands the old statue of the Virgin, her head cloaked in a hood of green moss. Jehanne steps toward the statue, strokes the velvet moss with the ball of her thumb, takes in the shimmering forest once more, then kneels down carefully before the statue, bowing her dark head, speaking softly as she brings her hands together in prayer. *Are you here?*

She remains this way for a long time, her eyes closed, her head bowed, waiting. Occasionally she shifts her haunches slightly or sighs, lowering her shoulders as if a slight change in posture might help her case. A lark sings out high and clear above her, its song piercing the upper vaults of the trees. The old branches lifting slowly and falling in the breeze, their leafy sleeves articulate, sad as fingers.

Later she lies on her belly on the forest floor, palms down, arms extended like Christ. The cool, nutty scent of leaves in her nostrils. *Won't you come?* she says. Tears leak from her eyes. The sun sets, a red ball sinking through the trees. The forest grows dim, cool, and menacing. Still she does not move.

CHAPTER FIFTEEN

'Where were you?' says her father when she comes in hours later, after dark. The family is gathered around the table, a brown ham gleaming in the firelight. Beside her father sits a plump, pug-nosed boy who stands when he sees her, grins like a fool.

Jehanne takes a step backward, blood roaring in her ears. Her mother stares at her. 'For heaven's sake, Jehannette, what's become of you?' Jehanne looks down. Her feet, her legs, are streaked with mud. A stiff hem of mud ringing the bottom of her dress. 'Why do you have leaves in your hair?'

She mumbles something about falling asleep in the fields and runs to her room. From there, she hears her mother calling her, but something holds her back. It is as if her feet are nailed to the floor.

She stands behind the door, listening to them talk. Her mother's high, unnatural laughter. Her father's forced, jovial public voice. After the boy leaves, her father comes into the room and hits her hard. Her nose begins to bleed. A feeling like a

32

knife jamming into her brain. 'What the hell is wrong with you? Don't you know a suitor when you see one?' He drags her by the hair into the main room and says to her mother. 'Look at this little bitch, this daughter of yours. What man would want her for a wife?'

Outside the moon is full. The great black shadow of the beech tree in the yard stretches across the bedroom floor and up the wall. 'He doesn't mean it,' her mother says, sitting on Jehanne's bed, holding her, stroking her hair, wiping the black crust of blood from her face with a damp cloth.

Jehanne is silent. She lets her mind wander until she sees the old beech tree in the garden twist and flex and burst into flame. The tree suddenly hot and alive, red and yellow and crackling with fire, reaching a branch into the house, breaking through the glass window in the main room (the treasured window broken!) and picking up her father, pulling him out into the darkness and holding him tight in those burning branches until he too catches fire, until he too is burning and screaming, then burning and silent, melting, crumbling to a pile of ash on the ground.

CHAPTER SIXTEEN

She grew older. She watched her body begin to change. Softness where there had been bones and sharp angles, hair, a musky smell from the hollows. Sadness too, in the afternoons. Pain like a sharp hook, rusting in her heart. Loneliness. Other times

33

joy. Wild soaring joy. Ten thousand birds singing inside her. She walked through the village in the violet light of dawn, swinging her arms, thinking, *Thank you, oh thank you!* Everything moving in her like wind, shaking her foundations.

It drove her father wild. Watching his child transform, grow powerful, secretive, defiant. As if an uncontrollable stranger were suddenly sleeping under his own roof. A stranger scheming to destroy his life.

Soon there were rules. Her father forbade her from going off into the woods by herself. Forbade her from the fields, the trees, the hills. 'No more running off,' he said. 'Do your chores, help your mother, go to church, be polite to the young men when they come calling, that's all.'

She had to think about the future, her mother said. Marriage. She was sixteen now. It was time. The word made her sick to her stomach. She watched the other girls her age, braiding flowers into their hair, pinching their cheeks, smiling shyly or picking up their skirts and dancing, showing off their knees for the boys. Competing over who would live with whom in which dark hovel, who would spend their lives plowing which burned-out field, making which gray stew in which sad hearth, having her hair torn out by which man, dying of which plague or beating or wretched childbirth . . . and she thought she'd rather die.

She'd rather be dead.

CHAPTER SEVENTEEN

Listen now, darling. It is time for you to know your purpose. It was Michael who told her. Michael who came one day while she was kneeling among the green shadows in the *bois chênu* with her eyes closed, face lifted, listening to the wind. It was afternoon. Suddenly the light was there, a torrent of feathered sunlight pouring through the trees, the deep Godvoice making the hairs on her arms stand up. *You must raise an army and drive the English from France. Take the Dauphin to be crowned King at Reims. This is God's command.*

Her mind rejected it at first. The words floated through her like underwater sounds, impossible to understand. Then, when she did understand, she ran into the trees and threw up, a yellow puddle on the ground.

It was as her father had dreamed. God had shown His wish in the dream—her father just hadn't understood. Jehanne said it was impossible, what He asked. Impossible. *I'm only a girl, a peasant. I know nothing of cannons or lances. I have no money. I can't even ride a horse. Please, ask me anything else. I'll do anything else!*

No.

This is God's mission, child. We will help you. God will help you. Go to the King, drive the English out of France. Crown the King.

She sobbed and ran from the forest. 'Leave me alone!' she cried. 'You ask too much.'

CHAPTER EIGHTEEN

The Church of St. Rêmy sat beside Jehanne's house, not twenty yards away. Separated only by a shaggy row of willows and a cemetery of leaning stones starred with pale green lichen. The church itself, a small peach stone building with a big wooden cross inside. In her mind's eye Jehanne pictured Christ stretched and lean as a cat on that cross, his wrists and ankles jeweled in blood, his sad, all-seeing eyes shining from behind the blades of his cheekbones, and seeing him there, she felt less alone. She began spending all of her time there, lying to her parents, saying she was going to work in the fields but instead creeping back behind the house and into the church, praying in a pew up near the altar.

It was very cold inside the church. The tips of her fingers went numb, turned white and mottled with lavender spots, but she stayed anyway. Eventually she forgot about the pain. Sometimes there were birds up in the eaves, pigeons fluttering and flapping in the shafts of sunlight that poured through the windows. And at sunset came the bells. She sat in the cold wooden pew with her head tilted back, her face lifted to the ceiling as the great bell rang and echoed through the high stone space, echoing off the walls, the high arches, the dim, shadowed corners of the nave, the rings of sound rippling through her body, her blood. In her mind she pictured a whole world of bells, all different sizes, ringing inside her. Big heavy bells in her ribs, her pelvis, her skull, tiny high-pitched

36

bells in her fingertips. Ringing and ringing. *And that is God too*, she thought. *That is you too*.

Up near the altar there was a window that was left open all day once summer came. Just outside of it sat the well that Jehanne's family shared with the church—a black stony hole that Jehanne had loved leaning over as a child, drinking in the cold, deep, earth air and the mossy stone smell, dropping pebbles down into the black shining water. Often she wished that she could fall in, down and down into the dark bottomless tunnel, swimming down through the water until she touched the ancient heart of the earth.

One day, while she was praying, Jehanne heard her mother's voice there by the well. There came a sudden bray of boyish laughter. Jehanne got up and walked to the window. She crouched on one side of it and peered past the leaded corner of the frame. Her mother was standing in the sun, pulling on the frayed well rope hand over hand and talking to a boy named Michel Le Buin. The miller's son. A blond, pimpled boy with an angry red chin and slicks of oil on either side of his nose. He walked around with a proud, haughty look on his face, as if he were very handsome and very rich. This infuriated Jehanne. Made her long to slap him. 'Such a long time since we've had a visit from you,' her mother was saying. 'I know Jehannette would love to see you.'

Jehanne backed away from the window, her arms cold. That night she did not sleep. She lay awake in her bed, staring up at the darkness and the dim wood beams in the ceiling that seemed like bars upon her future.

CHAPTER NINETEEN

Several days later Michel Le Buin came to dinner, bowing and sweating in a new green tunic. His hair was spit-combed across his forehead. He held a bouquet of vetch under his arm. Jehanne's mother welcomed him like a long-lost son. 'Such lovely flowers, Michel!'

He smiled, his greedy eyes on Jehanne, gleaming. 'They're for Jehannette.'

'How lovely. Jehannette, put them in water.'

When she did nothing, her father kicked her hard under the table. Spoke through his teeth. 'Jehanne, up. Now!'

Slowly she rose. She could feel the boy's eyes on her as she moved, inspecting her breasts, her neck.

'A fine young woman she's grown into,' he said.

'Hasn't she,' said her father.

After dinner she crouched like a thief beneath her bedroom window, her ears pricked, listening to the low chuckling voices outside. 'Not a typical beauty, of course,' her father said. 'But there's power in her. Spine. Good thing in a woman.' He was talking like a salesman, using the same voice he used when he talked about his pigs at market.

'I see that. Will she breed?'

Jehanne was caught by a sudden vision of herself held up by the ankles, turning in the air, the men discussing her hooves, her haunches.

'Oh yes. Did you see the hips on her? She's born for it.'

'Is there not some insolence in her?'

She could hear her father smiling in the night

air.

'Nothing that can't be corrected,' he said.

CHAPTER TWENTY

She ran very quickly through the dew-wet fields in the white mist of dawn, up into the woods, on and on until she thought her lungs would burst, and then she stopped and hid herself in the roots of a great gnarled black oak. The forest seemed not quite real to her yet, still emerging from the mist, the trees still half hidden, ghostly in the cool early light. Jehanne curled herself up tightly among the roots of the tree with her eyes closed and her head bowed, wondering, thinking, asking . . . *What would be the first step? I cannot go directly to the King. He would never see me.*

Soon the light began to spread in her bones. Then the low, thrilling thunder of Michael's voice: *Go to Vaucouleurs, little one. The Governor will give you a letter of introduction to the King. You will find supporters there.*

She wanted badly to answer him. Wanted badly to say, *Yes, I will do as you ask.* But when she tried to speak, no words came out. She watched silently as the light drained away. It was as if her mouth were filled with stones. 'Coward,' she said at last, spitting the words out. She stood up and dusted herself off. 'Stupid. Stupid coward.'

CHAPTER TWENTY-ONE

She spent the day walking blindly through the woods, praying for courage that did not come. Then, as she was making her way home through the hills above Domrémy late in the afternoon, she saw smoke. Fat black blooms rolling upward into the chalk-white sky. Not chimney smoke, too fast, too big for chimney smoke. Something else. Jehanne moved quickly to a ruined wall, tucked her red skirt between her legs and scrambled up the moss-bearded rocks until she was on top of them, looking down over the green countryside to the little neighboring village of Greux, where a clutch of houses by the river stood engulfed in flame. Wild orange sails of fire were billowing and snapping in the afternoon breeze, columns of black smoke pouring out of the windows, the houses themselves melting down to bone.

Heart hammering in her chest, Jehanne looked on to where the church tower of Greux was burning like an enormous candle, and farther still to where a lone black horse had burst from the village. Its back was on fire and it was running, screaming toward the river. Behind the wretched animal came a handful of men on horseback, moving fast through the high summer grass with torches in their hands, shouting and cheering as they raced along the back path toward the *bois chênu*. 'Oh no,' she said as the burning horse stumbled, then collapsed a few feet from the river. She jumped down off the wall and ran.

40

CHAPTER TWENTY-TWO

It was a few minutes before anyone in the village could understand what she was saying. 'Slow down,' said her mother, a hand on Jehanne's heaving back. 'Take a breath.'

Half an hour later they were on the old Roman road, all the residents of Domrémy and their best livestock, setting out in the blue twilight for the fortress town of Neufchâteau. The smell of smoke was heavy in the dusk now, the calves and horses nervous, sensing their masters' fear. Jehanne sat up in the cart beside her mother, who was clutching a speckled laying hen in her lap and wailing loudly. Hauviette and Mengette were in the wagon beside them, weeping too, clutching each other as if they were drowning, their faces crumpled, shining with tears. Jehanne regarded them coldly, thought them foolish. They had to go, that was all. They had to get to Neufchâteau as quickly as possible. Nothing else to think about, no point in crying. Just go. Fast. Now.

Speaking in a low, hard voice, she drove the horses forward into the darkness, and as she drove, she felt calm and clear. A thrilling feeling, as if she were poised on a tight rope above a deep ravine, walking slowly forward. All she had to do was keep paying attention, keep putting one foot in front of the other, keep seeing herself arriving at the other side, her foot touching solid ground. Then she would make it. *I've a gift for this*, she thought.

Her father and brothers were just ahead, herding the cows and sheep, and she could hear the panic in her brothers' voices as they spoke to the animals. Pierrelot's voice high and girlish, 'Go, damn it! Move!' Jean thrashing the cows with his stick. They'd bound the hooves of the animals with cloth so their march had an odd muffled sound. There was the usual creak and clatter of the wagons, but below it, a large, awkward dragging, as if a great sea creature were trying to pull itself up onto the beach.

'Go on,' said Jehanne's father to a yellow calf that had stopped in the road. An urgent, low force in his voice, his words hitting the air like hammers. 'Go on, damn you.' But the calf would not move. It dug its heels into the dirt, stiffened its legs and began to bawl. All the villagers around them stared, white as salt.

'Shut it up,' said one man. 'Shut it up, Goddamn it.'

'Shut up,' her father hissed at the animal. 'Shut up, shut up.' But the bawling only grew louder. Soon the animal was howling like a lost child. Her father rummaged furiously in his pocket. Suddenly he grabbed the creature's curling blond head and pulled it back. A blade flashed in the air, and abruptly the bawling stopped. The calf nodded its head and an apron of blood poured from its throat. Jehanne blinked and looked away. After a moment, the animal knelt in the road. Then it lay down. 'Let's go,' said her father.

She saw the forest rise up before her in a high mass of black trees and vines against the aquamarine sky. A tunnel of dark leaves leading inward, away from the twilight, and the trees looming taller in the gathering dark, their limbs growing monstrous and powerful, asserting

42

dominance over the land. The road itself was very old; it had once led all the way to Rome, and as they moved through the night forest, Jehanne's mother crossed herself and whispered the Paternoster, and all of the villagers grew quiet, the entire train of them silent but for the shuffling of feet and the snuffing of the animals, and as they rode, Jehanne found herself moving through an ancient dream of rage. Along both sides of the road she saw the souls of her murdered countrymen assembled, thousands upon thousands of them advancing in a slow ghostly parade through the trees. Gray-skinned, sad-eyed farmers and millers, smiths and carpenters, priests and cobblers, wives and whores, mothers, nuns, and hollow-eyed children, Catherine among them, Hemet among them, all of them walking, saying, *Avenge us. Avenge us, girl.*

*   *   *

Later came other voices. The chorus of three wild Godvoices in her ears. *Soon, darling, soon*, they sang. *Your season is coming.*

CHAPTER TWENTY-THREE

Jehanne and her family were among the first of the dusty, exhausted travelers to arrive in Neufchâteau that night, and so they were part of a group led by the innkeeper Madame La Rousse through the dark, manure-stinking streets of the town to her small half-timbered inn where they would stay for

43

several weeks, crowded in with the twelve other families from Domrémy, packed tightly as rabbits in a warren and waiting for the news that it was safe to return to their village. Jehanne's parents and her brothers bedded down on straw pallets by the hearth. Jehanne lodged in a small cupboard beneath the stairs. Her cloak rolled up for a pillow. A canopy of cobwebs overhead.

She spent little time there. Her mind was too impatient, too feverish for sleep. Each night she lay silent, eyes wide open in the darkness, waiting until the house was quiet, until she could hear her father snoring through the wall, and then she crept out of the inn and into the warm summer night. Up through the maze of dark cobbled streets she went, a small, barefoot figure moving quickly, thick calves, red cheeks, fierce eyes, up and up until she reached the northern wall and ducked into the turret staircase, her hands held out on either side, feeling her way along the cold stone walls until she came out on a parapet overlooking the vast night-blue countryside, the air heavy with the smell of grass and hay, the far-off hills spotlighted by a rind of moon.

Each night she hoped to see just the moon and dark hills before her to the north, just the deep, rolling world of blue, but every night there were fires. New fires. A fire where her home had once lain, her church, her heart. Four blazing orange monsters feasting on the dark shanks of the land.

You will pay, she thought as she watched it burn. *God will make you pay for this.*

CHAPTER TWENTY-FOUR

'Lord, we pray for the families of Domrémy, whose village has been so cruelly destroyed and who now seek shelter with us here in Neufchâteau.' The priest paused, wiped a white ball of spittle from his lips and continued. 'We pray that the terrible plague of the English invaders and the traitorous Burgundians be lifted from us and that France be permitted once again to toil and flourish in Your great and holy name.'

Jehanne knelt in the hot, overcrowded church among her fellow refugees and churchgoers, her head bowed, hands clasped tightly as she whispered a fervent prayer, oblivious to the stares and raised eyebrows of her fellow Christians. She knelt like that throughout the service, until the bells rang out, and the rest of the churchgoers began their slow march out of the building and through the front doors into the climbing July sunlight of the courtyard, where the wives of Neufchâteau had prepared a communal midday meal. Jehanne was hungry, could smell the hens roasting over the fires outside, but she continued praying. As her father passed by, he stopped, clapped his hand on her shoulder and said through gritted teeth, 'That's enough praying now, Jehannette.'

She looked up at him. 'I'm not finished yet.'

Her father's nostrils flared in disgust. 'Christ, you're an embarrassment,' he muttered under his breath.

'May God forgive you for swearing in His

45

house,' she said, her face so righteous that he itched to slap her, and would have done so had they not been in public.

Only when the church was deserted and the front doors closed did she stand. Her legs burning, her knees sore and red. The space was dim and cool now, forestlike, silent. Moving like a sleepwalker, she went to the front of the nave and knelt down before the altar and began to pray once more. Her heart ached now with remorse. *Dear God, forgive me for my rage toward my father and for my rage toward the English, whom I know are your creatures under Heaven as I am, although it often seems that they are not. Forgive me for my violent thoughts, and for my hunger to see them suffer as we do.*

A pause. Watching from the shadow of the vestry door stood the little bald priest in his black robes, transfixed by the strange sight before him. The girl kneeling in a shaft of sunlight, her face and hands raised to the sky, tears rolling down her cheeks. *And forgive me, please, for doubting you, Lord. Forgive me for not accepting without question your commands, forgive me for being so frightened. I want badly to do as you wish.*

Then silence. For a long time, silence.

She lay down on the floor and pressed her cheek against the cold, smooth stone. *Talk to me. Help me find the strength to do as you wish.* More silence. Silence forever, it seemed. The priest staring, frozen, unable to move.

At last came the opening in time. She loosened her grip on her mind, forgot herself, and in her forgetting she opened like a window to the sky. In poured the thrilling light, the joy. A golden burr in

46

her right eye and the spreading warmth in her cheek, along her neck, down her spine. The archangel spoke softly. *Learn to ride, little one. Teach yourself to ride*.

CHAPTER TWENTY-FIVE

It did not rain in Neufchâteau for three weeks. The air grew dry and dusty, the river shrank to a winding trickle in the red earth. Soon a thin red veil of dust covered everything in the town and all the countryside around it. Red dust on the tables and chairs and pots and pans and spoons and knives and windows, so thick on the windows on the front of Madame La Rousse's inn that one still, dull afternoon, Jehanne practiced writing her name with her finger on the glass. It was the only word she knew how to write, taught to her by Père Guillaume in Domrémy several years earlier. J-E-H-A-N-N-E-T-T-E, she wrote. But she did not recognize herself in the word any longer. It seemed to her the name of a stranger.

Dust and more dust, making the horses cough and the farmers out in the fields wipe their eyes again and again with their handkerchiefs. Soon the town's wells were running low and cups of water were being rationed out with care. Out in the fields, women began to clasp hands and kneel down and call to the old pagan gods for rain. 'O great Cernunnos,' they cried. 'We pray in your mighty name.'

When at last an armada of low, dark storm clouds appeared in the sky one afternoon, the townspeople were so busy putting buckets and tubs out to collect rainwater and pulling clothes off the drying lines that Jehanne saw an opportunity. Her father was setting up a second trough down by the barn for the animals, and her mother was pounding around upstairs with Madame La Rousse, closing the shutters about the inn, so she slipped unnoticed out of the front door and walked nonchalantly away from the house and down the hill, humming quietly to herself, as if she were on her way to church.

*   *   *

Down in the field just outside the western wall of the town, she crouched with her skirt knotted between her legs, watching a horse graze from twenty feet off. A thin, sad-looking creature with a dusty brown coat and hooves the size of church bells. Jehanne could smell the rain coming, the high, mineral scent in the air. The stiff wind moving over the grass. Dark violet clouds scudding across the sky. She clucked her tongue against the roof of her mouth and held her dirty hand out toward the animal, rubbing her fingers together as if she had a treat.

The horse stood with a pale fan of dried grass protruding from its mouth. Rotated its jaw, eyed her skeptically. For every step Jehanne took forward, the animal took one back. 'Come on,' she said. 'Come on, baby.' Overhead the wind riffled the trees, and the clouds moved like dark islands over the hills. Crouched motionless in the grass like a wildcat, eyes hooded, she waited until the animal lowered its great head to take another

48

mouthful, and then she sprang forward, hurling herself across the animal's back, clutching at its ragged mane as the startled creature reared up and pawed the air and bucked, shrieking and stomping the earth with its enormous hooves and shaking itself until at last Jehanne flew through the air like a rag doll, and the horse took off running across the field as if the Devil himself were on its heels.

CHAPTER TWENTY-SIX

In the morning she looked at her mother across the table and said, 'They need help feeding people up at the church. Can I go?'

The rain had stopped. Sunlight was pouring in the windows, and the world outside seemed sparkling and new, as if each of the leaves on the trees had been polished by hand. Jehanne longed to fling herself into it.

'There's a nice idea,' said Madame La Rousse, who was rolling dough by the stove, her hair tied up in a black cloth tower on her head.

Jehanne's mother glanced at her husband, who sat at the end of the table, hunched over a bowl of porridge, white twists of steam rising in the air. He did not look up, did not stop eating. He simply grunted and shrugged his shoulders, which Jehanne and her mother took to mean yes.

It was three days before the animal would allow her to mount again. Three days of lying to her mother and then waiting, chasing, ducking the animal's great punching hooves, being thrown into the mud, kicking the grass with impatience. On her

49

way to see the horse the third afternoon, Jehanne cut through the town market. She had a few silver coins her mother had given her for the church collection plate, and as she walked, she jingled them in her pocket. She stopped in front of a cart with piles of rope coiled like snakes on the ground before it. There were thin, fine flaxen coils and heavy tough ones made from hemp, some frayed, some clean and new, shining in the light like corn silk. Jehanne considered them. She bent down and fingered a sturdy medium-weight length, then stood and lifted the rope with her arms until it unwound to its full length, which was twice as tall as she was.

'I could think of some things to do with that,' said a voice behind her.

Jehanne turned. It was Michel Le Buin.

'Like what?' she said, her eyes cold, her heart itchy with hatred.

The oily-nosed boy pinched out a smile, scratched his neck. 'You'll just have to wait and see.'

Jehanne turned away and addressed the vendor, who was squatting like a monkey in the purple shade of the cart. 'How much for this,' she said, hoisting the rope.

'Three deniers.'

'How about one?'

'Settle at two.'

She looked at him, smiled. 'I've only got one and a half.'

The man scratched his beard. Considered the rope.

'Fair enough.'

'Any chance you could tie it into a set of reins for

50

me while you're at it?'

Jehanne was smiling beautifully now, her eyes shining like river stones.

The man looked away. Then he picked up the rope and began to fold it and knot it for her.

'Jehannette, if you don't marry me, I'm going to take you to court and sue you for breaking an oath.'

'I never made any oath.'

'Your father did.'

'He can say what he likes. Doesn't mean I'm going to do it.'

*   *   *

A dazzling high summer afternoon. A light wind rippling across the poppy fields. Cows dozing in the shade of the alders. In the westernmost field of Neufchâteau, far away from the river, Jehanne sat atop a split-rail fence with a bunch of clover hay in one hand and the rope in the other. The horse ignored her, flicked flies with his tail, until she quietly hopped off the fence and crouch-walked toward the animal with the hay held out before her in offering. Its ears twitched, a glossy black eye rolled toward her, but the horse remained still. 'Look what I got for you,' she said, lifting the hay to the animal's black lips.

A display of long yellow teeth and pink gums then, the horse's jaw rotating as it took the hay in, Jehanne moving slowly, slowly closer to the animal, cooing softly as she went. Slowly, ever so gently, she slipped the homemade reins over the great dusty head and manipulated the rope deep into the animal's mouth along with the hay, setting it in

51

behind the wet molars, and then creeping alongside the horse, taking hold of its mane and leaping smoothly up out of the grass, mounting it once more, this time calmly, and then gripping the sides of the horse so forcefully with her thighs and knees that when the animal bolted forward, she remained in place on its back, leaning over its long brown neck with her elbows dug in and the rope tight in her hands as the animal took off across the high green field, speaking softly in the animal's ear as it went, and guiding it with her reins until slowly its gait smoothed out to a long and fluid run, and they were moving as one through the grass in the clear summer afternoon with the earth thundering beneath them and the hills a blur of green all around, the enormous blue bowl of the sky overhead and the smell of clover in the air and the sun on their skins and she thought, *I can do this.*

CHAPTER TWENTY-SEVEN

A thick, pale man with slablike cheeks stood in the door of Madame La Rousse's inn, his eyes dull as wax. 'Summons for one Jehanne d'Arc, daughter of Zabillet and Jacques d'Arc to appear at the high court in Toul on November 16, 1428,' he said.

Jehanne's dark brows came together like crow's wings. 'What's the charge?'

'Charge brought by one Michel Le Buin of Domrémy, stating that mademoiselle has broken her solemn betrothal promise to enter with him into the most holy estate of marriage.'

Jehanne burst out laughing. She had not

thought Michel capable of it. She sat by the hearth with a long purple curl of turnip peel hanging from her knife, shaking her head. 'I never promised any such thing,' she said finally. She looked at her father. 'Did I, Papa?'

And this was more than her father could bear, the girl once again defying him, making a fool of him in front of a perfect stranger. His face swelled up with hatred, and he said that she was an arrogant bitch. Then he stood and punched her in the mouth.

When Jehanne opened her eyes, the world was tilting wildly above her. The table and chairs leaned at strange angles, everyone stood over her, tall as trees. Her mother was shrieking like she always shrieked. Useless. Her father was looking down from his great height, still red and pop-eyed, like a bull, his fists clenched, as if he expected her to say something more. But Jehanne remained still on the floor, and at last her father sat down in his chair. 'You had that coming,' he said, wiping his mouth with the back of a hand.

The messenger coughed, said it didn't matter what the truth was. 'You have to come to Toul to answer—' Abruptly he stopped speaking. Jehanne was on her feet and moving up behind her father with the kitchen knife flashing in her hand. The world red and rippling. She took his neck in the crook of her arm, pulled back his chin, and held the point of the blade against his tonsils.

Her mother screamed. 'Stop it!'

Jehanne leaned in close to her father's ear and spoke quietly. 'You ever touch me again, I'll kill you. Understand? I will slit your ugly throat.'

'Get off me,' he said.

Jehanne pressed the knife blade in deeper until a bright bead of blood appeared on his skin. Amazed at her own ferocity. 'Understand?'

Her father said that he did.

*   *   *

She spent the night outside, walking up and down through the hilly narrow streets of the town, trembling. For hours she knew nothing. Knew only the cold, damp air on her cheeks and the thrilling wind roaring in her head. She walked fast, blindly, walked until she came to the top of a steep hill where she stood breathing heavily, her nostrils red with cold as she looked down the crooked street. A flash of cobblestone shone in the torchlight outside a tall stone house. A chicken clucked softly in the darkness nearby. The roaring in her head had stopped now, and she felt tall and calm, standing in the darkness at the top of the hill, looking down at the rooftops below her. She knew then that it was possible. She felt as if someone had untied her. The wall of fear was gone.

Go to Vaucouleurs, said Catherine. *The man your father knows, Governor de Baudricourt, will give you the help you need*. And Jehanne saw how it would go then very clearly. She saw that she would go to Toul and answer the judge's foolish questions. She would make him believe her. Then she would leave Domrémy forever. She would go to Vaucouleurs, and she would find men to escort her to the Dauphin's castle in Chinon. She would go to war against the English. She would crown the rightful king.

CHAPTER TWENTY-EIGHT

In the end it was Durand who helped her escape. Durand who appeared that winter with his slumped, meaty shoulders and his high filthy black boots several months after Jehanne and her parents had returned to the charred remains of Domrémy. A month after the judge in Toul had heard Jehanne's testimony and declared her innocent of the charges brought by Michel Le Buin. Durand pulled up outside the house in his wagon on his way back from the market in Nancy, came lumbering across the frozen yard with a basket of green duck eggs in one hand and a fresh loaf of *sa fleur* bread under his arm.

Before he was halfway to the front door, Jehanne came hopping out over the hard icy ground in her bare feet, hugged her cousin hard, and dragged him over to the black stump that had once been a rhododendron by the side of the house. 'Listen, Uncle,' she whispered, shivering, her eyes feverishly bright. 'I need your help.'

For months she'd been trying to find a way out of Domrémy. Her voices whispering hot in her ears each day, *Go, little one! Go!* The English had laid siege to the city of Orléans in October, and the saints had been relentless ever since. Coming three or four times a day. Michael standing on the air before her in his wild, feathered sunlight, his brow pressed into long stern pleats, his eyes like burning stones. *You must make it to Chinon by mid-Lent if we are to save Orléans, little one. Go now. You must go now!* If she did not, he said, everything would be over. Orléans was the gateway to the last free part of the country, the last line of defense keeping the Goddons out of the unprotected heartland of the south. If the Goddons took Orléans, there would be nothing to keep them from taking the rest of France too.

Twice that autumn Claude had brought updates from Orléans to Domrémy. Tales of families hunting for rats by torchlight, drinking blood from the necks of their horses. 'Just when you thought it couldn't get worse,' Claude said. But there was none of the old storyteller's joy in him now. His cheeks had gone gray. His eyes were frightened.

They followed Jehanne into her dreams, the people of Orléans. Their sunken, purple-ringed eyes reproached her, pleaded with her until at last she could not eat or sleep at all, could do nothing but stand by the window in her father's house with her hands knotted together, staring at the empty road, praying to the empty road. *There must be a way. There must be a way.* When at last Durand appeared in Domrémy with his great toothy smile and the basket of eggs beside him in the wagon, it seemed as if she had conjured him right out of the dust and ashes, and the sun shone in her heart for the first time in months. 'My best girl!' he roared as she came across the yard.

But his face changed when she began to speak of her mission. Listening to her describe Saint Michael's orders to lead the Dauphin's army into battle against the English and crown the Dauphin Charles in Reims Cathedral, Durand turned increasingly pale. When he spoke, his voice was cold. 'Jehanne, stop. What are you talking about? Do you know what you're saying?'

Her eyes were very bright; there were hectic spots of red on her cheeks. 'Have you not heard the prophecy that France would be ruined by a woman and restored by a virgin from Lorraine?'

Durand laughed. 'And you think you're her?'

'I know that I am her.'

'You're out of your mind,' he said quietly.

'You believe a stranger in Rodez with bleeding hands and feet, but not your own cousin?'

'Not when my cousin tells me she wants to go get herself killed by the Goddons.'

'Uncle, I swear to you, by all that is holy, I speak the truth. I need you to take me to Sir Robert de Baudricourt's château in Vaucouleurs. There's no one else.'

'Baudricourt's not going to see you! Why would he? It's insane, what you're saying. You're a girl! A child! You can't go running around the country with soldiers, fighting wars, talking to kings. It's madness. They'll tear you apart.'

Jehanne looked at her cousin, and she felt the fire surge through her. Her sex, her fingertips, were glowing like stars. 'I am protected,' she said quietly. 'The Lord has said nothing shall harm me.'

Durand made a face. 'Don't say such things. And don't look at me that way, Jehanne. I can't help you.' He shook his head, rubbed his hand over his mouth. 'What do your parents say about all this? Do they know about this plan of yours?'

She said that they did not and could not. 'You know Papa. He'd kill me.'

'And who would blame him?' said Durand, throwing his hands out, his dark eyebrows raised high on his forehead.

Jehanne continued looking up at him, and

57

Durand could feel her will pulling at him like a fierce tide. She put her small brown hand on his arm. 'You have to help,' she said. 'Please. There's no one else.'

'No,' he said. 'Absolutely not. That's final.'

Jehanne kept asking. Again and again she asked, and again and again he refused. But each time there was a little less force in his voice. Looking into his young cousin's dark eyes, Durand began to feel slightly hypnotized. And the longer he looked at her, the more it began to seem to him that he *must* help her, that she was clearly in God's grace, and that to do anything else would be wrong, quite possibly an offense against the Almighty.

*   *   *

So Durand Laxart drove out of Domrémy with Jehanne crouched low in the back of his wagon, hidden beneath a filthy wool blanket—a cage of stinking chickens on one side of her, an enormous grinding stone on the other. It was a brutal January day. The air so cold it hurt to breathe, the bare black trees encased in ice, clattering in the wind. Overhead the sky was flat white, the sun steaming weakly from a hole inside of it. Jehanne pressed her small chapped hands together between her thighs, trying to keep warm.

She kept her head under the blanket, but she could see her house through the slats in the side of the wagon as it receded behind them—the burnt, stained, hunchbacked shape, the garden where He had first showed her His light, the ruined garden where her mother knelt now, hunched over the piles of ash and charcoal, digging for turnips amidst the ashes. *Good-bye house*, she thought as the cart rolled into the future. *Good-bye family. Good-bye* bois chênu . . .

Suddenly they all seemed unbearably dear to her. Even her father. Suddenly all she could remember was the love—her father taking her to pick strawberries at the edge of the *bois chênu*, giving her the sweetest ones. Or the way she would run out into the road to meet him at the end of the day when she was a child, leaping up into his great strong arms, shrieking with delight as he swung her around in a circle, her body's dark shadow stretching out hugely over the road, her hair flying out like a fan, and she would think, *Oh Papa! My Papa!*

She remembered not her mother's fear and cowardice, but the way she'd sung to her before bed at night. *Les troupeaux d'oiseaux descendent sur moi. Je salue les orioles, et le rossignol* . . . The way she'd brushed Jehanne's hair back off her forehead, her hand rough and warm and tender all at the same time, the musky fragrance of her neck as she bent down to kiss Jehanne good night. *Forgive me*, she thought. *Forgive me for leaving you.*

Through the wooden slats, her face striped in sunlight, she saw her village go by as if for the first time. The church with its charred black face and its sagging roof, Père Guillaume with his thin, wrinkled apple cheeks and his ugly, misshapen wool hat, taking a holly wreath down off of the door. She saw the dim cave of the smith's shop with its red fire glowing in the belly of the oven, the smith with his blackened face, his hammer on the anvil, a family of gray pigs huddled together

59

behind a split-rail fence in the frozen mud. In the square was the well where Quiet Paul had kissed her when she was ten, and at the well itself stood the mayor's daughter, Louise, in her fine green woolen dress, flashing her eyes at André Gachot. And the light Jehanne saw in Louise's eyes made her pine for a moment for a different sort of life entirely. A life like the one Catherine might have had—graceful and soft, protected. Making dresses and cakes, combing her children's hair, cutting violets in the garden. And it seemed strange to her that she should long for such a thing now, though she never had before in her life.

She waited until the wagon began to wind its way through the stiff yellow fields outside the village to raise herself up in the cart and let the blanket fall around her shoulders, the air stinging her face and ears as she looked out across the gray and brown winter patchwork of the countryside, out to the line of naked black elm trees on the hill with their long black branches reaching up against the January sky, the red eye of the sun sinking into the horizon. *And beyond that, Paradise*, she thought. *God's beautiful Paradise in the sky where my saints will lead me one day if I do as they say.*

CHAPTER TWENTY-NINE

It was dark when they arrived in Burey-le-Petit. At the house of the fawn. Jehanne had fallen asleep. Durand called to her from the front of the wagon, his voice disembodied, strange in the dark. 'You alive back there? We're almost home.' Jehanne, hoisted from a dream in which she was charging naked into battle without a sword, blinked and looked up at the cold black sky and the bright sprays of stars, and remembered that her journey had begun. She had taken the first impossible step.

The wagon was climbing slowly up a hill through the darkness, and the air was icy and fresh on her face, and as the night world unfolded around her, a powerful excitement crept over her skin. *It has begun*, she thought. She could hear the horses huffing up ahead as they labored slowly up the incline, and the clinking of their bits and the creaking of the wagon, and these seemed suddenly like new and thrilling sounds to her, like sounds she was hearing for the first time. And the night sky seemed like a new sky, filled with stars she'd never seen.

Durand's wife, Marie, stood at the door of the cracked house with narrowed eyes and her heavy white arms crossed over her chest. She was roundly pregnant and dressed in a thin, brown cotton shift, a gray blanket clutched about her shoulders. A look on her pale face as if she'd been drinking sour milk. 'You promised you'd be back by sunset,' she said to Durand.

Durand smiled and blushed and apologized all at once. 'I know I did, dear, and I'm sorry about it, but look, I've brought young Jehanne to stay with us for a patch.'

Jehanne's aunt regarded her bleakly. 'Why?'

Durand hurried Jehanne inside the house. 'I'll explain everything, don't worry. It's a great reason. A matter of great importance. Aren't you even going to say hello to her, Marie?'

'Hello, Jehanne,' said the woman without

smiling. She tucked in her lips. 'You knew,' she hissed at her husband as he passed. 'You knew tonight was the last night.'

'And it still is,' he said, kissing her on the shoulder. 'Don't you worry, Pony.'

'I poached a chicken for dinner. Of course it's cold now.'

Durand gave a nervous chuckle. 'Ah, cold chicken will suit Jehanne and me just fine, won't it, Jehanne?'

Jehanne said that it would, though her heart stung from Marie's cold reception. *She has never liked me. Well, I've never liked her either. Old shrew.*

*   *   *

After dinner Jehanne lay in a featherbed beside the hearth, watching the fawn, grown to an adult deer now, curled up asleep in its basket and the red coals that pulsed in the heart of the fire. She wondered if it was true what her brothers said, that Hell resembled such a place. Whole pulsing cities of fire, eternal burning. And as she watched those cities blaze in her mind's eye, her heart filled with shame for her earlier unkindness toward her aunt. *Forgive me*, she prayed. *Forgive my hateful thoughts toward Marie. I will try to love her better.*

Late in the night she awoke to a moaning. Low and ragged like a cow's. For a moment she was very frightened. None of the shapes in the room were familiar to her. She could not remember where she was. 'Oh,' said a voice. A woman's voice. 'Oh God.'

Then she knew. Lifting her chin slightly, she looked out beyond the featherbed across the room to her uncle's bed. She could see the dark shape of him, on his knees behind his wife. Their shadows thrown on the wall behind them, monstrous in the firelight. 'Yes. Oh God. Durand.'

The deer had lifted its head and was watching the couple, its face calm, impassive. Jehanne, face afire, watched too. Was fascinated in spite of herself. She could see Durand's hands on his wife's waist, her long curtain of hair swaying in the firelight, her face lifted to the ceiling, mouth slack, eyes closed. And it seemed to Jehanne that these were two people she'd never seen before—a secret Durand and Marie, kept hidden from the world. Hidden from everyone but each other.

'Oh,' she groaned, long and low. 'Oh.'

He lifted the dark curtain of her hair and twisted it in a knot around his hand. 'Say you're sorry for earlier.'

She tried to pull away from him then.

'Ah,' she said as he yanked her hair back, her profile rising clearly in the firelight. 'Ah, God,' she said, her voice cracking. She groaned and rose up, her back arching, her swollen belly and breasts in cameo against the flickering wall.

'Say it.'

'Forgive me,' she said at last, and then the man clasped her breasts and pulled her to him, burying his face in her neck.

*   *   *

Afterward they lay collapsed together in the dark, stroking each other, saying love words. Jehanne thought she had never heard people speak so tenderly to each other. And she lay there watching

63

the dying fire, wondering what she'd given up.

CHAPTER THIRTY

Vaucouleurs was like nothing Jehanne had ever seen. A tall stone city on a hill, circled by a high, thick wall and crowned with towers and turrets, its flags and banners snapping in the wind. 'Bit different from Domrémy, eh?' Durand said as they approached in the wagon. Another bitter cold day out, but this one was sunny too—the harsh, clear sunlight of winter. From a distance Vaucouleurs looked like a thing out of a fairy tale. Only when they drew closer did she see that it was a ruined thing too. The city had been besieged by the Burgundians over the summer, and everywhere there were red tiled rooftops caved in by cannonballs and walls streaked black with smoke. Windows with big, star-shaped holes in their centers, and great piles of rubble that had once been houses. *Filthy Goddons*, she thought as they rode among the ruins. *They'll pay for this*.

It was market day in Vaucouleurs. The air quivering with the hot buzz of commerce. Crowds of people packed into the winding cobblestone streets and the main square. More people than Jehanne had ever seen, shouting and jostling with their carts of goats and pigs, strings of rabbits hung up by their soft white feet, and sad-eyed trout still wet from the river. She watched as they passed baskets of brown, hay-flecked eggs and carrots with their frothing green hair, great wheels of cheese taller than she was and golden flats of honey glistening in the comb. People too—a squat, pink-skinned woman shouting with a tray of dried sardines that flashed silver in the light, a bony, blue-jawed man yanking a goat on a string, and the pock-marked farmer behind him, frowning at the small pile of coins in his hand.

An anxious hunger she saw carved into the faces in Vaucouleurs. A look you did not see in the country. Three dark lines across the brow, one carved into either side of the mouth as if by a knife. And a kind of theatre about it—the onion man's wide, desperate smile, the pale noblewoman with a hat like the sailing ship she'd seen in one of Claude's books sneering at Jehanne as she and Durand rode past in their cart. Suddenly Jehanne was aware of her greasy hair and dirty face, the red linen rag of her dress with its ripped seams and too-short sleeves, her boots with the soles worn through . . . She looked down at the black crescents of grime under her fingernails and tucked her hands into her lap. Then she went on looking, drinking in the hot, jostling energy, the spectacle. *Things get done here*, she thought. *Things can happen.*

CHAPTER THIRTY-ONE

The guards at Sir Robert's château laughed at her. Laughed like hyenas, their faces red and toothy, cruel. 'A magic virgin?' said one with a long knobby nose and a leering grin. 'Whyn't you come over here and work some magic on my cock, eh, darlin'?'

'How dare you!' said Jehanne, blushing. But that only made them laugh harder. 'Tell them I am the daughter of Jacques d'Arc from Domrémy. Sir Robert knows him. I demand that you take my message to him right away.' But even as she said it, she knew that was wrong too. *Now they will make you wait even longer.*

It was true. For four hours they made Jehanne and Durand wait in the freezing stone antechamber of the château. Their hands gray with cold, their breath coming out in great white plumes around them. Durand wondering what the hell he'd been thinking, agreeing to bring her there. But when at last he walked with Jehanne toward Sir Robert's chambers later that afternoon, passing knots of richly dressed knights and noblewomen in the public rooms, his heart swelled up once more. 'We'll show them,' he whispered to Jehanne. 'Sometimes God visits His miracles on us peasants too.'

Jehanne could not stop thinking about the guards. Their ugly red faces. Their loud, barking laughter. It was the first time she'd spoken of her mission to strangers, and as soon as she'd heard the words come out of her mouth, she'd known it was wrong. She'd done it all wrong. The words sounded hollow and unsure—not at all the way they felt inside of her. As she looked at the men's leering faces, she saw that they thought she was mad. A lunatic. A fool.

If she'd been rich, maybe, or a nun, educated and proper, they would not have laughed at her. Everyone knew and respected the visions of Colette de Corbie and Marie Robine of Avignon. Marie, who'd prophesied that a virgin from

Lorraine would appear on horseback and bear arms to deliver France from its enemies. But they were learned holy women, friends of the aristocracy. Not a dirty unlearned peasant from the cow pastures of Domrémy.

As she stood before Sir Robert in the pale stone grandeur of his receiving room, Jehanne's fear grew—a cold gargoyle hunched in her heart. She looked up at the corpulent bull stuffed into a blue satin tunic that was Sir Robert de Baudricourt, saw his elegantly carved mahogany chair and his oddly small, delicate feet turned out like a ballerina's on the bearskin rug. The gargoyle hissed, *Fool. He'll never believe you. If you're not careful, he'll throw you in prison for blasphemy. Burn you at the stake.* She opened her mouth to speak, but Jehanne found that no words would come out. Her cheeks and ears burned hot. The gargoyle had jumped to his feet and was shouting *Fool! Fool! You might as well just kill yourself, you stupid, stupid fool!*

At last Durand stepped forward and said, 'My cousin, Mademoiselle Jehanne d'Arc. Daughter of Jacques d'Arc, the representative from Domrémy whom Your Grace met with over the troubles there last year.'

Sir Robert licked his lips and peered down at Jehanne. 'Come closer, girl, I can't see you,' he said.

Jehanne could not move.

'Go on,' Durand whispered, nudging her.

Eventually she took a few stiff steps toward the Governor's chair. It was a fight to make her legs move. She felt as if she were wading through sand.

'Closer,' said the man, until at last she stood directly in front of him, smiling stupidly. 'Now, what is it that you want?'

Once more the words froze like rocks in her mouth.

'Well?'

'I know this will sound crazy,' she burst out at last. 'But I'm sent by our Lord. He wants you to write a letter to the Dauphin, reporting that God will send him help before mid-Lent.'

One of Sir Robert's eyebrows shot up, as if pulled by a string. 'And what Lord is this?'

Another pause.

'God.'

Sir Robert laughed for a long time, and when he was finished laughing, he lowered his purple eyelids and said, 'You can't be serious.'

Jehanne did not answer. She simply gazed at him, willing him to see what was in her heart. *See that this is not a jest . . . see that the future of France depends on me . . .*

Abruptly Sir Robert's eyes went cold. 'You've got a cheek, girl. You've got one hell of a cheek.'

Jehanne blinked. Fought the urge to run. She felt the Godself rise inside of her, felt the bold heat fill her, climbing up from her belly into her heart. 'That I do,' she said at last in a voice that sounded strange to her—a voice stronger and clearer than her own. 'Mark my words, sir, I won't leave Vaucouleurs until I have that letter.'

Sir Robert stared at her. Then he stared at her uncle who stood behind her, clutching his hat, his face as red as a tomato. 'Take this chit home and tell her father to give her a good beating,' he said. 'Girl like that needs to be hit.'

*   *   *

68

She stood in the long blue shadow of the château, facing her uncle, her jaw clenched. The temperature had dropped steeply while they were inside; a polar wind swiped at her ears and cheeks. The bones in her skull ached. Suddenly she felt very tired.

'Filthy pig,' said Durand, shaking his head. 'What does he know?'

'I'm not leaving,' Jehanne said, clutching the tops of her arms to keep warm.

Durand smiled sadly. 'That's very noble of you, dear, but how are you going to get him to change his mind?'

'God will tell me.' She looked down at the ground, studied the clear frozen puddle, inside of which a red leaf lay trapped. 'You can leave if you want to, but I'm staying.'

CHAPTER THIRTY-TWO

It was in Vaucouleurs that I became the Virgin. La Pucelle. Whatever was left of Jehannette, the cowardly daughter of Jacques d'Arc, died during those long winter months of waiting for Sir Robert's support. Slipped away and fell to the ground in a little pile of dry skin at my feet. And I became something else altogether. Something not quite human. For a virgin is not quite human. A virgin can walk through doors the others cannot. Her hand is a skeleton key.

Day after day in Vaucouleurs I let the voices tell me of the creature I must become. A symbol, pure and fierce. Simple as a blade of grass. Braver than a

69

lion. A marvel of conviction and rage and faith. The Maid of Lorraine. Believe that you are the Maid of Lorraine, the voices said. Know that you have always been the Maid of Lorraine.

CHAPTER THIRTY-THREE

When he saw that Jehanne would not be convinced to return to Domrémy, Durand took her to stay with his boyhood friend, Henri Le Royer and his wife Thérèse in Vaucouleurs. *Thérèse the Doubter*, Jehanne thinks, remembering.

She doesn't know what Durand said to convince them to let her stay. It must have been something about the voices. The mission. But she doesn't know. He made her wait, shivering in the wagon, blowing on her hands, while he spoke to them. An hour later they all came out of the house together, smiling very politely.

At first Thérèse had seemed pleased, even excited to have Jehanne in her home. Only later did she show her true colors . . . *like so many. Throwing daisies and gold coins at my feet while the sun was shining, but running for the hills at the first sign of thunder.*

The Le Royers lived in a pretty, orderly, half-timber house with painted red beams down at the end of a lane near the Porte de France. It delighted her at first, with its smells of wood shavings and bubbling stew, Henri and Thérèse smiling and waving from the doorway as Durand helped Jehanne down out of the wagon. Their faces fascinated and slightly terrified—as if she were a

70

unicorn they'd spotted in the forest.

Henri was a wheelwright, and there were dozens of wheels propped up neatly against the house like a thicket of wooden suns. As she made her way across the frozen yard toward the door, it comforted Jehanne to think of herself staying in a house surrounded by suns. *A good sign*, she thought, for her heart was still trembling from the terrible audience with Sir Robert. As they'd passed through the shadows of a covered bridge on the way to the Le Royers' house, she'd been seized by the desire to run away, run back to Domrémy forever and throw herself at her father's feet, crying *Forgive me! I'm a fool! I'm not special at all! Take me back! I'll do whatever you like, only let me stay!*

But she knew it was impossible. He'd kill me before the snow melts, she thought. He'd laugh as they put me in the ground.

Thérèse came forward first. Smiling and exclaiming. A plump, snub-nosed brunette with meaty brown cheeks and a deep, freckled bosom. 'Welcome!' she cried, embracing Jehanne, looking her over with her sharp green eyes as Durand and Henri looked on. 'We are so happy to have you with us.'

Thérèse's voice was high and stagey, her eyes so bright and hard with excitement they made Jehanne nervous, left her with the vague feeling that Thérèse had not seen her at all, but was instead seeing some idea of Jehanne that she'd created in her own mind. But just as quickly, Jehanne forgot about it, for she was tired and grateful for the welcome, the outpouring of cheerfulness and warmth. She did not want to question it.

Inside the main room of the house, near the hearth, stood a thin, yellow-skinned young woman with dark straight hair, a narrow, slot-like mouth, and a sharp, quivering chin. She was sweeping furiously. 'My sister-in-law, Letice,' Henri said to Jehanne as she stamped her slush-caked boots by the door. The young woman sent a swirling cloud of gray dust into the air and nodded without looking at Jehanne.

'A pleasure,' said Jehanne.

The woman regarded her with cold eyes. Said nothing. Then she turned back to her furious sweeping. Thérèse glanced at Jehanne and rolled her eyes.

Henri coughed into his fist. 'I'll just show you the room, then,' he said.

Jehanne followed Henri up a narrow stone staircase, its banister worn smooth as soap. The stairs were very steep, and Jehanne had to pull hard on the banister to get herself up them. She was panting when she reached the top.

'We thought you girls could sleep together in here,' he said in a nervous voice, ushering her into a clean, low-ceilinged room at the top of the stairs. 'You're right above the fireplace, so it's the warmest room in the house.' Inside the little room stood a big wooden four-poster bed with a straw mattress and a thick stack of gray woolen blankets laid neatly on top. There were long boughs of pine strewn across the floor, which made the room smell fresh and clean, and a pitcher of steaming water stood on a table by the window, beside a bowl. 'In case you want to wash,' said Henri, blushing. He had a shy, warm smile and a habit of

72

pressing his hands together as he spoke. 'I hope this will be all right.'

Jehanne nodded. 'It's very nice.'

Henri was staring at her with a strange, pent-up look on his face, as if he longed to ask her something. Jehanne waited politely, but he did not speak. After several moments he shook his head, as if coming out of a trance, and said, 'Now don't mind Letice, you hear? Her nose is just a bit out of joint.' He smiled and winked as he pulled the door closed behind him. 'She's used to being the holy one in the house.'

Thérèse was more direct. As soon as they'd finished supper, she drew Jehanne down beside the hearth and handed her a cup of hot spiced wine. Durand had already started off to Burey. 'I hate to do it, but Marie is waiting on me. The baby could come any time,' he'd said gruffly as Jehanne hugged him and hid her sudden flood of tears in the scratchy wool of his cloak. 'Be brave now,' he'd whispered as he hugged her back. 'Show 'em that fire the way you showed me back in Domrémy. They'll fall at your feet.' Now Jehanne took a sip of the wine and smiled politely at Thérèse, but before she could swallow, Thérèse grasped her hand tightly and was looking at her with hungry eyes. 'Do you think you can help us, dear? We've had such a bad time here these last months. I can't tell you what a time.'

Thérèse's sixteen-year-old son, André, had been killed during the siege of Vaucouleurs. The siege that Sir Robert had only been able to end by promising the Burgundians that the army of Vaucouleurs would stay out of the rest of the war. 'They shot him with a cannonball,' Thérèse said,

73

blinking and looking at the ceiling. 'We can't keep letting them get away with this. It's just—' She shook her head, unable to finish her sentence.

Jehanne was silent. Finally she said that she wanted badly to help the people of Vaucouleurs, but that there was nothing she could do until she had won Sir Robert's support. 'Judging from the way things went today, it could take a while.'

Thérèse squinted at her. 'You've seen him already?'

'Did Durand not tell you?'

Thérèse shook her head, a puzzled look on her face. 'He said it might be some time before Sir Robert would see you and that you needed a place to stay while you waited.'

Jehanne smiled and shook her head. 'We saw him this afternoon,' she said. 'He told Durand that I should be taken home and beaten.'

Thérèse laughed, a high, slightly alarmed sound. 'Goodness,' she said. 'That's not a very good start, is it?'

Jehanne said that it was not. 'I'll convince him though,' she said. 'I just need more time.'

Thérèse looked at her. Lowered her voice. 'I hate to say this, but from what I hear, the only women Sir Robert listens to are the ones he's sleeping with.'

Jehanne's nostrils flared. 'I can't do that.'

Thérèse blinked. 'Of course not,' she said hastily. 'I didn't mean to suggest . . .' Abruptly she smiled and clapped her hands against her thighs. Spoke in a bright, remote tone. 'Well, it's wonderful to have you here. I know we're going to be great friends.'

CHAPTER THIRTY-FOUR

It was weeks before Sir Robert would see her again. Cold, endless weeks. Rain pouring down every day. Darkness falling right after the midday meal. Jehanne fought the darkness in her own heart, the voices that promised disaster if she did not make it to Chinon before mid-Lent.

She spent most of her time in the church that sat beside Sir Robert's castle, praying. Up the long, steep cobbled hill she walked every day at dawn, her steps quick and intent, nimble as a goat. *Come, my love*, she thought. *Lend me your strength*.

People stared at her. Their eyes on her ragged red dress, her fevered face, her determined walk. She smiled at those who met her gaze, walked past the rest as if she didn't see them. She turned her eyes to the sky.

The church was a dark, shadowed place, built of brown stone with high and narrow green stained-glass windows and lit by a forest of tall, slender candles. Jehanne's boot heels tapped on the smooth stone floor as she walked toward the altar of Saint Michael, the taps echoing in the high rafters of the building, a thrilling, solemn sound that made her feel as if she were in a play. At the altar she lit a candle and added it to the flickering forest. Then she knelt and prayed, her breath coming out in small white puffs, the tender yellow candle flames trembling above her head.

And it was always after she'd surrendered that the saints would come. Always after she thought, *Well, maybe not today*, and accepted it, felt her

75

shoulders slump a little, let her heart sink back in its cage, that they came to her. The sudden bloom of light on her cheek, behind her eyes, the flood of warmth, their voices so tender. It was Margaret this day. Plump, fiery Margaret, standing in the air before her. *Hurry, cabbage. Blood is flowing in the streets of Orléans.*

What can I do? Sir Robert won't see me.

Be brave, lamb. Brave and fast. God will clear the way. Every path will be opened to you. Hurry now, no time to waste.

One afternoon, when she'd finished praying, Jehanne returned to the soldiers at the gate outside Sir Robert's fortress. Her heart shrank at the sight of them—their armor glinting in the sunlight, the memory of their cruel laughter ringing in her head. But she kept walking forward. *Enjoy yourself, darling*, Margaret sang out. *They're just boys after all. Show them your light; they'll never be able to resist.* Jehanne broke into a broad smile, her heart laughing at the lunacy of what she was doing, eyes bright, cheeks flushed as she came to stand before the group of knights and captains with their fine tall horses and their bright green tunics. 'Here I am again,' she said, raising her eyebrows and grinning. 'Think he'll see me today?'

'In your dreams, sweetheart,' one said.

The next day another said, 'What would Sir Robert want with a mad cowgirl?' But they enjoyed her too, the soldiers. The bold, feisty smile. The bald audacity of this cheeky, pretty farm girl. They ogled her, showed off with their swords, made rude offers, tested her to see what she was made of. 'I'll see you, honey. I've got just what you need . . .'

Jehanne laughed, rolled her eyes. But went

home feeling smashed under the skin. She woke late at night, sick with fear. Lay staring at the ceiling for hours while the woman beside her in the bed slept quietly.

But in the morning hope always rushed in anew, filling her heart with clean white sunlight. *Maybe today*.

CHAPTER THIRTY-FIVE

One day when Jehanne came home to the Le Royers', the main room was abuzz, ringing with talk and laughter. Three women were seated around the hearth, spinning and chattering. Thérèse was chopping carrots at the table. Letice sat beside her sister with a knot in her jaw, a strange hectic flush in her yellow face, scrubbing a turnip with her red bitten fingers. The room fell silent when Jehanne entered, the three women by the hearth gaping openly at her as if she'd sprouted a third eye in her forehead.

'Ah, there you are!' cried Thérèse loudly, a flutter of guilt in her voice. She introduced the women as Claudette, Mignon, and Paula. 'I was just telling the girls about your mission, Jehanne. Hope you don't mind.'

Jehanne stepped toward the hearth to rub her hands. She turned to face the women. 'No, it's all right.' Then she smiled wryly. 'I'll take all the help I can get.'

One of the women, a husky, low-browed brunette, gazed at her hungrily. That was Claudette. 'Is it true?' she asked. 'Are you really the Virgin from Marie Robine's prophecy? The one who's going to save us from the Goddons?'

'She is,' said Thérèse from the table. 'I knew the first time I saw her.'

'God speaks to you? And the saints too?'

Jehanne said that they did.

'Amazing,' breathed Claudette.

'In your dreams?' Paula asked, her voice sarcastic. She was a wry, heavy-jawed woman with a bitter purple mouth and long bony fingers. 'God talks to me in my dreams too. Doesn't make it real.'

'Doesn't make it false,' said Jehanne.

'They speak to her all the time,' said Thérèse. 'They have for the last five years.'

'Are they just beautiful?' said Claudette.

Jehanne nodded.

'Like in the church windows?' said Claudette.

Letice clicked her tongue and gave her head a hard little shake. Abruptly she set down her half-peeled turnip, dropped her knife with a clatter, and walked toward the door.

Her sister called after her. 'Leti,' she called, but Letice kept walking.

'Someone's time of the month, is it?' said Claudette.

Thérèse puffed up her cheeks with air and slowly exhaled. 'Ridiculous,' she said.

Claudette had eyes only for Jehanne. The Virgin. 'Tell me more,' she said. 'What do they say to you?'

Jehanne blushed. 'I'm forbidden to speak of it to anyone but the King.'

Claudette studied her. 'You have the *virtus* in you,' she said finally. 'I see it.'

78

'If only Sir Robert thought so.'

'What does it matter what that pig thinks?' said the third woman. A slim, urchin-faced creature with sad, bulging eyes and a light snow of pink freckles on her nose. Mignon.

'She needs an escort,' said Thérèse, pushing a line of orange carrot coins off her knife. 'And horses. She can't just trot off by herself through three hundred and fifty miles of Goddon territory. They'll string her up by her toes before she's gone ten miles.'

'I need a letter of introduction to the King too,' said Jehanne, who was pacing now in front of the fireplace. 'My voices say I have to be in Chinon by mid-Lent. That's only six weeks away. I have to leave here as soon as possible.'

Claudette nodded, frowned with approval. 'It's about time somebody did something.'

'I wish we could help,' said Mignon. 'Is there anything we can do?'

Jehanne stopped walking. She said that they could spread the word that the Virgin of Lorraine had come to win France back from the Goddons. 'But it must be fast. If Sir Robert does not help me get to the Dauphin soon, France will be lost for good.'

CHAPTER THIRTY-SIX

'Liar,' Letice hissed. It was nighttime. The house was dark. Jehanne was sitting in the room where she and Letice slept together, braiding her hair in the candlelight. Thérèse was still downstairs,

79

putting wood on the fire for the night. Letice came in, bringing with her a cold gust of air from the hall. She stood with her back against the door, her eyes black with hate. Jehanne looked up. Blinked.

'You're a filthy fucking liar,' Letice said.

'You think so?' Jehanne stood up and went at the girl head first, her hands knotted into fists, but before she reached her, Thérèse banged on the door, said, 'What's this? You girls locking me out now?'

CHAPTER THIRTY-SEVEN

Every morning Jehanne walked up the long hill to hear Mass in the brown stone church of Our Lady of the Vaults, and every morning a five-year-old altar boy named Grégoire watched her kneeling in the front pew, her hands clasped so tightly her knuckles were white, her face feverish, lifted to Heaven. Sometimes she wept, her eyes shining, her face wet with tears. Sometimes she spoke quietly to herself, as if in a trance. Everyone in the room noticed her, praying and whispering to her saints like one possessed. Praying as if her life depended on it. But only the boy was bold enough, untrained enough to stare nakedly at her throughout the service. Only the child watched with open fascination as Jehanne knelt in the sunlight, the motes dancing above her dark fevered head, chapped red lips moving, whispering, pleading, sighing. *Help me, Father. Lend me your strength.*

After the service he followed her down the dark stone staircase into the freezing high-vaulted crypt below the chapel. He watched her kneel once more in the damp shadows and pray at the shrine of the Virgin, her face so radiant that the boy thought he would do anything for her, follow her anywhere, just to be near her and the light pouring from her eyes.

At home that night, eating a bowl of lentils, he told his mother. 'There's a magic girl in church. I love her.'

'What?'

'She talks to God. And the saints. She's magic.'

'Finish your food,' the mother said.

But the next morning, when she dropped the boy off at church, the mother leaned down and whispered, 'So where's this magic girl of yours?'

The boy pointed to the girl in the red dress, kneeling in the front pew. 'There.'

'Her?'

'She's beautiful.'

'Not really,' said the mother. But she saw the heat in that round, uplifted face, the dark gleaming head, the radiant smile. She found it hard to look away.

'Why do you say she's magic?'

'Because she is.'

'No,' said the mother. 'She's just praying very hard.'

*   *   *

Later, in the street, the mother stood with a basket of leeks on her arm, talking to another woman in the sun. 'Have you seen that girl who goes back and forth to the church all the time? The crazy one?'

81

The woman nodded. 'Claudette met her the other day over at the Le Royers'. Says she's on a mission from God, no less.'

'Does she now?'

'Mission to go to the Dauphin, save France. Says there are three saints who talk to her, give her visions and the whole thing.'

The two women regarded each other with delighted frowns.

'You remember the prophecy Marie of Avignon made, that France would be ruined by a woman and restored by a Maid from Lorraine?'

'*Mmmm . . .*'

'She says she's the Maid.'

'God's Maid? Here to save France?'

The woman nodded.

'Oh, that's rich.'

Silence then. The mother regarded her leeks thoughtfully. 'Be great if it were true though, eh?'

'Thérèse believes her. Says she's honest as a nun.'

'Well. Pray God it's true. It would take a bloody miracle to save this country.'

CHAPTER THIRTY-EIGHT

Soon the Le Royers' house was packed full every afternoon with people wanting to see the girl who claimed to be the Maid of Lorraine. Hear about her mission for themselves. Mothers brought their colicky, red-faced infants and asked her to bless them; farmers brought cows and sheep that would not breed; a young man appeared with his face and

82

chest covered with black boils, begging to be healed. Jehanne refused. 'I have no healing powers,' she said. Still they lined up, begging for a touch, a word from the Holy Maid.

And still Sir Robert refused to see her. When she went to his château each day after her prayers, the soldiers shook their heads, shrugged. 'Sorry, darling. Can't do it for you.'

One evening, after everyone had left, Jehanne stood alone in her room, watching as a pack of dogs ran howling down the street. There were four or five of them, skinny, wild things, running fast and barking loudly—as if they were chasing something, though she could not see what they were chasing. Watching them, she grew very agitated. She looked down and saw that her fists were clenched tightly in front of her, her knuckles white as chalk. She began pacing back and forth. *I must have help. I must have someone to help me convince him.*

Abruptly she stopped walking and leaned against the cold windowpane, pressing her fingers over her eyes until dozens of yellow spots appeared. *Now! I must have someone right now!* She opened her eyes and looked out of the window into the road and the bare black trees, but there was no one there, only the dark huddled houses and the faint gleam of the wet cobbled street. She began pacing again, back and forth across the floorboards. *Oh, what's the point? What is the point?* She longed, suddenly, to fling herself out of the window, dash her head against the rocks in the street. 'How am I supposed to do this without any help?' she shouted at the ceiling. 'Tell me, how am I supposed to do this?'

She sighed and sank down on her bed. *I know nothing, Lord*, she thought. *You have chosen the wrong person for this mission. I have no idea what to do.*

CHAPTER THIRTY-NINE

The next afternoon, at the gate to Sir Robert's castle, there was a man Jehanne had never seen before. He was standing with the other soldiers—a tall olive-skinned young man with a long, sad face and bright gray eyes slightly too close together. He smiled when she looked at him, and when she smiled back, his eyes turned soft and helpless. His heart lay beating in her hands. His clothes were fine and clean—a heavy dark blue woolen captain's cloak with a thick silver clasp, tall brown leather boots—and as he walked toward her she thought, *Dear God, let him not say something embarrassing.*

When he was close enough that she could see the little silver links of his chain-mail, he stopped and squinted down at her. 'What is it exactly that you want with Sir Robert?'

Jehanne looked at the group of soldiers behind him, smiling broadly and elbowing each other. 'I'll tell you in private,' she said, and he followed her beneath the shadowed archway of the fortress gate. 'This will sound mad, but believe me, it's not.'

The man, whose name was Jean de Metz, gazed at her. Nodded.

When Jehanne had finished speaking, he smiled—a wry smile now, one eyebrow arched. He had expected something like this. Had heard the other soldiers talking about the mad little peasant and her talk of saving France. 'Has no one told you that the Dauphin is to be expelled from the kingdom, and that we are all doomed to become English?'

Jehanne looked at the man. 'Some have said it, but they are wrong.' She told him that she had to get to the Dauphin in Chinon before mid-Lent. 'Even if it means walking my legs down to stubs, I must get there, for I am the only one in the world who can regain the Kingdom of France.'

'Is that so?' he said, delighted by her audacity. She was the first person he'd heard talk of anything but outright surrender to the Goddons for months.

'I tell you with all the truth that is in my heart.'

'And if your heart is mad?' he asked. But his eyes were gentle.

'It is not,' she said quietly. 'I swear to you, I have no desire to carry out this mission. I would rather be home, spinning wool beside my mother in Domrémy. But I must obey my Lord's orders.'

That, he thought, *is a lie*. But a clever lie. It would not do to appear a bloodthirsty virgin, though this was exactly what excited Metz most about her. The fire. The urgency crackling around her like lightning. Metz asked the same question Sir Robert had asked her that first day. *The same question they all asked*. 'And who is your lord?'

'God,' she said.

Metz laughed softly through his nose. 'Lord help me, I believe you.' Then another laugh burst out of him, for he was amazed at his own words.

'You should.'

'You'll need escorts to take you, you know. It's three hundred and fifty miles between here and

85

Chinon. You can't travel that country alone.'

'Yes,' she said. 'I know.'

And to his great surprise, Metz found himself kneeling down before the girl, his heart banging wildly in his chest, as though he were about to propose marriage. 'Then I shall be one of them,' he declared.

*   *   *

Later that afternoon came her second believer: Bertrand de Poulegny. Short, thin, filthy Bertrand with graying corn-yellow hair and dark, wet, bulging eyes. Wax creeping out of his ears like moss. A crumpled clown's face. 'Won't get far with that green oaf helping you,' he said, falling in beside Jehanne as she walked through the gates of the château and began making her way down the long hill to the Le Royers. A strange one, Bertrand. Arrogant and innocent and desperate all at the same time. He was older than Metz by perhaps seven or eight years—a man in his mid-thirties with a slight hop in his step that gave him an eager, spritely aspect. A tragic twist to his mouth. Oddly endearing. 'I've actually been to Chinon,' he continued. 'I know the back roads, the forests to steer clear of. It's hellish country, you know. Burgundians and thieves, monsters all over.'

'I know,' Jehanne said, though she hadn't quite known the extent of it.

'Aren't you afraid?'

'No,' she said, lifting her chin a bit. She told him that God had given her this mission and that she knew He would clear the road for her. 'I was born for this.'

Bertrand grinned. Like Metz, he was a soldier—a man hungry to move and fight. He was tired of standing around in Vaucouleurs, sharpening his sword and listening to the bad news from Orléans roll in day after day. The girl's wild words and her pretty dark eyes excited him. When she spoke, he felt the walls of his world expanding. 'And what if I said I was born to guide you there?'

Jehanne was grinning now. 'I'd say you're welcome. The more escorts I have, the better.'

'We'll need money, you know,' he said. 'For horses and inns and such. Protection too. Have you got any?'

'Not a sol.'

Bertrand laughed. 'Me neither.' Then he threw his arms up into the sky and shouted, 'Dear bountiful God, if you love us, throw down some gold for our mission.'

Jehanne stared at him. 'Don't do that,' she said. 'It's not a joke.'

CHAPTER FORTY

They taught her how to fight. Metz and Bertrand. Taught her swords and shields and lancing down in the courtyard of Sir Robert's château while they waited for him to agree to see her again. They weren't serious about it at first. Jehanne sensed the men only agreed to it because they were bored—because showing a girl how to soldier seemed like more fun than another round of cards. But she was good, Jehanne. She learned fast. Had quick reflexes. Monstrous determination. Soon she had

Bertrand off his horse and down on the ground with her lance pointed at his wide brown eyes. Betrand shouting, 'Give, give! I give!'

Sir Robert's hunting partner, Vincent Duval, saw this happen. He stood beneath a rack of eight-point antlers in Sir Robert's sitting room, gazing out through the bay window into the courtyard below. A small, thoughtful man with a neat ring of silver hair around his bald skull. A man who was proud of his château on its high hill outside Vaucouleurs and the great garden of roses he'd planted around it that perfumed his bedroom all summer long. He was eager to keep them safe from the English. 'She's certainly got your men excited.'

Sir Robert came and stood beside him, stroking the stubble on his several chins and looking out to where Jehanne stood in the courtyard, talking with his soldiers. A strange, radiant day outside. It had rained earlier, and the cobblestones were still dark and shining, the sky itself a wild mix of dark gray storm clouds and brilliant yellow shafts of sunlight. Jehanne stood in a column of sun with the dark mountainous clouds massed behind her, her face bright, eager, her red skirt just visible beneath her cloak, her dark hair hanging down her back in two thick braids. Sir Robert cocked a brow, hoisted his belt up over his great drum-like belly.

Together they watched as Metz handed her a sword and adjusted her short fingers around the handle. Then Metz set his right hand on his hip and took a few dancing steps forward across the cobblestones, leading with his left foot and slicing the blade back and forth through the air as he went, finishing the dance with a sharp, elegant thrust. He turned and spoke to Jehanne, and a moment later she too came dancing across the cobblestones with one hand on her waist and the sword glinting in the sunlight, the red hem of her skirt swishing about her knees. She shouted 'Ha!' as she thrust her sword forward with a flourish, and Sir Robert shook his head. 'She's got stones, I'll say that.'

Duval squinted at the girl, who was clowning now, balancing the butt of the sword on her palm and walking forward slowly with the blade pointing toward the sky. 'The sheer oddness of the thing,' he said. 'A virgin sent by God to murder the English . . . something wonderful about it.'

Baudricourt snorted and turned away from the window. He squeezed the base of his nose, as if to remove some filth there. 'It's ridiculous. What's she going to do, put on a suit of armor and lead Charles's army in a charge?'

'They say she's got Metz and Poulegny offering to take her to him.'

Another snort. 'They're just thinking with their cocks.'

'Maybe.'

Sir Robert shook his head, walked away from the window. 'I'm not going to get behind this foolishness. France may be in bad shape, but we don't need some peasant girl telling us what to do.'

CHAPTER FORTY-ONE

One afternoon, when Jehanne had been in Vaucouleurs for about a month, a messenger appeared at the Le Royers' house. An enormous black man in a splendid yellow satin tunic and thick gold hoop earrings. His skin was very dark, almost purple. Gleaming like an eggplant. His features composed and elegant, still as stone. Thérèse gasped out loud at the sight of him and took a few steps back. 'Oh, I . . . can I help you?' she said at last.

The man introduced himself as a messenger from the Duke of Lorraine. 'I bear an invitation for the Maid,' he said in a deep melodious voice. His words shocked Jehanne, who sat at the table with Metz and Poulegny; they made her ears and arms prickle with delight. She could not believe that anyone in Nancy had ever heard of her, much less the Duke himself. 'I am the Maid,' she said.

The messenger said that the Duke was gravely ill and that his doctors expected him to die within the month. 'He has heard of the Maid's great healing powers, and hopes perhaps . . .'

Jehanne shook her head. 'I have no such powers.'

The messenger appeared not to hear her. 'The Duke would be most grateful.'

Bertrand leaned over and whispered in Jehanne's ear. 'He's *very* rich, the Duke. Couldn't hurt to meet him . . .'

CHAPTER FORTY-TWO

For a long time now Jehanne had been longing to shed her dress and braids. Reminders of the scared peasant girl from Domrémy. The coward. But it

90

was Metz who got her to do it. The afternoon before they left for Lorraine, she sat in her bedroom, packing her things into a blanket. Metz came and poked his head in the open door. 'Almost ready?'

Jehanne nodded and reached for the red dress that lay folded beside her on the bed.

Metz opened his mouth. Then closed it. Then opened it again. 'You can't wear that,' he said. 'Not to travel.' He was silent for a moment. 'Not for any of the things you're talking about doing, actually.'

A strange sensation then. Joy and terror at once. Her heart glowing, her belly cold. To dress as a member of the opposite sex was expressly forbidden by the Bible. A sin punishable by death. A cold spider walked down her spine. It was happening. It had begun. She asked Metz what she should wear instead, knowing what his answer would be. 'Let me lend you some clothes,' he said. 'It's better if you travel as one of us.'

The costume that Metz presented her with consisted of an old pair of black woolen leggings with holes in the feet and a scratchy gray wool tunic that smelled of mildew. A pair of tall, ancient brown boots that looked as if they'd been dug up out of the earth. 'Sorry they're not finer,' he said, blushing. 'My servant Jean's the only one of us sized small enough to fit you.'

Jehanne smiled, thinking it was all in better shape than her old red dress.

And she knew when she took her dress off, that it was for the last time. She knew she'd never put it on again. She folded it tenderly and put it on the blanket with the rest of her things. *Good-bye, Jehannette*, she thought. *Good-bye, old life.*

The hose felt strange at first. She'd never worn them before. It was odd to have the wool snug like that, right up against her sex. The seams biting into the tops of her thighs. Odd to feel the loose, rough cloth of the tunic brushing lightly against her nipples instead of the snug linen bodice she was used to. The sleeves hung down past her hands like bells, the hose bunched at the ankles. But it delighted her too. It transformed her, made her into someone else, a creature of her own invention. Not Jehanne, daughter of Jacques and Zabillet d'Arc of Domrémy, but Jehanne the Virgin, Child of God. And it seemed to her that she had crossed a bridge of some kind. Left one world behind and moved forward into another.

The room was full of people when she walked back into it. News spread fast in Vaucouleurs. The women gasped and crossed themselves when they saw her, for it was illegal to dress as a member of the opposite sex. Not just forbidden by the Bible, but an offense punishable by death. Henri looked at the ground. Letice stood next to Thérèse, whispering in her ear. A wicked look of delight in her eyes. Thérèse was pale as salt, her head pulled back like a turtle's. Metz stared with hot eyes, followed her legs in their black stockings as she crossed the room. 'Oh, wonderful!' he said. 'That's bloody wonderful!'

'Get a pair of scissors.'

'No, Jehanne,' said Thérèse. 'You mustn't.'

Jehanne looked at her calmly. 'My council has approved it. Do you question the word of God?'

Afterward the pile of hair on the floor was so large it looked as if a wild animal had collapsed there. 'Jesus help us,' said Letice, crossing herself

92

and staring down at the mass of dark curls everyone had always said was Jehanne's best feature. It was beautiful, the hair. Dark brown like a block of mahogany, with bronze lights in it. 'You have stars in your hair,' her mother had said once while she braided it. 'Tiny gold stars.' But Jehanne liked herself better without it.

They walked her over to a window and Bertrand brought her the little shard of mirror he used for shaving, and there she was, all neck and dark eyes and mouth. The bangs short, chopped across the forehead, her hair curling up over her ears. A bird she was then, free and light and new and clean, the chill air on her neck, the past left behind her on the floor.

CHAPTER FORTY-THREE

That night Jehanne dreamed of wagons. A great tower of wagons, all piled up on top of each other. An evil tower, it was clear. There were long, sharp wooden stakes sticking out of it from all sides, like porcupine quills. In the dream, French soldiers dressed in long pink skirts and big pink hats that covered their eyes were running up the tower and hurling themselves onto the stakes. It was all strangely well organized, like a dance. A group of maybe ten soldiers would get together in a circle around the tower, then silver trumpets would sound, and they would run and throw themselves onto the stakes at the same time, the long wooden poles thrusting out, red and wet, from their backs. Once the men were dead, other soldiers came and lifted the bodies off the stakes and carried them away on wooden boards. Then a general—also in a long pink skirt and a pink hat—gave the order, and another group circled up and waited for the sound of the trumpets.

When she awoke in the morning, she knew what it meant. She ran up to the château, grabbed Metz's arm and said, 'Tell Sir Robert that France will suffer a terrible defeat at Rouvray tomorrow. Ask him how many more men need to die before he listens to me.'

CHAPTER FORTY-FOUR

They rode to see the Duke of Lorraine at his palace in Nancy. An unreal place with gleaming gold-leaf ceilings and swans floating in the moat, a greenhouse full of potted orange trees. Jehanne walked among them, sniffing the air, thought she'd never smelled anything so sweet. As they were led toward the Duke's quarters, Bertrand kept looking over at her, as if to say, *Is this real? Are we actually here?*

But the Duke himself was horrible. Useless. A terrifying man with a large yellow head that sagged like an old gourd and a gleaming mink blanket pulled up to his chin. A stink of rotten meat hovering around him. A bluish scum over his eyes. As soon as he learned that Jehanne could not heal him, he lost interest, did not want to hear about her voices, her mission to save France. He let his sagging head fall back on the pillow. Rolled his eyes to the fire that raged in the hearth beside him.

'There is no saving France,' he said. 'France died years ago.'

'I assure you, Duke,' Jehanne replied. 'France is not dead.'

But the old man would not look at her. Would only stare into the red light of the fire that roared beside his bed, his breathing slow and wet, as if he had jelly in his throat. When Jehanne spoke again, he cut her off in the middle of her sentence with a wave of his hand. 'Give her five livres and the old black rouncey out in the stables,' he said to his servant. 'Then leave me alone.'

'Couple of pennies and a horse that moves slower than I do,' Bertrand fumed on the way home. 'Why give us anything at all?'

*   *   *

But it did something, that trip. It changed things for the people of Vaucouleurs. When they saw Jehanne come riding back into town after her travels with her cropped hair and her windburned face, her boy's clothes, her sword at her side, and Sir Robert's two soldiers behind her (Metz and Poulegny, no less—good, solid men), she became real to them in a way she had not been before. It was clear: She was a warrior, a soldier of God. And as they watched her, they realized they had missed her during the two weeks she'd been gone, missed the bright, hopeful feeling they got in their hearts whenever they saw her walking up the hill to the chapel each morning. As she rode past their houses with the two knights behind her, people came running out into the streets and cheered, 'The Maid! The Maid returns!' Jehanne stopped her horse and allowed herself to feel for a moment the swelling wind of goodwill that was rising up around her, the sense of things gathering and shifting. *Perhaps*, she thought. *Perhaps*.

CHAPTER FORTY-FIVE

There was an open bottle of red wine on the table when they entered the Le Royers' house. Thérèse was sitting at the table with a half-empty glass in front of her, furiously plucking feathers from a pheasant, its blue neck exposed on her knee. Letice was spinning by the fire, her eyes bright. A strange little smile on her face. 'Curate was here to see you,' Thérèse said. Her eyes flashed. Her voice was cold. 'Says they want to perform an exorcism tomorrow, make sure you're not a witch. I said, "How do I know what she is?"'

'Thérèse,' said Henri.

She ignored him. 'Seemed like a normal enough girl at first, praying, God-fearing, but now, with this going about in boy's clothes, cutting off the hair, riding about the countryside unchaperoned with soldiers, I don't know.' She gave her head a fierce little shake. 'It's not right,' she said.

The word *exorcism* was all Jehanne heard. It froze her blood.

Metz stepped forward. 'Well of course they want to do an exorcism, ma'am. Have to make sure the girl's not sent by the Devil, don't they?' He smiled, but Thérèse's face remained set. 'We've known this would most likely happen,' he said finally.

'I didn't know, and I don't like it,' Thérèse said.

There was a new look about her—as if her eyes were closed, although they were not. 'I tried to help her out, Durand being an old friend of Henri's and all, but it's six weeks now she's been sitting around my house, filling the air with her holy-mission nonsense, not lifting a finger to help with the cooking and cleaning, running around the countryside acting like she's so bloody important . . .' She turned and looked at Jehanne with narrow eyes. 'How long 'til you admit it's just a lie, a crazy bid for attention, and go home where you belong?'

Jehanne flushed deeply. 'It is no lie, madam. And as for why I've stayed this long, you yourself said I was welcome to stay as long as it took.'

'Not six bloody weeks!'

Jehanne said that if they did not want her there, she would leave.

Henri put his hand on her shoulder. 'Now don't be hasty, Jehanne.' Then to his wife: 'We did say she could stay.'

'We didn't know she'd turn into this,' she said, flinging out her hand at Jehanne.

*   *   *

Jehanne spent the night in the church. It was cold, but a better cold than the cold at the Le Royers' house. She begged her saints to come to her, but they did not appear. There was only the drumming of rain on the roof. Rain pelting the stained glass, drilling into the mud of the churchyard. She watched the long blue shadows of the columns and arches in the candlelight, the tall black shadows of the trees outside, shaking in the wind. And she understood then what the old King had said about

97

feeling as if he were made of glass. *If someone touches me, I'll shatter into a thousand pieces.*

*   *   *

When she woke up, a long slant of sunlight was pouring in through the high window and she could feel its warmth on her cheek. Metz was there, shaking her shoulder and smiling down at her with his long sad face, his warm gray eyes. 'Guess what?' he said.

CHAPTER FORTY-SIX

Sir Robert had heard about the defeat of the French troops at Rouvray. The Battle of the Herrings, they were calling it. And it was as Jehanne had dreamed the night before she left for Nancy. A disaster. Three thousand French noblemen defeated by a small convoy bound for the English troops at Orléans. Three thousand of France's most famous warriors against three hundred English wagons full of dried fish.

All the most highly decorated generals had volunteered to march upon Rouvray: La Hire, Poton de Xaintrailles, the Bastard of Orléans, and the King's own army, led by young Count de Clermont. It should have been an easy victory, a joke. But no, it was as she had dreamed: a slaughter. Poton, La Hire, the Bastard, and their men riding in from Orléans in a thunder of horses and armor, their bright flags snapping in the winter wind as they arrived outside Rouvray with their men, hot to fight—only to find Clermont and the King's army nowhere in sight. 'Clermont, that ass,' Sir Robert said, shaking his head. 'While he and his idiots were busy plundering Rouvray's cellars, the English convoy arrived, caught sight of the Orléans men lying in wait, and started digging themselves in for a fight.' The Orléans men had requested permission to attack the convoy without Clermont, but he refused. Clermont had been so greedy to see his first big battle that he made them all wait for him while the English got themselves beautifully entrenched, circling their wagons and planting sharp spikes that stuck out on all sides, so when at last the French forces attacked, they charged straight at the spikes in a great crush, impaling themselves row after row after row. 'A massacre,' Sir Robert said, his jaw set, eyes lowered as if he were watching the battle unfold as he spoke. 'Another pathetic massacre.'

He raised his eyes to look at Jehanne, who stood before him. 'How did you know?' he said. There was a difference in him that day. He still looked like an old bull, but something had changed. The doors in his eyes had opened. 'How did you know that would happen?'

'A dream.'

He nodded, rubbed his lip with his index finger. 'Tell me about this dream. Did God speak to you in it?'

'I'm forbidden to say more.'

The Governor squinted at her for a long moment, his finger pressed against the hollow in the center of his top lip. 'You are something, Jehannette from Domrémy, I'll give you that.'

'I am the Maid of Lorraine, sir. I was born for

this.'

Sir Robert shook his head. 'Whatever you are, you've gotten a lot of people in this town very excited. You'd better hope you don't disappoint them.'

Jehanne's heart bounced in her chest. 'Does that mean you'll send me to Chinon, sir?'

'I'm considering it.'

CHAPTER FORTY-SEVEN

That afternoon Thérèse came to Jehanne where she knelt, praying in the church, and begged her to return to the house. 'I was wrong to doubt you,' she said, gripping her apron as she spoke. 'It's just been so strange—all this.'

Jehanne was silent. *You heard about Rouvray. About my meeting with Sir Robert. That's the only reason you're here.*

'You know,' she continued, 'the way I was raised, it's a sin worthy of hanging for a woman to go around in boy's clothes . . . it's just . . . not done.'

'God Himself has instructed me to do it, and I will continue.'

Thérèse nodded. Her eyes were bright with tears. 'Of course,' she said. 'Of course you should, but won't you come home now, please? I hate seeing you here in the cold like this.'

People are terrible, weak as sheep, thought Jehanne. But eventually she allowed Thérèse to throw a shawl over her shoulders and they walked out of the church and down the long hill to the house.

100

The curate, Jean Fournier, said they needed to exorcise her. Make certain that she was not a fiend of the Devil. He'd appeared, frowning in the Le Royers' doorway, that evening, rain splashing on his hat, staining his purple houppelande. On one side of him stood Sir Robert, Sir Robert with his eyes bright and strange. On the other side stood a boy, thin and wrecked with pimples. A long triangular face, eyes on either side of his skull, like a goat. Jehanne dropped her bowl of porridge on the floor when she saw them. A cold rush shot through her bowels. 'Father!' cried Thérèse, jumping up. 'What an honor!' But Jehanne knew it was no honor they'd come to do her.

Jehanne knew the curate. She'd confessed to him every morning for the last two months. She knew his thick, pale hands with the swollen red knuckles, knew the sight of them placing the wafer, *Body of Christ*, on her tongue, holding the silver communion cup as she drank, *Blood of Christ*, wiping the rim with the white linen cloth afterward. But the curate did not seem to know her now. He looked at her with cold, righteous eyes. As if he were looking down upon her from a very great distance. As if he had never seen her before in his life.

'We have business with Jehanne,' Sir Robert said to Thérèse. 'Leave us, this is private.'

The curate turned to the boy, spoke quietly, words she could not hear. The boy set his sack down on the table and took out a gold bowl wrapped in flannel and a small glass bottle of water. He set the bowl down on the table, poured some water into it, and lifted it toward the curate with both hands.

Jehanne stood up. 'Don't do that. I won't be part of it.'

Metz had warned her that an exorcism was likely, but she had not believed it. *They wouldn't*, she thought. *Not to me.*

But the curate was walking toward her now, holding the bowl out in front of him, murmuring Latin. '*Ecce Crucem Domini, fugite partes adversae . . .*'

Jehanne stepped backward. 'Father, do not do this,' she said, fighting to keep her voice steady.

'Can't be sending a witch to meet the King, can we?' said Sir Robert.

Her pride rose up then, a spiky black animal waking inside her, screeching. That they could think she was from the Devil, that anyone might imagine her a witch . . . she started toward the priest. 'You know I'm not a witch, Father. I've confessed to you every day for the last two months.'

'Witches are often excellent liars,' said Sir Robert.

The curate continued. 'I command you, unclean spirit, whoever you are, along with all your minions now attacking this servant of God—'

'Please, Father,' said Jehanne, kneeling down at the curate's feet, pressing her face against his shins, her heart roaring in her chest. 'You know there is no unclean spirit in me.'

But the curate was in a trance, chanting his holy words. 'By the mysteries of the incarnation, passion, resurrection, and ascension of our Lord

Jesus Christ, by the descent of the Holy Spirit, by the coming of our Lord for judgment, that you tell me by some sign of your name, and the day and hour of your departure. I command you, moreover, to obey me to the letter, I who am minister of God despite my unworthiness—'

'Father!'

'. . . nor shall you be emboldened to harm in any way this creature of God, or the bystanders, or any of their possessions.'

She was clutching the curate's legs now, sobbing as she looked up at him. She knew what happened to those who were exorcised. Whether they found you to be a witch or not didn't matter. You were marked for life. A freak. An outcast. 'I beg you.'

Sir Robert stood with his lips pursed, eyes narrowed, arms crossed over his chest. 'Throw some water on her, Father. See what happens.'

The curate lifted the gold bowl and dipped his fingers in the water. 'We drive you from us, whoever you may be, unclean spirits, all satanic powers, all infernal invaders . . .' He lifted his hand and flicked the water onto Jehanne. All eyes in the room, watching, waiting for her to go up in smoke.

But she did not go up in smoke. She only wept. 'Oh Jesus,' she cried. 'Help me, Jesus.'

'Thus cursed dragon and you, diabolical legions—'

'All right, that's enough,' said Sir Robert. 'She's not a witch.'

CHAPTER FORTY-EIGHT

'I began to fear the church that day,' she says to Massieu in the monstrous darkness of the tower. 'I still loved it, but I began to fear it too.' A shadow went over her heart when she thought of it. The curate coming toward her in his purple robe. The red look in his eyes. *They wanted to kill you*, she thought. *They wanted your blood.*

PART II

CHAPTER ONE

Quickly now, the voices were saying. *Go quickly, little one. No one can touch you!* So she rode with her men across the cold yellow fields and the gray hills outside of Vaucouleurs, toward the King in Chinon.

A large crowd had gathered in Vaucouleurs to see her off that afternoon. It was a miserable day, freezing and rainy, fog creeping down the streets and swallowing up the rooftops. But still they'd come—hundreds of them, gathered together at the Porte de France, gaping and cheering and shoving each other, lifting children on their shoulders to see the Maid, the holy peasant on the black horse, possibly mad, dressed up as a boy, on her way to save France.

The townspeople had bought her a new set of clothes for her journey. Once word had gotten around that Sir Robert was supporting Jehanne's mission, they'd pooled money to have an outfit made that actually fit her. A simple thing, an outfit any young man in her village might have worn: a thick black wool tunic with sleeves that did not hang below her fingers, some good brown woolen hose without holes in the feet, and snug leggings that laced up the front. Also, tall leather boots with spurs, a heavy gray cape, and a black felt cap with her name stitched crookedly in the back in red thread: Jehanne, the Maid. *Every day I become more real*, she thought as she looked at her new clothes. *Every day I go further from my father. Further from the fury and the mud of Domrémy.*

As she rode through the crowds, Jehanne saw the Le Royers and Durand and Marie standing off to one side, huddled together in the rain, waving and weeping and smiling, their noses red with cold. Durand and Marie had come to the Le Royers' house earlier that morning to say their proper good-byes, Marie with a squalling, pink-faced infant wrapped like a mummy in her arms, looking exhausted but satisfied. A look on her face as she nursed the child that said, *Until you do this, you'll never know what real love is*. Durand had been a wreck. Durand laughing, then weeping, when he saw Jehanne come down the stairs with her short hair and her boy's clothes. 'God help you,' he sobbed into her neck. 'I hope I've done the right thing, helping you.'

Jehanne hugged him, thanked him for all he'd done, but she felt stiff, awkward, as if she were performing a pantomime. She did not like saying good-bye to him in front of so many people.

'God bless you, darling,' Thérèse screamed now as Jehanne rode past. 'God bless the Maid of Lorraine!' And the crowds around her cheered and cried, 'God bless the Maid of Lorraine!'

Jehanne knew it wasn't about her, the love pouring out of the crowd. She knew it was about God—the thought of God alive inside of the girl, God here among them now—that made them all scream like that. But it was thrilling anyway. Every hair on her body stood up. She felt as if she were painted with light.

*　　　*　　　*

There were six men who escorted her to Chinon,

circling her in a kind of protective horseshoe as they rode: Metz and Bertrand; the King's wiry little messenger, Colet de Vienne; the archer Richard; and the two freckled servant brothers, Julian and Jean de Honnecourt, who, Jehanne knew, hated her from the beginning. Their looks said so when she met them outside the Le Royers' house that morning. Bold, sneering looks, openly disrespectful. 'How those breeches feel on you, ma'am?' the older one, Julian, said when no one was listening. His teeth were white and very large, and his hair was orange and bushy like sheep's wool. Everything about him repulsed her. 'Nice and tight, eh?'

'They'll feel a lot better when we get to Chinon,' she said dryly, as she climbed up onto the mounting stone and pulled her horse's girth tight.

'Bet they will,' said the boy, his younger brother laughing behind a large freckled hand.

It took them eleven days to reach the King. A cold, treacherous ride through the worst of the Burgundian territory. Much of the countryside was flooded from the long winter rains—the pine forests turned into icy swamps, the rivers grown ferocious as lions. Crashing white rivers, very hard to cross. 'One of them almost swallowed you up,' Metz said later, although Jehanne knew it wouldn't. Yes, it snatched her off her horse and sucked her under with its freezing tongue, slammed her head against the rocky bottom, and rolled her over again and again, her lungs exploding in her chest, a red ribbon of blood rising from her skull. But she'd known the river would not be the end of her. She'd known Metz would dive down and rescue her, grab her under the arms, and drag her up onto the shore, both of them lying there, gasping like beached fish as Colet led their frightened horses toward the banks. So she let the river roll her again and again, let it slam her and toss her along its jagged corridors, her face calm, her eyes open, watching the storm of silver bubbles raging around her, thinking, *Soon now, God will pull me up. Very soon a hand will appear* . . .

They traveled mostly by night, in the dark, so they would not be seen. By day, they slept in caves and barns and ruined churches, curled up like dogs beneath their cloaks, their boots still on, hugging one another for warmth. Jehanne slept little. An hour, perhaps two, and then she was awake, her eyes wide open, the voices saying, *Go, darling, go!*

She could feel the Godhead growing inside her now, growing and spreading like a secret plant. Feeding her and feeding off of her, its roots fusing with her bones, its delicate tendrils sprouting in her fingers. And as it grew, her wisdom grew, until she knew that the winds were with her and the stars in the night sky were with her, until she knew that holy rivers were coursing through her veins and ancient caves of knowledge were yawning open inside her skull, and she loved God then in a way she never would again, for her love was the naïve, untested love of a new bride—perfumed and dreamlike. Blind as a mole.

Rarely was she afraid. War had run wild through the lands they were crossing—war jumping from house to house, from village to village, with its enormous torch, laughing as it tore the world apart, but the more Jehanne saw of war, the more eager she became to fight. As she rode, images

110

burned themselves into her brain: a family hung from the branches of an oak tree, their blue feet dangling above the ground like wax flowers. Their eyes black, popped out like a crab's eyes. Another day a herd of starving cows lay wailing in the road—their sad maiden's eyes raised to the sky, their bellies swollen up tight as drums. A parade of horrors shouting at her, pleading with her. One day Jehanne saw a naked woman on the steps of a burned-down church, eating dirt. Stuffing it in her mouth greedily, as if it were a butter tart, shrieking when Jehanne tried to approach her. Shrieking as they rode away. And later that same night, Burgundians. A pack of Burgundians riding right past Jehanne and her men as they hid in the forest. Bertrand had spotted them first—a string of yellow torch flames streaking through the darkness. 'Christ!' he said, snuffing his own torch quickly and hustling the others off the road and into the woods. They waited there, still as statues, holding their breath in the dark, praying silently as the riders approached. *Please, Father. Help us.*

Drunk and shouting the men came, laughing and swearing, their faces red with drink. As they rode past, Jehanne saw a lumpy burlap sack tied with rope to the back of one of the horses. A pair of bare pink feet at one end, bouncing terribly on the back of the horse. When a muffled shriek came, the rider laughed, shouted, 'Not long now, darling! Not long now!'

After the men had passed, Jehanne and her little party waited for an hour before riding on. All of them trembling, too stunned to speak. 'Jesus,' said Bertrand, rubbing his hands over his face.

Jehanne looked at her hands. 'God's wrath will

be upon them soon enough,' she said.

CHAPTER TWO

There was darkness within the group too. The darkness of the Honnecourt brothers, freckled and defiant, elbowing each other behind Jehanne's back, laughing at her. On the first night of their journey, they had ridden through the Saulx-Noire forest, and Colet and Richard had been very upset about this. 'Place is full of witches,' Colet said, his face pale as chalk.

Jehanne said that there were no such things as witches, and that they should not be afraid, for God was protecting them.

Julian scoffed. 'God my ass,' he said.

His brother giggled, then pretended to be coughing.

Jehanne stared at him very hard and said that no man in her party was to blaspheme the Lord. 'You do it again, I'll stick my sword in your heart, understand?'

Julian made a girlish face and fluttered his hands in the air, a mockery of fear. Then Metz looked sharply at him and his brother until they both stopped smiling, and the group continued through the forest and down into a deep, wooded ravine.

The muddy track led steeply downhill through a tunnel of crooked beech trees, and soon the riding grew difficult. Jehanne's horse began to slip and stumble in the mud and rocks, the animal snorting and panting and pawing the earth, desperate to find purchase. A sharp wind had come up, a cruel hand on her back, forcing her downward into the mouth of the ravine. 'Look, let me ride ahead of you,' said Colet at last. 'Watch how I do it.'

But as he moved his horse ahead of hers, Jehanne saw that Julian was waiting behind Colet, leering at her. He rode close behind her as they continued down the hill, snickering whenever her horse stumbled. And the forest seemed an evil place then. The bare black trees blocked out the night sky, and the wind made the branches creak and moan, and when the others were far enough ahead, Julian drew his horse up almost beside Jehanne's and spoke quietly, so only she could hear: 'You ought to feel right at home in here,' he said in a soft, ugly voice, 'being a witch and all.'

Jehanne gripped her reins. 'If you think I'm a witch, you shouldn't be here.'

'Don't have much choice though, do I? Got to go where the boss goes.'

'I'm not a witch.'

Julian smiled innocently. But as Jehanne rode ahead of him, she heard him hiss once more, 'Witch.'

CHAPTER THREE

Other kinds of darkness too. Darkness of a sweeter kind with Metz. One night, when they were deep into the Goddon lands, they stopped at the abbey of Saint-Urbain. A famous place. A known refuge for anyone in need of shelter—criminals, pilgrims, wandering monks, runaways. It stood in black silhouette against the gray night sky, a tall stone fortress with a bell tower, perched high on a cliff above the Marne River. On the way up to the gate, Metz rode alongside Jehanne and smiled gently. 'No sense anyone knowing you're a girl, right?' She nodded and let him pull her hood up over her head, her ears blushing as he did, the base of her spine glowing with pleasure.

She knew he wanted her. She knew it and liked it. In spite of herself, she liked it. The heat of his adoring eyes on her skin. His warm hand on her waist, helping her off of her horse. When a monk appeared at the abbey gate to let them in, she kept her head down as Metz had instructed her to and stared at the brown rain-pocked puddles on the ground as Colet showed the monk their letter of introduction from Sir Robert. It was very cold. She could not feel her hands. She made fists and hit them hard against her legs, but it made no difference. As soon as the monk had turned away, Metz smiled shyly and handed her his fur-lined gloves.

The monk led them through the big wooden gate and across a wet cobbled courtyard, into a dormitory where there was a large, long room with a big fire blazing at one end. It was all she could do not to run at the fire. There was hardly any furniture in the room: a small wooden table and two little rough-hewn wooden chairs by the window. Also a bed. One big bed pulled up close to the fireplace, piled high with blankets. Jehanne went and held her hands in front of the fire. She tried not to look at the bed, but she knew everyone else was looking.

'Well now, this isn't half bad,' said Bertrand,

dropping his satchel onto the floor and stretching his arms over his head.

Julian and his brother smiled at each other. Then they smiled horribly at Jehanne.

When the monk left to get them some food, the younger Honnecourt bolted the door behind him. A sharp electricity took over the room. Jehanne looked up at the six men who stood around her, their wet faces flickering in the torchlight, and for a moment they all saw it: her body naked and spread wide on the mattress, her wrists and ankles tied to the bedposts, the men taking their turns with her, cheering one another on, leaping onto her like dogs, bucking and howling in the firelight.

'This should be interesting,' said Julian, raising his eyebrows.

Metz slapped the back of his head very hard, and Julian stumbled a few exaggerated steps forward. 'You say another word, you'll sleep in the bottom of that river.'

Jehanne walked over to the bed and crossed her arms over her chest and looked at it. After a moment, she turned toward Metz and Bertrand. 'Can I trust you two to protect me in the night?'

The two men glanced at each other. Bertrand nodded quickly, a sharp soldier's nod. 'Of course,' he said.

Metz looked at Jehanne. He nodded, but his eyes said something else.

'All right then, you and Bertrand and I will take the bed,' she said, her breath coming out in long white banners. 'The rest of you can bunk down by the hearth.'

*   *   *

115

Deep in the night she awoke tumbling inside a wave of desire. She was aware of only the feeling at first. Just the hunger rinsing through her half-asleep body, the splendid heat of another body pressed up against hers . . . whose body? *God's*, she thought, only God could make her feel this way. Only gradually did she realize that it was Metz who was pressed against her beneath the heavy woolen cloak, breathing quietly into her hair, his thick erection pressed into her back.

And it was not so much that she was disappointed to realize it was Metz, as she was disappointed to realize that because it was not God or any of the saints, she must stop it. It couldn't go further. By the hearth, a tall black figure moved back and forth quietly, throwing logs onto the crackling red flames. And she knew that no one else knew what was happening to her. It was a secret. She lay still and closed her eyes, breathing, unwilling to let go of the sensation just yet—the hardness of him against her back, pressing gently, the smell of wood smoke and damp stone and skin in the air. She could tell by Metz's breathing that he was awake. On the other side of her, Bertrand was snoring lightly. Curled on his side with his fist pressed against his cheek like a child.

Abruptly she turned her body so that she lay flat on her back, her face very close to Metz's face. When she spoke, her voice was hard, low, emotionless. 'If you go further, it will be the end of everything. Do you hear me?'

For several moments there was silence. Jehanne felt like weeping. *Ignore me, ignore me. I didn't mean it*. But at last, Metz too shifted and lay on his

116

back. His voice came through the darkness. 'I hear you.'

CHAPTER FOUR

My angel, the voice said. *My brave little angel. No one is as brave as you are. No one is as pure.*

She knelt by the river in a small cove, surrounded by bare brown willows. She could see the abbey up above on the bluff, the black church spire rising up like a knife against the pale gray sky, and she knelt there among the trees and the dark, rushing water and held out her arms to embrace the air, lifted her face to drink the sky.

Michael was there with her, the golden light rinsing through her, his enormous voice melting her bones. *My darling, my brave, perfect little angel.*

It's very hard, she said. *So much temptation.*

Yes, but you resisted. You were so strong. He held her closely in his arms and gazed down at her with his stern lion's face, his sad ancient eyes. *My love. My strong, brave little love.*

Yes. I am yours. Only yours.

You must hurry now, little one. There isn't much time. He stroked her cheek tenderly, and then he held her very close and whispered, *You'll be dead in two years.*

CHAPTER FIVE

They rode on toward Chinon that evening in the frigid blue dusk. A silent single file, led by torchlight. Jehanne slumped over her horse, staring listlessly at the ground as they moved over the frozen fields and toward the high black hills, each of the riders silent for different reasons.

Dead. Dead in two years. At first she had thought she must have misunderstood. What? she had said, terror roaring in her ears. *What?* And then, *Oh no.* All the strength had gone out of her. She fell to the ground.

For a long time she wept. Let the terror wash over her, carry her out to sea. Everything finished. No husband. No children. No home. Ever. She had never wanted these things before, had thought she would never want them, but now she did want them. Desperately. She lay curled on the riverbank, clutching her womb. As if someone had stabbed her there.

Never allowed to know love, to grow beyond a girl, a child.

Later came questions. *How will I die? Will I be killed in battle? In my bed? Will I suffer greatly? Oh God, please let me not suffer greatly.* But he would not say more. He just kept holding her, pouring his sunlight into her, spinning the golden web around her.

But for the first time Jehanne did not want the light. Would not allow it to soothe her, make her forget. She wanted only the salt blue water of sorrow, its low, broken voice singing, rocking her as she wept.

Eventually, when she was worn out from crying, when the sobs had stopped and she lay exhausted and calm on the riverbank, a voice rose up inside of her. *Of course, death. Did you think you were going to get out of this alive?*

Oh, but knowing, Jehanne thought. *Knowing is different. Knowing changes everything.*

*   *   *

Metz and Bertrand and the others had seen it happen. They saw her kneeling there by the flooded brown river, praying. They had been standing outside the abbey, readying their horses for the journey, when Metz looked idly down toward the water and saw Jehanne there, kneeling on the bank with her arms outstretched, her face shining, tears streaming down her cheeks.

'What the hell, Metz?' said Bertrand a few minutes later, for Metz had dropped his pack on the ground and let his horse wander off. He was standing at the edge of the bluff, staring down at the girl, and soon Bertrand was beside him. Eventually the other men came too. They watched Jehanne speaking silently to the heavens, the strange radiant tears going down her face, and they watched too when her face crumpled suddenly, as if she'd been hit, and she collapsed to the ground.

'Should we help her?' Bertrand had whispered, but Metz shook his head. They kept watching, watching her slim back heaving as she sobbed, her hands clawing at the sand, her face turning up to the sky from time to time, raging at the sky until at last the sobs quieted and she grew still. Slowly she

119

wiped her eyes and sat up. She stayed there, holding her knees and watching the river, and when at last she stood and began walking back up the hill, Julian de Honnecourt had cried out, 'Oh dear Jesus, forgive me!' and ran stumbling down the road to meet her. He knelt down before her, clutched her hand very tightly and gazed up at her with his strange pale green eyes and sobbed, 'Please forgive me for doubting you, holy Virgin. Forgive me, please, I beg you.'

Jehanne wiped her cheek and looked down at him with her swollen eyes. 'I forgive you, but you are an idiot,' she said.

*　　　*　　　*

The men were different with her after that. The Honnecourts did not mock her anymore. Metz stopped looking at her with lustful eyes. The day by the river frightened him, she saw. Killed his desire. But in its place came awe. Awe and tenderness. When they ran out of food one afternoon, Richard the archer went out into the forest and came back holding up two dead squirrels by the tails. Bertrand roasted them over the fire on a stick and brought them to Jehanne. 'What about you?' she said. 'We're fine,' said Julian, all of them nodding, insisting until at last she ate. Another day, when she went to go to sleep, she found that Colet had rolled up his fine brown woolen tunic and left it beside her cloak to use as a pillow.

Often, as they rode, the men remembered what they'd seen that day by the river at Saint-Urbain. They thought to themselves, *She is sent by God!*

120

She is going to save France! And the world seemed to pulse with magic then. Each man felt that he knew his purpose in the world, felt that it was his sacred duty to deliver the Maid safely to the King in Chinon, and they felt honored to have been chosen for such a task.

For Jehanne, it was love that changed. Love shed its enchantment, its perfume. It stood naked before her now in a bright cold light, showing all of its ugliness, its cruelty. The terrible sacrifice it would require. The blood.

And because love changed, her world changed too. The world became a stark place, very simple. There was the mission, and there were two years to complete it. That was all. Everything else arranged itself around these two facts. It was still beautiful, the world—in some ways it was more beautiful than before—but death stood behind the blue sky now. Death stood behind the flowers. And when the saints sang, a cold snake slithered through her stomach. The hairs on her neck stood up.

No time.

CHAPTER SIX

I never saw them again, once we reached Chinon. Not really. Not the way I saw them when we were together on our journey, riding through the wilderness, close as brothers. Riding together, eating together, sleeping together, curled up against the freezing wind, hearing one another snore and cough and sigh, shout out in our nightmares. Whisper our prayers. I never knew their breath again, their

121

tenderness, their jokes, their bravery. The wooly sheep smell of Metz's hair when it was wet. The way Bertrand would start blinking very quickly when he got excited in conversation. Occasionally I would see them. I saw Metz on the street once in Tours, saw Bertrand from time to time during the fighting, but it was never the same. We were different people by then. Different people in different worlds, waving at each other from opposite shores.

I tried to keep them with me in Chinon, tried to bring them with me to the castle. I said they were my men, my protectors, my family. I could not be without them. But the King's messenger would not listen. 'Just the Maid,' he said. 'If you are what you say, you won't need protectors.' So I went alone up the hill to see the King. I left my family behind.

I was always leaving my family behind.

CHAPTER SEVEN

It was not as they said, her first meeting with the King. She did not miraculously recognize him in the great hall at Chinon. The great Armagnac dukes and courtiers and knights were not there, standing on tiptoe, looking on in their furs and jewels beneath the flickering chandeliers. There was no grand public event. Their first meeting was a secret.

A few hours after Jehanne and her men had arrived in Chinon, the King's messenger came to the inn near the river where she and the others were finishing supper. Metz and Bertrand speedily dismantling a brown roasted chicken, Jehanne

122

picking at a piece of bread. *Better to be hungry. Keep the senses sharp.*

'You are to come with me to the castle at once,' the messenger said.

'What about my men?' she said.

No. It was impossible. 'I cannot stress enough the need for secrecy at this moment.'

Her stomach went cold. She felt as if she'd been slapped. She looked at Metz and Bertrand across the table, their pale, stunned faces. 'I'll be back soon,' she said at last, forcing herself to smile as she pulled her stiff, mud-caked boots back on. But even as she spoke, a voice in her bones said: *You'll never see them again.*

They were too stunned to say much, too stunned to do more than hug her awkwardly, mumble their good-byes. Metz stood watching, holding on to the doorway of the inn so as not to fall to his knees.

*   *   *

When they were outside, the messenger handed Jehanne a cloak, said she must wear it. 'Keep your face down,' he said. 'Don't let anyone see you.' Jehanne had disliked him on sight: a thick, bullet-headed man with a wide gap between his front teeth and an ugly, wet smile. He made her sit in front of him on the horse and insisted on keeping his big sweating hands on her waist as they rode toward the castle. 'I have just ridden eleven days across the countryside, sir,' Jehanne said. 'I know very well how to sit a horse.' But he ignored her. His sweating hands stayed where they were.

They followed a long, narrow, zigzagging road uphill through the town and the high curling

123

forests above the town toward the pale gold cliffs where Chinon Castle loomed over the valley with its towers and dark slate-roofed turrets, its winding walls sprawling along the clifftops. It was evening now, the hour when the air is violet and everything else stands out in silhouette, black and sharp. A landscape in cameo. Jehanne kept trying to look and see the castle towers up on the cliffs, but every time she tried, the man pulled the hood back down over her face so she could not see anything. 'You want trouble?'

Jehanne said that she did not.

They did not enter the castle by the main gate. Instead they went through a battered green door in the outer wall, and then up a long drafty flight of stone steps and out into a darkening courtyard. There the castle towers rose darkly overhead as Jehanne and the messenger passed by a stone chapel and a monstrous old oak tree, and at last they entered a tower in the far corner of the courtyard, overlooking the dim blue valley and the town of Chinon, the broad river Loire winding through it, thick with white reefs of ice.

Inside the tower, five or six people were sitting around an ornately carved mahogany table. It was a strange room, small and dark, even with the fire going. There were nets of cobwebs in the corners, a close, mossy smell in the air as if it were never used. They all stared at Jehanne as she came through the doorway and pushed back the awful hood at last. 'This is her, then?' said a fat woman in a tall red cone hat with its veil folded back like a dinner napkin, her bright dark eyes flashing. On her finger, an emerald the size of a walnut.

A man in a blue tunic with a faded gold fleur-de-lis embroidered on the chest nodded, stepped forward, and cleared his throat. 'Your majesties, may I present Jehanne d'Arc. The Maid of Lorraine.'

He introduced the Dauphin first. Charles VII. The uncrowned king. *As soon as I saw him, I knew he'd betray me.* She saw it in his face: in the small, shifting eyes; the pale, weak chin; uncertainty wafting off of him like perfume. The words flashed in her mind like lightning: *He'll be the death of me.* A complete knowledge. Instantaneous. Fear drenching her insides, blood draining from her face as the judgment was laid out in her heart like cards on a table: He's a jellyfish, spineless, no conviction, no will of his own. A broken man.

Still she knelt down before him, steadied herself. Still the mission must continue. She kissed the hem of the King's houppelande—a tattered yellow silk thing, stinking of mildew—and gazed up at him. 'Gentle Dauphin, I bring you good news and hope.'

The King said nothing. Regarded her briefly, then rubbed the side of his long drooping nose and nodded at the courtier to continue with the introductions.

Next came Yolande. The Queen of Sicily. The Dauphin's mother-in-law. Yolande in the red cone hat and the fat emerald, nodding gravely. Her eyes bright and black as currants. Her hands small and white, tufted with dimples. 'If you are in fact the Maid of Lorraine, we will have much use for you,' she said.

Finally, La Trémöille. The King's Chamberlain, Georges de La Trémöille. *Jealous, wicked La Trémöille.* He was the King's chief counsel. An

125

enormous bald mountain of a man in a black velvet tunic, fatter even than the Queen of Sicily. Thick gold rings on his fingers. A slow, reptilian glitter in his eyes. He did not smile when they were introduced. He simply glanced at Jehanne for a moment from under his sagging eyelids. Then he looked away, nostrils flaring. As if he were offended to be in the same room with her.

Jehanne hardly noticed. Jehanne could think of nothing but the King. The narrow balding head, the weak, shifting eyes. The sullen, petulant mouth. *My betrayer.* She felt as if the walls of the room were closing in around her. *What did you expect? A tall, strapping thing with blond curls and a gold crown? A hero to help you complete your mission?* And she saw then that she had. She had expected something like that. And she saw that she had expected him to love her. To recognize her immediately as God's Messenger, his long-awaited savior, and welcome her with grateful, open arms. She had not expected to see her death.

The Queen of Sicily came toward Jehanne, her eyes sharp, searching. She took Jehanne's chin in her hand and looked at her, turning her face, first to the left and then to the right. 'Does not appear to be mad,' she said at last to no one in particular. 'But of course appearances can be deceiving.'

She questioned the girl, the same questions everyone asked. *Tell me about your voices, your mission, your family, your visions. Are you truly a virgin? How do you know it's God's voice you hear and not the Devil's? How do you know you're not possessed?*

As she answered, Jehanne could feel the Dauphin watching her. From time to time he

126

raised an eyebrow and sighed loudly, as if he were bored. But he did not speak.

'What sign can you make to prove that you are sent by God?' Yolande asked.

Jehanne was silent. She wanted to run, to get away from these strange, cold people and never return. *Bold!* Michael whispered. *Answer boldly, love!* As he spoke, his fury flooded through her, the fire rising up from her belly to her chest until she felt like biting the air. 'Majesty, take me to Orléans and I'll show you the signs you want,' she said. Her voice loud, arrogant. 'Take me to Orléans and I will show you the greatest victory France has seen in a thousand years.'

La Trémöille's eyes went wide. 'The gall,' he said.

'It is not gall. It is God's will.'

Yolande smiled, a long, thin smile, like a dolphin's. 'Perhaps it is,' she murmured.

'Well, if it's not, you'll be killed,' said La Trémöille mildly, from under lowered lids. 'We don't take kindly to pretenders here in Chinon.'

CHAPTER EIGHT

'The room they gave me at the castle was very beautiful,' she says to Massieu, her head tilted back against the cell wall, a sad smile on her face. Neither of them has any idea what time it is. The tower is dark as a well. Massieu's candle is still burning, though it's lower now, a yellow pool of wax shines and quivers around its base. 'Very beautiful and very cold. A million miles from the rest of the world.'

Her room had sat at the top of another tower, Coudray Keep. It had three diamond-paned windows that looked out over the Loire countryside. Heavy moss green velvet curtains pooled on the floor, a thick satin comforter gleamed on the bed. Even the chamber pot under her bed was painted with delicate green vines and flowers—finer than any dish she'd ever eaten from. That evening, when she was alone in her room, Jehanne picked it up and turned it around in her hands, looking at it in the candlelight. *All this is very dangerous.*

She stood up and walked over to the windows. Looked down through the blue valley at the little rooftops in the town of Chinon, the little silver river flashing in the moonlight, the hills and barns beyond—barns so tiny she could crush them between her fingertips. *This is why we don't seem real to them. This is why nothing about us seems real to them.*

They would not allow her to sleep alone there. 'Your hosts at Coudray Keep will be Monsieur and Madame du Bellier,' the Queen had said. 'They'll see to it that you have everything you need.'

And it was Madame du Bellier who had greeted Jehanne after the interrogation and took her to her quarters. Short, quivering Madame du Bellier with a stiff red-gold halo of hair that puffed out from beneath her cone hat and hands that smelled of vinegar. Cheerful and nervous at the same time. As if she were very excited to be near Jehanne, but also afraid she might bite. 'I'll be keeping you company at night so you don't get too lonely all by yourself,' she said as she led Jehanne through a bare winter garden toward the tower, the square hedges wrapped up in burlap against the frost. Jehanne knew what that meant. *Someone watching me at all times*, she thought. *Someone to tell them everything I do.*

In the middle of the night, the golden light woke her. Margaret was there, rising like a sun from behind the wardrobe, her eyes burning, her pink mouth stern beneath the shadow of her mustache. *Be careful!* she said. *Don't get comfortable here. Don't let it go to your head.*

Oh no, Jehanne said. *Never.*

Easy to say now. Wait until it's been a few months. Wait until you're used to sleeping in that soft bed with the feather quilt and the hot bricks down at the bottom, keeping your toes warm. How will you feel about returning to the mud then?

Keep me humble! Please, Jesus, keep me humble!

She tried to go back to sleep, but she could not. Madame du Bellier was snoring softly, steadily in the bed beside her. Outside, hard rain was banging against the windows. Jehanne kept thinking about Metz and Bertrand and the others. Wishing she were back with them. *Back in the forest, riding toward God . . .*

Jehanne got up and went to the fireplace, watched the fire burning low and red in its iron cradle. She took her old woolen cape from its hook and wrapped it around her. Then she lay down on the floor and curled herself up in front of the hearth. The floor was cold and hard, but at last she slept there. *Better than that wicked bed. Anything is better than that beautiful, wicked bed.*

CHAPTER NINE

In the beginning Charles was terrible to her. Cold and rude. His small pig's eyes narrowed in doubt. Suspicion rising off him like smoke. He summoned her to him the day after she had arrived at the castle. Two pages in faded blue-velvet tunics with fraying gold fleur-de-lis embroidery led her through the wrapped, bare gardens to the south wing of the castle: The King's apartments.

Charles sat in a tall leather chair by the window with the Chamberlain standing behind him. La Trémöille's enormous shadow falling over the Dauphin like a cloak. Charles looked at Jehanne with his lips pursed tightly, as if they'd been sewn together. 'You may have convinced my mother-in-law of this foolishness,' he said. 'But you have not convinced us of anything. Why should we believe you are what you say?'

'Because it is the truth,' she said.

La Trémöille's face curdled like milk, but Charles squinted, looking at her. 'Do you know how many people come here saying they've had holy visions, saying God has sent them to me?'

'I know things about you that no one else knows,' she said. 'Things only God could know.'

La Trémöille rolled his eyes.

'Tell me, why would God choose you, a peasant girl, an illiterate, when he could act through anyone, the most learned man on the planet?' said Charles.

'Perhaps a learned man was not what He needed for this mission.'

130

Charles leaned forward, peering at her, his spindly hands clasped together on his knees. 'What do you know about me? What is it you think you know?'

'You would have me say in front of another?'

'I am the King's closest advisor,' La Trémöille said. 'There is nothing he does not discuss with me.'

'What I have to say is only for your ears, Dauphin.'

How La Trémöille stared at her then! His eyes shining with hate.

Jehanne kept her eyes on the Dauphin. There was a long, raging silence.

'That'll be all for now, Pucelle,' Charles said finally. 'Leave us.'

Jehanne left the room, but when she was halfway down the hall, she stopped. 'I left my hat. Wait for me,' she said to the page, and headed back in the direction from which she'd come. As she approached the door, she heard the Dauphin's high, nervous voice coming from inside. 'Still, I think it's worth hearing her out at some point, Georges,' he laughed. 'I mean, at this point, why not, really?'

Silence.

'Well,' the Dauphin said at last, his voice rising several octaves. 'Don't you think?'

'No, I don't,' said La Trémöille. 'I think this whole thing is just more of your ridiculous nonsense. The fact that you allowed her to be brought here at all is an embarrassment.'

Silence. The scrape of a chair.

'I don't see why you get to speak to me that way, I really don't.'

131

Again silence.

Then La Trémöille: 'I get to speak to you that way because you owe me six hundred thousand livres. And because without me, you'd be dead.'

* * *

When Jehanne returned to her room after chapel that afternoon, there was a note waiting for her on her bed. 'Will you read it for me?' she asked Madame du Bellier.

It was from La Trémöille. There were just three lines. A meaningless, spidery black thicket of shapes to Jeanne's unschooled eyes. 'Oh,' said Madame du Bellier as she scanned the letter, her hand going to her mouth.

'What is it?'

'Oh, it's—there must be some misunderstanding. This can't be for you.'

'What does it say?'

She looked at Jehanne, her head thrown back, as if she'd been struck by a sharp wind. After several moments she spoke. 'It says: "You will suffer for this, Jehanne d'Arc. You will suffer in ways you cannot imagine."'

CHAPTER TEN

She spent the night in the chapel under the fretful watch of Madame du Bellier. Praying and weeping while Madame du Bellier sat stiffly near the entrance to the chapel, doing needlepoint, acting as if she could not hear everything. *Oh please!*

132

Jehanne sobbed. *Oh please, won't you come? Tell me how to make him listen. I am so afraid.*

Silence.

After a time Madame du Bellier stood and approached the girl, who had at last stopped praying and simply lay sobbing on the floor of the chapel. 'Come, darling,' she said, touching Jehanne's shoulder. 'It's all right now. Nothing's going to happen tonight. Come, let's get you into bed with some hot milk.'

'If only my men were here,' Jehanne said. 'I'd feel safe then. Why won't they let my men come and be with me?'

Madame du Bellier looked at her, stroked her hair. 'Soon enough you'll have new men,' she said. 'Make a friend of the King, and he'll have the best men in France keeping you safe.'

'Trémöille's threatened,' Madame du Bellier said later, once it had become clear that Jehanne would not sleep that night. Would only pace back and forth before the low, red fire, cracking her knuckles and saying *What shall I do? What shall I do?* 'He's very jealous. Very possessive of the King. I've seen it before, with others here at court. Others who are gone now. He hates the idea of anyone knowing more about Charles than he does.' She looked into the fire. 'You must find a way to befriend him, Jehanne. Make him see that you are not a threat.'

Jehanne stopped walking. 'That man will never be a friend of mine.'

CHAPTER ELEVEN

The next morning two pages ran through the castle in opposite directions. The first clutched a letter from the Maid to the King, as dictated to Madame du Bellier. It read: *Gentle Dauphin, if you love your country at all, I beg you, come to me this night in my chambers. Let me deliver the message that God has commanded me to bring you. Come alone, Dauphin. I beg you.*

The second page bore a letter from the Maid to Trémöille. It read: *You do not scare me. God and God alone will decide who among us suffers.*

CHAPTER TWELVE

She was awakened in the night by a sharp banging at her door. It was the Dauphin, clutching a long tattered fox-fur coat at the neck, his eyes wide. His hands trembling. 'Let me in quickly. I can't be seen here.'

'But Madame,' Jehanne said, nodding to the plump older woman who lay snoring softly in her bed.

'Tell her she has to go,' he said. 'Tell her she can come back in an hour.'

Jehanne woke the sleeping woman, and when she was gone, she and Charles sat down in the two tall chairs by the fire. The Dauphin stared at the little bed Jehanne had made for herself on the floor: her cloak and a pillow in front of the hearth.

'Our bed is not to your liking?' he asked as he laid his fur over the back of the chair.

'I am a warrior,' Jehanne explained solemnly, as she had explained earlier to an offended-looking Madame du Bellier. 'Warriors sleep on the ground so as always to be ready for battle.'

Metz had told her that on the way to Chinon. 'Never get too comfortable,' he said. 'You get comfortable, it's all over.' Bertrand roared when he heard that. 'What do you know about war, stripling?' Metz blushed red to the tops of his ears, and when at last he admitted that he'd read it in a book ('I've read a great many books about war and chivalry, for your information'), Jehanne and Bertrand looked at each other over the fire and then burst out laughing. But the words had stayed with her. She believed them.

The Dauphin looked at her. Then he took a deep breath through his nose and said, 'Tell me, what is this secret you cannot say in front of the Chamberlain?'

'I saw you in a dream.' He'd been in a castle by a river. 'Luges, Laches?' she asked.

'Loches,' said Charles. 'The summer castle.'

'But it wasn't summer anymore,' she said. In the dream, the leaves were red and yellow on the trees and there was an edge of chill in the air. It was evening. The Dauphin walked into the oratory by himself, knelt down before the altar, and begged God for guidance. 'You asked that if you were in fact the rightful heir to the throne of France, that God would keep you and protect you until such time as you could safely ascend it. Then you prayed that if you were not the rightful heir, that God would permit you to escape to Spain or

135

Scotland and take refuge there instead of being put to death in prison.'

When she had finished talking, Charles was very pale. He looked so vulnerable that she suddenly felt sorry for him. 'But how could you know that?' he said. 'No one knows about that.'

'Let me help you, Dauphin. You have been wronged these last years. Let me give you the help you deserve.'

He blinked several times. Scratched his nose. 'Do you say you know the truth of my paternity?'

She took his hand, held his chilled blue fingers in hers. 'You are no bastard, Sire. You're the King's true son and heir. You alone are the rightful ruler of France.'

CHAPTER THIRTEEN

They spent six weeks interrogating her, examining her. First the churchmen of Chinon in their tall black hats, then the churchmen of Poitiers in their tall red hats. All of them staring at her, pelting her with questions. *How do you know it's God who speaks to you? How do you know you're not possessed? Why do you dress as a man? How do we know you're not a witch? What spells do you know? What curses? What magic?*

Yolande was always there, watching from the corner, with her veil folded back. Watching, listening, taking notes in a small leather book. Whenever Jehanne said something brash, Yolande smiled, the left side of her mouth curling up, a little black dimple appearing in her cheek, so

Jehanne spoke brashly often. 'No one in the world can save France but me,' she said one day. 'I wish it were not so, but it is so, and you must use me quickly, for I will last little more than a year.'

How Yolande stared then!

'How do you know that?' the Queen asked.

'My voices tell me many things, Your Majesty. Not all of them pleasant.'

* * *

One day Madame du Bellier woke Jehanne up before dawn, the light from a candle flickering over her face in the darkness. 'Here, put this on, darling,' she said, handing the girl a long white nightgown. 'The Queen's physician is going to examine you.'

'Why?' said Jehanne, still half asleep as the woman helped her into the gown and wrapped Jehanne's cloak around her shoulders. 'Nothing to worry about, they just want to make sure you're healthy.'

She brought Jehanne to a room in the castle she had not seen before. 'Be strong now,' Madame du Bellier said, looking away. She squeezed Jehanne's hand, then left. In the room there was a bed with a sheet thrown over it. Yolande stood near the bed with five or six women around her, all of them with solemn, stiff-looking faces. A hard, unseeing look in their eyes that made Jehanne think of the exorcism in Vaucouleurs. 'We have to examine you, you understand,' Yolande said. 'Make sure you're really a virgin.'

Jehanne took a step backward. 'I am indeed a virgin, Majesty. I give you my word.'

'Nevertheless, we must be sure.'

Jehanne blinked. Stammered. 'Where is the doctor?'

One of the women stepped forward. 'I am Madame de Gaucourt,' she said. A tall, angular creature—thin as a grasshopper with a long, hooked nose, lavender skin. 'I will be examining you.'

'I thought it was a doctor,' Jehanne said, taking another step back.

'Madame de Gaucourt is the wife of one of my most trusted advisors,' the Queen said. 'It's best for a woman to do this.'

'Be a good girl now and this will all be over quickly,' Madame de Gaucourt said. She told Jehanne to lie down on the bed, and when Jehanne had done so, she lifted the girl's skirt up around her waist and spread her legs open.

'Bend your knees.'

A terrible feeling, the cold air on her tenderest part, the women gathered around, staring as if they expected a hissing cobra to emerge from between her legs. 'Majesty, I swear,' Jehanne cried. 'No man has touched me there.'

Madame de Gaucourt rolled up her sleeves. Spoke for the group: 'That may be, but we must see for ourselves.'

She held a long metal spoon in her hand that glinted in the light.

'What's that?'

'It'll be over soon. Just think about the God you say has sent you here.'

Her scream, when it came, echoed through the castle corridors, made the cooks in the kitchen jump. 'Now, now,' said Gaucourt. Taking her time, fidgeting. Jehanne began to weep. Great fat tears rolled slowly down her face. 'All right,' Gaucourt said finally, her hand slick as if it had been dipped in jelly. 'She's pure. No one's had her.' She wiped the instrument clean on her apron, smearing it with bright blood. 'Amazing,' she said, looking down at Jehanne. 'A peasant like you, keeping it all this time.'

*　　*　　*

A thousand examinations, it seemed. A doctor with peeling lips looking her over for marks of the Devil, a tiny theologian with yellow hands who wanted her to recite prayers, the Bishop and his men in their long black robes peering into her eyes, asking the same questions the other men of the cloth had asked: How do you *know* it's God? Show us a sign. Where is your proof?

Again and again they said that they needed to be sure. Jehanne could think only of the poor people in Orléans, starving, eating rats and dogs. Sucking on stones to keep the hunger pangs at bay. She felt like shouting, 'People are dying! Let me go save them!'

CHAPTER FOURTEEN

The dauphin attended Jehanne's daily interrogations in Poitiers, but unlike Yolande, he never spoke. Seemed to pay little attention to the proceedings. Several times he fell asleep, snoring loudly in his chair. Other times he doodled on a piece of paper, not bothering to hide what he was doing. Jehanne's heart sank whenever she looked at him. She had hoped, after the night in her room . . . But no, it was worse now. His eyes were flat, inscrutable. His face closed. A wall.

One day he came in very late, well after the proceedings had begun. Everyone stood, watching him walk his slow, slouching walk across the room, his stained pink-satin houppelande billowing behind him like a sail as he fell into a chair beside Yolande. He had deep brown bags under his eyes, and his hair was so greasy it looked wet. He smelled as if he had bathed in wine. Jehanne grew furious at the sight of him. Disgust rose up in her, hot and wild. *How can you call yourself King? They should cut you into pieces, drag you through the streets.*

'You say your voices tell you that God wishes to free the people of France from their present calamity,' one of the churchmen said. A small man with a bristly white beard and a large brown mole on his cheek. His lips were pressed together tightly, as if he were hiding gold in his mouth. 'But if He wishes to free them, surely it is not necessary for Him to use an army.'

Jehanne stood up and banged her fist on the table. 'For God's sake, the soldiers will fight, and God will give the victory!'

The churchmen looked aghast. Charles blinked. *Well, that's the end of me*, she thought. *Tonight I sleep in the dungeon.* But Yolande was smiling. A radiant smile, like a bouquet of flowers flung high in the air. 'Thank you, Jehanne,' she said. 'You may leave us now.'

'It's not his fault,' Yolande said later. 'The King has had it worse than anyone.' She and Jehanne were walking together through the castle's outer courtyard that overlooked the valley. It was early in the morning. The sky chill and white. Pale scarves of fog still nestled among the budding hills. Already Jehanne knew some things about Yolande from Madame du Bellier. Yolande owned vast estates in Anjou, land she did not want destroyed by the English. Yolande was rich. 'Owns half of Spain,' said Madame du Bellier. 'She's worth more than Charles and La Trémöille combined.' In her message, Yolande had said: 'There are some things you must understand about the King if you are to help him.'

He'd had a terrible life, she said, from the start. First the mad father, murdering his own knights, throwing his shit against the windows of the Louvre, thinking he was made of glass. Then the Whore Queen Isabeau, betraying him, her own son, disowning him, proclaiming him a bastard in public, not the King's son at all—making a fool of him in front of the entire country. 'A monster, that woman,' Yolande said. 'She should be killed.'

As she spoke, Yolande's face changed. Suddenly she looked older. Older and darker. As if a shadow had passed beneath her skin. 'And so much death around him . . . always death, at every turn.' There had been four Dauphins in line for the throne before Charles. Four older brothers who now lay with their arms crossed over their chests in the Abbey at Saint-Denis: Charles, Charles, Louis, and John. The first two hadn't made it out of childhood. The last two died suddenly, as youths, while in the Duke of Burgundy's care. 'He said it was illness both times,' Yolande said. 'But of course it was a lie. He poisoned them, Burgundy. Poisoned them to get them out of his way.'

Jehanne was staring now, but the Queen did not seem to notice. She seemed to be somewhere else. 'I took Charles away then. I had to. He was already engaged to my daughter; I had come to think of him as a son. We left Paris in secret, by night. It was in the middle of the riots. Burgundy was trying to take over the city, and I knew if he got his hands on Charles, he'd kill him the way he did his brothers. So I took him. I got him out, took him down to my castle in Provence.'

The Whore Queen had been furious when she heard. She demanded Charles be returned at once, her fastest messenger galloping over the yellow fields outside Paris with the Queen's shouting letter rolled up in his pouch. Yolande responded with a letter of her own:

We have not nurtured and cherished this one for you to make him die like his brothers or to go mad like his father, or to become English like you. I keep him for my own. Come and take him away, if you dare.

Isabeau had not dared. 'But,' Yolande said, her eyes far away, 'something else happened, something terrible.' Two of Charles's counselors, Tanneguy du Chastel and Pierre de Giac, had secretly plotted revenge against the Duke of Burgundy for murdering the Mad King's brother, the Duke of Orléans, years earlier. 'Charles had no idea. He was young; they used him,' Yolande said. They told the Dauphin to request a peaceful meeting with Burgundy on the old bridge at Montereau, and then they cut Burgundy's head off right in front of him. Blood coming out in ropes, the head arcing through the air and rolling to rest at Charles's feet. Charles screaming in horror. 'He had no idea,' Yolande said, 'but of course no one believed him.' All of Burgundy blamed Charles for the death. The dead Duke's son, Philip the Good, declared civil war on the royal family. The Burgundians versus the Armagnacs. Swore he would not rest until young Charles was dead.

'So poor Charles lives in fear now,' Yolande said. He was afraid of everything. He hated crossing bridges, feared for his life whenever he entered any public place. Hated strangers and crowds. Made two different men taste his wine before he would drink it. Even consulted with his astrologer every evening before he slept. 'Very bad stars tonight,' he would say, and then he'd vanish into his quarters for three or four days. No one allowed in or out. 'Lockup,' he called it. 'I've been in lockup.'

There was a good man under there, fiercely intelligent, Yolande said. And kind. But damaged too, in need of healing. 'You must be patient with him,' Yolande said. 'It has been raining in his heart for as long as he can remember.'

Jehanne nodded.

'What about La Trémöille?' she said finally.

Yolande looked at her. 'What *about* La Trémöille?'

'I don't think he likes me.'

'No, I don't imagine he does. Nevertheless, as

long as you do what you've promised us, you have nothing to fear from La Trémöille.'

*   *   *

The next afternoon Jehanne walked up to the Dauphin after the interrogations were finished and asked him to accompany her to church. 'We have much praying to do if we are to save this country, Dauphin.'

He looked at her, three pleats tucked between his eyebrows. 'Why do you not call me King?'

'I'll call you King as soon as I have you crowned in Reims.'

The Dauphin laughed at her, the absurdity. The monstrous arrogance. But it excited him too, being around that kind of confidence. He agreed to pray with her. Yes, an excellent idea. He walked with her down the hill to the Rose Chapel and sat beside her throughout the Mass, watching her in the candlelight. After a time, he got to his knees and bowed his own head.

From then on, he accompanied her to the chapel every day. Sat beside her in the freezing pink-marble room and prayed, marveled at how strong he felt when he was next to her there—her faith, the certainty rising off of her like heat, warming him, making him think, *Perhaps. Perhaps it is possible*.

When he was alone, without her, his hope vanished quickly. Evaporated like water before his eyes, returning him to the howling desert of his old life. The desert where everyone he loved had died or betrayed him. The desert where La Trémöille was King and he was a slave, cowering and mewling on his knees, begging for mercy. And so Charles stayed by Jehanne's side, drinking in her light, beating back the desert. And when he prayed, he prayed that God would make him strong. Strong enough to keep defying La Trémöille. Strong enough to be King.

*   *   *

A month later the churchmen of Poitiers declared that they could find no evil in Jehanne. 'We see no reason why, in view of the imminent danger to France, the girl should not be permitted to help the King and go to Orléans.'

'Finally!' crowed Yolande. She said they must return to Chinon at once. Must get to work. It was the end of March. The earth was beginning to soften and give off a cool, metallic, claylike scent. The daffodils were leaping up alongside the road. And as the pointed slate-roofed towers of Chinon Castle came into view from their carriage, Yolande clenched her hands into two plump white fists. Looked at Jehanne and Charles with blazing eyes. 'Now we have a chance! Now we will give them a fight!'

CHAPTER FIFTEEN

It was right after that that they introduced me at court. Yolande's idea. Yolande, who was so quick to use me.

She had said that it was time to arrange an official meeting between the Maid and the King before all the nobles and knights of court. It was essential. 'We must show them your power. Show them the miracles you're capable of.'

'But I have no miracles,' Jehanne said. 'You know that, Majesty.'

Yolande smiled calmly. 'What I know is that if you want the knights of France to fight like lions for you, you must prove to them that you are sent by God.'

'Is the word of God Himself not proof enough?'

'No. It is not.'

* * *

Several days later Jehanne stood beneath the flickering chandelier at the entrance to the great hall, her heart hammering in her chest, waiting for the lie to begin. The room before her was packed full of nobles and courtiers in furs and jeweled tunics, hats like sailing ships. Hundreds of knights, their armor gleaming in the torchlight. Most of them craning their necks, up on tiptoe, staring at her, trying to catch a glimpse.

She knew it was wrong. She'd refused to do it at first, said it was impossible. Her saints would never approve. But they would not listen. 'It's the only way,' Yolande said. 'She's right,' said La Trémoïlle, eyes glittering. 'It must be done.' Listening to them, Jehanne felt as if she were in a little boat, surrounded by threatening green waves, high as mountains. 'One display of God's power will do more than a thousand explanations ever could,' Yolande said. 'Trust me on this, my dear.'

In the end Jehanne did as they instructed. She took off the nice new clothes Yolande had had

146

tailors make for her in Poitiers and put on her old dirty ones. The filthy brown hose and the stained black tunic from Vaucouleurs. She let Yolande smear mud on her cheeks and her hands, mud in her hair. 'I want them to see you as I first did,' Yolande said, smiling. 'An urchin stumbled out of the wilderness.'

When the Queen was finished, Jehanne let Madame du Bellier guide her in secret down a long dripping tunnel that ran underneath the castle to the apartment of a slim, silken-voiced man who was introduced to her as Count Louis de Vendôme. 'He will take you to the King,' she said.

The man was holding a small silver goblet full of amber-colored liquid. 'I have something that will calm your nerves, if you like,' he said.

Jehanne said that she did not want it, though her palms were sweating. Her mouth dry as dust. 'Let's just go,' she said miserably.

When the trumpets sounded, Jehanne and Vendôme walked together into the great hall. And it was as Yolande had said it would be: The Comte de Clermont was sitting there, on Charles's throne, wearing Charles's hat, smiling stupidly. Playing the King. As the Count led Jehanne toward him, she repeated Yolande's instructions in her head: *Remember, they all think you're seeing Charles for the first time. They'll think he's trying to trick you. Testing you to see if you'll fall for the phony king. So let Vendôme take you up to the throne, and when you're in front of Clermont, stop and look at him for a moment. Then say out loud: 'But this is not the King of France.' After that, turn and walk back through the crowd until you see Charles, who will be standing with La Trémöille on the left side. Go to*

147

him, kneel down, kiss the hem of his robe, and say, 'Most noble Dauphin, I am sent by God to bring aid to you and your kingdom.' Then we will have them! Yolande had crowed. Then they will be eating from the palms of our hands!

She did it. The charade. She did it perfectly. Exactly as Yolande had instructed. When she said, 'But this is not the King of France,' everyone in the crowd gasped. And when she turned and walked over to Charles and knelt down before him, they gasped again, even louder this time, and she heard a buzz of whispers and talk around her. *How does she know? How could she possibly know? Incredible. Amazing.*

Charles played his part. 'It is not I who am the King, Jehanne. *There* is the King,' he said, pointing to Clermont.

'In God's name, noble prince,' Jehanne said. 'It is you and none other.'

Jehanne felt like she was going to throw up. Swallowed hot bile down her throat. Repeated what she'd said to him that day in his apartment so many weeks ago: 'Sire, if I tell you things so secret that you and God alone are privy to them, will you believe that I am sent by God?'

Charles nodded like a puppet.

Both of us just puppets.

'I must tell you in private,' she said.

As instructed, they walked together to the little oriel beside the fireplace and Jehanne repeated the things that she had already told Charles six weeks earlier—about the dream at Loches and the truth of his paternity and the details of God's mission—and Charles pretended to be shocked and amazed to hear them, and as she spoke,

Jehanne's skin went cold as ice. *O wrong,* Catherine said. *O wrong, very wrong!* Jehanne could not bear it. She knelt down suddenly and clutched Charles's hand. 'Look at me,' she said, staring into his small pale eyes. 'It is all true. Do you know that? Forget this sham. Do you understand that I speak God's truth?'

Tears sprang to his eyes. He squeezed her hands back. 'I do believe you,' he whispered. 'God bless you, I do.'

CHAPTER SIXTEEN

People started coming then. From all over the countryside they came to the river town of Chinon in hopes of seeing the famous Maid. The Savior of France. Hundreds and soon thousands of them, traveling by foot, by horse, by carriage, over the red-dirt roads of France in the cold April rains, their faces shining with hope, curiosity, and even among the doubters, an eagerness to see what it was all about, everyone wanting to see for themselves.

One morning Madame du Bellier drew back the curtains and let the sun flood into the darkness of the girl's room. A clear, bright, early spring morning, all the world washed clean by the rain. Crowds of screaming people had gathered down below, were pressing at the castle gates, hundreds of them. Madame du Bellier opened the window, heard the roars of the crowd, the clatter of wagons, and the clocking of hooves as horses and their riders moved across the wooden drawbridge, one man whistling, high and sweet as a songbird.

'What are they all doing?' Jehanne said, coming up behind her, still rubbing her eyes.

The woman laid a hand on the girl's shoulder. 'They're here to see you,' she said.

Jehanne stared down at the sea of people. 'No,' she said finally. 'It's Him they want.'

Later in the afternoon Madame du Bellier brought her a letter that had been delivered from town. It was from Metz and Bertrand.

> We heard about your very great success at Poitiers and with the King at court, and so we send our congratulations and very best wishes, and also send the news that we are going to Blois now to join up with the King's army so we can have the honor of fighting for you in Orléans.

'Oh,' Jehanne said, weeping, holding her hand over her mouth. 'Oh.'

CHAPTER SEVENTEEN

A frenzy of activity now. Training, meetings, strategies for Orléans. The official meeting between Charles and the Maid had been a great success, Yolande said. The knights were chomping at the bit to fight. 'I've never seen anything like it. They've got wildfires in their eyes!'

Every morning Jehanne and Charles were brought to Yolande's apartments for briefings with the war counselors, generals, and famous

150

mercenaries who were flooding in from all over France, begging to meet the Maid. Yolande tacked a big yellow map of Orléans up on the wall, and the men told how it was: Where the Goddon fortresses were strong, and where they might be taken. 'Diarrhea hit them hard this winter, so they're weak right now,' one general said. A short, ferocious-looking man with a web of scars over his face and a red-velvet cloak covered in little silver bells that tinkled when he walked. 'One hard push could send them running for the hills.'

'One wrong push could be the end of France,' said Charles.

The general made a face.

'I'm saying we must plan very carefully,' Charles said. 'We need a perfect plan.'

The general looked at Jehanne, then winked, as if to say, *Screw plans. Let's do the hard push!*

A tutor came in to work with Charles on his public speaking and to help him with his stammer. 'Can't have a king with a stammer,' Yolande said. They made him do all kinds of things—walk with a stack of books on his head to improve his posture, pluck his eyebrows so they did not hang so heavily over his eyes. One morning when Jehanne came in, he had an entirely new set of clothes on. A splendid mink-trimmed turquoise-brocade tunic and new tight black stockings and high polished black boots. His narrow little bird's shoulders looked much broader in the new tunic, and when he noticed Jehanne staring at them, he blushed and said, 'Padding.'

They'd become close by then, Charles and Jehanne. There was an appealing haplessness about Charles that touched her. She could see that

151

he was trying to become strong, to find his dignity. But it was his clumsy attempts that endeared him to her. How he sat beside her in the chapel with his teeth chattering like dice in his head, swearing he was not cold. How deeply he blushed when Jehanne spoke of victory over the Goddons, as if it were thrilling but possibly dangerous to even think such a thing. In the afternoons Jehanne trained down in the jousting ring with Charles's cousin, the Duke of Alençon, and often, as they walked there after chapel, Charles would take a little hopping step beside her and gaze at her with wide, childish eyes. 'How will it all happen again, Pucelle? Tell me again.' Or he would grip her hand suddenly, with tears in his eyes, and say, 'Truly? Shall I truly be king?'

CHAPTER EIGHTEEN

At times she had nightmares. In the worst one she was galloping across the long snowfields on her horse, and the violent joy was rushing inside her, and the ten thousand soldiers were thundering behind her, but this time, when they reached the enemy forest, all of their horses disappeared. They were forced to keep running on foot, in their armor and their long, pointed metal shoes. Suddenly Charles popped up in front of her and said, 'You have to carry me; it's the law. You have to carry me on your shoulders.' Jehanne's heart filled with dread when he said this, but she understood that she could not refuse. So she lifted the Dauphin up onto her shoulders and began running again through the forest, and it was even more difficult for her to run now because he was very heavy and he kept slapping her head and jerking her reins in different directions. 'Go left!' he shouted. 'Now right! Now left, you stupid fool! Left, I said! Do you understand nothing?' Jehanne knew that the only way out of the forest was to run straight ahead as fast as she could, and she kept begging the Dauphin to let her do this. 'Please,' she cried, weeping and staggering under the weight of him. 'Please, let me show you.' But the Dauphin just became more annoyed and began hissing, 'Shut up, just shut up.' Soon they came to a clearing in the trees. In the middle stood a high, dark, stone tower. It was much colder there and there were strange white and gray birds flying overhead. Birds the girl had never seen before. 'Ah, at last!' the Dauphin shouted. He hopped off the girl's shoulders and opened the big wooden door to the tower. Inside was a long, dark, winding stone staircase. 'Here we go,' he said, smiling and holding the door open for her. 'Just leave your clothes here with me. I'll take care of them.' Jehanne did not want to go into the tower, and she told the Dauphin this. 'Please,' she said. 'Please don't make me.' She gripped the door frame with both hands and crouched down low like an animal, digging her heels into the ground. 'Go on, I'll be right behind you,' he said, smiling at her with terrible pointed black teeth and pushing her forward. 'You'll be perfectly safe, my dear.'

She'd awoken panting and drenched in sweat. She got up and ran downstairs to the chapel in her bare feet. And she knelt there, weeping in the dark, until at last Catherine and Margaret

153

appeared, hovering above her like two golden moths. *Hush now, darling,* whispered Catherine, pouring her sunlight in the girl's ear. *We're here.*

I'm going to die! she cried, the dream so real, so sharp that it was as if Michael had never told her that day beside the river, as if she were hearing it for the first time. *I'm going to die!*

CHAPTER NINETEEN

Alençon was the only one she could talk to. The only one who made sense to her. The Duke of Alençon. *Mon beau Duc.* He was Charles's first cousin—a general in his early twenties with thick, bristly black hair and dark, hooded eyes, an odd roughness in his features, as if they had been carved from a block of wood. His father had been a famous warrior, killed terribly at Agincourt. Alençon himself had been held prisoner by the English for five years before Jehanne met him. Locked up in a tower in Arras, living on bread and water and mice he hunted in his cell. Finally his family had scraped the money together to ransom him, but it ruined them to do it. They had to sell off all of their lands, their jewelry, paintings, everything. He returned to his château in the Loire to find it stripped bare, just the most basic furniture left. A few tables and chairs scattered about like bones. Everything else gone. Like Jehanne, he too was hungry for vengeance. 'The Duke is the only man in France who hates the English more than you do,' Charles said.

Alençon hated court too. Had no interest. After

all that time alone in a tower, he knew what it was like to look around at one of Charles's obscene dinner parties and think, 'Who are these vultures? These stupid, laughing people?' Like Jehanne, he preferred to move. To ride and joust and hunt. Sleep outside under the trees. Cook your meat over a fire. Kill the Goddons. Drive them out of France.

He was better on a horse than anyone Jehanne had ever seen. There was no separation between him and his animal when they rode. No hint of effort. They simply flew across the fields. He did not talk much, was comfortable in his skin, in his silence. But when he did talk, when he was among friends or speaking to his men—he was open and easy and good-natured. When it mattered. None of this chattering, this 'Well, have you heard . . .' Nothing wasted.

She knew she wanted him. From the beginning it was clear. She could not pretend otherwise—not with herself. Not when the thought of his skin, his dark, waiting eyes, kept her up at night. Often when she was away from him, she would think, *He's not really so handsome. He's actually quite odd looking.* But when she was near him, she ached for him as a starving man aches for food.

It was a different sort of wanting from the way she'd wanted Metz. Deeper, more alarming. Alençon did not surrender when she looked at him. His eyes were hot and silent. Holding her.

It never ceased to amaze Jehanne that he was the Dauphin's first cousin. The first time she'd met him, she and Charles had been together in Charles's chambers, and Alençon had come in the door and lifted Charles off his feet as he hugged

155

him. 'So where is this miraculous peasant?' he said, kissing his cousin on both cheeks.

'I'm right here, Your Grace,' said Jehanne, who stood by the window in a dark blue tunic, looking unusually clean and lovely.

'So you are,' said the Duke, grinning. 'I hope I'm not interrupting.'

'Oh no, you are welcome, my good Duke,' she said, coming toward him, looking at him. Unable to stop looking at him. 'I need all the royal blood on my side that I can get.'

Charles and Alençon had grown up together, been friends since they were children. And through Alençon she'd seen a different side of the Dauphin too, for Charles was easy and relaxed around his cousin in a way he never was otherwise. He laughed more, would let Alençon tease him, could be witty himself, charming even. He wasn't a fool, Charles. He was just unsure. Unsure of everything.

She knew from the beginning that nothing could happen between them. Alençon was married, and Jehanne too, in her way, was married. But it did not mean that she did not want him, did not come to love him. It was a thing kept secret, flowing silently beneath everything like an underground river.

CHAPTER TWENTY

It was very hard to hear my voices in the castle. Much harder than in the forest, among the oaks and the long pale sunlight. The sunlight of the bois chênu. *They still came to me, but it took longer, and they*

156

were quieter, much harder to hear. I had to listen very closely. At first I thought it was because the castle walls were so thick—very deep, old, stone walls and so many of them, wall after wall after wall, blocking out the world, the light. But later I knew that it was the air inside the castle too. The air was packed tightly with gossip, thoughts, plans, schemes. Murder. The air in the castle was as loud as a hive.

CHAPTER TWENTY-ONE

The day after Alençon arrived at Chinon, he stood with the Dauphin in the *berfois* overlooking the jousting ring, watching Jehanne tilt and ride. It was a cold, bright, clear day. The sky a pale sparkling aqua, a flock of black starlings overhead, diving and swooping through the air. Charles had taken Jehanne to his armory that morning and had her outfitted with a lance and shield and some chainmail. He'd also lent her a dapple-gray horse that put the black rouncy she'd received from the Duke of Lorraine to shame. Now the little Maid flew across the ring like a shot, her chin jutted out, her lance glinting in the sunlight, the red dirt about her horse's hooves jumping into the air. 'Holy Mary,' the Duke said as Jehanne drove her lance through the heart of the straw man that stood at the end of the ring.

'Isn't she wonderful?' said Charles.

'Oh, all those farm girls can ride,' La Trémöille said, rolling his eyes. 'For Christ's sake, they bring their damned horses into the house and sleep with them all winter long.'

Alençon was not listening. Alençon was watching the girl. 'I think I'll join her,' he said, handing La Trémöille his cloak and jumping the ring's fence. Half an hour later he entered the ring, outfitted on horseback and carrying a lance. 'Shall we have a go?'

Jehanne, slowing her horse, grinned and shouted, 'Ah, a worthy opponent at last!'

An hour later she had him off his horse, lying in the middle of the ring, the tip of her lance kissing his throat.

*   *   *

'She's unbelievable,' Alençon said that evening, as he and the Dauphin and La Trémöille shared a bottle of wine in the Dauphin's chambers. His eyes were shining. 'It's hard to believe she's real.'

La Trémöille raised an eyebrow. 'Yes,' he said. 'It certainly is.'

CHAPTER TWENTY-TWO

They spent the month together. Jehanne and Charles and Alençon. Riding together, practicing jousting and swordplay, studying attack strategies for Orléans. 'If you want anyone to listen to you, you have to know these things,' Alençon said. Charles refused to participate in the war play. He was a very good horseman, but he wouldn't go near a sword or a lance. He shivered visibly at the sight of Alençon's poleax. 'None of that battle stuff for me,' he said. But he rode with them down by the river and through the curling, new-green vineyards in the warm spring afternoons, when Alençon sang in his low, clear voice:

O I love to see up on the field,
The knights and horses in their battle array,
And I tell you nothing thrills me, dear,
As when my men shout, 'On! We die this day!'

'What a horrible song!' said Charles, laughing, but as he watched their three long shadows advance together before them on the road, he felt that he was among friends for perhaps the first time.

A sweet, thrilling moment in their lives. A kind of tender, delicately balanced friendship between them: Jehanne and Alençon lavishing their attention on Charles, making sure always to keep him in the center, always included. Charles, shining from all the attention, oblivious. A friendship like a soap bubble. Destined to burst.

CHAPTER TWENTY-THREE

One day in Chinon Charles had summoned Jehanne to meet him in the Tour des Chiens. The Dogs' Tower. He stood surrounded by a dozen pointers, stroking their black silken skulls and ears, cooing 'Yes, yes, my darlings' as they leaped on him and licked the salt from his thin, violet palms.

'Never seen a whole tower just for dogs before,' Jehanne said.

The Dauphin glanced up, grinning. Blushing.

'Oh, this is nothing,' he said. 'My mother kept a whole zoo at the palace in Paris. Full of lions, baboons, crocodiles, snakes.' He waved his hand in the air. 'Every crazy creature you can imagine. I think she liked them better than people, if you want to know the truth.' He smiled, spoke to a dog with pursed lips, scratching behind its ears. 'Didn't she, Pansy? Yes, I think she did.'

At last he straightened up and turned to Jehanne. 'So, I've been thinking, with all this training going on, what do you propose to do in Orléans, exactly?'

Jehanne grinned, cocked her head. 'I'll lead them in battle, Dauphin. Fight the English until they are destroyed.'

Charles blinked. 'But surely you yourself don't mean to be down there on the field with the soldiers in . . . in the fighting?'

A big grin then. The dark brows rising, spreading like a crow's wings. 'Oh yes, Sire. That's exactly what I mean.'

'On horseback?'

'Yes, Dauphin.'

Charles was staring now, his heart hammering. 'With a sword?'

'Of course.'

'You actually plan to fight?'

'I plan to do whatever God tells me to do. I know He will have me out on the battlefield. It seems best if I have a sword.'

Silence then. The Dauphin watched her through narrowed eyes. Picturing it. A terrifying, marvelous image: The possessed witch-girl on horseback, leading an army of ten thousand men. An image so potent that a jet of reptilian blood shot through his veins. Reptilian blood singing, *You'll be King. You'll be King. You'll be King!* He smiled. 'You'll scare them to death.'

'I hope so,' she said.

*   *   *

Several days later she stood illuminated by fire in the armorer's dim workshop in Tours. A small black stick figure with her arms held out crosswise, the red forge flames glowing with prophecy behind her. The armorer wrapped a length of measuring ribbon around her arm and scribbled down a figure on a scrap of wood. 'She'll for sure be the smallest suit I ever made,' he said. Slowly he circled the girl. Lassoing the ribbon around her neck and bust and chest and hips. Hands trembling as he went.

'Make her the finest too,' said Alençon. He was seated in a chair in the corner, watching Jehanne with delighted eyes. The air between them charged, electric. Her skin tingling beneath his gaze. 'I will,' said the man, who had stopped working and was staring at her with enormous wondering eyes.

'I'm not going to fly away,' she said, laughing.

'No, mademoiselle. Of course not,' he said, though he did not look at all certain.

*   *   *

Later, while she and Alençon were riding back from the armorer's, several people ran by them very quickly. She looked up and saw that a great number of people were running, all in the same direction. All of them with excited, hungry looks

161

on their faces. 'An execution,' said Alençon.

They followed the running crowds until they came to the town square. It was full of people. People crammed together, talking and watching, fathers with children up on their shoulders, old women in their headscarves, craning their necks, looking toward the center of the square. Some leaned out of windows. Others stood up on rooftops, perched like birds. In the center of the square there was a large platform and on the platform stood a wooden post with a long arm sticking out. A noose hung from the arm. A long, silent O of rope, dangling in the air. A woman nearby was selling baked potatoes.

Jehanne watched a wagon move slowly through the crowd. The executioner in a pointed black hood sat up front, holding the reins. His face hidden. In the cart behind him crouched a figure in a ragged gown, clutching something the girl could not see. A woman, old and wrinkled, her head shaved. Her face like a white raisin. The crowd was cheering now. The crowd was wild.

Slowly the man in the black hood led the prisoner up the stairs. Jehanne saw then that she was holding an orange cat very tightly against her. Up on the platform a man read something out loud from a scroll, and the executioner set the noose around the old woman's neck. He took the cat from the old woman, stroked it several times, and then twisted the animal's head around on its neck. A swift, firm gesture. Like wringing out a towel. The animal jerked once, twice, and was still.

The executioner handed the dead animal back to the old woman, who was screaming now. A high, wild scream, like an eagle's. The crowd screamed back, ecstatic.

Alençon looked at Jehanne. Her face was blank. Expressionless.

'They'll do that to me one day,' she said.

Alençon blinked. 'Don't say that,' he said, taking her by the arm. 'Come on, let's get out of here.'

*   *   *

When Jehanne's armor was completed, Charles went to the armorer's to watch her try it on. 'She's for sure the smallest one I ever made,' the smith said again as he finished buckling the last greave about her shin. Jehanne stood there in her shining white metal suit. 'It's beautiful,' she said.

It was lovely, finely made, with jointed plates for the knees and elbows and a short embellished steel skirt, split in the middle so she could ride. The King walked around her, frowning. 'Not bad. Of course they do better work in Paris, but I think this will suit our purposes. How does it feel? Can you walk?'

'Oh yes,' she said, taking a few stiff steps forward in her long pointed metal shoes.

'Is it very heavy? Are you ready to take it off?'

'Oh no,' she said, beaming. 'I'm never taking it off.'

*   *   *

It was terribly heavy, the armor. Sixty-five pounds, the armorer said. And hot. Like walking around in a coffin. I had to bind my breasts to protect them from the metal. They wrapped twenty feet of linen around me every morning, very tight, fastened with a big steel

163

brooch. But even then there are places you can't protect. Your thighs. Your hips. You've never seen bruises until you've fought in a suit of armor for a few days. Your whole body turns purple and black. After a while, you can't even remember what your skin looked like before. It seems that it's always been like that, ever since you were born.

It does something too, the armor. It's not just that it protects you. It changes you, separates you from the world. From other people. Puts you on a different level. A very simple level. There's only one thing to do in a suit of armor, and that's to fight. So that's what you do. You fight. And sometimes you kill.

*　　　*　　　*

Next came the sword. Charles had offered to have the smith in Tours make one for her, but Jehanne refused. 'I know what sword I want,' she said.

On the way to Chinon they'd stopped at the little town of Sainte-Catherine-de-Fierbois. Jehanne had wanted to pray at the shrine there. To visit with her saint. A strange sort of shrine. Full of old weapons and armor. Long rusted ropes of chain hung from the rafters. Thousand-year-old axes crossed on the walls. 'Catherine is the patron saint of grateful knights and escaped prisoners,' the priest there had said, pointing out the manacles of the nobleman Cazin du Boys who'd been taken prisoner by the Burgundians, along with the garrison of Beaumont-sur-Oise. 'Fellow went to sleep praying to Saint Catherine and woke up the next morning to find his cage door wide open and all the guards asleep,' said the red-nosed

164

priest. Jehanne walked among the weapons, touching rust-spotted blades and handles, fascinated. The priest noticed her interest and said, 'You know Charles Martel?'

Jehanne did know Charles Martel. Everyone in France knew Charles Martel. The Hammer they called him. He'd driven the Muslims out of France seven hundred years ago. Martel and twenty-five thousand Frenchmen versus eighty thousand blue-turbaned Saracens. A miraculous victory. Invaders with faces dark as hatchets and long black beards had swarmed down over the country like bees, their blood arrogant from twenty years of victories over the Persians, the Romans. Eyes glittering with dreams of conquering all Europe. Martel killed that glitter. Put an end to those dreams. Martel sent them screaming for the trees.

'His sword's buried up behind the altar. So no one steals it.'

Jehanne looked at him. 'It's really his?'

The man nodded, solemn. 'I've seen it with my own eyes. Big gorgeous thing. Five crosses engraved in the handle just like they say in the books.'

*　　　*　　　*

Yolande loved the idea. 'Perfect!' she cried, and sent a messenger to the shrine in Fierbois to fetch the famous sword.

'It should be behind the altar,' said Jehanne, 'buried a few inches underground.'

The messenger looked at her. 'How do you know it's there?'

'Her voices told her,' said Yolande quickly,

165

before Jehanne could say anything. 'They say it is the sword of Charles Martel that will drive the English out of France.'

Jehanne looked at Yolande. Was silent.

'Why did you say that?' Jehanne asked after the messenger left. 'My voices said nothing about the sword.'

Yolande looked at her. 'You must trust me, Jehanne. We must use every opportunity we can to convince the people that you are sent by God.'

Jehanne looked at her feet. Did not speak.

She let it happen. She did not like it, but she let it happen. Let Yolande spread the tale of the Maid's miraculous sword throughout the kingdom. The famous sword of Charles Martel, revealed to her by her saints in the shrine of Saint Catherine. The sword with which Charles Martel had driven the Saracens out of France seven hundred years earlier. As the Maid would drive the English out of France now. And when the rusted old sword was taken to an ironsmith in Tours for repair and the smith cried out that the rust 'just fell away, like magic,' leaving the sword a gleaming steel thing, sharp and strong, Yolande crowed, 'You see, a miracle! It was meant to be yours, my dear.'

'It's no miracle,' Jehanne said. But no one around her was listening.

*   *   *

She loved her standard better. Did not feel a flush of shame when she looked at it, felt only the Godhead shining inside her. It took six women three long days and nights to sew her standard. All of them hunched over a round table by the hearth

166

at the head seamstress's house, their hair pulled back into tight braided buns, their long fine needles glinting in the firelight. The standard was made of thick, double-faced white satin and trimmed with golden fringe. Each side was embroidered with the words Jesu Maria above an image of Christ seated on the globe and supported by two winged angels. Golden lilies were scattered across the background. The women worked like mules to get it done in time, sewing in a kind of intent, focused ecstasy, their hearts singing *She's come, she's come, she's come!* as their needles dipped in and out of the gleaming material, whip-stitching the lily stems and sewing the angel's eyes up with French knots, their blood jumping with the wildness of it all, the miraculous peasant, the virgin on horseback galloping over the fragrant spring meadows to save France, and the fact that they too got to be a part of it, and so they sewed until their fingers cramped into claws and their lower backs howled in pain, getting up only to splash cold water on their faces or to run quickly outside and around the house in the chill air to keep themselves awake through the night, rubbing their arms and staring up at the moon as they moved through the damp grass, exhausted and exhilarated, happy as dogs.

CHAPTER TWENTY-FOUR

The fire was leaping brightly inside Jehanne now, making her radiant, irresistible, the flames spreading quickly, igniting in the hearts of everyone she met. No one could resist. *More*, their

167

hearts said. *Yes, yes. More*.

It was mid-April. The weather had grown warm by then, the bright, new greens of spring were spreading across the countryside, the roadsides crowded with crocuses and lilies. Jehanne rode in her new armor, with her rapidly growing entourage behind her as they went to meet the Dauphin's army in Blois. There were ten of them now, riding beneath her new banner. The Duke of Alençon was joined by her new equerry, Jean d'Aulon, a tall, beefy, dented man whom the Dauphin had sent to manage the rest of the Maid's newly acquired staff: two squires, two pages, two heralds, and her chaplain, an Augustinian monk named Jean Pasquerel. A youth not more than twenty, with a shining bowl of light brown hair atop his head and jagged eagle's features. 'I met your mother at Le Puy,' he had said when he first approached Jehanne in Tours. She'd been at an inn with Aulon and Alençon, planning the ride to Blois.

'My mother?' Jehanne asked. The words stopped her in her tracks. A wave of love and sorrow rose and crashed inside of her. It would not be correct to say that she'd forgotten she had a mother, but it had been a very long time since she had thought of herself as someone who had a mother. 'She thought you should have a chaplain, so she sent me,' the young monk explained, shrugging and smiling shyly. His eyes adoring.

'Actually, she sent both of us,' said a man, stepping out from behind the door. It was Bertrand, filthy as usual and grinning like a monkey.

'Bertrand!' she shouted, running at him like a

168

child, delighted to see a known face. 'I thought you were in Blois.'

The man nodded. 'Have been. Just went over to Le Puy for the holiday.'

Jehannne looked at him. 'And Metz? Is he here too?'

Bertrand shook his head. Said Metz had gone back to Vaucouleurs. 'Couldn't stand the thought of watching you fight,' he said quietly. 'Said the worry would kill him.'

'Oh,' said Jehanne, looking at the ground. Then she looked back at Bertrand. 'Well, I'm glad you're here,' she said.

Bertrand fished something from his pocket and handed it to her. 'Your mother sent this too.'

'My ring!' Jehanne cried, for it was the little gold ring her mother had given her on her thirteenth birthday—the year she became a woman. It had the words Jesu Maria engraved on the inside. She stared at it, pressed it against her heart, then slid it on her finger and kissed it. She grabbed Bertrand's hand and squeezed it very tightly. 'It's so good to see you,' she said, tears pouring down her face before she could stop them.

They'd met up by coincidence, Bertrand and Jean Pasquerel and Jehanne's mother. All three had gone to Le Puy on Good Friday to see the famous Black Virgin, and afterward they'd got to talking on the shrine steps. 'She's very proud of you,' Bertrand said. 'She was beaming.'

'You told her about—everything?'

Bertrand nodded. 'It made her famous in Le Puy, once it got around that she was the Maid's mother. You should have seen the crowds. People trying to touch her, asking for a lock of her hair, the whole thing.'

Jehanne blushed. Looked away. 'And you told her I'm all right?'

Bertrand nodded. 'Of course she's terrified about this whole Orléans bit, the idea of her daughter going to war, but she's very proud too. She said they knew it was coming, she and your father. They dreamed it.'

'Right,' Jehanne said stiffly, looking at the ground.

*   *   *

Now, on this warm April day as they headed toward Blois, the young monk rode alongside Jehanne, gazing at her in her gleaming armor and shaking his head. 'I can't believe this is really happening,' he said.

'That's two of us,' said Aulon.

'This is the day the Maid arrived to lead the King's army,' the monk said in a dreamy voice, almost to himself.

'*Ach*, enough of that,' said Jehanne, throwing a hand in the air as if to push such foolishness away, and kicking her horse onward. Soon the city of Blois appeared before them, built atop a pair of steep hills that rose up out of the countryside like two great camel humps. Jehanne and her men first saw those two camel humps from a hilltop a mile away. And even from that distance they could see the enormous camp of Charles's army spreading out around the outer walls of the city—a great sea of canvas tents and huts and men, thousands and thousands of men, and their horses and livestock and flags and weapons spread out from the base of the two hills, and though her face remained a mask of bravery, though she had made light of the day's significance with the young monk, her heart went cold at the sight of it. *Oh my God, it's real.*

PART III

CHAPTER ONE

Bertrand had been at Agincourt. The Slaughter he called it. He'd told them about it one night back in the wintertime, during their journey from Vaucouleurs to Chinon. It had been raining very hard outside, and they'd stopped to take shelter in a cave Colet had found. A lucky find, that cave. It was large enough that they could bring the horses inside with them, large enough that they could have a fire. After they'd fed the horses and shared the last dried sausage between them, they sat around, warming themselves and listening to the water drilling into the earth outside. A ferocious rain. The water roaring down as if a dam in the sky had broken.

After a while, Richard looked up from sharpening an arrowhead and said he could not wait to spill Goddon blood in Orléans. Both Honnecourt brothers perked up at this. 'First Goddon I kill, I'm going to keep his ears. Wear them on a necklace,' said Julian, whose father had been killed during the siege of Vaucouleurs. Jean thought about this for a minute, his eyes gleaming in the firelight. Then he said, 'First one I kill, I'm going to take the whole head. Dry it out and bring it home to Mama for a Christmas present.'

Bertrand made a face. 'Yeah. It all sounds grand and fun now,' he said, 'but you get out there on the field and there isn't one thing grand or fun about it.' He said that he had been at the Battle of Agincourt.

'You were there?' said Jehanne, staring.

175

'Worst day of my life.'

'What happened?' Jehanne asked, leaning forward.

Bertrand shrugged. 'It was supposed to be an easy victory. The Goddons had been pounding us for six months straight, and we knew they were worn out,' he said. 'Winter was coming, and they were marching back toward their ships in Calais, so we decided to go after them. Easy enough to find them, really. All you had to do was follow the burning farmhouses.

'There were only seven or eight thousand of them, and they'd already marched two hundred and fifty miles in just over a fortnight. A crazy pace Henry had going, trying to get home before the snow flew. Something like fourteen miles a day. And we knew it was taking its toll. Dysentery was spreading like fire through the troops and they were out of food. Eating onion bulbs for supper. Four thousand of their men had died that week alone. The ones that were still standing were just desperate to get on their ships and go home.'

Bertrand smiled. 'We thought, *Well, now here finally is a chance to teach these bastards a lesson.* And you should have seen the army Albret had assembled. Prettiest thing you've ever seen. Twenty thousand Frenchmen, all the great princes. Bourbon, the Old Duke of Alençon, Orléans, Brittany. More nobles than I've ever seen in one place. All with their gleaming armor and swords and their big Spanish horses. Just an amazing sight.

'So we set up to head them off at a strip of land between two small woods. One was Agincourt, and the other was Tramecourt. It was the end of October and just awful weather, bitter cold and

176

rainy, a lot like it is now. But we barely noticed it we were so riled up. I remember the night before we fought, we were all sitting up drinking by the fire, laughing about how much money we were going to make from all the Goddon ransoms. I was strutting around like an idiot, telling how my wife had said, 'Bertrand, you don't bring me home a fur coat, we're through.' We were all of us like that that night, cocky as dogs.'

Bertrand shook his head and took a long sip of his wine. 'It was the field itself that killed us. Just a sea of mud, so thick it took half an hour to walk ten feet. It was like trying to walk through tar. You stepped in and sank right up to your knees. That and the longbows. They were the other thing. As I said, we were set up north of the English, between these two small woods, so the field itself was very narrow, and here we were with our cavalry all ready out front, and our men at arms behind with their lances and axes and flails, and I don't know if you've ever seen what a rain of arrows looks like, but there is just no fighting it. At least we haven't figured out how to fight it yet. Those English— they may be pigs, but by God they're good archers. And their bows are so much bigger than ours. If you stood one of our archers next to one of theirs and told them both to shoot, you'd laugh at the result. Their arrows would go three or four times as far as ours. Just leave us in the dust.

'At any rate, there we are, twenty thousand men—the best warriors in France—and we're all suited up in our armor, and charging out to fight on our beautiful horses, but suddenly, when we're about three hundred yards away from their front line, the sky goes black, and the next thing you know, there's this sound, this kind of *shum, shum, shum* all around, and our horses start dropping left and right, horses just screaming and bolting and going down all over, their eyes rolled back white in their heads, the arrows taking them down by the dozens. And then, the animals that did make it as far as the Goddons' front line ended up running up on these huge six-foot stakes they'd planted out front. Bastards tore right through their hearts. Worst waste of horseflesh I've ever seen.

'So then the men-at-arms come up and we try to go at them on foot, but as I said, the damned armor was a disaster in all that mud. We might as well have been trying to walk around in coffins. So there we are lurching about in the mud and rain, trying to just make it to the front lines, and already the English have us surrounded on both sides and are forcing us so tightly together we can barely move, much less swing our axes, and all the while these arrows are raining down, *shum, shum, shum,* and everyone around me is dying, only we're packed so tight that the bodies can't even fall, so when I look around, all I see are these dead eyes, these terrible frozen faces, staring into nowhere. Worst feeling I ever had. Like waking up inside a nightmare.

'From there, it just got worse. When we finally hit the front lines, we knocked them back at first— just plowed some of them straight off their feet, we were so furious. But it didn't last. As soon as Henry saw how slow we were, he halted his archers and sent his whole army charging at us on foot, which was smart because his men had realized it would be death to wear armor in all that mud. Most of them didn't even have helmets on. They just came at us running, mostly barefoot, all painted up with mud and blood and their hose rolled up to their knees, swinging their hatchets and axes and mallets and flails, taking off heads left and right. I remember first seeing Henry out there running around in his gold helmet with rubies all over it, swinging his claymore and howling and knocking all these poor armored-up men over, and you know, once you get tipped in one of those things, you're like a crab flipped on its back. It's over. So here's Henry and his men knocking them over and then pulling up mens' helmets and popping their eyeballs out with their knives, and then leaving them there to drown or suffocate. A lot of men died just because they couldn't get out from under the ones who'd fallen on top of them.

'But those of our men who could fight fought so well. The Old Duke of Alençon was like the Devil himself out there, whipping his ax into a Duke's head, splitting it open like a pumpkin. At one point, he had the King himself down on his knees. I saw that happen. He was standing over Henry, and he'd even managed to swipe a floret off his crown, but then out of nowhere came this monstrous black-haired knight, all grinning and blood-drunk, his eyes rolled back in his head, and he swings his flail into the Old Duke's mouth and when he takes it out, there's this big, wet, red mess where Alençon's face had been, and the monster's howling and laughing, and he's in such a frenzy that when his Goddon friend comes up to him, he grabs a knife and cuts his throat, thinking he's French.

'Anyway, it didn't take long after that. Within an

hour, maybe even half an hour, our two front lines were destroyed. The bodies were piled up higher than my head. Those of us who were left ran into the forest and watched the Goddons go through the field, kicking over the bodies and taking weapons and digging around under their armor for gold and rings and knives. A terrible mess of screaming coming from the fallen men. The bastards.

'Eventually our reinforcements arrived. We were just about to go back out on the field when Ysembart d'Azincourt came roaring out of the forest with about a thousand peasants behind him and attacked Henry's camp, started running off with all kinds of loot. They were awful-looking wretches—looked like they hadn't eaten in years. I remember seeing one beggar, filthiest animal you ever saw, all decked out in Henry's velvet and ermine cloak and gold chains and whatnot, dancing around the campground with a ham in his hand, swishing his coat this way and that, singing, 'Hee hee, I'm King Henry come to murder the French.' Another one came running out of Henry's tent with a pug dog under each arm, poor things howling like babies. Well, at some point Henry must have seen what was going on because the next thing he did was order his men to kill all of the French prisoners they'd already taken in battle. Princes, dukes, counts, all of them. The archers went around running them through with lances, splitting their heads open with poleaxes so their brains spilled out on the ground. Then all of the unarmed nobles surrendered, and they rounded them up and corralled them into this straw house in their camp, barred the door, and set the thing on fire. There were at least forty men in there, screaming. Screams like I never heard before. I remember, once the thing had caught fire, some of them managed to break through the wall, so there were these poor flaming bastards stumbling out into the open and running around in circles, staggering, pleading for someone to help them. The English just laughing.

'No one had the stomach to fight after that. All the French who were still alive just rode off the battlefield. The English came back and rounded up the few nobles that were still alive—the ones they could get big ransoms for. Anyone else who was still breathing on the battlefield got their throat cut. Ten thousand Frenchmen they killed that day. Some of the best warriors you've ever seen. Something like three dukes, five counts, ninety barons and the constable himself—all dead. Fifteen hundred knights too. They say that Henry made the nobles he'd taken prisoner wait on his dinner table that night. They say the heads of the rest of our nobles were set up on stakes around Henry's table, as if the Goddons hadn't done enough.

'I've never seen anything like it. It was like Henry took all the rules we'd agreed to live by and threw them in the mud. All the old rules of war and fair conduct, he acted like none of them had ever existed. Like we'd all been born savages, and anyone who didn't fight like a savage was a bloody fool. I remember thanking God my father wasn't there to see that fight because if he had been, I think it would have killed him where he stood.

'The war that Henry fought, it turned everyone, all of us into animals. Blood-drunk monsters.

That's what fighting without rules does to you. You become creatures who will do anything to win. Creatures who run on spilled blood. And the trouble is, once the fighting's over, you come to find there's no man left inside you anymore. You're just an old hollowed-out shell, no sense of right or wrong, fair or unfair. You're just cleaned out, lost, wondering what happened to you.'

'That or you're a murderer,' said Colet, his slim face gleaming whitely in the firelight. 'Get so used to killing you can't do anything else.'

'True enough,' said Bertrand.

Jehanne was sitting on the ground beside Metz, wrapped in a half-wet blanket. Thinking. She thought that what Bertrand said was true and good, but lower down, some reptilian part of her said, *We'll have to fight like they do. This chivalry stuff will be the end of us. The rules have changed. We change with them, or we die.* Realizing that she was thinking this, she folded up the thought. *No,* she told herself. *It isn't true.*

But she did not throw the thought away. She simply folded it up and buried it in a room of her soul that she did not like to visit.

*   *   *

Now, as she rode toward the camp in Blois, she thought again of Agincourt. But this time she did not think about *how* she would fight. She thought only that she would fight. That she could not wait to fight. *Oh God, I am your vessel. Oh God, I am your holy wrath.*

CHAPTER TWO

She loved the camp. The moment she rode into it, she knew: *This is where I belong. I am a warrior. I belong in war.* Exhilaration roaring through her as she rode through the muddy sea of tents and men and flags. Smell of saltpeter and gunpowder firing her blood.

Sunlight glinting on pointed metal boots.

She loved the corrals of the tall warhorses and the armories with their black mountains of cannonballs out front. Loved the young squires squatting on their haunches down by the broad green river, singing as they washed their masters' swords and shields. Loved the archers out in the clover fields, shooting their arrows into yellow straw men, the archers suddenly dropping their bows and staring as she rode past them in her bright silver armor with the Jesu Maria banner held high, running toward her now, all of them running to get a better look, running and then shouting, *The Maid! The Maid! The Maid is come!*

She knew almost nothing of their protocols and strategies, their tactics of war. Nor did she care. She was their fire, the fire that had gone out during all the decades of defeat, the roar and fury they'd lost. The single-minded will to win.

Take command immediately, Michael whispered as she continued alongside Alençon through the camp. *If you don't lay down the rules right now, they will never follow you*. And so Jehanne heard her own voice become deep and calm as she greeted her new generals, and so it was that she became another self then, a warrior self. No more pleading peasant girl. She was the Maid, born to lead her men to triumph.

Two men approached on horses. 'Ah, La Hire,' Alençon said, pointing toward the man's black-and-white flag.

'La Hire?' asked Jehanne, who had grown up hearing stories about him. La Hire, the great, fearless general. La Hire, the Fury. 'That's La Hire?'

'The one in the red cloak,' Alençon said, nodding at a small bald man sitting atop a splendid gray horse. He was dressed in a red-velvet cloak that glittered oddly in the sunlight and made a merry, tinkling sound as he rode. As he came closer, Jehanne could see the little silver bells on it.

'I've seen him before,' she said, remembering him from one of Yolande's meetings at Chinon. He was the one who'd winked at her, as if to say *Screw plans. Let's do the hard push*.

La Hire, Jehanne knew, had fought in all the great battles, Agincourt, Rouvray. A legendary mercenary, famous for his arrogance, his rages, his fearlessness in the field.

'It's very good that he's here,' Alençon said. 'He left Orléans for a while after the disaster at Rouvray. We were afraid we'd lost him for good.'

As La Hire drew closer, Jehanne recognized his shaved head and brown, leathery face, the light web of scars all over his cheeks and neck. Bright, intense blue eyes, like chips of sky. 'He says the bells let the enemy know Death is coming,' said Alençon, smiling and nodding at the warrior.

'Hail to the Maid,' La Hire shouted. He was always shouting. 'God fucking bless you, child.'

184

She nodded, ground her sharp upper tooth against the one below it. Heard it squeak. *Wait until you can tell them all at once*, she thought.

'And you, General.'

The man's eyebrows went up and he grinned a white, snapping grin, as if he'd taken a bite out of the air. 'Ready to go kill some English?'

Her blood shouted *Yes!*, but she said something different. 'If it comes to that,' she said. 'I hope it won't.'

'*Pssh*,' said La Hire, blowing air out of his cheeks. 'If you can make 'em go away just by asking, you're no bloody saint, you're the fucking Almighty Himself!'

This time she could not hold her tongue. 'I won't have swearing like that in my army,' she said. 'If we are going to ask for God's help, we must abide by His rules.'

La Hire laughed—a short, sharp bark. 'Clearly you've never spent much time around soldiers,' he said.

'Clearly you've never fought with God on your side,' she said.

The man looked at her then, his eyes cold. 'You know nothing about what I've done,' he said.

Jehanne was silent. 'Fair enough,' she said. 'You understand that I need to address the men immediately. Is there a place where I can do that?'

La Hire continued looking at her with his sharp blue eyes. 'Sure, sure,' he said, recovering, turning his horse. 'But let's go get you settled up at the château first, then you can speak to the men first thing in the morning.'

Jehanne did not move.

'Come on, then.'

'I need to address them now.'

The warrior studied her. She felt the fury in him, on a tight leash at the moment but there just below the surface, waiting. He rubbed his lips, squinted. 'They're off duty, half of them drunk by now, you know.'

'All the more reason for me to speak to them.'

The man's mouth curled up on one side. 'You're a fierce little thing, aren't you?'

'Yes.'

The other side of his mouth curling up now. 'Ha!' he shouted, wheeling his horse. 'I like it! Follow me, Fierce Virgin!'

CHAPTER THREE

She stood in the gathering twilight, surrounded by six bright torches on a wooden stage that had been erected at one end of the camp. Dusk was falling and the campfires were being lit in the dim fields. Huge orange blooms pulsing up in the darkness, and around them thousands of French and Scottish and Spanish soldiers standing and sitting and cheering at the sight of the small, bright-eyed girl with her glinting steel suit and her dark cap of boy's hair, and among them in the twilight, she saw flashes of danger, the long hair and gleaming shoulders of the whores with their red skirts and filthy bare feet, the dice games and card games, men staggering, reeling with drink. The air smelled of smoke and fresh straw and roasting meat, and Jehanne could feel the wildness in the men rising as the night drew down, and she felt the hair on the back of her neck rise up, and wondered if she was, in fact, mad to believe they would listen to her.

It was a while before they were silent. Ten, perhaps fifteen minutes of cheering, wild shouts, and roars just at the sight of her—Jehanne standing before them in her shining armor, her round face beaming, her eyes promising silently: *Yes, friends, help has arrived. God's love has arrived. Now we will triumph.* The strangeness of the image, the sheer fact of this impossible creature was enough to transfix them, stir them into a frenzy of joy and rage. By the time they were silent, there was hardly need for words.

In her bones, Jehanne understood this. Understood that much of her power lay in the outrageous picture she presented, the unspoiled peasant virgin—almost a child—riding down out of the fields of Lorraine to drag France up out of Hell, to restore France to her former glory. It stopped them in their tracks. And so she stood silently before them, beaming, loving them, and she could see their faces transforming before her, the jeers giving way to fascination, hope, doubts trampled by a rush of wonder as they gazed upon her, roaring and screaming her name, the men so moved that it was as if Christ Himself stood before them.

She held up her hand and waited for silence. Prayed silently, *Help me, Father* . . . And she could feel the golden light pouring through her then, could feel the night open itself like a dark flower around her, could feel herself dissolving into the sea of people, into the white moon overhead and the black rustling forest behind and the blue hills rolling in the distance, and when she spoke, her voice was loud and clear, and it seemed that God Himself was whispering in her ear.

'I bring you great news, my friends, my brave and noble soldiers of France,' she began. 'After so many years of suffering, God has come to our aid.' A huge storm of cheering forced her to pause. When it died down, she continued. 'He has sent me to tell you that now is the time for us to defeat the English, and He has promised to help us in our fight. Those of you who ride to Orléans and fight with me will fight with all of God's might and love behind us, and victory will be ours, provided . . .' More wild cheering now. 'Provided we obey His conditions . . .'

Again she was forced to stop. Again the roaring from the crowd grew so loud she could not continue. The men were wild with excitement, pressing up against the stage, shouting, cheering. Her words did not matter. They wanted simply to stand before her, to drink in her light. Hope had bubbled up like a spring inside of them, and they felt that there was nothing they could not do so long as she was there to guide them.

This ended as soon as Jehanne began to shout her conditions. 'For we must become God's warriors now, men, and to become God's warriors, we must make our hearts pure as snow. And so there will be no swearing, no betting, no drunkenness, no whores, no looting, no ransoms in God's army,' she said. 'And every man must hear Mass and make his confession before battle.'

Abrupt silence. Silence for what seemed like an eternity. Followed by a galloping chorus of boos.

'What about killing? Can we do that?' someone shouted.

'That's crazy,' called another.

'Or what?' shouted a boy with small, shiny black eyes. A face like a weasel.

'Or we will be defeated!' Jehanne shouted. 'The English will destroy us and France will be lost forever.'

More silence.

She let the words sink in, smiled gently. 'We cannot expect God's help unless we show our love and respect for Him at all times. We are God's soldiers now, and we must behave as such,' she said. Again she did not know where the words came from. She listened, amazed, as they came out of her, clear and strong and sensible—words, it seemed, that no man could argue with.

CHAPTER FOUR

Later that evening, as Jehanne was walking through the darkness toward her tent, she heard men talking by a fire. 'Don't see why I should confess, I'm going to Hell anyway,' said a general she'd met briefly at dinner, Poton de Xaintrailles. A thick, stubborn-looking man with fluffy yellow hair like chick feathers and narrow pea-green eyes. Cheeks red as a sunset. He was sitting with La Hire and several other captains, poking at the fire with a long stick. She knew he did not like her. He'd refused to look her in the eyes when they were introduced, and when the girl referred to the men as 'my army,' he gave a great ugly snort.

'Good point,' said La Hire. 'If I start confessing now, I'll be talking for all eternity.'

She stepped forward into the firelight. 'You'll confess before battle. It's what God demands.'

Poton looked at her, his eyes flat, inscrutable—like a cat's. 'You know how many men I've killed?'

'No, and I don't want to know,' she said calmly. 'What I do know is that confession will be held before every battle from here on out. And if you don't like it, you can find another army to fight for.'

A ripple of delight went through the men. They liked her toughness. It made them feel safe. But Poton, she saw, was not won over. Poton remained with his obstinate red face, staring at the girl as if he wished her dead. And it was some time too before the others began to behave. Several days, in which they tested her constantly, in which she had to be stern as a bishop. 'Fucking Christ,' La Hire shouted one night when he sliced his thumb open while cutting into a sausage. Blood plushing out as if from a spigot. '*Uh!*'

Jehanne shouted back, one index finger up, eyebrows raised. 'What was that?'

La Hire scowled, muttered. 'Sorry.'

Or Alençon, losing a game of cards one night after dinner. 'Cocksucker!' he cried, then he blushed deeply. 'Sorry, Jehanne.'

La Hire jumped up then. 'No, it's fucking impossible.' He stomped around the campfire, his face knotted up, ugly in the light. 'You don't understand what kind of men you're dealing with here. A fine swear word is life's blood with us; you can't pretend we're choirboys, for fuck's sake!'

'I am under no illusions that you're a choirboy, La Hire,' she said, 'but if you don't follow my orders, we will lose this war. It's as simple as that.'

190

Eventually they came to an agreement. She told them they could use any curse words they liked as long as they did not involve God or Christ or the Virgin Mary or sex. 'Make them up,' she said. 'Like what?' said La Hire. 'Give us an example.' It took her a few minutes. 'Son of a goat,' she said finally. 'That's ridiculous,' said La Hire. But somehow it stuck. The whole next day Alençon and La Hire went around saying it. 'Hello, you son of a goat!' 'Nice day, eh, son of a goat?'

Another day she took on the prostitutes. Early in the morning, when the air was cool and the tents were still shrouded in mist, she rode through the camp with six soldiers behind her, shouting orders that startled her with their ferocity. 'All whores must leave these premises immediately. Come out at the order of the Maid and depart now, or prepare to face God's wrath.'

Fifteen minutes later, when no women had emerged from the tents, Jehanne jumped down off her horse into the mud, shouted 'Follow me' to her men, and began storming through the tent flaps, kicking at bedrolls and pulling up blankets. She found a great number of whores there, some still sleeping, their pale limbs entwined with their soldiers', some hiding in trunks, some in disguise, hastily dressed up like soldiers in tunics and leggings, with charcoal mustaches painted above their lips. When some of the men complained that the women were their fiancées and intendeds, women they dearly loved, Jehanne smiled and said, 'Well, find a priest to marry you by sundown and they're welcome to stay.'

There were no weddings by sundown, but there were large packs of ragged painted women departing the camp that day, some of them weeping and waving and blowing kisses at their men as they went, others spitting and cursing the Maid as they walked, saying, 'Goddamn righteous bitch. Who in the hell does she think she is?'

CHAPTER FIVE

One afternoon two young men came into the main room of the Bear Inn in Blois, where Jehanne was going over a list of provisions with Aulon. Both of them carried heavy burlap sacks. They were filthy, their hair matted, streaks of dirt on their cheeks, their faces sagging with fatigue. Jehanne stood up, stared. 'What are you doing here?'

'Look at you now,' said the older one, gaping at her short hair, her fine red woolen tunic, her high polished leather boots.

The younger boy smiled shyly, revealing a chipped tooth. 'Any room for your old brothers in the Maid's army?'

Their father had sent them. 'He stayed mad about you leaving all winter,' said Pierrelot. 'But as soon as he heard you'd be leading the mission to Orléans, he came around.' Not a gradual shift. An abrupt one. Overnight Jacques decided that Jehanne was a saint and an angel and always had been. He walked through the streets of Domrémy and Vaucouleurs with his chest puffed out, bragging that he was the Maid's father. That he'd known she was destined for greatness from the moment she was born. If you had told him that he once hated his daughter and beat her black and blue, he would have stared at you, utterly baffled, as if he had no idea what you were talking about. 'He said to tell you he's very proud,' said Pierrelot.

Jehanne nodded. 'Now he is,' she said, gazing bitterly at the ground.

'You're quite the hero of the family these days,' said Jean in a sour tone. 'No one talks of anything else.'

Pierrelot stepped forward and hugged her hard. 'It is so good to see you,' he said. 'Will you let us stay?'

Jehanne hugged him back. Was surprised how good it felt to hug her own flesh. Her brother. 'Of course,' she said. 'Of course you can stay.'

*　　　*　　　*

Yolande was next. Yolande coming across the ripening spring fields in her blue wooden carriage with gold fleurs-de-lis painted on the doors. The wagon rocking and jutting in the mud, the rocks, the fat Queen's face glazed with sweat as she hauled herself down the little wooden steps and onto the wet green field where Jehanne awaited her. 'They say you've stopped the men from cursing, got them going to Mass twice a day,' she said to Jehanne. 'Kicked all the whores out of camp.'

It was a warm, breezy late April morning, and they were touring the provisions for Orléans together. Yolande had personally ordered five thousand pounds of beans and seventeen hundred pigs as her donation to the relief of Orléans, and now she stood at the entrance to a great fenced field, counting the pigs herself as farmers herded

193

them inside in groups of ten.

'Wasn't easy,' Jehanne said. 'I found a pack of them dressed up in leggings and boots like men, with beards and muttonchops drawn on their cheeks.'

Yolande chortled, a juicy, rolling, fat woman's laugh. 'I wish I'd seen that,' she said, patting her forehead with a folded white handkerchief. She wore a faded black cotton dress that pulled at the seams, and there were dark ovals of sweat beneath her arms. But somehow, Jehanne thought, it didn't matter with Yolande the way it did with the Dauphin. Yolande looked like a queen anyway. 'My, look at the size of that one there,' she said, pointing to a gray-spotted pink beast that was nearly as tall as a cow.

The girl smiled. 'It's a generous donation you're making, Your Highness.'

The Queen nodded.

'I don't know if Alençon told you, but the army could use some more cannons. I don't suppose—'

Yolande shook her head. Glanced at the sea of pigs milling in the mud and sunlight. 'I used the last of my credit to buy those swine.'

'I see,' Jehanne said.

The Queen looked at her sharply. 'We won't get a second chance here, you understand? We are too poor, and the men's hearts are too beaten down to face another defeat. If you don't succeed on the first go, it will be over. England will devour this country for good.'

'I know,' Jehanne said. 'There isn't time.'

The fat Queen peered at her for several moments. 'What it must be like for you . . . I cannot imagine.'

194

The girl smiled sadly at her. 'Mostly, it's wonderful.'

CHAPTER SIX

Next came Gilles. The Monster. Jehanne watched him ride into camp one morning with his splendid private army—his arrival a spectacle. It was the singing she'd heard first. A choir of sunburnt little boys dressed in white robes with blue velvet trim had come walking up the muddy camp road, singing in Breton, their high, angelic voices flying above the camp. Behind them marched a glittering circus of people. First the musicians with their polished silver trumpets, then the churchmen, led by a hunchbacked old Bishop in a tall, tear-shaped hat and a red houppelande with a squirrel-fur collar. Behind him, the Archdeacon and a flock of chaplains in black and gold robes. Jehanne glanced at Alençon as a skinny-necked juggler walked past, tossing golden balls, and raised her eyebrows at the spectacle. 'Strange man, the Baron,' Alençon said quietly. 'Hell of a brave soldier, but there's something off about him.'

Jehanne nodded absently, continued staring.

'He likes the battles too much,' Alençon continued. 'The blood.'

Jehanne laughed. 'I'm not sure if that's a problem right now. We need all the men eager to spill Goddon blood that we can find.'

Alençon glanced at her.

Baron Gilles de Rais, Jehanne learned, had become famous as a great military hero thanks to

195

his bravery in the Breton wars. He was fearless, it was said. Fearless and handsome. Thrillingly rich. Now she watched as his private army of three hundred knights rode through the camp—all of them on thoroughbreds, their polished armor glittering in the morning sun, their doublets bearing the gold and black and blue Rais coat of arms, their lances pointing toward the sky. The Baron himself led them, dressed in black velvet and seated atop a splendid black stallion. He was a tall, thin man with shiny blue-black hair and full red lips, his shoulders thrown back like a dancer's. He looked beautiful and haughty and absurd, Jehanne thought. Like someone who thought his life was a play. But when the young Baron noticed her watching him, his dark eyes went wide, and there passed from him a look of such intense vulnerability that all of the pomp and frippery suddenly seemed sad and somehow desperate to her, and Jehanne found herself in the strange position of feeling sorry for the second richest man in France.

He invited them to his camp for dinner that night. Jehanne and the generals. *Un petit d'ner*, said the Baron's pretty, gold-haired page, his lips pink and shining, swollen like blisters. At sunset Jehanne and La Hire and Alençon walked up the hill together toward the city of gold-trimmed blue tents that the Rais camp had erected near the gates of Blois that afternoon. 'Bloody peacock,' scoffed La Hire as they walked among the billowing tents in the soft evening breeze. The sky overhead was streaked thickly with red clouds. The whole scene had the feel of a dream.

'Have you seen him on the battlefield?' said

196

Alençon.

'Oh yes,' said La Hire. 'He's Hell's own demon with a knife. But all this,' he said, waving a hand. 'Who does he think he is? God?'

'If only we had some of that money,' Jehanne said, staring as a pair of servants wheeled an enormous organ past them in a cloud of dust, gold angels floating among the pipes, the jade and pearl knobs gleaming in the late-day sunlight.

'What would you do with it?' said La Hire, grinning.

'Buy more cannons,' she said. 'A lot more.'

*   *   *

The Baron stayed beside Jehanne all night. Hardly spoke to anyone else. 'I cannot tell you how I have been looking forward to this, dear Maid,' he said when Alençon introduced them. He was dressed in a long leopard-fur cloak, his posture inclined slightly toward her, his dark eyes glowing. He had, Jehanne saw as he kissed her hand, extraordinarily long eyelashes—thick, black, curling lashes that a girl would have cherished. And a sprinkling of pale brown freckles across his nose, which somehow surprised her. 'I believe we have much in common,' he said.

Jehanne scratched her neck. 'Oh?'

'Like you, I am a passionate servant of our Lord,' he said, eyes shining. 'But thus far, He has not honored me with the extraordinary communications He has bestowed upon you.'

Jehanne smiled tightly. 'Thank you for coming.'

The Baron leaned in closer. Lowered his voice. 'I too am a student of prophecies and

197

constellations, séances to banish the demons, the Dark Ones, alchemies to harness nature's bounties,' he smiled, his eyes pulling at her like magnets. 'We made gold in my kitchen last week.'

'I'm not interested in any of that,' Jehanne said, seeing clearly that he was mad, but feeling slightly hypnotized by him nonetheless.

'Still, perhaps at some point you will honor me with a conversation about your visions? Your voices?'

'I don't talk about them unless I have to.'

'No, of course not.' The Baron smiled back at her, undaunted. 'But perhaps at some point you will share your secrets.'

'Probably not,' said Jehanne.

She was seated next to him at dinner. Several times during the meal, La Hire, who was seated on the Baron's other side, tried to engage him in conversation, but the Baron waved his hand, as if to bat a fly away. 'Tell me what it was like,' he said after they'd eaten, and the platters of stork bones were being cleared away. The Baron had had several glasses of hippocras by that point, and his voice was deep and velvety, purring. Jehanne felt as if she were sitting beside a tiger. 'Talking to God . . . seeing the saints with your own eyes . . . you must tell me.'

'No,' Jehanne said. She drank deeply from her water glass.

Rais laughed out loud. 'Just no?' he said. 'Just like that?'

'Just like that,' she said, fine hairs of pleasure and pride tickling her insides.

He stared at her. 'I can't remember the last time someone said no to me.'

'I said no to you once already, when we met,' Jehanne said.

The Baron was silent, looking at her. 'Careful,' he whispered. 'I'll start worshipping you.'

Jehanne blinked. 'If you want to help, you can buy three new cannons for my army. We need them. But I won't tell you about my voices in return. If you buy the cannons for us, you give to the future of France. Nothing else.' Jehanne stood up and nodded at Alençon, who was watching. 'My good Duke, would you be so kind as to walk me back to the château?'

*   *   *

'He's charming, I'll say that,' Jehanne said as they walked uphill together through the spring darkness. 'Crazy, but charming.'

'I don't like him,' the Duke said.

Jehanne smiled, the pleasure of Alençon's jealousy running over her skin. 'His money's good. His army's good.'

The Duke was silent. But when he left her at her door in the château, he said, 'Be careful, Jehanne. He's dangerous.'

*   *   *

Several days later, sixty black horses appeared outside of Jehanne's tent, pulling three enormous cannons. The boy with the obscene pink mouth stood and read from a scroll. *For the future of France, from the Baron Gilles de Rais, April 26, 1429.* The boy looked at her. 'My lord also instructs me to tell the Pucelle that if she should

199

require anything else for her holy mission, he will
be very happy to provide it.'

CHAPTER SEVEN

You must warn them, Catherine said in the night.
She was sitting on the side of Jehanne's bed,
stroking the girl's cheek, her breath sweet as
oranges. *Warn them before you spill their blood.*

Yes, Jehanne said. *Yes, I will.*

The next morning Jehanne took her oily-nosed
page, Raymond, into the pine forest behind the
stage and dictated a letter to the English at
Orléans.

To you, Henry, King of England, and to you,
Duke of Bedford, who call yourself Regent of
France, obey the King of Heaven and
abandon your siege. Surrender to the Maid
sent by God the keys of all the good towns
which you have taken and violated in France.
Take yourself off to your own land, for God's
sake, or else await tiding from the Maid,
whom you will soon see, to your hurt.

La Hire snorted with delight when she showed it
to him. A smile breaking through the web of scars.
'Should give them a good chuckle.'

'Why?'

He laughed. 'Because it's fucking funny,
sweetheart.'

The fire rose then. She slapped him hard across
the face. 'This is not a joke.'

200

'Hey,' said La Hire blinking, throwing up his hands. 'Enough.'

'I'll say what's enough,' said Jehanne.

That evening Jehanne sent Ambleville, her small, freckled herald, to Orléans to deliver the letter to the English generals. A week later he still had not returned, and there was no reply from the English. Only a hysterical letter from Ambleville's fiancée in Orléans, saying he'd planned to spend the night at her family's house but had never appeared. 'Bastards are holding him captive,' said Alençon.

They never saw him again.

CHAPTER EIGHT

They rode out from Blois toward Orléans on the twenty-seventh of April. Jehanne and her army of four thousand men. Men come from all over France to fight with her. Soldiers and civilians alike, swept up i1n a wave of righteous fury as they marched north alongside the Loire, the priests in the lead, singing *Veni Creator Spiritus*. Behind them came the enormous company of monks and generals, the soldiers and the train of supplies for the people of Orléans: six hundred wagons piled high with beans and bread, axes and sulfur and grain. Animals by the hundreds, cows, pigs, sheep, chickens, all herded by peasant boys, grinning as they walked, passing skins of wine between them.

The weather was growing warmer now, softer every day. There was a raw green smell in the air, the cool bitter smell of soil, onion grass. Clusters of tulips swayed alongside the road. The long sadness of winter was finally in retreat. You could feel it in the men, the sudden jolt of life that comes with the first warm weather. Jehanne rode out in front beside Rais, conscious, suddenly, of her dirty face, her borrowed horse. The Baron sat atop the gleaming black stallion he called Nutcracker, his long white manicured hands holding the reins loosely in his lap, a big diamond ring on his finger.

'How are you today, dear Maid?' he asked.

She shrugged. She was already sweating. 'This armor will kill me before the Goddons get the chance.'

He smiled. 'I don't think it was meant to be slept in.'

She knew they all mocked her for sleeping in her armor. Knew it and did not care. It was the only way she felt safe sleeping among them in the night. A virgin among four thousand soldiers. Even now, she could feel the Baron watching her with his hungry eyes. Saying that one day she must come visit him at his castle in Brittany, Machecoul. He talked about his life there, the chapel with the gold-leaf ceilings, the petits fours, the frescoes, the marvelous choir boys, and as he talked, she thought, *Why is he so desperate to impress me?* She looked at him, said nothing.

The Baron coughed, changed the subject. 'Have you thought about what our strategy should be once we reach Orléans? Has your council spoken to you about this yet?'

Jehanne was silent for several minutes. At last she said, 'My strategy is, we're going to find the English and ask them to surrender. If they do not surrender, we're going to destroy them.'

Later that afternoon, when the sun stood straight over them in the sky, Rais sat fanning himself with his black velvet hat. 'God's blood, what I'd do for a lake to jump in,' he said.

Jehanne turned, spoke sharply: 'Do not take the name of God in vain, my lord. Take back your words right now.'

Rais smiled in disbelief, eyes wide. As if he'd been told a good, but possibly offensive, joke.

She stared back at him, did not blink.

'All right, I take it back,' he said, raising his hands in mock surrender.

'It's not a joke,' she said. 'God won't help us if we make light of His power.'

'No, I—of course, but—'

She cut him off. 'And I promise you, if He doesn't help us, we're all going to die.' She shook her head, clucked her tongue. 'This is the whole problem,' she said sadly. 'We say we love Him, and we beg and weep and pray for His help, and then we turn around and curse Him or evoke His name over something silly like wanting a swim. How can He possibly believe we're taking Him seriously?'

'But I meant no harm. I wasn't think—'

'I know you weren't,' she interrupted, 'but He wants us to think. Why should He take us seriously if we don't take Him seriously? If you invoke the greatest power in the universe every time you feel like a swim? Look at this country. Our last king was a madman and a murderer, and his wife was so greedy and heartless that she bartered away her own country to the English. Our armies go around

203

whoring and looting the churches and stealing from the peasants. Our nobles are so busy drinking and going to balls and squabbling over land and screwing each other that the English have stolen our own country right out from under us. And the peasants are in such a state of terror and despair that they've all abandoned their villages and taken to worshipping the Devil, gone to live in the woods like wolves.' Her eyes flashed. 'And you ask why, why is God allowing this to happen? What else can He do? He gave us the gift of life, the gift of this beautiful world, and we're making a mockery of it.'

The Baron lowered his gaze, flushing. 'Many sin because they are in despair.'

'But that's when they should be praying,' Jehanne said. 'If their despair has so overtaken them that they are without hope and can no longer live as decent human beings, nor even ask for His forgiveness, how can God help them? If they cannot open their hearts to Him, if all they do is drink and sleep with whores and rob people and curse God's name, how can He possibly help? How can He believe that we want anything except to die in misery?'

Jehanne was aglow, her cheeks red as fruit. The Baron sat gazing at her with the eyes of a child.

CHAPTER NINE

A three-day journey to Orléans. They camped in the fields at night, stopping an hour before sundown, when the sky was deep pink, and taking their horses down to the river for water. They splashed the cold river water on their faces, their filthy necks. Often Jehanne took her boots off and stood in the icy water in her stockinged feet, numbing her blisters, wishing she could unbind her aching breasts. Soon the sky grew dark and the fires blazed like great orange lamps strung across the countryside as far as the eye could see. Around each fire sat a group of men, eating stew, sharpening their swords, passing pouches of wine back and forth, a tangible happiness among them as they sat under the stars, away from their homes, their fields, their wives, men among men, alive and free and on their way to fight for their freedom, for their country, for God. Suddenly no one knew what lay around the next corner or over the next hill. No one knew if they'd be alive in a week. And there was so much beauty to life because of it, so much intoxication in the blue night grass and the lowing cattle, the rustling trees, the breathing night forest, the high, wild sky, and the men's faces shining in the light of the campfire, some of them singing low bawdy songs about wenches and fools, and in former times there would have been whores among them, tossing their hair, flashing their shoulders in the firelight, but now there were none. In the night Michael came to her and whispered, *You do well, darling. You have them all spellbound. They'll do anything for you now.*

*   *   *

In the chill light of dawn on the last morning of their journey, Alençon stood over Jehanne in her tent, grinning. 'Ready to go kill some English?' he said, extending a hand. Stiffly she raised her arm,

205

allowed him to pull her upright in the enormous metal suit. When she was standing, she lifted her metal arm and rubbed her neck. Nodded her head back and then forward. Shook the dust out of her hair. 'Ow,' she said.

Alençon watched her.

'You all right?'

Jehanne nodded. 'Let's go kill some English.'

The priests said Mass for the entire army and passed communion in a damp field, among the thousands of men, as was done on days when battle was foreseen. Front and center, Jehanne knelt, her dark head bowed, her armor shining, Jean and Pierrelot on either side of her. La Hire and Rais and Alençon and Poton kneeling behind her. *And what would you think of this, Father?* she wondered. *Would you still be proud if you were here now? Or would you hate me the moment you saw me in front of all these fine warriors? Hate that it was I and not you leading them on?* She closed her eyes and opened her mouth, and the priest placed the piece of bread on her tongue. She swallowed the Body of Christ. Felt his love rinse through her like sunlight. Then the priest wiped the edge of the chalice with a handkerchief and placed the gleaming rim of the cup between her lips. He tipped the cup and she drank the wine. She swallowed the Blood of Christ; she remembered his sacrifice, the thin, pitiful body hung up on the crucifix in the desert heat, the glory of his sacrifice, and as she did, she felt the lifeblood surge through her. *'Spiritus sancti, spiritus sancti,'* droned the priests. Then she prayed. *Let me get it right.*

She wanted to confront the English right away— as soon as they reached Orléans. That was how she'd seen it in her dream. That was what the voices had said. *Be bold!* They needed to go straight to Talbot's forts north of the city and tell them to surrender. If they refused, she would attack before they had a chance to call for reinforcements. 'We must strike hard and fast,' she said to the generals before they left camp that morning.

She spent the day preparing herself for it. The fighting. The horror. They'd ridden all morning in the climbing spring sun and soon were sweating in their heavy steel suits. As they rode up and down through the rough, hilly country, Jehanne warned herself of what lay ahead. She sat on the back of her horse in that killing armor, the steel biting into her armpits and thighs, thinking, *You are going to see Hell today. Hell like you can't imagine. Men and horses are going to scream and bleed and die, and when they do, you must not waver, Jehanne. You must shout and charge and hold your banner high. Remind your men that they are fighting for France, for the life of France, and for their own lives. Remember it is God's will*, she thought. *Remember what they will do to all of France if they have the chance. It is us or them.*

By mealtime, the wind had come up and heavy purple clouds had blotted out the morning sun. The day had grown cold and threatening. *Angry*, the girl thought, her heart roaring in her chest. *Angry like me.* They stopped briefly to eat and water the horses, but she could not eat, nor could she calm herself enough to sit down. She walked slowly back and forth in the monstrous armor, the red rage rising up inside her. She thought, *This is who I am now. This is who I must be. God's*

Righteous Beast.

But there was no fight that day. Her generals betrayed her. They didn't take her to the English forts north of the river at all. They led her to the wrong side. The south side, across the river from Orléans, and far east of the city. Miles away from Talbot and his main forts. It was some time before she realized it. They'd paused on a high ridge outside Orléans to survey the territory. From there she'd been able to see the near-complete ring of Talbot's forts and the enormous city itself. Orléans sat along the northern banks of the Loire, surrounded by high, thick walls, its tall fortress towers rising in black, pointed silhouette against the gray sky. Long funnels of dark smoke rose up from the English forts that circled the besieged city. There was only one gate they hadn't managed to seal off yet. That was the Burgundy Gate, on the far southeastern end of the city.

Jehanne had no interest in this area—she wanted to ride straight into the heart of the action. That was what she'd seen in her dream. Cross the river into La Beauce, go to the English encampments, confront, attack. In the war council the night before, she'd stabbed her finger at Talbot's forts on the map and said, 'There, that's where I want to strike.' Poton nodded and said, 'That's where we're headed,' and even smiled at her for the first time.

But it was not where they were headed. Instead they'd stayed on the south side of the river, only bringing the troops and the great, dusty, ambling train of supply wagons and animals to a halt once they were a ways beyond Orléans and miles away from the key English forts. 'What's going on?'

Jehanne shouted when she saw what was happening. It was raining by this time. Thin, cold streams of water were sliding down the girl's neck beneath her armor. Her saddle was growing slippery. Kicking her horse, she galloped up to the front of the caravan where Poton and La Hire were riding side by side. 'We're on the wrong side of the river! What are you doing? There's not even a bridge here!'

And here was Poton's second smile. Poton, with his yellow chicken-feather hair plastered to his forehead, his neck thick and red. 'Surely you didn't mean to attack the English forts today—not before we've delivered the provisions to all those hungry people inside the city . . .'

'Of course that's what I meant!' Jehanne shouted. 'The council stated plainly that we are to confront the Goddons right away.' Michael had said, *Go straight to Talbot. Demand surrender. If he refuses, attack.*

'Ah,' Poton said, rubbing his chin, clearly enjoying himself. 'Well, it seems we've had a misunderstanding then, because I have instructions here from the Bastard of Orléans himself to stay on the south side of the river and ride well beyond the city walls so that the supplies can be ferried across the river and then sneaked into the city through the Burgundy Gate after twilight.' He nodded with his chin, down to the riverbank where scores of boats were waiting.

'But if we wait, they'll have a chance to prepare. Call in reinforcements from all over. We'll lose our whole advantage.'

Poton regarded her with flat eyes. 'The Bastard should be here at any moment now to greet us. If you like, you can take it up with him.'

She understood then. She saw that she was the only one who had planned to fight that day. She was alone. A fool who'd been kept out of the generals' most important conversations, excluded from their true opinions, their plans. The red, underwater feeling flooded through her. She screamed as she had never screamed before. 'How dare you?' she screamed at the men. 'How dare you disobey me?'

'The Bastard ordered it,' said La Hire in a sharp voice. 'He said this way was best.'

'The Bastard knows nothing!' she shouted. 'These were my orders from God, do you understand me? God said we were to fight today!'

Across the rain-pocked river came a little wooden skiff, and at the head of it stood a husky, wide-jawed man with a long, thin elegant nose and a dark, neatly shaven goatee. Sad brown poet's eyes. A broad, winning smile. He was dressed in armor and a gray cloak with beaver trim. Beside him stood a wolfhound, snout pressed into the wind. As the boat advanced into the shallows, the dog jumped down and ran splashing, barking toward the riverbank. The man came behind him, beaming as he strode through the muddy brown shallows, water streaming from his armor. Jehanne knew it was the Bastard. The Old Duke of Orléans' illegitimate son. Alençon had told her about him. The Bastard's brother, the new Duke of Orléans, was being held prisoner in the Tower of London, and in his absence, the Bastard had stepped in as the city's chief defender. Most of Orléans' other nobles had fled after the defeat at Rouvray, but the Bastard had stayed on to fight. 'A true pleasure!'

he bellowed as he came toward Jehanne, arms spread wide.

She spat at his feet. Her face red, jaw set. Eyes of a bear. 'Are you the Bastard of Orléans?'

He stopped walking. Blinked. His dark eyebrows bunched together. 'I am,' he said, 'and I rejoice at your coming. Have I offended you?'

'Did you give the order that I should come here instead of going straight to the English?'

His smile faded. 'I did. My council decided that this was the wisest way.'

Poton looked at her, his yellow eyes delighted.

'The council of God is wiser than yours, Bastard,' she said, her ears red. Burning. 'I bring you better help than any knight or city. I bring you the help of the King of Heaven!'

A great cheer erupted from the waiting soldiers at these words. 'The Maid! The Maid!' they roared. No one could speak over the chorus as it spread through the ranks. 'The Maid! The Maid!'

'I am grateful for it, madam,' the Bastard finally said. His voice was deep and rough, like wagon wheels going over gravel. 'But we need to get these provisions inside the city walls first. My people are starving.'

'They'll be worse than starving if we don't get the English out soon,' she said. Jehanne turned her back then and lurched away from him in her armor. She did not trust herself to speak further.

CHAPTER TEN

Along the banks of the gray, wind-roughed river sat two dozen motley wood boats and barges, bobbing and tipping in the water like corks. Jehanne stood at the top of the bank, watching the wind. It was blowing directly at them, hard from the north. After a moment the Baron de Rais came and stood beside her. 'Idiots,' he said. He nodded at the herds of pigs and sheep and cows they'd brought, the wagons piled high with wheat and dried herring and beans. 'Of course they can't go anywhere in this wind.' He opened his mouth, showed his teeth like a horse. 'If it makes you feel any better, I wanted to fight today too,' he said. 'My blood was up too.'

Jehanne walked blindly away from Rais, struggling against the rain and wind as she made her way down the muddy riverbank to the edge of the water. She stood there for maybe half an hour, studying the water, the dark violet sky, the trees blowing toward her. *Make it change*, she thought, closing her eyes. *Make it change*.

'Why's she in such a temper?' said Raoul de Gaucourt. He was the Captain of Orléans—a barrel-chested, ginger-haired man with thin, crooked legs who had joined Rais on the upper bank. He stood watching the girl, his thick, furred hands planted on his hips, long tufts of ginger fur sprouting from the collar of his chainmail.

'Her blood was up,' said Rais. 'She was ready to fight.'

Gaucourt looked at him. 'Forgive me, Baron,

but is she not here as more of an inspiration for our men? A restorer of the spirit?'

'She thinks she's our leader.'

The man laughed, looked over at Jehanne, who was crouched on her heels with her hands in the mud, staring at the river. Frowned. 'Uppity little bitch, isn't she?'

Rais's head swiveled around slowly, like an owl's. His voice was soft. 'You speak that way about her again, I'll cut your head off.'

'Fuck you,' said Gaucourt. He stared at Rais. 'Are you crazy?'

Rais smiled. 'Oh yes,' he said. 'I am crazy.'

* * *

The change, when it came, was abrupt. One moment the water was pushing toward Jehanne on the riverbank, slapping loudly at the dock's wooden legs, the next moment it was pushing away, rows of stiff silver waves suddenly turning toward the opposite shore, as if a great hand had tugged at the surface of the river from a distance. Jehanne looked around her with wide eyes at the trees, the fields, the poppies, the flags all leaning suddenly toward Orléans. Above her, on the hill, she heard the men begin to shout. She saw people running toward her, laughing and shouting and cheering, skidding in the mud.

Flashes then, pictures like lightning. Rais running along the sandy flats toward her, sinking to his knees, saying 'My God' as the boats' sails swelled full as moons. Alençon turning, staring at Jehanne as if she'd sprouted wings. Pierrelot and Jean, who'd been loading up the boats, turning in unison to look her, white faced, as if they were carved from soap. 'Holy Christ,' shouted the Bastard, laughing. 'You little genius!' The wind was full upon him now, blowing his dark hair back, blowing the trees back, lifting the corners of the tarpaulins in the caravan, making them flap in the wind. On the hill beyond, a shepherd boy ran slowly against the wind toward a barn, moving in slow motion, his black hat clapped to his head. A few moments later the pack of boats set off across the river with their white sails unfurled like a flock of enormous birds. The Bastard came skidding down the muddy bank toward Jehanne. Shaking his head, smiling. He extended his arm to her, shouted 'Come here!' and pulled her up the bank with him to stand before the vast army. 'Behold, the Maid!' he shouted, throwing his arm out, and the cheering was so loud that for a time it was impossible to speak.

CHAPTER ELEVEN

He wanted to take her immediately into Orléans. 'The people are wild to see you,' he said.

She refused. She did not want to be separated from her army. She was afraid that if she left them, it would all fall apart. 'What about my men?'

'I don't have enough boats to get them all across today,' the Bastard said. 'They'll have to go back and camp in the woods. They can't stay here. It's almost dark; the Goddons will be out patrolling soon. It's too dangerous.'

Jehanne's jaw knotted. 'I can't leave my men,'

214

she said. 'I can't.'

He did not understand. He looked at Jehanne with his big excited face, his warm brown eyes, eager to carry this sign of hope to his people. 'They'll be fine, dear Maid. You'll see them in a few days. Please, let us give you a proper bed for the night, a good hot meal.'

'I can't leave them, Bastard. I won't.'

The Baron walked up then, smiling calmly, his eyes very bright. 'If I might speak to the Maid alone for a moment,' he said. He walked Jehanne away from the Bastard, smiled tenderly. 'I know you don't want to leave them. I understand. But they can't stay here; it's too dangerous.'

'I'll go with them, then.'

'Do you really think that's a good idea? You're exhausted. You almost fell off your horse this afternoon you were so tired. Why not get some rest? Save your strength for the battle?'

'They'll go straight to the whores if I'm not there.'

'No, they won't.'

'Why not? I'm not such a fool to think that a week of Christian living has turned four thousand soldiers into saints.'

'Because I'll go with them,' Rais said. 'I'll take them back into the forest to make camp for a few days. I'll make sure that Mass is said and that they all confess. I'll have my men keep the whores away. We can keep them in line.'

Jehanne looked at him, her eyes fearful. 'I want your word.'

'You have it. I'll bring them back as soon as I can.'

She believed him. She knew he would do as she

215

asked.

CHAPTER TWELVE

Through the deep blue twilight they rode, Jehanne, the Bastard, Alençon, La Hire, Gaucourt, and Poton, followed by their attendants and a company of nobles, marching along the long winding dirt road that led up from the river where they'd docked and across the dim fields to the high-walled city, the black cameo of its fortress towers thrown against the evening sky, the long funnels of siege smoke rising behind them. They entered through the Burgundy Gate, the Maid appearing before the people of that long-besieged city like an apparition on her great white charger, her white banner held high, the words Jesu Maria emblazoned across it. Below, the image of Christ, two angels, and the lilies of France. Beside her, the Bastard, and behind, a crowd of knights, squires, captains, soldiers, and citizens carrying torches, shouting her name. 'The Maid!' they cried. 'The Maid!' Women weeping and reaching out to touch the girl, men with wide-eyed children on their shoulders, buckled old women waving, sobbing, from their balconies, youths shoving through the crowd, howling, their frenzy to feel the holiness so great that one of the torches tipped and set fire to the long white pennant. An orange flame climbing quickly up the silken fringe. The crowd let out a collective gasp. 'Fire,' shouted someone. Calmly Jehanne turned toward the flame. Then she spurred her horse forward and in a single deft

216

move twirled the banner around its pole, extinguishing it easily, gracefully. She stared, astonished at her own dexterity. A wild cheer went up around her, people gazing with crazed eyes, as if God Himself rode among them, performing miracles. She looked at the Bastard. Eyes wide. Terrified. The Bastard smiled. 'Get used to it.'

An uproar so enormous that it swept beyond the walls of the city, out across the dark Loire to the forts of Les Tourelles and Les Augustins on the southern bank, where the cold and huddled English soldiers looked at one another in silence, crossed themselves, and prayed that God would deliver them from the rage of the French witch.

All through the town they followed her, cheering and singing as they went past the Regnard Gate and up through leaning narrow buildings until they arrived at the Rue des Tameliers. Here they turned and funneled down the narrow cobbled street until at last Jehanne and her escorts came to the tall half-timber house of the town's treasurer, Monsieur Boucher. The Bastard had apologized for not being able to host her at his château, which, he explained, had been blasted so many times by English cannons that the roof now let more rain in than it kept out. And so it was Boucher's fine house—a leaning red-brick behemoth of five stories with dark beams crisscrossed in great Xs across its face and a high, steep, red-shingled roof. Their host stood next to his wife in the doorway, both of them wide-eyed, nervous, beside themselves with excitement. 'Such an honor,' shouted Clothilde Boucher above the noise, stumbling over herself as her guests, pushed by the wild crowd behind them, nearly fell inside.

The husband bolted the door fast behind them, the crowd outside still roaring, shouting her name.

Jehanne stood inside the treasurer's freshly swept parlor, pale and stunned. Clutching Pierrelot's shoulder for support. 'I can't hear anything,' she shouted. 'From all the screaming. I can't hear anything.'

Madame Boucher led her toward the hearth with a motherly smile. 'That's all right. We'll take care of you now, dear.'

Jehanne sank down on a bench by the fire. Closed her eyes, let her shoulders sag. 'I could use some bread.'

In the hearth a goat was turning on a spit, roasting in celebration of the Maid's arrival. 'We've prepared a fine supper for you,' said Madame, nodding at the black, slim-ankled beast gleaming in the hearth, its charred eyes popped and raised to Heaven, its limbs stretched gracefully above the red flames. 'Our last goat,' she said proudly. 'We saved it especially.'

'Just some bread, please,' Jehanne said. 'And a cup of wine.'

A powerful glance passed between Monsieur and Madame Boucher. 'You've got to eat more than that, my dear. Got to keep your strength up.'

Jehanne sat on the bench with her cheeks sunk in her hands. Limp. Her eyes off somewhere inside the hearth.

'She doesn't have the stomach,' Pierrelot said. 'The rest of us can help with that goat though.'

Madame Boucher stopped staring at her guest, remembered her merchant-lady manners. 'Of course,' she said. 'Let me fetch some bread.'

They sat around a great wood table in the

218

firelight with the black goat before them. Jehanne and her escorts, Monsieur and Madame Boucher, and their child, Charlotte. All devouring the goat, hands and faces shining with grease. 'Wonderful meat, ma'am,' said Jean d'Aulon, licking his chin. Jehanne sat small and owl-eyed between the great beefy shoulders of Aulon and Pierre, silent, saying nothing and hearing very little. The child stared at her throughout the meal. Finally she asked, 'Are you a girl or a boy?'

The father reached out and slapped the child on the head. The mother went pop-eyed with horror. 'Charlotte! That's a rude question.'

Jehanne smiled, coming back to them. Floating back to earth.

'I'm a girl,' she told the child. 'Like you.'

'Why are you dressed like a boy, then?'

'Because I have a boy's job to do.'

'Is that why your hair's gone too?'

Jehanne rubbed her bare neck, smiled. 'Yes, it is. That's why my hair's gone too.'

They shared a bed that night. She and the eight-year-old, Charlotte. A small, blond, biscuit-smelling child who, in the deep of the night, nestled up against Jehanne as if they were mother and daughter. Jehanne kept waking up in the darkness, her heart swelling in her chest for the warm, sleeping creature beside her. For the children she herself would never have. Her womb ached as she looked down at the plump white face in the dim light of early morning. The tiny freckles on her chin. Small hands curled in soft doughy fists. Small breaths coming in and out in the darkness. Jehanne ran her hand once over the child's head, smoothing the gold-white hair down at her temple, watching the little chest rise and fall. Then abruptly she blinked twice, pulled herself away from the child, and turned to face the wall.

CHAPTER THIRTEEN

In the morning she sent another letter to Lord Talbot, calling once more for the English to quit the siege, to surrender all the cities and territories in France that they had occupied, and return to England. If they refused, she promised, 'Beware! I shall raise a war cry against you that will last for a thousand years.'

Again they kept her herald. The reply came from an English herald instead, stating that they would burn her when they got hold of her, calling her a stupid cowgirl and a whore and a witch. When Jehanne heard it, her face flushed red. Tears brimmed in her eyes, the Godhead roared in fury. 'Bastards,' she said, wiping her face. She walked through the dim-shadowed room out into the sunlight and the cobblestones. Pierrelot followed her. 'Where are you going?'

She did not reply. Instead she shouted at Aulon, who'd been a prisoner of the Goddons for two years and spoke good English. 'I need to go to Les Tourelles right now.'

They rode very fast through the city until they came to the ruined southern bridge that had once led across the river into the enormous fort of Les Tourelles. It rose up before them, its two thick towers crowded with English archers. Not so long ago Les Tourelles had been the pride of Orléans—

an impenetrable fortress that guarded the city's main bridge. But Talbot and his men had captured the fort early on in the siege by digging a series of underground tunnels and attacking from below. And the outraged people of Orléans responded by destroying the bridge with a storm of fire and cannonballs to keep the English from crossing over into the city.

'Go on,' Jehanne said, kicking her horse out onto the stone wreck of the bridge. The horse stepped daintily among the cobbles, then stopped when they came to the ruined edge of the bridge midway across the river. Below the dark green river water rushed and swirled in white eddies around the great stone legs of the bridge. Even from the opposite bank the two towers blocked out the sky. She raised her hands to her mouth: 'Surrender to me, English! Surrender now, in the name of God.'

Imagine this: a small, pink-cheeked peasant girl in men's clothes, seated atop a big roan and shouting at England's greatest generals, telling five thousand of England's fiercest warriors to give up and go home. 'Go home or face your death.' On top of the high crenellated towers of Les Tourelles the English soldiers perched like cats, enjoying the spectacle, smiling and laughing at her. Some pulled up their tunics and pissed high, shining arcs down into the river. Others preferred to shout slurs.

'Go home, whore.'

'Stupid bloody slut.'

Aulon translated. Then stopped, refused to continue. 'You don't need to hear this.'

She wept. Horrified. Weeping, furious at herself for weeping. Amazed how much the words hurt

221

her. 'How dare you?' she screamed. 'How dare you say that to me?'

Laughter then. High-girl-voice mimicry. 'How dare you say that to me?'

'Bloody fucking cowgirl.'

'Crazy little cunt.'

Aulon took hold of her arm. 'Let's go home,' he said gently. Jehanne yanked her arm away and stared at him, her face a mask of hate.

*   *   *

Shortly before dawn they woke her. The room was aflame, as if the sun had suddenly risen from behind the hulking wardrobe. Jehanne lay pinned to her bed, eyes wide. *Attack soon, my love. Soon. It must be soon*, said Michael. Margaret was there too, Margaret with the wildfires in her eyes. *Armor your tender heart, cabbage*, she said. *Raise your sword and drive the Goddons out.*

I wish they would listen to me, Jehanne said. *I wish they would just leave . . .*

They will not leave until you make them leave. You must make them leave.

I'm scared. I don't want to fight.

God is with you. Lay down your fear and rest in His palm. Let Him carry you forward. Let Him show you what must be done.

I know what must be done, the girl sobbed.

Silence then. A rustle of feathered sunlight in the high corner of the room.

Oh, don't go yet, she cried. *Stay with me, please. Will you please stay with me tonight?*

Already they were fading into the air.

Go soon, darling. Go soon.

CHAPTER FOURTEEN

'We have to attack. My voices say now.' She stood, eyes blazing, across from the Bastard in the cold, stone war room of his ruined château, her small brown hands laid flat on the great parchment map of Orléans that lay before them on the table. Around the table stood the other generals. All of them crowded around the map. 'Let's not be hasty, my dear,' the Bastard said.

'Perhaps you will allow us to fill you in on the extremely complicated workings of this situation first,' said Gaucourt, his mouth curling slightly. His freckled lips repulsed her.

A bitter cold gray morning, as if spring had never come. A fire of damp green wood hissed and smoked in the hearth. A cold wind blew in through a hole in the roof. Jehanne looked at the men. 'Your workings mean nothing,' she said. 'My council says the time is now.'

'I understand that,' said the Bastard, 'and we are most grateful for your council, but Lord Fastolf is riding toward Talbot with reinforcements as we speak. They'll be here before we can take any of their forts. We must wait on more men. I've got the garrisons from Gien and Montargis and Château-Renard on the way. We'll attack once they're here.'

La Hire made a face. 'Fat lot of good that will do.'

Jehanne stared at the Bastard. 'The Baron de Rais has just returned with our army. I tell you, we are enough.'

'Only half of those men are soldiers,' said

223

Gaucourt. 'The rest are just farmers with pitchforks.'

'An angry farmer is better than a soldier for hire any day.'

Gaucourt shook his head. 'I agree with the Bastard. We can't risk a botched attack.'

La Hire bunched up his lips, cocked his head. 'I don't see why not,' he said. 'It's not like things are going to get any easier once Fastolf's here.'

Alençon nodded. 'Indeed.'

'Look, I don't think you understand how thoroughly they have us boxed in here,' the Bastard said to Jehanne. He stabbed his finger at the waxy yellow map, pointing out the black squares of the English forts that had almost completely encircled the city. 'Now they've fortified the church of Saint Loup, and they're planning to seal off the Burgundy Gate from there. If they succeed, we're finished,' the Bastard said. 'No one will be able to get in or out.'

'So we take Saint Loup first,' said Jehanne.

'When more troops arrive, and we know where Fastolf is, then we take Saint Loup.'

La Hire and Alençon glanced at each other. Jehanne leaned in very close and put her finger in the Bastard's face. 'Bastard, in God's name, the moment Fastolf arrives, you will let me know. If he gets through without my hearing of it, I promise I will cut out your heart and swallow it whole.'

Rais laughed.

The Bastard gaped at her. 'You're out of your mind.'

'No. I'm telling you the will of God.'

CHAPTER FIFTEEN

She woke up shouting. It was later that afternoon, in her room at the Bouchers' house. Jean Pasquerel was dozing in a chair by the hearth with his Bible resting on his chest. Aulon was snoring loudly on the floor. *It's begun*, Michael whispered. *The blood of France is flowing in Saint Loup. Hurry, love. They've begun without you.* Jehanne was so shocked she could not see clearly; her body seemed to act on its own.

'Raymond!' she screamed. 'Where is my armor? Bring me my armor! Come get me dressed right now!' Someone else seemed to be shouting through her mouth. Aulon sat straight up, blinked at her. 'What's happened?' he said. 'They're fighting,' Jehanne screamed. She ran out in her bare feet into the hall. She felt like a puppet, pulled by strings. 'Raymond, Mugot, where are you?'

She ran to the window and looked down into the street for her two pages. Two men were walking slowly up the cobblestone hill, leaning on each other as if drunk. One had an arrow coming out of his throat. He was making loud gurgling sounds. As if he were trying to cough. The other man's arm was gone entirely below the elbow. He clutched a piece of cloth to the stub, but the cloth was soaked a dark ruby red, and as he moved along the street, blood dripped through his fingers onto the stones. 'Sylvie,' he called in a ragged voice. 'Sylvie.'

Madame Boucher came running up the stairs toward Jehanne, panting. 'What is it? What's

225

happened?' Charlotte came up the stairs behind her. Jehanne could hear Aulon in the other room, fumbling with his boots.

'They're fighting without me,' Jehanne shouted. 'Where is Mugot? Where is my armor? Get me dressed! Someone get me dressed!'

Madame Boucher looked at her. 'I know where it is,' she said in a calm voice. 'Stay here, Charlotte and I will help you.' She looked at her daughter. 'Come with me.'

They worked quickly, binding Jehanne's breasts with linen strips and then helping her into her heavy chainmail shirt, buckling the silver breast plate and the harness onto her chest, fastening the besagews under her arms and the greaves onto her shins. The heavy steel gauntlets onto her small hands. She could hear a woman wailing out in the street. 'Oh, Luke. Oh, Jesus, help us.' Suddenly the front door banged open and Mugot burst in. 'I'm here,' he shouted.

'You're too late,' Jehanne snapped.

She left the house so quickly she forgot her standard. Mugot had to pass it through the window to her down in the street. 'Follow me to the Burgundy Gate!' Jehanne shouted, and she rode the white horse so quickly down the street that sparks flew from its hooves.

CHAPTER SIXTEEN

The men were already in retreat when she arrived at Saint Loup. She saw French soldiers running across the fields toward her, swarms of them

226

running and riding down the hill away from the fortress, running and riding for the Burgundy Gate. At the sight of them, the fire rushed through her, hot and wild. She watched herself stand up in her stirrups, watched the hot possession come into her eyes, watched herself scream, 'No, men! We will not retreat today!' Jehanne screaming at the bloody, mud-painted men coming across the fields toward her and screaming too at the fresh troops she saw beneath a row of maples. Hundreds of soldiers and militia men with their horses and ladders and hatchets and axes on the ground nearby. Poton with a great crowd of mercenaries. Rais with his Breton knights and archers. Men who had not fought yet that day. She saw herself raise her standard high and wave it across the blue sky, and in a bold voice she shouted, 'On your horses, men of France. This day is ours. Saint Loup is ours, men! Ride with me!'

The rest comes back to her in pictures, as if she were looking down on herself from the air. She watches the girl in armor ride across the trampled green, shouting words she has never heard before, orders and exhortations that have never occurred to her. *Fight with me now. Fight for your lives. God is with us, men. This is our chance. Get behind me and ride for France, for your families, for your lives. Get these bastards out of our country, men, out of our land. Run toward them, raise your hammers and axes and take their heads, their hearts, their eyes, their livers. Show them that we will not stand for their thievery and greed any longer. Show them that this is your land and that you fight for it with all of God's mighty strength behind you.*

And at the sight of the furious galloping girl in

227

her bright armor with the white satin banner of God held high over her head, a collective ripple went through the men. A surge of fury like a wave washed over them, carried them forward. Alençon looked at his knights with hot eyes and shouted, 'You heard her, men. *Avant!*'

La Hire was already on his horse, holding the animal's reins tight in one hand as it pranced and flared its red nostrils. He laughed. 'Here we go,' he said.

'*Avant!*' shouted Rais, running to his horse, and then they were shouting orders at their knights and at the uninjured retreating men on the fields who were so moved by the sight of the girl that they too turned on their heels to follow her, screaming back toward the fortress.

Down the hill they went, a thunder of hooves and battle cries, swinging their axes and claymores and hatchets, some faces already painted red with blood, others red with fury, until suddenly a black rain of arrows from the sky was upon them, and the dapple-gray warhorse that was running beside Jehanne screamed and jerked its head toward her, an arrow sunk deep in its shining black eye. But there was no fear inside her now. Only a wild heightening of the senses as the saints chanted in the girl's ears, *Go go go go go go go*, and the holy fury pounded in her like a drum as she shouted, *On, men! On! Today is ours!* The men surged forward, leaping from their horses when they neared the old church and swarming like a colony of silver ants toward the high palisades and the corps of English soldiers who were standing guard outside.

It all happened very quickly. A brief, ferocious

fight. The English were so stunned by the sight of the wild-eyed Maid galloping toward them on horseback and the sudden roaring charge of soldiers behind her that they fell easily, quickly to the French. La Hire, roaring like a bear, cut five Goddon throats in the first three minutes. Rais, howling, staved a Goddon's head in half with his great jeweled ax and watched, delighted, as the wet, pink brains fell out onto the ground. Alençon sprang from his horse upon the shoulders of an enormous, bullet-headed Goddon, knocked him into the mud, grabbed the man's great spiked hammer, and slammed it in his red mouth, shouting, 'There! Die, fiend!'

Very quickly, the ground was red with blood, the air loud with the groans and screams of the dying. La Hire's men lifted a wooden ladder to the wall of the church, set it into the stones, and scrambled up it to the wooden walkways of the palisades. There, a row of filthy-armored English guards stood in a line, passing a pot of spitting oil to a horse-faced redheaded man who stood above the ladder, leering down at the climbing Frenchmen. 'Pour!' shouted an English soldier, and a golden wave of oil splashed onto the face of La Hire's young page, Daniel, who fell shrieking to the ground. 'Pour!' the English soldier shouted again, but before the horse-faced man had a chance to pour again, La Hire swung his long ax and hacked into his pale neck, sending the red head spinning high into the air and down into the mass of warring men below.

Running along the rooftops, Rais caught sight of a plump, sweating boy glancing over his shoulder as he hoisted himself up onto the high crenellated wall of the bell tower. He laughed and caught the

229

boy's ankle. 'Where you going, fatty?' he said. He pulled the boy toward him, tickled his ribs, and the boy fell shrieking backward through the air, down inside the inner courtyard of the church where the rest of the English soldiers were running and screaming in sudden panic, trying desperately to escape.

Jehanne stood at the foot of the ladders, shouting her soldiers on, filling them with her fire. 'Up, men! Up now! Saint Loup is ours! The day is ours!' and she was focused so intently on urging her men forward that she did not watch where she was walking and stepped directly onto a caltrop. She looked down to see a wet, red, metal spike sticking out of the top of her foot. 'Oh,' she said, sitting down sideways on the ground.

'Get her off the field,' Alençon shouted to Aulon, as he knelt beside her, his face freckled with blood.

But Jehanne would not hear of it. 'I'm fine,' she said, clutching Alençon's shoulder as she pulled the sharp weapon out of her foot. 'Let go of me. I'm fine.'

Now, Michael was whispering, *Now now now*. And so she struggled to her feet and went on. Pushed her men away and charged up a ladder with the white Jesu Maria banner in her hand, waving it above the men's heads, and seeing the muddy battlefield below thick with blood and the bodies of dead Goddons, she shouted, 'Follow me now, men! Everyone over the wall. Saint Loup is ours!'

A frenzy then. So many Frenchmen scrambled up the ladders and down the stairs of the keep into the courtyard that the English inside didn't stand a chance. Six of them were pushed from the ramparts with cut throats or pierced hearts, their silver-suited bodies landing with a thud on the floor of the courtyard, and as soon as the Goddons looked up and saw the hundreds of Frenchmen descending upon them, they laid down their weapons, raised their hands high above their heads, and shouted, 'Surrender, we surrender!' One boy, shaking, sobbing, backed against the wall, crying, 'Please, Jesus, I surrender!'

Jehanne looked with wild eyes at Rais. So much adrenaline was coursing through her she felt as if she were floating above the ground. 'What's he saying?' she shouted. 'I can't understand.'

'They're surrendering,' said Rais, laughing. He pulled his curved dagger from a dead man's eye, the rubies in its hilt catching the sunlight. 'It's over. They surrender.'

*   *   *

Then came the wildness. The French soldiers running wild through the church, screaming and laughing and tackling one another, throwing their metal helmets and shields on the ground. Shouting, bouncing, drunk with joy and adrenaline—astonished to find themselves alive among so many of the dead. Jehanne felt it too, thought she'd faint from the thrill of it. Alive. She was alive.

She walked around like this, blindly, for perhaps half an hour after the Goddons surrendered, stunned and marveling at the sudden miracle of life, the fresh sweet air in her lungs, the delicate brown beauty of her hand, the glittering blue sky

231

overhead. Everything ringing slightly, everything unreal, tilted and glowing, much brighter than usual, as if she were looking at a painting. 'Oh my,' she said quietly. 'Oh my, oh my.'

Some time later she found herself sitting on the ground in a pool of blood with her legs stuck out in front of her like a rag doll, staring blindly at a pile of bodies stacked up against the church wall. Up until then she had not seen them. Had seen only a group of colorful shapes, a mountain of silver and mud and bright red paint. Among the shapes, a few sharp details—a plump, unmoving hand with a gold crest ring shining amidst a nest of dark knuckle fur, a man kneeling and moaning, holding the shining brown purse of his liver carefully in front of him—but they had no meaning. It was just far-away pictures, just a long, blurred tapestry on the far side of an enormous silent canyon.

And then suddenly, it wasn't. She heard a strange, wet snoring sound to her left, and she saw a thin, curly-haired Goddon with a prominent Adam's apple lying on the ground beside her with blood pumping steadily out of his chest. She saw his chapped yellow lips moving. 'Car-face,' he seemed to be saying. 'Need car-face.'

Slowly Jehanne got up and walked over to him. She knelt beside him and took his hand. 'What is it?' she said. 'Tell me what you need.'

The man licked his yellow lips, then said it again. 'Car-face.'

Jehanne repeated the word silently to herself. Then abruptly she stood up and shouted, 'Get the priests in here right now. These men need to confess.'

232

She spent the night sitting in the church of Sainte-Croix. Staring straight ahead of her. She did not pray. She did not sleep. She sat in the pew, staring, thinking, *Why don't I feel anything?*

CHAPTER SEVENTEEN

In the beginning I was not upset. I was too excited to be upset. You have to understand what it's like, charging all at once like that, throwing yourself into that madness. That sea of fury and death. You know only that you must get through, that if you do not fight your way through the wall of men in front of you, they will devour you. So you fight as you can, as you must, with your sword, your teeth, your hands. You'll do anything to make it through, to make it stop. Anything at all.

It takes you over, war. As soon as you enter the field, you become part of the great Red Machine, a wheel inside the great Red Machine, rolling and rolling forward, fighting your way toward silence. Stillness. There is no thinking, no time for consideration. There is only doing what you must do in the moment, what seems best in the moment. And there's a beauty to it, working like that, letting the ancient instinct take over, the drive that says fight or die. Kill or die.

It happens so fast. At once very fast and very, very slowly. As if your body is moving faster than it's ever moved, and at the same time a hand inside your mind is very slowly, calmly sketching a picture of

233

everything that happens. Recording everything. And only after it's over, only once the great Red Machine has ground to a halt, do you know what you've done. No, even that's not true, because after it's ground to a halt, the fire is still racing through you. Maybe you drop your weapon, maybe you start dancing around, dancing and shouting and laughing and banging up against the other men, screaming because you're alive, more alive than you've ever been. You've killed them, and you're still alive, and it's a long time before that fire burns down and you find yourself sitting in a corner, staring blindly at a tall silver and red pile in front of you, and only when you realize that the pile is a pile of the dead, do you begin to understand what you've done. You don't feel it yet, but the name is there in your head. The name that tells you who you are. The truest self, the one you can never know until you've fought. You see that you are the one who fights. You see that you are the one who kills.

CHAPTER EIGHTEEN

It happened very quickly after that. In a week it was over. They took Les Augustins in one day, Les Tourelles in two. The day after Saint Loup was the Day of Ascension, and Jehanne declared that they would not fight on a holy day. Instead she sent another letter to the English, had her archer shoot it up over the walls into Les Tourelles. The English soldiers just laughed, called her names, threw rotten cabbages at her. Rais was with Jehanne and Aulon that day, seated beside her on his stallion at the edge of the ruined bridge as her archer let the arrow fly. When Aulon repeated the names they called her, Rais turned white as salt. 'Who dares say such things to the Maid?' he shouted, the cords in his neck standing out like wires. They laughed at him too, but they shouted their names out anyway. 'Thomas Parry and John Cotter,' they cried.

Two days later they were found hung from a tall sycamore tree outside the city walls. Each one naked, with his sex stuffed in his mouth, his eyes black, popped out like crab's eyes. She knew Rais did it. Knew, and was horrified, but was also secretly flattered. He claimed he knew nothing—claimed he was up at Dunois' château all night. La Hire backed him up, said they were playing cards together. But she knew. 'Why did you do it?' she said. 'Why would you do such a thing?'

Rais smiled, his sable collar dark against his pale, mad face. 'My dear, I have no idea what you're talking about.'

They kept fighting. The war dream went on. A strange time, that time in Orléans. The power was so high in her, she hardly needed to sleep, to eat. Could only think of going forward, of fighting on and on until the red rage left her, until the saints were silent. Until the red rage was spent. And she knew that if she did, nothing would stop them. She knew they would win.

Several times her troops got scared—tried to run. Two days after Saint Loup, as Jehanne and Alençon and La Hire and their men were crossing the river to attack Les Augustins, the bushes along the riverbank began to shake, as if they had come alive. A moment later a whole swarm of Goddons came roaring out, splashing through the clear golden shallows with their swords raised,

235

screaming bloody murder. Jehanne and her troops had not been prepared at all. They were still a mile off from Les Augustins. She could not believe the English had found them.

A wildly hot day. Bizarre for early May. The sun was standing straight overhead, glaring down, so they'd stopped for water. Jehanne and Alençon were standing together in the shade of an oak tree, sharing water from his wineskin. The soldiers were down by the river's edge, filling up their leather caps and helmets with river water and pouring it over their heads and their horses' heads. Jehanne caught sight of Bertrand, with his wild yellow curls, drinking water from a steel boot. He waved and shouted, 'Hurrah, Pucelle!' and she was waving back at him when it happened. As soon as the men caught sight of the Goddons coming across the water with their axes out, they ran—started scrambling up the banks and onto their horses and running toward the little makeshift bridge the militia had made of boats and pontoons the night before. A rush of men so powerful that even Bertrand and others who wanted to fight were swept along with it. Men dropping their helmets, stumbling, scrambling up on their horses and running toward the bridge to the mainland, huffing and pushing each other. 'Go! Hurry up! Fuck's sake, get out of my way.'

Again the fire rose up inside of her. The Godhead shouted through her mouth as she ran down the riverbank after them, the long white banner of God in her hand. 'No! Turn and fight, men!' A loud, hard shout. Ferocious. The girl in armor, eyes aflame. 'Turn and fight now! Let God's wrath rise up in your breast and let it drive

236

you forward to destroy those bastards who would steal our land and make us their slaves!' And it was as she opened her mouth to shout again that a man ran up behind her, picked her up, and pressed a knife against her throat. 'Hello, sweetie,' he said, his breath hot in her ear.

La Hire saw it happen. La Hire, who'd been at the mouth of the bridge, trying to block the men from retreating, saw and stood up very quickly in his stirrups. Shouted, 'They've got the Maid!'

As one, both the French soldiers on the riverbank and the English soldiers in the shallows turned to see the thick Goddon soldier on the riverbank holding the kicking girl in the air, stroking her cheek with the blade of his knife. A moment trapped in amber. Both armies watching, still as statues. Watching as Jehanne kicked and screamed. Watching as she went abruptly silent and still. Then watching as Alençon broke from behind an oak tree and ran at the Goddon from the side like a bull, knocking him over into the sand and pulling his meaty arm away from Jehanne's neck long enough to push her into a fringe of weeds, then jumping on top of the Goddon and plunging his little hand ax into the man's forehead.

Later Alençon would say that the roar of the French soldiers that sounded then was 'like the roar of ten thousand lions.' A roar that shook the trees and made the river jump its banks. And the French charge that followed was so ferocious that it resembled a glinting metallic sea, rolling and surging across the island and spilling out into the river toward the advancing Goddons, and even La Hire's heart drew back at the sight of the army's fury, and seeing it, feeling the sudden hot surge in the air, scores of approaching Orléans militiamen and Scots and Spanish mercenaries leaped from the pontoon bridge and ran through the shallow water with their swords raised to join the French charge, howling and screaming with such force that the English simply turned and ran at the sight of them, up the riverbanks and across the fields toward the fort of Les Augustins.

*   *   *

Jehanne lay very still in the grass where Alençon had dragged her, out of the way of the onslaught. Her face was gray. Her lips an alarming lavender. Alençon knelt beside her and held his palm above her mouth. 'Oh God,' he said. He began to unbuckle her breastplate, his fingers trembling.

Abruptly she coughed and blinked. 'Where's my horse?' she said.

Alençon laughed. A laugh and a sob at the same time. 'Right here,' he said. 'Tied up right where you left him.'

It was sheer will that did it. Sheer will that drove Jehanne and the French army to charge toward Les Augustins. They knew they were outnumbered by perhaps a thousand men, but they could not be held back now. Their bones were screaming for blood, for vengeance, for seventy years of wrongs to be righted, and it was this long-withheld fury that drove them across the river shallows and up the banks after the English, drove them over the brilliant green May fields toward the palisades that surrounded the old monastery, swinging their axes and flails and morning stars and hammers

238

and kitchen knives, professional soldiers and militiamen, farmers and carpenters alike, riding side by side, swept along by the same mad and holy fire, some falling in the great black rain of arrows that met them as they charged toward the monastery, men screaming and horses screaming and stumbling and falling, but most of them making it, most of them leaping off their horses when they drew closer to the outer works of the fort and hacking into the charge of fresh English knights that ran out of the monastery to greet them. And only when the French had fought their way through those knights, only when they began to call for the battering ram to be brought forward so they could break down the great wooden door that led inside the monastery, did they see the enormous armored giant who stood guarding the entrance like a mountain, ready to destroy any Frenchman who came near.

'Jesus Christ,' said the Bastard, stopping dead in his tracks. A man over seven feet tall and thick as an oak tree stood in front of the entrance of Les Augustins with a thick, curling, dark beard and a red shield with a white cross on his chest, a great spiked hammer in his hand. 'A monster,' Rais said in an admiring voice.

They were crouched in a dim outer ditch before the earthen works of the monastery. It was afternoon. La Hire and his men had joined a remaining corps of militia who were running up to the walls and setting fires at the base of the fort, attempting to send the whole compound up in a blaze.

Jehanne and Rais and Alençon were focused on the giant—on finding a way to get past him. After a time Poton joined them with two Spanish soldiers, Alphonse de Partada and Miguel del Toro, who, upon seeing the monster, simply stopped and stared. 'Christ, how are we ever going to get past that?' Poton said. Partada stood smiling. Partada, with two black thumbs hanging from a piece of rawhide around his neck, a wild light in his eyes.

'Any ideas are welcome,' the Maid said.

CHAPTER NINETEEN

They tried first to shoot the giant with flaming arrows, lining Rais' six best archers up in a ditch in front of the earthen works and signaling them to shoot all at once. But they were too far away. The arrows all buried themselves, smoking, in the ground several yards in front of the giant, causing him to roar with ugly laughter. 'We're going to have to use a culverin,' Poton said, his feathered yellow hair lifting in the breeze. 'And even the gunner's going to have to get closer to get a good shot . . . I don't see how we can do that without sending him out in the open.'

Jehanne saw. In a flash of vision she saw. 'We need to distract them,' she said, the Godvoice speaking through her mouth. 'A few of us need to run straight toward that beast.' The girl's eyes wide from the madness of what she was saying. She looked at the boy who stood beside the culverin. The *couleuvriner*. A slight young man of sixteen with keen dark eyes and enormous hands. He had killed forty-two Goddons in Orléans that winter with his culverin. Was something of a legend among the French and Goddons alike. The Bastard called him the Wrath of God. 'You see? You wait 'til all the English are watching us, then get yourself into position while we're still running.'

Poton was staring at Jehanne. Staring at her as if he'd never seen her before. 'You'll be killed,' he said.

She smiled at him. 'No. They won't catch me.'

Jehanne looked at the Wrath. 'As long as you hit him before we get to the door, we should be all right. And while you're at it, try and blast a few holes in the door too, so we can get inside easier.'

'I like,' said Partada in bad French.

'It's suicide,' said Rais, his eyes glittering.

'You don't have to do this,' said Alençon, his face white around the mouth.

'Oh yes, I do,' said Jehanne, jumping up and grabbing her standard. 'Because this is how we're going to win.' She looked at Partada and del Toro. 'Are you with me?'

They said that they were.

'Don't miss,' Jehanne said to the Wrath, who looked at her as if he were offended by the suggestion that he could.

*   *   *

Side by side the three of them set off running toward the fortress in the late afternoon light. Jehanne in the middle, running without her helmet or her boots, running barefoot and holding her white banner high, the soldiers flanking her on either side, their swords out, prepared to fight. The field was muddy under Jehanne's feet, and her armor weighed half as much as she did, but the holy, violent joy moving through her was so hot and wild that she hardly noticed, running through the mud and corpses and broken arrows like a gazelle, her two soldiers huffing and grinning beside her as the soldiers on both sides of the battlefield stared with wide eyes. It was so mad, the stunt, so wild and absurd, that it gave the three runners a shimmer of immortality, the air around them pulsing and electric. The French cannons shouted loudly behind them, a ferocious, bone-jangling sound, and immediately she could smell the bitter smoke of gunpowder in the air, could sense the great stone balls hurtling through the blue air above her head, see them crashing into the ground all around her, but it didn't frighten her. Everything seemed slowed down, almost calm, although she was running faster than she had ever run in her life. She smiled, hearing the saints chanting in her ears, *Yesyesyesyesyesyesyes!*, and watching as the first cannonball arrived at the fortress, tearing a long hole through the mighty door as if it were made of paper, and then the second cannonball sailed toward the stunned, wide-eyed giant, slamming into his enormous armored chest and blowing him backward amidst the splinters of the door. 'Jesus!' Partada shouted as the third cannonball crashed into the fortress wall. By the time they reached the great door, only half of it remained, and Partada and del Toro ran easily through. Jehanne stood before it, waving her banner and shouting to the rest of her army, 'Charge now, men! Les Augustins is ours!' and watching as La Hire and the great silver mass of his army came charging across the field to slaughter the Englishmen within.

CHAPTER TWENTY

'Poton loved me after that,' she says to Massieu. 'He went around telling everyone I was the bravest person on God's green earth, but, in truth, I was not a very good soldier. I did not have the coordination, that panther's grace that the best warriors have. La Hire with one hand tied behind his back was more lethal than I ever was with a sword. But I understood about surprise, which most of the others did not. I knew that catching the Goddons off guard, doing what they least expected, was a thousand times better than the best battle plan any general could come up with. With surprise, you can beat any odds.'

Alençon had taught her that. Back in the winter, when they were riding to Poitiers. Charles and Yolande had gone together in the carriage, but she and Alençon had decided to go on horseback. It was a gray, breezy day, and she was very happy to be away from the castle, riding fast and free over the countryside in the fresh cold air, and as they went, Alençon told her about Charles Martel—how Charles Martel had defeated the Saracen invaders at the Battle of Tours.

'There were eighty thousand of those black bastards,' Alençon said. 'But the Hammer knew just what to do with them.' The Arabs, he said, had outnumbered the French three to one, so Charles had taken his soldiers and packed them in tight, like a glacier, on top of a high, wooded plain outside Tours. This forced the Saracens to charge uphill and through a dense thicket of trees before they could start their attack, exhausting their horses. 'The Arabs never knew what hit them,' said Alençon. 'Here they come, panting and red-faced up the hill, and the French are there waiting for them, cool as bishops with their axes and flails out, ready to tear them up and grind them small.'

Jehanne laughed.

'That was the Hammer's brilliance—he knew that surprise is the key to victory. Throw 'em off balance and you're halfway home.'

'Is that the trick, then?' Jehanne had said, grinning.

'It's one of them,' said Alençon.

So when it came time to attack Les Tourelles, she wanted to attack immediately. That night, as she and her men stood watching Les Augustins burn—a ragged, red cathedral of fire reflected in the dark, rippling river—she said, 'We'll attack first thing tomorrow. They won't expect that. They'll expect us to wait for reinforcements. So we'll sneak up, take Les Tourelles at dawn.'

But several hours later a messenger appeared at the Bouchers' house, saying the Bastard and his council had decided that once again they must wait for more troops to arrive before they attacked Les Tourelles. 'Les Tourelles is impossible,' the Bastard wrote. 'It will be impossible for us to get inside without more men. We must wait until the reinforcements get here.'

The same as always, she thought. *Wait. Wait. Always wait.* Jehanne, who had been sitting at a table looking over a map of Les Tourelles, shoved the map away from her, got on her horse, and rode up to the Bastard's château. She walked into the

244

dining hall, where the Bastard sat with Gaucourt eating roast beef, their greasy hands shining in the candlelight. 'Ah, Jehanne,' said the Bastard, smiling. 'We were just talking about you.'

Jehanne did not smile. 'Where is the Baron?' she said.

'God knows,' said Gaucourt. 'Last I saw, he was down by the river, passing out chocolate and hippocras to the choirboys.'

'Letting off steam like everyone else,' said the Bastard. 'What do you want with him?'

'I want him to fight with me tomorrow.'

The Bastard frowned. 'Did you not receive my letter informing you that the council decided not to fight tomorrow?'

'Bastard, you have been in your council and I in mine,' Jehanne said, 'and believe me, the council of the Lord will be carried out and will prevail.'

'And what exactly does the council of the Lord suggest?'

She looked at him with cold eyes. 'We take Les Tourelles at dawn.'

CHAPTER TWENTY-ONE

'I knew I'd be injured the next day.'

'How did you know? Did the saints tell you?'

'No. I dreamed it.'

'Tell me,' says Massieu. 'Tell me how you dreamed it.'

It happened the way it always did. She had seen a sudden picture, very clear and specific—an arrow tearing through her breast. And with it came a

245

ferocious pain—pain like she'd never felt before. She woke up panting, her shirt soaked with sweat. 'Watch out for me today,' she told Pasquerel when she confessed to him that morning. 'A Goddon archer will get me today.'

Pasquerel blinked. 'Not kill you?' he whispered.

'I don't know,' she said. 'Let's hope not.'

'Did you know you were going to win?' Massieu asks.

'Yes. I knew we were going to win. And I knew both sides would suffer terrible losses that day . . . but I did not know how terrible.' She looks away from him then, her eyes following a white shaft of moonlight slicing across the tunnel of stones. 'I did not know that . . .'

'I'm sorry.'

'I don't want to talk about the war anymore,' she says abruptly in a flat voice. 'I'm tired. I need to sleep.'

'Of course,' says Massieu, getting up and gathering his cloak around him, hiding the disappointment in his eyes.

CHAPTER TWENTY-TWO

But in the night the war comes back to her anyway. Comes crashing through the walls of her cell, crouches like a wolf on her chest, panting, poisoning her dreams. It's Bertrand she sees first, Bertrand with his corn-yellow curls, his crumpled jester's face, walking into her camp with a huge shad in a net—the fish still alive and wet with its sad, jellied eyes, its pearly scales shining in the early light—Bertrand grinning as he laid his prize on the ground at her feet. 'Thought you could use a good breakfast,' he said. Bertrand fairly hopping with delight at his catch.

But she'd been too nervous to eat. Could not even think of eating. So she winked at him, said, 'Let's save it for tonight, eh? I'll bring back a Goddon to serve it up for us.'

'Ah, even better!' Bertrand had said. 'A victory fish.'

And it was the victory fish that Bertrand was thinking of later that morning as he scrambled up a ladder to the top of the high ramparts that surrounded the two enormous black towers of Les Tourelles. The victory fish he was thinking of when he reached the top of the wall and turned around to watch Jehanne, who stood halfway up a nearby ladder, screaming at the men below to hurry up, and so he did not see the spiked iron ball that came arcing neatly through the blue sky and buried itself in his skull. And he did not hear Jehanne screaming as he lost his hold on the ladder and fell silently to the ground. 'Oh Bertrand!' she screamed. 'Bertrand!'

She was not wearing a helmet that day. She had wanted the men to see her eyes, her face, as they fought. And her face was radiant as she urged her men on, up, and over the ramparts, as she cried, 'Fight for your families, men! Fight for your freedom!' but the radiance vanished when she saw Bertrand fall. The sight of Bertrand lying on his back, his arms flung out on either side of him, his head a ball of blood, snuffed the light in her eyes. Killed all thought of care or self-defense, and it was then, as she stood on her ladder, looking down

247

at her friend, that an arrow came whistling from below and buried itself in her back.

CHAPTER TWENTY-THREE

When she awoke, she was lying on her side. A wild pain inside her, as if a bolt of lightning was being pulled very slowly through her chest. There was a circle of drawn faces looking down at her, and beyond them, a flash of leaves and blue sky. 'Bertrand?' she said.

Aulon shook his head. 'No,' he said, wiping her forehead with a damp cloth. 'You rest now. You took a bad hit.'

She remembered the arrow. When she looked down, she could just see the tip of the head pushing out of her neck. Blood ran thickly down her breast.

Rais knelt beside her, a strange glitter in his eyes. 'So she is mortal after all,' he murmured. 'Shall I pull it out for you?'

'No,' she said. 'Aulon will do it. But you need to help hold me down.'

'Yes, let me do that,' Rais said. He was hovering over her with a green bottle in his hand, looking as if he longed to lean in and drink her blood. 'Would you like some hippocras for the pain?'

'No.' She looked at Aulon. Her breath was coming in hard little pants. 'Just break off the shaft in back. Go as close to the skin as you can.'

The first time Aulon grabbed the arrow, Jehanne fainted. They poured water over her face to revive her, and when she came to, she reached for the green bottle and drank deeply, the alcohol traveling down her throat like a tangled string of fire. Rais gripped her shoulders more tightly this time. Aulon knelt beside her and took hold of the arrow shaft with both hands—one near the entry wound, the other back near the fletching. Jehanne was clutching Rais' hand so hard it had turned white.

When Aulon snapped the arrow, Jehanne fainted again. Again they revived her with water. When she came to, she sat up and said, 'I'll do the rest.' She looked at Aulon. 'You and Gilles just hold me steady.'

The men knelt on either side of her. The arrowhead was protruding from her neck, just above the collarbone. But it hadn't completely emerged. Only the tip was visible. The rest lay beneath a jutting tent of flesh. 'You'll have to cut the skin so I can get the head out,' she said, handing Aulon her knife. 'Cut both sides, like a seam.'

Rais picked up one of his leather gloves and handed it to her. 'Bite down on this.'

But as Aulon made the cut, Jehanne spat out the glove and screamed like an eagle. A sound so outrageous that both Aulon's and Rais's heads jerked back as if they'd been slapped.

'Do you want to rest?' Aulon asked when she was quieter.

'No,' she said, the skin around her mouth white. 'Just hold me tight. As tight as you can.'

Once more they rearranged themselves. Aulon seated himself with one arm around her waist and his chest pressed against her back. Rais sat on the other side, facing her, his shoulder pressed into her chest. With her thumb and forefinger she dug into the neck hole, grabbed hold of the arrowhead, and pulled it out until it made a deep sucking sound and stuck out several inches from her neck like a bolt.

Jehanne was screaming so loudly that both men had closed their eyes and were squinting against the sound of it—as if they were walking into a tornado.

'Let me help you,' said Aulon.

Jehanne shook her head. She wiped her hand on her hose and then, with a firm, hard motion, she gripped the shaft in her right fist and yanked it out of her neck. 'Fuck,' she said as blood pumped out of her neck. Then she fainted.

CHAPTER TWENTY-FOUR

When she awoke, the sky was streaked with the violet blue and hot orange of sunset and the chamomile was glowing in the field around her and a cool breeze had come down from the hills. She was alone beneath a tree, on a hilltop a little ways off from the battlefield. Her horse grazed in the grass nearby. She touched her wound, which the men had dressed with olive oil and cotton. She could smell the fruity scent of the oil and the heavy, pungent scent of blood from the battlefield.

She got up and walked until she could see the two massive black towers of Les Tourelles and the maze of outer works and ditches and ramparts that surrounded it. The French soldiers still had not gotten inside. She could see them climbing over the high earthen walls like ants. *The men still launching themselves up the ladders and fighting along the tops of the walls, the men still falling through the air like birds . . .*

Many French soldiers had died trying to get over the wall that day. She saw them as she rode down the hill toward the field where the Bastard stood—hundreds of corpses pulled off the field and lined up to one side. *So many feet*, Jehanne thought as she rode past, watching the long rows of bodies in their silver suits, the suits glinting in the last rays of sunlight, their long metal shoes pointing upward to the sky.

The Bastard frowned when he saw her. 'What are you doing here? You should be resting.'

Jehanne shrugged. 'A scratch,' she said, smiling.

'We should quit for tonight. The men are exhausted. They've been fighting for thirteen hours without a break. None of them has had a thing to eat all day.' He gestured out toward the dimming countryside. 'It'll be too dark to see soon anyway.'

'I need to speak with my council first,' she said. 'Call for a break so the men can eat something. I'll be back in an hour.'

She knelt in a vineyard a little ways off from the fighting. Knelt in the crumbled dirt among the rows of dusky blue grape leaves with her eyes closed, listening to the leaves rustling around her, smelling the campfires being lit in the distance and the cool mineral smell of the dirt. She looked at the sky. *Show me your will, my Lord. What would you have me do?*

CHAPTER TWENTY-FIVE

When she returned to the field half an hour later, her eyes were blazing. The Godhead was pounding inside her, hot as a sun. 'Now is the time, men,' she shouted as she stood before her troops in the flickering torchlight. 'My council tells me now is the time for us to take Les Tourelles. The English have their guard down. They think we're finished for the day; they think we're all going to go home and have our dinners; but, by God, we will show them that we have just begun! We must charge like tigers now, men, charge with all the fire and fury in our hearts and with the power of almighty God at our backs, and when we charge, watch me closely, for when my standard touches the rampart, I promise, Les Tourelles will be yours.'

A great roar erupted from the men as they rode through the twilight toward the great fortress, Jehanne running out in front of the troops with her white banner waving, not even feeling her armor as she ran down into a ditch at the base of the rampart, feeling only the chill night air on her face and the wildfire of God blazing inside her, and when at last the tip of her banner touched the rampart of the fort, she turned toward her men and shouted, 'Go up now. It's all yours!'

A speedy assault. The French ran up the ladders and leaped over the walls, catching the English while they were still loading their bows and groping around in the dark for their weapons. Jehanne, halfway up a ladder, kept hearing Rais above, laughing and shouting 'Die, pigs! Die!' A

252

bloody fight, but no worse than the ones that had gone before it. No, it was what happened next, on the bridge, that bothered her. The bridge was the thing she could not forget.

During the night, a group of citizens in Orléans had gathered up a mountain of scrap wood—ladders and boards and old wagon wheels and old doors, any flat piece of wood they could find—and built a high wooden walkway with ropes and pulleys that spanned the gap between the city wall and the destroyed bridge that led directly into the northern side of Les Tourelles. It was a wild-looking thing, stretching crooked and spindly and misshapen over the rushing green river. When La Hire and Alençon and Rais and their men finally made it over the southern walls of the fort, a group of armed militia men from Orléans crept out along the bridge in single file, high above the river, toward the unguarded northern wall of the fort, stepping easily and quickly off the mongrel bridge and then charging through the doors and windows of the fort toward the unsuspecting English inside.

CHAPTER TWENTY-SIX

'We cornered them,' she says. 'Because of the bridge, we were able to corner them inside the fort. By the time they realized what was happening, it was too late.' The Goddons had panicked. They'd lowered the drawbridge that led from Les Tourelles to the mainland, and dozens of knights and generals stampeded out onto the bridge with their hands up, shouting, 'Surrender, surrender!'—

not realizing that the worst still lay ahead. For the Orléans soldiers had loaded up a barge below the drawbridge with pitch and bundles of sticks and straw and oil-soaked rags and had set the drawbridge on fire from below, and almost immediately the entire bridge burst into flame.

She'd seen it happen. She was standing on the northern bank of the river, and she saw the fire, lapping at the wooden legs of the drawbridge, the long yellow flames rising up and spreading fast along the planks of the bridge itself, devouring it, until there came a deep, ugly crack and a groan, and the drawbridge collapsed, sending the entire crowd of heavily armored men cascading into the river. She saw immediately that they were doomed. Because of their armor they were doomed. And she watched helplessly as they thrashed around in the river in their monstrous metal suits, grabbing at each other and calling 'Help, help!' as the weight of their armor dragged them beneath the surface one by one until only two knights were visible.

One was very fat and had thrown his arms around the neck of a much smaller boy who had managed somehow to get out of his metal suit and was trying to swim to shore. 'Get off me!' the boy screamed, thrashing in vain against the big, armored knight who was clutching his neck. 'Get off! Get off!' he cried as the big man thrashed and pushed the boy's head under water. As soon as the boy was under the surface, the big armored man began to sink too, flailing his silver arms in the air and then sinking under himself until the surface of the river was completely still.

A moment later the boy came up gasping, blue-faced. 'Swim here!' Jehanne cried, waving her arms. 'Swim here!' The boy looked up and began to crawl slowly through the water toward her, but after he had taken a few strokes, he was jerked sharply beneath the surface again. 'Jesus!' she cried as his head disappeared into the green water, leaving only one arm waving frantically, and then no arm—just a bouquet of white bubbles—and finally nothing at all.

La Hire stood beside Jehanne, shaking his head. 'Fortune in ransoms lost right there.'

She raised her head, looked at him. 'How can you say such a thing?'

La Hire stared back. Spoke calmly. 'Because I don't see the point in crying over a bunch of animals who've spent the last nine months trying to kill me.'

'Just because they're animals doesn't mean we have to be.'

La Hire looked at her for a long time.

'You think you're not? You think you're any less of an animal because you order others to do the killing for you?'

'I do as God commands.'

La Hire spat. 'Then God's a bloody animal too.'

*   *   *

She did not speak to La Hire for a long time after that. She avoided him. It was easy enough to do. The siege was over. On May eighth, the morning after the French had taken Les Tourelles, the English army rode away. A curious, ferocious retreat. First the Goddons had lined up in the field outside the still-burning skeleton of Les Tourelles

255

in full battle dress, as if prepared to fight. 'We will not attack on a Sunday,' said the Maid, but she led her army out to face them anyway. One by one they lined up their ponies opposite the English, lances at the ready, a herd of steel-faced monsters. 'If they attack, you may fight, but only if they attack,' she said. An hour passed, the two weary armies facing each other in a mysterious game of chicken. No one moving.

Eventually the commander of the English army shouted something and waved his arm backward. Then he turned his horse and rode away from the field toward Meung-sur-Loire, and his army followed him.

'Look at that,' said Poton quietly.

'My God, you did it,' laughed the Bastard, picking Jehanne up and spinning her around in his arms as the great storm of men and horses retreated across the fields and away from Orléans. 'You little genius. You did it!'

CHAPTER TWENTY-SEVEN

When the people of Orléans learned that the siege had been lifted, their joy was so great that life was given over completely to rejoicing for a week. A seemingly endless string of parades and feasts and dancing and tributes with Jehanne as the deity around which everything revolved. The image everyone longed to revere and bow down to. And so she stood, as if at the center of a storm, watching in a kind of trance while thousands of townspeople swirled and roared around her,

256

chanting her name and carrying her in a chair above their heads as they danced and wept and threw roses and made toasts; and the weather was beautiful all that week, sunny and soft and clear, the hills green and lacy, the lilies and tulips in full bloom and the smell of lilacs in the air; and Jehanne seemed part of this great flowering spring, seemed to have created it especially for them. As she sat among them—those thousands and thousands of shining eyes—smiling and waving within that strange communal trance of love, she thought how enormous man's hunger for God was, how desperately we want the thing that we can bow down to and worship, the thing that makes us open our hearts up completely, the thing that unleashes all of our awe and wonder. And it frightened her a little, for she knew very well that she was not God, knew that the people were worshipping nothing but a lamp in which God had chosen to burn for a short time, and she tried to tell them this many times, but they would not listen to her, they did not want to hear. They wanted simply to be near her, to drink in the light that was pouring from her, to sing of her miracles and her triumphs. And it was heady stuff, all this communal worship, and perhaps we should not blame Jehanne too much for forgetting sometimes that she was just the lamp, and for forgetting that one day the holy fire might go away, because who in ecstasy, in the throes of love, can ever remember the gray, lonesome days, and who among us does not hope with all their hearts that somehow, by some miracle, such love might go on forever?

CHAPTER TWENTY-EIGHT

The day after their victory, while the people of Orléans were beginning to sing and dance and drink in the streets, Alençon came up to Jehanne, grinning. The sight of his dark, smiling face made her take a step forward. 'How are you feeling, my Maid?'

Jehanne smiled. 'Better now.'

'Catch any stray arrows today?'

'Not yet, you?'

'Care to take a walk down to the river with me?'

They walked down to a place where the river was broad and flat and milky green, and they sat on its bank in the grass beside the drowsy willows that hung out over the water, and were silent together, watching the late-day sunlight and the dragonflies skimming and humming above the river. As they sat, Alençon picked up her hand and held it in his own. 'It's nice to see you without all that armor on,' he said. Then he said her name, tasting the word. *Jehanne*. He reached up, touched her cheek.

There came the sound of laughter nearby. Bright, girl's laughter, followed a moment later by the girl herself with honey blond curls, coming down the hill toward the river, great with child. Behind her a tall, thin boy followed, loping, catching her hand and pulling her against him. A passionate embrace, long. His hands in her hair, her body pressed hard against him. The couple unaware of their audience.

Watching them, Jehanne stiffened, felt a high wall spring up around her. *Dead in two years,*

Michael whispered. Pale as china, she smiled tightly, withdrew her hand from Alençon's. 'We should be getting back,' she said.

Alençon gazed up at her, smiling tenderly. 'No, we shouldn't.'

'Yes,' she said, standing up and brushing the grass from her lap. 'We should.'

PART IV

CHAPTER ONE

'I'm so happy I could kiss you,' Charles said when Jehanne brought him the news of their victory at Orléans. 'Truly you must be the Daughter of God,' he said, squeezing her hands, his small eyes shining, his orange houppelande billowing in the warm May breeze. They were standing in Charles's garden at Loches, and beyond the walls they could hear the voices of hundreds of peasants who'd gathered there, shouting, 'Pucelle! Pucelle! Pucelle!'

Jehanne wanted to take Charles to Reims right away. *Crown him fast*, Margaret said. *He's nothing without that crown*. And she knew it had to be done in Reims. Every French king since Clovis had been crowned in Reims. The French people would never accept a king unless he'd been crowned in the cathedral there. But here, Charles's old timidity returned. 'It's too dangerous,' he said, shaking his head. 'There are still too many Goddon strongholds between Chinon and Reims.'

He made Jehanne and her generals wait there in Loches for two weeks just to hear him say that. Said he was meeting with his council the whole time, but there were parties every night. She would hear the laughter, the music coming across the lawn, see Charles staggering around with La Trémöille, both of them drunk, laughing like fools. All the while Margaret chanted in her head: *Daughter of God, go go go. I will help you, go!*

Finally she could not wait anymore. Her men were growing restless. They needed to keep their momentum, fight while their blood was hot. She walked in on Charles and his council one morning—just walked in, didn't wait for the page to announce her. She knelt down and threw her arms around his legs. 'Oh, do not hold council for so long, my Dauphin!' she said. 'But come with me to Reims and accept a worthy crown.'

She tried to convince him that it was safe to go, that now was the time while the men were full of triumph, while the Goddons were cowering in their caves, terrified of the Maid who'd snatched Orléans so quickly, so easily, back from them. But he would not listen. 'Secure the Loire first, little Maid,' the Dauphin said. 'Make sure the way is clear, then I will go.'

CHAPTER TWO

Jehanne and Alençon returned to Orléans to gather their army. It had grown into an enormous thing by then. A whole continent of warriors, ecstatic, hungry for battle. In the two weeks they'd been gone, men had poured in from all over the country until there were two thousand knights, plus their squires and pages, plus archers and foot soldiers. Then there were the civilians. Who knows how many? Two or three thousand, La Hire said. 'Soon there won't be anyone left in the villages to rescue,' he joked.

The King had put Alençon in charge of the military command, though he was ordered to 'seek the Maid's counsel in all matters.' And with them came the generals: The Bastard and Rais and

Poton and La Hire in the lead. Rais 'pouring money into the army like a madman,' Alençon said. 'Now that the Queen's coffers are dry.' Rais feeding all the soldiers three times a day, buying new armor and artillery and horses. 'I've never seen such spending in my life.'

'We are very grateful, Baron,' Jehanne said when she came upon Rais in the camp one morning.

He was atop his stallion, with a ragged young boy seated in front of him, holding the pommel. The boy was perhaps six or seven with beautiful, sleepy black eyes and bare feet, his face dirty as the bottom of a shoe. 'Ah, Pucelle,' he said. 'The pleasure is mine.' He tousled the boy's hair. 'Thomas here and I were just on our way to find ourselves some breakfast, weren't we?'

The boy nodded.

Jehanne looked at Rais. 'I'm still not going to tell you about the voices,' she said.

The Baron laughed, his red lips curling up like a girl's. 'We shall see about that, little Maid,' he said. 'We shall see.'

*   *   *

By the time they rode out of the city in early June, there were more than eight thousand men riding behind her. Eight thousand men hearing Mass, confessing every morning. Eight thousand men without wine or women or cards to distract them, sober and eager to carry out the will of God.

They went first to Jargeau, then to Meung, then to Beaugency. All Goddon-occupied towns along the Loire. All fast, easy sieges: They took Jargeau

265

in two days, Meung in one day, Beaugency in two. 'Child's play!' La Hire shouted as he planted his flag atop the bridge at Meung. In Beaugency, they didn't even have to fight. The mayor came out with his hands up, waving a white shirt above his bald, pink head, shouting, 'Surrender! Please! We surrender!'

But from the beginning Jehanne sensed Patay would be different. *Patay*, she thinks, pictures flashing in her mind. The sea of corpses, the screaming horses.

Patay, my great triumph.
Patay, the killing place.

CHAPTER THREE

Toward evening, after the victory at Beaugency, a messenger had come flying into the French camp. A young, sunburned boy, very thin, all neck and elbows and flopping blond hair, his horse gasping, lathered with sweat. He said that Fastolf was nearby with an army of five thousand reinforcements from Paris. Fresh, trained soldiers, thousands of longbowmen. They'd joined up with Talbot and his men, and were hiding out somewhere in the forests north of Patay. No one knew exactly where. 'I saw them as they passed through Meung,' the boy said. 'I never seen so many longbowmen in my life.'

'Oh no,' said Mugot.

Jehanne turned, looked at him.

'They're just waiting there,' the boy said, his voice high, hysterical. 'Waiting to slaughter us.'

266

'Don't be an idiot,' she said. 'We just have to find them before they find us.'

The Bastard shook his head. Said they could not handle an open battle. 'Not with all those longbows. They'll destroy us.'

'No, they won't,' said Jehanne. She closed her eyes and turned her face to the sky. When she opened her eyes several moments later, they were blazing. 'This will be our greatest victory,' she said.

CHAPTER FOUR

We rode toward Patay. The men were afraid, but I said it must be done. My voices were clear. We must overtake them. We must hunt them down and overtake them.

When they started to get close, Jehanne sent scouts ahead—sixty or seventy of them fanning out through the forest, looking for the Goddon camp. Alençon and La Hire had the vanguard ready to fight, and they were waiting in the forest when two of the trackers came tearing back through the pines an hour later with red faces, shouting, 'We saw them! Holy Christ, we saw them! They're right here! The whole army!'

The English were camped in a valley not five hundred yards away, under a good cover of woods and brush. 'We never would've seen them,' said the breathless scout, 'but all of a sudden Paul and I hear all this shouting and yelling, and we can tell it's the Goddons just from their ugly accents, so we go running through the woods toward the voices, and when we get close, we hide behind some trees, and we see this huge red stag run past like its tail's on fire—a gorgeous beast, seven or eight points on him at least—and he goes galloping up over the hill, and a minute later about twenty Goddons come chasing after him, shooting at him. So Paul and I ran back to see where they'd come from, and the next thing you know, there's the whole Goddon army right there in front of us—most of 'em barely even awake yet, still walking around in their underwear and bare feet, eating their breakfast sausages.'

Jehanne saw it in her mind's eye: Three thousand Goddons still rubbing sleep from their eyes, their armor scattered all around them, gleaming in the new morning sun, their breastplates and helmets and the long-jointed silver fingers of their gauntlets lying useless on the ground . . . 'We must attack right now,' she said in a loud, hard voice. *Surprise them! Surprise is the key!*

She sent La Hire and Rais riding ahead with the vanguard to attack the camp immediately. She and Alençon and the Bastard and Poton stayed back with the rear guard, waiting to launch the second wave.

But there was no second wave. By the time Jehanne rode forward with her troops into the battlefield an hour later, it was over. A field littered with corpses and wandering, riderless horses. Fastolf had panicked, had run off into the woods with a handful of his men. All that was left were horses and bodies. A sea of two thousand dead and dying English. A small handful of dead French. No fighting. No rising fury, no voices saying *Gogogogogo*, no brave dash for survival, no hot rush of joy at finding yourself still alive when it

268

was over. Just your own soldiers standing and all the others fallen. Two thousand men cut down in less than half an hour. The dying calling out for their mothers and wives, calling out for God.

As she rode across the field, Jehanne saw a boy dragging himself toward her on his hands. His right leg was trailing behind him, the left one was gone, a lake of blood pulsed behind him. He regarded her with huge blue eyes. 'Wait,' said Jehanne, climbing down off her horse and running toward him.

'I'm all right,' he said. 'I can get up.' As if to prove his point, he pushed himself up onto his one knee and knelt before Jehanne for a moment in a swirling skirt of blood. 'See.' He smiled, wiped his cheek. Then his eyes went white in his head, and he fell to the ground.

She heard a scream then. A different scream from the others. It was coming from somewhere off to her left. Abruptly it cut off. She squinted, looked in that direction, and saw more bodies, also a sagging barn at the edge of the field. Like a sleepwalker she moved toward the barn, stepping over the bodies, not even noticing them, pulled as if by a hook through the barn door and into the dim, mote-filled sunlight where she heard now a low slapping sound that she followed into a stable where a boy leaned over a pile of hay with his dark head fallen forward into the sunlight, making a slow snoring sound in his throat. Very close behind him knelt a radiant, naked Gilles de Rais with a wet beard of blood, running his hands through a pile of objects on the hay, which Jehanne realized were the boy's stomach and intestines and liver.

The boy groaned. Blood poured from his

mouth. 'I know, my love,' said Rais, stroking the boy's face, pressing his cheek against the boy's cheek, painting his face with the boy's blood. The Baron closed his eyes. 'Oh Father, we ask that you carry this beautiful soul with you to Heaven now . . . we ask that you raise him up to your throne and embrace him in your everlasting love . . .' Very slowly, Jehanne backed away from the door and made her way back through the barn. Gilles de Rais never looked up.

Outside, Jehanne walked blindly across the field, seeing only Rais' bloody smile in front of her, and so she did not notice the wild-eyed Goddon who broke from the woods to her left and came running at her, tackling her from behind and locking his arm around her neck as they fell together to the ground. And she did not think when she pulled her little knife from its scabbard and sank it into the man's throat. And she did not think when she pulled the knife out of his neck and then stabbed him there eight more times, twisting the knife and screaming 'Die!' until the man stopped moving.

CHAPTER FIVE

I remember flowers and I remember people. People as far as I could see outside the cathedral, an ocean of them packed into the streets, up on the roofs, and on wagons and bridges, standing on the hills outside of town. It was more people than I had ever seen or would ever see again, all of them shouting and crying and cheering, and the sky full of flowers, petals

270

swirling and falling as the King came out in his new crown and splendid robes, and I remember that there were parties afterward, parties for weeks, it seemed, and I remember that I smiled and that I tried to be happy, but I was not happy.

*   *   *

I was not happy.

CHAPTER SIX

After Patay, Charles had come to meet them at Saint-Benôt-sur-Loire. He said they could go to Reims now. 'You've done it,' he said as she walked toward him, his lips trembling, his eyes shining with tears. 'You miraculous creature, you've done it.'

'God did it,' Jehanne said, thinking of the dead man with the knife in his throat. Thinking, *But who did that? Did He or did I?*

A strange time. *The time of celebrations and lies.* A sense of shadows gathering, viciousness whispered behind her back, plots made in hallways and staircases, a sinking feeling beneath the revelry. Death standing, smiling, behind the banquet feast. She found herself longing for home, longing for her mother and the sheep and the fields of Domrémy, the safety of the *bois chênu*.

At moments, for hours at a time, the people's joy buoyed her up, carried her along like a ship surging over the sea, for it was not the people who disliked her. To the people, she was the Daughter

271

of God, she deserved to be worshipped and adored. They came flooding into Gien from all across the country to join the great procession through the summer countryside toward Reims until Jehanne's army alone consisted of ten thousand men, all of them willing to fight without pay, to be a part of the Maid's holy mission. No, it was the churchmen and the King's counselors, La Trémöille and his friends, who frightened her, who made the hairs on the back of her neck stand up. They were the ones who glanced at her sideways at the banquets, who pinched their lips and shook their heads when they saw the Dauphin asking her for advice.

The coronation only made it worse. They hated the fact that she'd entered the great cathedral right beside Charles in his bare feet and nightshirt, carrying her white banner and walking next to him as they made their way down the marble aisle toward the altar while La Hire and Alençon and the Bastard and Rais walked behind, Rais carrying the flag of France, the *oriflamme*, Rais whom Charles would name Marshal of France later that day. They hated the fact that she'd remained beside the King throughout the ceremony, watching as the Archbishop anointed him with the sacred oil and then dressed him in the long purple-velvet houppelande with the ermine mantle, watching as the Archbishop slid the gold ring over Charles's thin finger and lowered the golden crown on his small, bumpy head. They hated that she'd stepped up near Charles in the nave as he turned to face his people as their king, and more than anything, oh, more than anything, they hated that the loudest roaring of the day came when the Maid

272

stepped forward and took her place at his side.

She had heard the churchman behind her gasp when she did it, heard a sharp, ugly cough from La Trémöille. But she would not step back. She stood beside Charles, both of them weeping, and she thought, *I did this. I, the peasant girl, and God inside me, together we did it. It's real.*

Afterward, when the sky was full of flowers and the streets of Reims were flooded with people, she saw one of the churchmen and La Trémöille whispering together outside the cathedral, whispering and glancing over at her, and when she saw them, a dark shadow passed over her heart. A voice in her head said, *Yes, I will die soon.*

CHAPTER SEVEN

Jehanne sat beside the King at the feast that followed the coronation at the Palace of Tau and at all the celebrations that took place that week. Jehanne smiling and talking, laughing, receiving her admirers, the steady stream of people who came to her with shining eyes, kneeling and bowing their heads. 'Astonishing,' they said as platters of oysters and songbirds were laid on the table. 'Never have such wonders been done, never on the earth.' Gamely she told stories of the triumphs and Orléans and Patay. The flaming boat full of pitch burning down the drawbridge. Glasdale and all his knights falling into the river at Les Tourelles. The great red stag that led them to triumph in Patay. But once the compliments were finished, once the adulation had spent itself, what was there to say?

273

'What next?' they asked, and Jehanne said, 'Paris is next. On to Paris.' But the King looked away when she said this, coughed into his hand, and grimaced, muttered, 'We'll see.'

Everyone admired her, but no one much liked her. No one dared ask her to dance. When she spoke of God, the churchmen looked at her with naked envy. When she spoke of more war, the courtiers looked nervous, hesitant. It was too much to speak of more. To speak of Paris. What had happened was so astonishing, so completely beyond belief that no one dared to think of *more*.

She understood. Part of her understood. She saw the necessity of it. A rest. But her blood wanted only to be on a horse, fighting, completing her mission, charging toward the horizon, charging away from the accusing eyes of the dead man whose throat she'd cut, the man who woke her every night at Reims saying, *You'll join me soon enough, witch. Soon enough you'll be one of us too*.

She had no place in celebrations, in breathing and letting it all sink in. She sat beside the King and smiled gamely, lifted her glass of watered-down wine for toasts, told herself, *Enjoy this, relax, it is necessary*, but it was not possible for her. As the glasses clinked and glittered, as Charles caressed his new mistress's plump white shoulder and the generals leaned back in their chairs and waxed nostalgic about the joy of sleeping out under the stars, about how they had almost retreated at Saint Loup and how they killed the giant at Augustins, the war drums inside Jehanne beat hard. Not voices now, but drums pounding: *Gogogogogogogo*. Drums pounding: *Notimenotimenotime*. At times, when she was alone, they grew wild, desperate. She stood before the gilded oval mirror in her bedroom at Loches, looked at herself and said: 'You'll be finished in a year. You must complete your mission. Take Paris now, while you can.'

And later, when she lay awake at night in her splendid silken bed, staring at the ceiling, it seemed that only Christ would understand this peculiar and lonesome sadness, this terrible knowing that the end is near, this desperation to do what must be done before the curtain falls, while those around you, those who could not possibly know the future, want only to ride the pleasure while it lasts, to celebrate how far they'd come and be grateful for it. To live.

CHAPTER EIGHT

The day after the coronation Jehanne dictated a letter to Philip, the Duke of Burgundy.

> Prince of Burgundy, I pray of you—I beg and humbly supplicate—that you make no more war with the holy kingdom of France. Withdraw your people swiftly from the towns and fortresses of this holy kingdom, and on behalf of the gentle King of France, I say he is ready to make peace with you, by his honor.

She knew Burgundy would not surrender. She knew Burgundy would never leave Paris until he was dragged out by the hair. But she knew too that she must ask. *Give them a chance*, Catherine had said in Orléans. Catherine, who had not spoken to her since Patay. Not one of the saints had spoken to her since Patay.

She did not consult with the King or anyone else before she sent the letter. She sent her own herald to deliver it to Paris.

The Duke did not respond.

CHAPTER NINE

The King rose from his bed in the early light at Château-Thierry. Left behind the smooth, curving back and tiny rose-brown nipples of his new mistress, and walked into his sitting room in his white nightdress, hair trailing down his back in thin, oiled tentacles. He sat quietly by the window, watching the mist rise off the river. Georges de La Trémöille found him there. 'Well, King, what will you do now?'

'Whatever the Maid's council tells us, I imagine.'

La Trémöille looked at Charles. 'Really?'

'What would you suggest, La Trémöille?'

La Trémöille pursed his lips. 'All respect to the Maid, Majesty, but if you keep letting a seventeen-year-old holy freak lead you around by the nose, it's going to be difficult for the rest of Europe to take you seriously. Why not use your new power to negotiate a bit with Burgundy? Why waste all this money on battle when you're already sunk to the neck in debt? Why kill when you can make peace with words? Why not show the people what a wise and powerful king they've crowned, show them that you will end this war like the nobleman that you are?'

CHAPTER TEN

Under a hot, damp, green sky, Jehanne paced the roof of the castle, unable to keep still. 'This is insane,' she said. 'You cannot do this. Burgundy will never honor any truce you make with him. You know that.'

The King stood nearby, gazing into the fish pool, watching the trout he was going to eat for dinner as they moved slowly through the water, their thick gray backs shining in the sun. 'He's just buying himself time,' she continued, her face very red. 'He's trying to keep us from attacking while he fortifies the city, you know it.'

'What I know, Maid, is that we are in a very different position with the English now than we have been in some time, and if there's any way to use our advantage to create peace, I want to find it.'

'But Burgundy doesn't believe in peace,' Jehanne said. 'He's proven it over and over again. You know this. You've seen it as well as I have. He has no idea of honor or fairness, all he cares about is snatching as much of France as he can.'

The King turned his head, looked off toward the frothing green vineyard on a nearby hill. 'There is much that you cannot possibly understand about the ruling of a country,' he said quietly. 'And while I am eternally grateful for all that you've done for France, I am also asking you to trust me when I say that negotiating for peace is the best course of action for now.'

Jehanne rubbed her hands over her face. 'But we're in such a good position right now; after the coronation and all the victories we had this summer, the English are terrified of us. I know we could take Paris if we attacked now. I know it!'

The King continued looking at the vineyard. Studying it as if he might find wisdom there. 'Be that as it may, my order to you is to rest and enjoy your victory for a time now. Let me consider carefully the best way to proceed.'

Jehanne opened her mouth to speak, but the King shook his head. 'That will be all now, Pucelle. Thank you.'

CHAPTER ELEVEN

The action, when they finally took it, was a slow zigzag of advancing and retreating in the general direction of Paris. A perfect map of the King's uncertainty. When Jehanne got his ear, poured some of God's fire into it, they surged forward. When La Trémöille was there, whispering silken words of negotiation and appeasement, they fell back. No one could tell what Charles would do next. Would he retreat to the Loire, or would he travel to Paris after all? No one knew. More than anything, it seemed, he was enjoying being king. Enjoying traveling through all the towns, soaking in the worship, the adoration after all those years in the shadows. All the towns that the English had occupied brought him their keys that

278

summer. Soissons, Laon, Créchy-en-Brie, Provins, Coulomiers, they all came back. Pledged their allegiance to France.

There were huge crowds wherever they went. Enormous. In one village it took them six hours to go half a mile. Hundreds, sometimes thousands, of people would line up in the roads, thronging Jehanne and the King as they rode through, shouting and reaching out to touch the King's hands, thinking that the Holy Ampoule had given him the power to cure the sick, the blind, the crippled. Reaching out to Jehanne, believing her the Daughter of God, begging her to touch them, to cure them of plague, blindness, leprosy, syphilis, sterility. 'I can't do anything,' she said, but they didn't listen. 'Just one touch, Pucelle,' they said. 'Just one.'

It took them thirty-six days to reach the outskirts of Paris, the town of Compiègne, and by then, many of the Maid's best knights had grown restless and drifted off, returned home to their harvests, their wives, their families. The Bastard and La Hire left in mid-August. 'Sorry, darling, but I'll grow old waiting around for Charlie to get his balls up,' La Hire said, hugging her hard, the bells on his cloak jingling as if there were something to be happy about. Pierrelot stayed on. 'I'll stop when you stop,' he said to Jehanne, but Jean left, saying the family needed him in Domrémy. 'Someone's got to keep old Jacques in line,' he said in a joking tone, but no one laughed.

The first hints of autumn had begun to surface by then. A few orange trees among all the green, a chill edge in the air some evenings—and as it happened, the men's thoughts returned to their real lives. Cows. Taxes. Wheat. Sex. Wine. You could feel it: the miraculous summer coming to a close. The days growing shorter. The grand momentum slowly but surely dissolving.

CHAPTER TWELVE

It was the letter from Bedford that changed things. The letter that the Duke of Bedford sent to us in Compiègne at the end of August. A page of insults. He called the King a bastard and a murderer. Called me a dissolute whore. Said if Charles and I wanted Paris, we would have to fight him for it. It was a provocation, obviously. He was nearby with his troops, we knew that. He was spoiling for a fight. But Charles refused. Would not consider it. Would not even respond to the Duke's letter.

I behaved very badly then. I wept and shouted, said he was gutless, a coward—anything I could think of, anything to get him angry, to make him fight back, but he just stood there looking at me, very quiet. I could see that I exhausted him. Could see he was growing tired of me. 'Be patient, Jehanne,' he said. 'We're having good talks with Burgundy. Let's see what a little diplomacy will do.'

Three days later we learned that thirty-five hundred English knights were marching toward Paris to fortify the city. That was what the truce accomplished. That was what his diplomacy did. It gave Burgundy enough time to turn his city into a fortress. And still Charles refused to fight. The next week Charles and Burgundy made yet another truce.

280

CHAPTER THIRTEEN

The fire outside of Alençon's tent burned sideways in the wind. A ragged red flag swaying and shifting in the night. Jehanne was sitting on a log, staring into the fire, when Alençon stepped outside and saw her there. He held a dented pewter cup of wine in one hand. 'What are you doing, little Maid?' he said.

She looked up at him, flames crackling and dancing behind her head like a halo of fire, her cheeks flushed with heat. 'We could just go,' she said.

The Duke smiled, sat down on the log beside her, stretched his legs out in front of him toward the heat. 'To Paris?'

She nodded. Picked up a stick and poked idly at the coals. 'Who knows when the King will stop with this truce nonsense. We're losing men every day. We need to go now.'

'You want to go without his permission?'

'What can he do to us? If we lose, he'll scold us. If we win, he'll kiss our feet.'

The Duke scratched his chin. Closed his eyes, drinking in the heat of the fire. 'He could do more than scold us, you know.'

'He won't. He likes you too much and he's too afraid of me.' She turned her face toward him. 'I can't stand this anymore. Paris is just sitting there, waiting for us to grab it, while the King frets and second-guesses himself. All of my voices tell me now is the time; we must act, Duke. I'll never forgive myself if we don't.'

281

'We can't take the King's army. The Baron de Rais and Poton will come with their men, of course, but that makes us five hundred at best.'

'I don't want the Baron,' she said.

Alençon smiled. 'Without him, we are nothing. Hardly enough to take a bridge, much less a city.'

She nodded. Was silent for a time.

'So five hundred, then,' she said at last.

'It's not many. I don't know if it's enough.'

She touched his cheek. 'You forget the angels.'

The Duke smiled. 'And how many angels are there with us?'

'More than you can count,' she said.

CHAPTER FOURTEEN

They rode out a few days later, just before dawn. Jehanne and Alençon and their corps of warriors. Poton with his troop of ragged mercenaries. Gilles de Rais with his glittering circus. Jehanne could not look at Rais. Could not speak to him. She turned her horse and rode away when she saw him coming toward her. 'Hail, Pucelle!' he shouted. Jehanne did not respond.

It was a clear, windy autumn day. The first real chill was in the air, and Jehanne's horse was frisking and straining to run beneath her. She looked over at Alençon, who rode up grinning alongside her and kicked his horse into a canter, so she urged her horse forward as well, and soon she and Alençon were galloping over the sloping yellow fields, racing through the golden rod toward the rounded hills; and the sky was very blue and the air smelled of wood smoke and the wind was roaring across her face as she rode, roaring cold and fresh through her hair, and it seemed to her that the old magic was upon them then. That they were righteous and blessed, and on their way to carry out God's dearest wish. *Surely He'll protect us*, she thought. *Surely this is His wish*.

They made camp outside of Paris, in the town of Saint-Denis. Jehanne and Alençon and Rais and Poton and their five hundred soldiers. On their first night there, she awoke to the sound of laughter. High, flowering laughter floating out across the night field. Girl's laughter. And something else too. A drum. She sat up and pushed back her blanket. Her eyes wide, her ears snapped open like a cat's. Into the blackness she peered, the high yellow campfires blooming like otherworldly tulips against the deep night sky. Again the laughter. Jehanne's nostrils flared. Quickly she scrambled to her feet, picked up her sword, and followed the sound through the tall grass. Creeping. Silent. Ahead to the left, through a stand of pines, she saw a fire larger than the rest, a raging fire around which a motley crowd of soldiers had assembled, and around which a young brown-skinned woman danced to the drum in a long red skirt, feet bare, dark curling hair long and loose and gilded in the firelight, shoulders and teeth gleaming as she went around the flames, skirts pulled up in her fists, her throat long and smooth, as a small, smiling man patted the drum with the heels of his hands and the soldiers cheered and laughed.

She walked into the circle. Walked up to the dancing girl in the red skirt. 'What are you doing here?'

The girl was not impressed. 'What does it look like?'

'We're just having a bit of fun, Maid,' said one of the soldiers.

'You know whores are forbidden in my camp.'

'Why, because the men have to remain pure for battle?' the woman said in a scornful tone.

Jehanne looked at her.

The dancer spat on the ground. 'Everyone knows you don't have the guts to attack Paris.'

Jehanne smiled, then raised her sword over her head and hit the woman with the flat of it so hard that the sword broke in half. The woman fell to the ground. Everyone around the campfire stood frozen, eyes wide as coins. Jehanne stared back at them. 'I said no whores in camp.'

*   *   *

Jehanne sighs now, leans her head against the wall of her cell. 'I knew it was wrong,' she says. 'I knew I would pay for it. But the fire in my blood was so strong. All the months of waiting on the King, of watching my beautiful army drift away, of sitting around in those ridiculous castles, waiting. I could not bear it anymore. I knew my power was fading; I could feel the magic draining out of me little by little every day. A terrible feeling. Like watching your own blood pour out of your body. And I did not know why. I prayed more than ever before. I lay on the floor in the churches for hours, begging for guidance, for help, for strength. But something had broken. The winds had changed. And all I knew was that I had to recapture Paris, that the

English had to be run out of France, that this was what God had instructed me to do, and that no one seemed willing to listen to me anymore. The King went back to being a coward, the soldiers went back to their whoring and drinking. It was as if they could only bear so much holiness in their lives. As if they suddenly had to go back to being animals again, and no matter what I said or how many times I told them God could not help them if they behaved this way, they would not listen. They wanted wine, rest, women, laughter, food. They'd had as much of God as they could bear.'

CHAPTER FIFTEEN

The Duke of Alençon was standing in her tent when she awoke. Unshaven, unwashed, a dark look in his eyes. Jehanne sat up, rubbed her eyes, blinked. 'Is it true?' he said.

'Is what true?'

'About the whore?'

'What did they say?'

The Duke glanced at the floor. Then back at Jehanne. 'That you hit her so hard over the head your sword broke in half. She may not live, Jehanne.'

She looked away from him, her ears ringing with blood.

'Did you do it?'

Suddenly her face broke and tears poured down her cheeks. She nodded, pressed her fingers against her eyes.

'What were you thinking?'

'I didn't mean to hit her that hard,' she said, sobbing. 'They know they aren't allowed to have whores in camp.'

The Duke knelt down beside her and laid his hand on her shoulder.

She looked up at him with red eyes. Spoke in choked, sodden words. 'Nobody listens to me anymore.'

CHAPTER SIXTEEN

She stood in the high pines along the eastern edge of the camp that ran downhill toward the river. She had a place there. A small clearing just above the riverbank where the earth was carpeted in brown pine needles, and the trees were very tall and very old, and there, in that same place, were some young pine saplings with their feathery, light green needles, fernlike in their delicacy, fanning out silently in the still cool air with the old alligator bark of the ancient trees behind them and the long golden river sliding over the rocks beyond. In this place, the black branch of one thick old tree reached out far over the river, and its smallest branches trailed along the surface like fingers, and the light fell and glittered wonderfully on the water, and she could feel her God there, inside of her, could be gentled and calmed by Him as she watched the sun pour down in long shafts and then splinter out across the surface of the water like shards of a shattered mirror. She rested her hand against the rough trunk of the tree and then leaned her whole body against it, soaking in the silence, the curious comfort of leaning up against something so old, listening to the never-ending movement of the water. After a long time, she knelt down and pressed her palms against the earth. She bowed her head. *Forgive me*, she said. *Forgive my wickedness. My temper. My violence. My impatience*. Her shoulders slumped. *Please forgive me*.

CHAPTER SEVENTEEN

'It occurs to me, Charles, that we could go ahead and let the Maid attack Paris.'

'Is that not what you've been advising me against for the last month, Georges?'

'Indeed it is, but I've realized that there are several things we have not properly considered here.'

'And what are those?'

'The first is that the Maid is actually very popular in Paris. Far more popular than you. Possibly more popular than Burgundy too.'

'*Mmm*.'

'So it occurred to me that if she does manage to get inside the city, the people might well rally behind her and put her on the throne instead of you. Perhaps that's even what she's hoping for.'

'That's insane.'

La Trémöille shook his head. 'Paris is afraid of you and your family, Charles. They believe your parents destroyed their country. Whereas the Maid, well, the Maid has accomplished a great deal of good for France in a very short period of time.'

287

'What is your point, Georges?'

La Trémöille smiled. Stroked his lips with two fingers. Knew he was conjuring terrible memories from Charles's childhood now. The older brothers poisoned by Burgundy, the whore mother shaming him throughout the city, disinheriting him, calling him a bastard, the poor mad father shrieking in the halls of the Louvre. 'Well, it seems to me that it would be best for all concerned if the Maid did not succeed in her attack on Paris.'

Charles cocked an eyebrow. 'She doesn't have much chance of it without my army behind her.'

'Indeed. But if she attacks Paris without your support, that's not going to look very good for you either. People will say, "Why did he not support the Maid? It's his fault that she lost."'

Charles was silent for a little while. Thinking. 'So either way it's terrible. If she gets into Paris, there's a good chance the people will put her on the throne. And if she fails, everyone will blame me . . . as always . . .' Charles closed his eyes, pressed his fingertips against his eyelids. 'Oh Jesus.'

'Yes. But this morning I thought, *Well. What if our army goes along with the Maid to Paris, marches right up to the walls with her, but doesn't attack? Is secretly forbidden from attacking?*

Charles blinked.

'So she attacks with just the five hundred men she's got now?'

'Yes.'

'Then she will fail and her reputation will be ruined, but—'

La Trémöille smiled. 'None of it will be your fault.'

CHAPTER EIGHTEEN

'Somehow Alençon convinced Charles to bring the army to us in Saint-Denis. I don't know how. He rode away from camp one day, and when he returned, his eyes were very bright, and he came running toward my tent. "Guess where I've been."'

Jehanne smiles. 'He was so kind, Alençon. He tried so hard.' She exhales, regards Massieu in the blue predawn light. The old priest nods, looks as if he might weep. 'But there was something off about it from the start. The King's army came along with us, but not one of them would look me in the eye. Men who just a few weeks earlier were kneeling at my feet. Calling me the Daughter of God. Calling themselves the Maid's Army. None of them would look me in the eye now. At some point I realized that Charles must have ordered them not to attack. 'Humor her. Go with her to Paris. See how things are there. But do not, under any circumstances, attack.' I could feel it. They were no longer mine. Not the way they'd been in Orléans. I tried to lead them on anyway, shouted at them to fight for their freedom, begged them to fight for their freedom, but the whole time I knew it was falling apart. I knew my days were numbered.'

CHAPTER NINETEEN

They attacked paris on September the eighth. The Festival of the Nativity of the Virgin. A holy day. A

289

day, which, in previous times, Jehanne would have declared off-limits for fighting. But such piety did not seem possible to her now. The soldiers were restless. The generals were pushing to attack. 'If we don't hurry, we'll lose our chance,' said Poton. 'This is it.' The fire inside her was roaring, desperate, the drum pounding a steady chant: *attack, attack, attack.*

She begged her saints for guidance, but they did not come. *Please*, she said, kneeling at the chapel in Saint-Denis. *I fear that if we do not attack tomorrow, we'll never get another chance. The King changes his mind so often it's a miracle they're here right now . . .*

But the voices did not come. The light did not come.

She wept. Screamed, *Where are you?*

Why won't you come?

CHAPTER TWENTY

They approached the city very early in the morning, through the pig markets that lay outside the city walls, under a light gray drizzle. A maze of wooden pens and troughs and ramshackle barns, the mud-painted animals watching as the soldiers rode through on their horses, the water in the troughs rippling out in circles as the weight of the moving army shook the earth. 'Today we take Paris,' said Mugot, beaming as he rode alongside Jehanne.

'Yes,' she said, tousling the gold mushroom cap of her page's hair.

It was promising at first. They were thousands of men on this clear, early autumn day, all in good armor, all armed with their wooden shields and culverins, their lances and bows and swords. Their wagons piled high with trembling gray mountains of gunpowder, and as they neared the city walls, there arose for a moment a shimmer of the old glory in the air. A cry went up among the men as they rode. 'She will put the King in Paris if it is left to her!'

Moving in neat, glittering rows, they packed in tightly about the high, gray-stone city walls, atop which its silent defenders stood, lined up like birds on a wire to greet them. Dark heads, near black in the distance, with the sun not fully overhead yet, faces unseen, only a long row of heads and shoulders, and the menacing glint of their weapons. Between the French soldiers and the wall lay a broad green moat, its surface velvety with algae. Silently the line of men waited at the top of the wall, watching, their faces dark, closed like stones.

The moat was very deep; they had to build a bridge to get across it. The men passed wood forward from the back of the army—large bundles of logs and branches weighed down with rocks, whole carts and rock-filled barrels were fed into the moat until a bizarre makeshift bridge began to rise from the water—green and monstrous, like a shipwreck raised from the bottom of the sea. When it was finished, Jehanne ordered the men across with their ladders and cannons and culverins, and then she hopped down off her horse and walked up to stand alongside them at the edge of the moat. She pressed her fingers into a cone around her

291

mouth and shouted up at the Goddons on the wall: 'Men of Paris, yield to us quickly, for Jesus' sake. For if you do not yield before night, we will enter by force and you will all be put to death without mercy.'

The sound of laughter floated down slowly from the top of the wall. Behind it a chorus of disembodied voices, echoing in the air.

'Go back home, you crazy cunt.'

Then a volley of explosions cracked open the air, and a rain of iron cannonballs fell onto the soldiers near the edge of the moat. Alençon's cousin Richard stood beside him one moment, loading his bow, and the next, a cannonball buried itself so deep in his head that only the top of the black ball could be seen, rising up from his skull like a wicked tumor. 'Oh,' the man said, blinking. Then he fell down. Behind him the red sun sank into the hills, the sky gray as ash. 'Jesus, Richard!' cried Alençon, kneeling beside him, his face freckled with blood. But the man was no longer breathing.

Beside Jehanne, Poton and Rais rolled a catapult into place. Rais, eyes dangerously alight, set the arm of the catapult, then picked up a pitch-covered rock and placed it into the bowl of the machine. He grabbed his page's torch and touched it to the rock. 'Now, burn,' said Rais, smiling as the ball burst into a globe of orange fire.

A moment later the fireball was soaring through the blue sky, and then stopping very abruptly as it entered the ribcage of one of the Burgundian archers on top of the wall. For a moment the man stood motionless on the wall, his chest illuminated as if his heart had caught fire. Then he tipped forward and fell through the air.

A splash like a wild, white flower rose up out of the green moat. Then the white flower collapsed, sank into rolling waves of foam. And the water was still and green again.

'Bloody bitch,' someone shouted from high on the wall. Jehanne looked up in the direction of the shout, and as she did, she felt a white-hot flash of pain in her leg. She looked down. An iron crossbow bolt was sticking out of her thigh. Her thigh seemed oddly distant from her, as if she had risen above her own body. An ugly thing, the bolt, thick and black and sharp, like the tooth of a monster. Blood was pumping out around it like oil, red and alive. 'The Maid!' cried Mugot. 'The Maid's hit.' He ran toward her, the lovely white silk of her standard waving behind him like a flag above the sea of blood and death, and then his face changed suddenly, as if his skin had been torn downward. Surprise, then shock. His skin gone gray. The air around him whizzing terribly.

A bolt had nailed his foot to the ground. The boy looked down in amazement, then raised the visor of his helmet, and as he did, another bolt sank into the center of his forehead. That bolt, Jehanne would think later, was like a third eye foreseeing a black and terrible future. 'Oh no,' he said. A long tear of blood ran down his face.

'Mugot!' Jehanne cried.

The men around Jehanne stood frozen as the page attempted to move forward. He took a step to the left, and then the bolt pulled him backward, made him wheel his arms like a drunk working to steady himself. 'Sorry,' he said, as blood poured from his ears. He sat down, the white banner sinking into the mud beside him.

Overhead the black sky continued spitting down arrows, a waterfall of arrows and cannonballs pouring over the Paris wall and raining death upon the French. The King's army remained at a safe distance. Did not attack. The men up on the ladders had stopped climbing and were looking back toward where Jehanne stood beside the fallen boy and the fallen standard.

'Don't stop!' she cried. 'Keep going! Keep going!'

Rais stepped in. 'Don't be an idiot, Jehanne. You're hurt.'

'Get away from me,' she screamed. Her face white, bloodless. 'Get away from me.'

He ignored her, picked her up, and cradled her as he would a child as he shoved through the raging sea of men and arrows, making his way toward the earthen ramparts that were the first line of the city's defenses. Jehanne fought him, kicking and sobbing. 'Don't touch me. Don't you dare touch me.'

The Baron looked at her. Then he looked at Poton. 'Poor thing's lost her mind,' he said.

*   *   *

The soldiers continued their doomed attack on Paris until night fell, but they came no closer to getting over the wall and inside the city. When he saw the pale skull of the moon rise over the hills, Alençon threw his longbow on the ground and ordered their retreat. 'Eight hours of fighting and still not one Frenchman over the walls,' he said to Poton as they watched the slow parade of weary,

294

mud-caked troops riding back through the earthen works and ditches.

'Would have helped if the King's bloody men had lent a hand!' spat Poton. He picked up his long ax and threw it into the moat.

Gilles de Rais was looking at the sky. 'And so the spell is broken,' he said quietly.

Alençon's head snapped toward Rais. 'Don't say that!' he said. 'Don't you dare say that.'

The Baron laughed, gestured toward the royal army as it disappeared in the distance. Then he looked to the Maid, who lay motionless beneath a blanket in a wagon. 'Whether I say it or not, it's still the truth.'

Slowly the rest of the French soldiers retreated through the pig market, their shoulders slumped, the bodies of the wounded soldiers folded over the backs of horses, and the bodies of the dead piled high in the wagons, their stray, bloody hands and steel-tipped boots dangling over the sides, bouncing lightly with the jolts of the wagon, as if they were waving a half-hearted good-bye.

CHAPTER TWENTY-ONE

She woke in the pale first light to an aching leg and no memory of why it ached. It had been too dark to pitch the tents when they made camp, so they'd built a scattering of campfires in a long, flat meadow several miles outside the city and slept around them, wrapped in the cloaks and blankets they had with them. The temperature had dropped in the night—Jehanne's cheeks and nose were red with cold, and when she opened her eyes, she saw that the field around her was blue and soft with dew, and that her blanket wore a pale skin of dew and that the dew also hung in the trees alongside the meadow, making them seem like a world of ghosts dissolving in the first light.

She reached down and touched her thigh. Felt that it was wrapped tightly in cloth. When she touched the cloth on the top part of her thigh, she felt a sticky dampness that sent a chill down her spine. Now she remembered. The failure. Her failed promise to enter Paris.

She closed her eyes and let her head fall back against the cloak she'd folded up on the grass and used as a pillow. When she opened her eyes a little while later, she gazed up at the pale blue-white sky and thought how recently such a sky had seemed like the sky of a new and powerful France. Her France. A place of God and faith and victory. *No more*, she thought. *Not anymore . . .*

*   *   *

'Maybe I wanted it too badly,' she says to Massieu. 'Maybe it mattered too much. Maybe God saw that I had become afraid of dying, afraid of losing my power. Maybe the power had corrupted me, made me proud and vain and arrogant, and so He decided to take it away. I don't know. I am only human. But why keep filling me with the urge to fight, filling me full of such wild fighting fire that I could hardly sit still, and then thwart me at every turn until I knew not how to serve Him or whom to trust? Why not let the fire die out, why not let me return to my mother and Domrémy and the sheep?

'Oh, I cannot tell you the pain of it, what it felt like to have all that warrior fire raging inside, all that hunger to run and ride and fight, my blood singing, *Go, go, go,* and yet not being able to go. Being cut down, betrayed, humiliated over and over again every day when all I ever wanted was to serve Him, to carry out the mission He'd given me.

'Maybe I was too hungry. Maybe I was too proud. Oh, but I was only seventeen, Lord. Why would you not forgive me my flaws? Why punish me for the very urges and fires you poured into me?'

CHAPTER TWENTY-TWO

In the morning she shook Alençon's blanketed shoulder until he snorted and sat up suddenly. 'What is it?' he said, a wild look in his eyes, as if wolves had been chasing him through his dreams.

'Let's go. We have to attack again.'

The Duke rubbed his eyes. Looked at her. 'We don't have enough men. It's impossible.'

'For God, nothing is impossible,' she said.

He sighed. Looked at her. 'What do your voices say?'

Jehanne did not answer.

They were quiet for some time.

'It will be over for me if I fail now,' she said at last, looking at him. 'Everything will be over if I fail.'

'You don't know that.'

'Yes I do.'

It was a small company of warriors that rode out

of camp that morning. Jehanne and Alençon and perhaps seventy others, looking more like exhausted wanderers than great knights and generals of war. Gilles de Rais was not among them. Gilles de Rais and his men had ridden off that morning without a word.

They did not approach Paris by the pig market this time. Instead they rode to a place several miles down the river, where Alençon's men had constructed another bridge several days earlier.

It lay before them, a rough, crooked wood structure that rose over an expanse of glittering green water and landed on a bank of Paris that was barely walled or even fortified, for the deep, broad Seine had seemed a worthy defense by itself. Jehanne let out a whoop of joy when she saw it. 'It's wonderful,' she said. She looked at Alençon with shining eyes. 'Oh, my Duke, you are a worthy man.'

She turned and beamed at the men. 'Now we shall have them, men!' she shouted. 'Paris will be ours this day!'

The Duke looked at the ground. As he did, there came the sound of hoofbeats behind them. He and Jehanne turned toward the road, where a man dressed in a blue satin tunic embroidered with a gold fleur-de-lis was riding toward them on a small chestnut pony. 'Message from the King,' he said, when he and the panting horse stood before them. A small, fox-faced man with large, moist eyes that began to look almost tearful as he took in the bridge and the small troop of warriors. He pulled a scroll from a sack on his saddle, unrolled it with a long W of regret carved in his forehead, and read: 'I, King Charles VII of France, command

298

that the Maid and the Duke of Alençon and their men return immediately to Saint-Denis where a matter of great urgency awaits them.'

The girl glanced at Alençon. Then she turned to the messenger. 'We're about to mount an attack here. What is this matter of great urgency that requires our immediate return to Saint-Denis?'

'His Majesty did not say,' said the sad-eyed man. 'I'm sorry.'

*   *   *

Later that night they learned what had required their immediate return. Jehanne and the Duke and their knights were gathered around the campfire in Saint-Denis, eating in heavy silence when a boy, breathless and red-faced, ran into the flickering circle of firelight and stood panting with his hands on his knees. When he could speak, he said, 'They've burned the Duke of Alençon's bridge. The King's men have burned down the Duke's bridge.'

Jehanne looked at him. 'You lie.'

'I do not,' said the boy. 'I stayed behind to see what would happen, as the Duke himself instructed me to, and around sunset I saw them ride in and douse it with oil and light it on fire with their torches,' he said. 'I swear on my mother's life. The bridge is gone, it's just smoking cinders now. The river has washed most of it away.'

Jehanne looked at Alençon, her heart banging in her chest.

'He would not do that,' Alençon said. 'Charles would not do that.'

The messenger put his hands out in front of

him, as if to ward off a blow. 'I'm just telling what I saw, Your Grace. They say the King's preparing to return to the castle at Loches in the morning,' the messenger continued. 'I rode past their camp. They're packing everything up.'

A knot of fury appeared in Jehanne's jaw, and her nostrils flared wide, like those of a horse. 'That bastard,' she spat. She threw her stick down in the fire and walked off into the darkness.

CHAPTER TWENTY-THREE

She spent the night alone in the forest. Wandering blindly through the spindled black world of shadows in the high old pines, screaming a deep and terrible animal scream, as if her own infant had been gutted before her eyes. Through the dark corridors of the trees she walked, howling those raw, inhuman sounds, screaming for hours, for years, it seemed, until at last she collapsed at the base of an evergreen and wept, her armored back heaving, her face pressed against the trunk of the old tree as if it might whisper an explanation to her, as if it might lift her into its arms and gentle her against the unfathomable night. 'Oh God,' she whispered. 'What am I to do?'

CHAPTER TWENTY-FOUR

In the morning, the rain fell softly through the layered branches of the pines and down onto

Jehanne's cheeks and hair. She stood, wiped her face with her hands, and then walked out of the forest. Her eyes were cool, as if she bore no relation to the creature that had grieved so wildly in the night. The camp was still silent when she reached it. The low, dying fires hissing and steaming faintly in the rain, the men lying on their backs with their mouths open, some with empty wine casks in their hands, others with whores, their limbs entangled, oblivious to the rain. Jehanne continued walking. When she reached her own campsite, she packed a sack of clothes, saddled her horse, and rode down the wet red-dirt road into the village of Saint-Denis.

A silent ride. The world had changed overnight. It felt distant to her now. Foreign. For the first time she saw God nowhere. The fields were just fields, green and damp. The trees, just trees, wood and leaves. The sky gray and flat and having nothing to do with her. None of it having anything to do with her. And there was comfort in this somehow, in the numbness, the cool remove. A strange relief in seeing the world around her as simply a world of things, no Godthings or magical things, not loving things or beautiful things. Simply things. They did not touch her. They were nothing to do with her.

The rain dripped quietly off the slate roof of the old abbey church in Saint-Denis and the high, crooked oaks that sheltered it. Jehanne stood in her armor, still as a scarecrow at the altar of the famous church, a small, sturdy figure cast in silver. The church was dim in the rain that day, and she enjoyed the fact that it no longer sang to her. That the stained windows did not throw rainbows on her face and that the flicker of candles no longer filled her with the urge to weep with joy. And she thought that even if it had been a glorious day, a day of sunlight and warm spring breezes flowing through the open windows and green trees rustling outside, she would not have cared. She looked at the many rusted suits of armor that hung on the walls of the church. Hundreds of them, ghostly metal war shells that had been shed and donated by those knights wounded in defense of France, to honor the King and the realm. *Warrior selves hung up to rest. Warriors saying this life is finished, I have no more use for this hard metal skin, for this killing suit I donned in the name of God and France. Take it from me.*

Slowly she lifted her silver helmet from her head and laid it on the stone floor before the altar. After that came her breastplate and her greaves, her gauntlets and her besagews and her chain mail, until it all lay on the floor before her in a metal heap, lifeless, surrendered, and Jehanne stood in her brown linen tunic and stockings, small and pale, looking at the armor with cold eyes, as if it belonged to someone else.

CHAPTER TWENTY-FIVE

Most of the volunteers had left already, had decided to make their own way back to their homes in time for the harvest. And so it was perhaps just two hundred men who rode sullenly out of Saint-Denis along the southbound road, some cracking jokes about finally getting back to their sweet Loire pussy, about sleeping in a decent bed, about getting a decent breakfast of ham and eggs and fresh hot bread. But most of them were silent, watching the mud puddles in the road before them, their mouths pressed into expressions of bitterness and regret.

Jehanne remained calm, expressionless even, when they reached Gien several weeks later and the King announced that the army would be disbanded. And she remained calm in a private meeting in his castle, where he informed Jehanne and Alençon that they were dangerous influences on each other and were forbidden from ever fighting together again. 'Separate now and let me never hear that you have reunited lest you face certain death,' he said.

Even at these words, Jehanne flinched only slightly. Then the stone face returned. A stone face that remained as she and Alençon stood together outside the castle while his carriage was packed by the servants. Remained until the driver was in his seat and the horses were pawing the earth, and at last Jehanne brought herself to look him in the eye. 'I'm sorry,' she said.

Alençon shook his head, smiled. 'There is nothing to be sorry for.'

'Well,' Jehanne said, looking off at the trees. 'It's all over now.'

'Only for a little while,' Alençon said. 'Just until Charles gets over his temper.'

Jehanne understood then. Saw that he could not bear to admit otherwise. And so she forced herself to smile. 'Until next time, then,' she said. She stepped forward stiffly to shake his hand.

The Duke made a face and pulled her tightly

303

against him. He held her for a long time, breathing in the scent of her hair. 'Jehanne,' he said, as she pulled away from him.

She smiled. Touched his cheek. 'Until next time,' she said again. Then she turned and walked away very quickly so that he would not see her weep.

CHAPTER TWENTY-SIX

She spent the rest of the autumn with the King and his court, wandering from castle to castle, waiting for her wounds to heal. Pierrelot and Aulon remained with her through that aimless season. Loches, Meung-sur-Yèvre, Bourges, Saint-Pierre-le-Moutier. They stayed only a week or two in each place, until the stench of shit and sweat and rotting food overwhelmed them, and then they moved on. Leaving their green watermelon rinds and mutton bones on the floor for the animals that would inevitably take up residence there in their absence. The King was polite, but kept his distance. No longer did they pray together in the Rose Chapel. No longer did they ride their horses along the river.

Jehanne slept badly, awkwardly, in her fine soft bed. She had terrible nightmares, fought a thousand losing battles in her sleep, saw Bertrand and Mugot die again and again, saw Gilles in all his monstrosity, rode through fields of the dead in her sleep, woke screaming in the night. In the daytime, she let servants bathe and tend to her wound with clean hot water and fresh linen bandages. She

304

accepted visits from various noble well-wishers and gawkers. She smiled grimly through countless royal ceremonies and rituals, biting down hard on her cheek to keep herself from falling asleep.

In Bourges she stayed for several weeks as the guest of Marguerite La Tourolde and her husband, René de Pouligny, the King's treasurer. She went to church each morning with her hostess, listened numbly to the sermon. The words sliding past her like water, sounds without meaning. Afterward, crowds of women came and gathered around her, smiling hungrily. When they spoke, they stuttered and blushed and trembled and begged her to bless their rosaries. 'An honor, dear Maid.' 'A joy,' they said, kissing her hands, the hem of her skirt. 'Marguerite has told us so much about you,' one said, falling to her knees. 'Would you touch my beads, Maid?'

'Touch them yourself,' she said. 'God will heed your prayers better than mine.'

One afternoon Marguerite took her to the bathhouse in town. 'I dare say it's a spiritual experience,' Marguerite said. Jehanne sat naked and sweating in that strange, steaming cave until she thought her lungs would burst. Then she stood, reached into a bucket, and splashed cold water on her face. A feeling like lightning cracking in her brain. Jehanne gasped, blinked at the icy water, shaking it off her face. When she opened her eyes, Madame La Tourolde was staring at her backside. 'What happened to you?'

The girl looked over her shoulder at her own buttocks, which were pale as flour and covered with an angry red riot of sores and blisters and dark purple scars from past offenses. Jehanne blushed and touched her left buttock. 'From the armor,' she said, sitting down quickly. 'And the saddles.'

The woman frowned. 'But why hasn't anyone tended these for you?'

Jehanne shrugged. 'Nothing to do for saddle sores but wait for them to heal.'

'But you must rub oil on the ones that have closed up. Otherwise you'll get awful scars.'

She regarded the woman bleakly. 'Madam, aside from you, no one's ever seen that part of me naked. I don't expect anyone ever will.'

'But your husband. Surely one day . . .'

Jehanne set her jaw and stood up. 'I'm hot,' she said. 'I need some air.'

*　　　*　　　*

A strange, unreal time for Jehanne. And stranger still when she returned to Charles's castle at Loches. Every day hundreds of visitors lined up outside the castle walls to meet Jehanne, begged her to kiss their ailing infants, their blind eyes, their crippled legs. Others appeared at the castle, claiming to be holy women and vision-seeing daughters of God with messages for the King.

One cold day in October, a woman named Catherine de La Rochelle came to see Jehanne. She bore a letter from the King, asking the Maid to speak to her and see if she was legitimate. A strange-looking creature—long-necked and heavy-hipped, like a gourd, with wide, hectic green-gold eyes and a slight tremble when she spoke. Jehanne sensed immediately that she was a liar. The woman claimed to have been visited every night for the last six months by an angel in white who instructed her to go to the King and tell him of a secret cave filled with gold that God intended for him to pay his army. Jehanne's eyes flickered at the mention of money for further battles. 'You say she comes every night?'

'Oh yes!' the woman said.

For two nights Jehanne sat in a little chair beside the woman's bed, forcing herself to stay awake, but the angel in white did not appear. On the second night, the woman awoke around midnight and raised herself up on her elbow, smiling a sly little smile. She smelled like rotten mushrooms. 'You must be awfully cold out there. Would you not like to come and share the bed with me? 'Tis nice and warm.'

'I'm fine here.'

She gazed at Jehanne with beseeching eyes. 'Maybe if you told me of one of your visions . . .'

Jehanne looked at her.

'I am so longing to hear what it was like for you. The saints, the angels coming to you in the night, whispering in your ear.' The green-gold eyes were shining, a desperate, hungry light in them. 'Won't you tell me? Won't you come get warm in bed and tell me?'

Jehanne stood up. 'You're a filthy liar.'

A gasp from the woman. 'Oh no, never! I just hoped you might say a little bit. I just—' A sob coming in her throat then. 'Oh, God forgive me. I wanted to meet you so badly, to talk to you, to hear—'

'Get out of here,' said Jehanne, her heart suddenly furious, insulted, that she should be reduced to this, interviewing false prophets while

France so desperately needed her help. She walked to the door and slammed it shut behind her.

* * *

Increasingly, as the wound healed, the blessed numbness that had tranquilized Jehanne's heart diminished. She began to feel restless, to dream of riding in the hills and sleeping outside under her blanket with the cold, fresh night air on her face and the enormous swirling night world of stars and darkness overhead. Sometimes, when she could not sleep, she stood by her window and looked out at the sky and the dim, humped, blue-black countryside, and it amazed her how much smaller the night sky seemed when seen through a window. And though she knew it was the same sky she'd known when she'd slept with her men outside in the fields, it did not seem to her like the same sky at all. She did not feel a part of this sky, as she felt when she slept out in the open beneath its enormous dark shoulders. She did not feel it pulsing in her blood the way it had the night before a battle when she knew it might be the last night, the last stars, she ever saw. And she understood the strange beauty of war then, the way it brings the world to life for its participants, makes each moment shimmer simply because it exists, makes each blade of grass a marvel, makes the humblest gruel seem a delicacy, the trip of a squirrel up a tree trunk an adventure, a thing of wonder. And she saw then that she missed the war, that she'd felt at home in it, among the filthy soldiers and the horses and the fires and the trees, in a way she'd never felt anywhere else. In war, she'd had a purpose. She had belonged. She'd known why she was alive. In court, she was just a curiosity, one of the King's collectibles, sitting on a shelf.

CHAPTER TWENTY-SEVEN

By november she could walk without pain or assistance, so she began to sit in the opulent, chilly little limestone chapel three or four or hours at a time, praying and confessing to the priest and begging her voices to come to her. For so long now they'd been silent. Since Patay.

*   *   *

One day, as she sat in the dim, silent nave with her eyes closed and her face raised like a plate to the sky, Michael appeared. The great lion's face gazing down on her, the sunlight rinsing through her as if he'd never been gone. *It's almost over now, my love. The Burgundians will take you prisoner before Midsummer.*

What? Jehanne said, blinking. Then weeping. *What?*

By Midsummer it will be over. Be not afraid, but go willingly. God will help you.

Oh, no, she said, folding her hands in her lap.

After a moment she said: *Please let them kill me straightaway when I'm taken. Please don't let them torture me.*

Go willingly, my love. Trust in God and He will help you.

CHAPTER TWENTY-EIGHT

I begged Charles to let me fight. Let me attack Paris once more. I told him my voices had assured a victory. 'Dauphin, you must listen to me,' I said. 'My time is almost over.' But he refused. Or rather, La Trémöille refused. La Trémöille said: 'Would that be the same sort of victory they promised you in September? The one that cost us five hundred thousand francs and almost a thousand men, and got us nothing?'

They wanted to keep negotiating with Burgundy. 'We're getting close now,' Charles said. 'With any luck, we'll soon settle this whole thing without spilling another drop of blood.'

I could not let that stand. 'You and I both know Burgundy will never hand over Paris willingly.'

Charles flapped his white hands in the air. He'd become a much more elegant creature by then, in his green silk slippers with the rosettes, his golden mink collar and green silk orle. But it all fell away when he flapped his hands like that. He was the same scared, spineless thing he'd always been. I knew it and he knew it. 'Well, we must try, mustn't we?' he said weakly. 'France has never been a bloodthirsty country and she's not going to become one if I can help it.'

I knelt down at his feet. Pressed my face against his knees. 'Oh Sire, do you truly think me bloodthirsty? Do you really believe that of me?'

Charles looked away. 'You're always in such a rush, Jehanne. This is the fate of a country we're talking about. There are many things that must be taken into account.'

310

'But I'll be gone by Midsummer. My voices have said it. It'll all be over for me.'

'Nonsense,' said La Trémöille with a chilly smile. 'We all know your voices aren't always correct.'

'They are this time,' I said.

*   *   *

A week later they called me back into the King's chambers. It was snowing outside. It had been snowing all day. Charles and La Trémöille were sitting by the fire, playing backgammon. Outside the world was silent as death. 'We've decided there are some towns along the Loire we'd like you to take back from the Burgundians after all,' La Trémöille said, smiling.

He wanted to get rid of me. I see that now. He sent me to Saint-Pierre-le-Moutier and La Charité in all that snow with hardly any men or weapons. I didn't care. I was glad to get out of there. And somehow we actually took Saint-Pierre, so then they became very excited about our taking the second town too. I sent word that I needed more men, more weapons, powder, saltpeter, sulfur, arrows. La Trémöille wrote back promising he'd send them, but when we reached La Charité, there was nothing there. Not one thing. I don't think Charles knew anything about it. I remember the weather was terrible. So cold it hurt to breathe, and the wind was whipping around, and there were no reinforcements at all, so yes, that siege was hopeless. Of course it was hopeless. After a month, the King called me back to La Trémöille's castle at Sully-sur-Loire. They made me a knight that Christmas. Jehanne du Lys. That was my name now. Charles passed a law saying that no one in Domrémy

311

would have to pay taxes ever again. He gave me a mink cape. A splendid thing lined in crimson satin. Also a coat of arms with a sword holding up a golden crown. It didn't matter. That was the worst Christmas of my life. I wished I were dead that Christmas.

*　　*　　*

In the spring I received word that there was trouble up around Lagny. The Burgundians had started harassing the town, even though the truce was officially still on until Easter. 'A bloody mess up there,' Pierrelot said. So he and Aulon and I left the castle without telling anyone. We went up to Lagny and fought with the garrison there against the English. We had a good victory, and then a few weeks later another one at Melun. I sent word to Charles, telling him of our success, begging for more men and supplies, but nothing arrived. Nothing. Not even a thank-you. Then, in the middle of May, I received word that Burgundy had surrounded Compiègne with a couple of hundred soldiers. This was two days after the people of Compiègne had held a feast in my honor. Burgundy had already taken the little village of Margny, which lay right across the river from Compiègne. He was closing in fast. So I decided to fight. I knew it was crazy. I knew I would lose. I had hardly any men with me, hardly any artillery, but I thought, Better to fall while fighting than to waste away in La Trémöille's castle. Anything is better than that.

CHAPTER TWENTY-NINE

They rode single file through the forest—a dark ride, hardly any moon in the sky. Their torches bobbed up and down as they galloped alongside the river, a long string of yellow flames smeared across the dark water. It was still dark when they sneaked into the town. They went directly to the château of the commander there, Guillaume de Flavy, and Jehanne's men slept for a few hours on the floor in his great hall. Jehanne prayed. Jehanne paced. In the morning they planned to join up with the soldiers of Compiègne and attack Margny on horseback.

Shortly before she met up with her men, she went to church and prayed for several hours. Once more the voices did not come, but when she opened her eyes, a little girl was standing in front of her, blinking. She was perhaps four or five. Thick auburn helmet of hair, plump knees, eyes like green apples. She said her name was Catherine. 'Are you the Maid?'

Jehanne nodded, said that she was.

'Are you going to save us from evil Burgundy?'

'I'm going to try,' said Jehanne.

'When you come back, you can come to my house for dinner,' the girl said. 'My mother said it's all right.'

Jehanne smiled. 'I don't think I'll be coming back,' she said.

*   *   *

Her eyes were very bright that morning as she addressed her men, her voice loud and clear. She rode before them in her armor and her splendid doublet of red and gold silk, and as she looked into their sunburned faces, the fire rose up inside her once more, and she shouted, 'Today is the day we take back Margny, men. Today is the day we secure the bridge to keep the Goddons out of our beloved Compiègne. Fight boldly with me now, Men of God, and I promise you, we will triumph!'

The men let out a great roar. Jehanne kicked her horse, and they rode through the city gates, across the wooden bridge, and then up the long green hill toward Margny, and soon the church bells of Margny were ringing in wild alarm, and the Burgundians were shouting 'Attack! Attack!' and they came charging out of the city in packs, still pulling on their helmets and shields. And the French fought very well until an enormous swarm of Burgundian reinforcements arrived suddenly, coming at them on foot from all sides, and swinging their axes and swords, and there seemed to be a vicious fury in the Burgundian soldiers that day as they ran out of the town toward the Frenchmen, driving their axes into the horses' chests and necks, laughing as the animals stumbled and knelt, screaming. 'You're finished, witch,' shouted one enormous man with a long white scar like lightning down his face, and as he shouted, he swung his ax into the face of Poton's page.

Jehanne saw that her men and their horses were falling all around her, and they had begun to retreat, running downhill en masse toward the river. 'No,' she shouted as men ran by her down the banks and across the drawbridge into

Compiègne. 'Don't run! Stay and fight!' But even Aulon and Pierrelot had begun galloping back toward Compiègne, and Jehanne rode after them, shouting that they must keep fighting even as her horse stumbled over the bodies of so many dead horses and men, and soon a pack of Burgundians was closing in on her, chasing her onto a boggy field down by the river, and Pierrelot shouted, 'Make for the drawbridge,' and Jehanne wheeled her horse and made for the drawbridge where her men were flooding into the city, but before they could reach the bridge, the great iron lattice of the portcullis began to come clanking down, and though some men inside the city walls were shouting, 'Hurry, Maid, for God's sake, hurry,' others were shouting, 'Forget that crazy bitch, she'll get us all killed,' and so she watched as the drawbridge gate slammed down, turning her horse this way and that as the Burgundian soldiers closed in around her and Pierrelot and Aulon, leering and laughing and prodding, yanking first Pierrelot off his horse and then Aulon as Jehanne screamed and her horse reared, and then one soldier took an ax to her horse's front leg, and the horse knelt screaming, and Pierrelot shouted, 'Jehanne!' and then another soldier grabbed Jehanne's arm, and she fell to the ground, and the Burgundians closed in around her.

PART V

CHAPTER ONE

'That's it,' she says to Massieu. 'You know the rest.'

Dawn is coming now. The cell a softer shade of blue, a few pale strips of light falling in through the roof. Jehanne traces the rough weave of her wool dress with her fingertip. Smiles oddly.

The priest blinks. 'But why didn't Charles ransom you? How could he sit by and let you be sold to the English?'

Jehanne is still staring at the floor. 'I'm tired,' she says suddenly. 'We'll speak more tomorrow.' She glances up at him, asking with her eyes for his forgiveness, his understanding.

'I should sleep myself. Those goons will be awake soon.'

Jehanne smiles a little. 'The goons,' she says. 'Yes, they will.'

Massieu peers at her closely. 'Are you all right, dear?'

No, she thinks. *I am not all right at all*. But here Jehanne takes hold of herself. Takes herself in hand. There are things Massieu must not know. Things she cannot bear for him to know. 'Yes,' she says, her smile calm and firm. 'I'm fine. Just tired.'

'You get some rest, then,' he says, groaning and getting to his feet. 'I'll see you tomorrow night.'

'Yes,' Jehanne says. 'See you then.'

*   *   *

And so she is alone once more with the snoring guards. Alone with Berwoit and his bandaged

319

hand. Berwoit whom she bit like a dog the day before, breaking the skin, biting down through the tough muscle, drawing blood. A horrible taste, his blood in her mouth. She'd spat it out violently, as if it were poison.

She had thought to frighten him. Had begun by growling low in her throat, baring her teeth like a dog as he came toward her in the cell. She thought if she frightened him, he might stop. Might be scared away. *But they do not stop. They never stop.* She squeezes her eyes closed, fumbles about in her mind for another memory. *Something from the old days . . .*

When it does not come, when nothing comes but the howling silence of her saints, God turning away from her, closing his eyes to her, Jehanne lies down on the floor of her cell and pulls her blanket over her shoulders, up tightly to her chin.

CHAPTER TWO

For a long time she'd had hope. She was certain she'd escape or be rescued. As soon as Charles heard she'd been captured, he'd pay her ransom. Or else he'd send his men up north to storm the castle and set her and Pierrelot and Aulon free, return them to the safety of the Loire. La Trémöille, she knew, would let her rot, but not the King. 'Charles will have us out of here in a week,' Aulon whispered from the cell he and Pierrelot shared next to hers. 'We'll be back in the Loire by Midsummer's Eve, mark my words.'

Her first night in captivity Jehanne was so sure

320

of this she fairly glowed with arrogance when the Duke of Burgundy came to see her in the tower at Beaulieu Castle. 'Finally got yourself caught,' he said, smiling over Jehanne, who lay on the floor, her face a swollen landscape of purple and black bruises, her hands and ankles bound up with rope.

She looked up at him, her lip curled. 'Not that you had anything to do with it.'

A broader smile from the Duke, his eyes glittering, feverish. 'Nevertheless, here you are, the invincible Maid, fallen at last.'

Jehanne regarded him with cold eyes. 'The King will ransom me soon enough.'

'I wouldn't be too sure about that. From what I hear, the Dauphin will be quite delighted to let you stay where you are.'

'Liar,' she said. She was certain that he was just bluffing, trying to make her squirm.

The Duke squatted down by the bars, peered through them at Jehanne. 'You're just a little runt of a thing, aren't you? Just a cocky little peasant with a head full of crazy ideas.'

Jehanne looked at him. 'The people of France think me none too crazy.'

'The people of France are a bunch of ignorant fools.' He cocked his head, smiled. Spoke in a crooning voice. 'Imagine so much trouble from a mad little cowgirl dressed up in a suit of armor . . .' He stroked her plump, still-childish cheek with his finger.

Jehanne flinched. 'Don't touch me.'

'Well, you had a good run, I'll give you that,' he said. 'Put up a hell of a fight for a while there.'

'Hardly a fight at all. Your men ran screaming like chickens.'

The Duke laughed. 'Need I remind you of all the defeats you've suffered in the last year?'

'Chickens are chickens,' Jehanne said. 'They'll run again soon enough.'

'You think so?' said the Duke. 'Let's see what you say after you've been locked up for another month or two. After the guards have had a chance to play with you a little bit. Shall we?'

She held his gaze, smiled. Then she sucked in her cheeks and spat a gob of phlegm squarely onto the toe of the Duke's gleaming left boot.

He regarded it. Took a handkerchief out of his pocket and wiped it off. Then regarded Jehanne calmly. 'You'll regret that.'

'I doubt it.'

The next day Jean de Luxembourg stood outside her cell. He was a tall, thin man with a narrow, quizzical face, a blond wedge of hair. His eyes were very bright green, his head cocked slightly to one side. It was his land she'd been captured on. She was his prisoner. 'You've made the Duke of Burgundy very angry, you know,' he said. His voice was elegant, calm as a priest's. 'What on earth did you say to him?'

'Maybe you should ask what he said to me.'

Luxembourg smiled. 'Oh, I'm sure he was horrible. He hates you as much as the English do. If it were up to him, you'd be boiled in oil and served up on his breakfast platter tomorrow morning.'

Jehanne was silent, waiting for the waves in her stomach to subside. 'And you?' she said at last. 'What do you plan to do with me?'

Luxembourg looked at her, pursed his lips. 'I don't know yet. Burgundy wants me to sell you off to the English as soon as possible, but that seems a bit rash to me. Perhaps your King will be willing to pay more.'

'I know he will,' Jehanne said, her eyes lighting up.

*   *   *

But there had been no word from the King. The kind, rabbit-eyed woman who brought Jehanne her food each day told her that people were marching all over France with lit candles, demanding the Maid's release, but still Charles was silent. His silence growing heavier and heavier each day until Jehanne could not help but remember her first meeting with him. *He'll be the death of you.* The certainty in her bones. There were no more visits from Luxembourg. Just days and days alone in the dark cell, wondering, begging the saints to come to her, praying, trying to find her way back to the secret room of her childhood, the *bois chênu*, where she'd been safe.

One morning toward the end of summer, when the air was very hot and wet, two guards came and opened up the door to Aulon and Pierrelot's cell. 'Looks like you cunts are free to go,' one said as he led the two men out into the corridor. But when Pierrelot said, 'What about my sister?' the guards just laughed. 'That one's not going anywhere.' And so they'd had to shout their good-byes as the guards dragged them down the hallway. 'We'll be back, Jehanne!' Aulon had shouted. Which made the guards laugh even harder.

The next day, as the rabbit-eyed woman set Jehanne's porridge on the floor, she glanced over her shoulder, then leaned in close and whispered, 'You must try to escape from here. The Duke is planning to sell you to the English.'

Jehanne stared at her. 'But that can't be,' she said. 'Has he heard nothing from the King? He said he would wait and see what the King offered.'

The woman looked at the girl, her eyes bright with pity. 'I heard him say it myself, child.'

CHAPTER THREE

She tried. When the guard came in to take her chamber pot that evening, she hid behind the wooden door, then ran out into the hall and locked him into her cell, the guard barking like a furious dog as she ran down the dark tower stairs two at a time, down and out into the warm August twilight. There was an orchard of peach trees to the right of the tower, and the smell of rotting peaches was very strong in the air as she ran blindly away from the castle. Soon she was into the orchard itself. Rows and rows of trees in the gathering dusk, and just beyond them, she could see salvation: a stone wall she could climb over. Then woods. Woods where she could hide.

She made it halfway through the orchard before another guard caught her. Her bare feet kept sinking into the soft, rotting peaches on the ground, and it was difficult to run fast. She kept slipping, stumbling. Soon she could hear the big guard huffing and grunting behind her, the sound getting louder and louder until at last he caught hold of her tunic and fell upon her, brought her crashing to the ground, saying, 'Oh no, you don't.'

She thought it was over, thought she would be taken to England right away, tortured, killed. But it did not happen. *Instead God put his hand around the little flame of hope in my heart once more, and the flame steadied itself.*

CHAPTER FOUR

The grand black-lacquer carriage of the Demoiselle of Luxembourg thundered through a high tunnel of lime green elm trees, drawn by four splendid chestnut ponies, their silken hindquarters gleaming in the afternoon sun. At the main entrance to Beaulieu Castle, the carriage came to a halt and four footmen alighted and opened the door to the cab. Out came a gray silk slipper, followed by the great rustling silk skirts of the Demoiselle herself. A tall, elegant blond in her fifties, with a long, thin nose and skin translucent as rice paper. She stepped lightly and quickly across the cobblestones and made her way inside the castle. There to greet her stood her nephew Jean, who bowed low before her and smiled nervously. 'Where is she?' said the lady.

Jehanne sat tied to a chair in a dim dungeon cell, her lips tight, eyes raging. The guards had been making fun of her failed attempt at escape. 'Little fool slipping around in the orchard. Why didn't you just use your broomstick, darling?'

'That's enough,' said the Demoiselle, and the men were silent. She stepped forward and looked at Jehanne for several moments. A puzzled expression on her face, as if she could not quite believe that the filthy, crop-haired urchin before her was the great and famous savior of France. Then she turned to her nephew, who stood back a bit, looking nervous. 'But she can't be more than fourteen.'

'She's eighteen.'

Jehanne watched both of them, said nothing.

The Demoiselle's skirts rustled once more as she stepped farther into the cave. 'You have my great respect,' she said to Jehanne. 'You have done things no woman on earth has ever dreamed of. Things no human on earth has ever dreamed of.'

Jehanne was silent, eyes hooded.

The Demoiselle turned toward her nephew. Spoke in a cold voice. 'You've always been callous, Jean, ever since you were a child. But this is a new low even for you.'

Luxembourg looked at the floor, red spots rising on his cheeks.

'She can't stay here. I won't have it. Have your men bring her to me at Beaurevoir at once. I'll look after her until we decide what's to become of her.'

'But Aunt—'

'This is not a discussion, Jean.'

The Demoiselle took Jehanne away to Château Beaurevoir in the north. A great sprawling place with a red-tile roof and a great old pine forest around it. The Demoiselle put her in a different sort of tower room altogether. This one cozy and luxurious, with a thick gray-velvet quilt on the bed and a fireplace, a view of the Demoiselle's gardens down below. There were bars on the window, but on the other side of the bars were the blooming

326

roses with their full pink skirts, their perfume climbing up the tower walls and through Jehanne's window in the night.

A prettier brand of captivity. Still, the doors were locked.

*　　　*　　　*

The Demoiselle had no children of her own. Her husband had died when she was young, and she'd never married again. 'I regret not having them though,' she said. 'When one gets older, one begins to see things differently.' She came to visit Jehanne in her room every afternoon, taught her to play backgammon, read to her, asked her questions about the girl's saints, her revelations. After a time, she began to bring her friends to visit Jehanne as well. The Three Jehannes. The Demoiselle, whose name was Jehanne de Luxembourg. Her nephew's wife, Jeanne de Béthune. And Jean's stepdaughter, Jeanne de Bar. A trio of bright-eyed ladies with their fine silk dresses, their rapt, childlike fascination with the Maid. *How was it when He first appeared to you? Did you know it was Him from the beginning? Were you not terrified during the battles, with all those men dying around you? All that blood?*

But no one was as fascinated with her as the Demoiselle. 'To think, no education at all,' she would say, gazing hungrily at Jehanne. 'Just the instincts of a genius and the heart of a lion.' Soon the Demoiselle was saying she wanted to keep the girl with her there at Beaurevoir, to civilize her, teach her to read. Turn her into a lady. One afternoon she brought an armful of dresses into

Jehanne's room—one brown silk, one soft blue wool with a square neck, one apricot velvet, the color shimmering in the afternoon light—and laid them out on her bed. 'If you'll just think about wearing one, dear, it will make everything so much easier.' The Demoiselle planned to convince her nephew not to ransom Jehanne, to let her stay on with the Demoiselle as a kind of companion. 'A protégé,' the Demoiselle said. 'But he has to believe you want to live peacefully, reasonably. He has to believe you would not be a threat.'

Jehanne walked over and looked at the dresses on the bed. They seemed like beautiful but somehow dangerous objects. Things that would be deadly for her to touch.

'I understand that the boy's clothes were right for war and all that—time,' the Demoiselle said over Jehanne's silence. 'But it's not necessary anymore.' She smiled at Jehanne fondly. 'And you're so pretty too—if only you'd let people see it.'

Jehanne looked at the elegant powdered woman, at the dresses, at the apple tart a servant had placed on the table. She told herself that the Demoiselle's idea of prison was far better than anyone else's so far. But she could not make herself move closer to the dresses, could not make herself touch them. 'It's not time yet,' she said finally. 'I have to wait until the voices tell me to.'

The Demoiselle's lips twitched in annoyance. 'You know it only makes things worse for you.'

'I know it must seem that way to you.'

The woman studied her for a moment. 'But why? No one would ever harm you here.'

Jehanne's eyes turned hard. Cold. 'One of your

knights shoved his hand up my shirt the other day. What do you call that?'

'Who?'

'The young one with the curly black hair. He brought me dinner.'

'Aimond?'

'He was surprised when I pushed him away. Told me I should count myself lucky to have attracted his attentions. Told me only freaks married God.'

The next day the young knight Aimond de Macy was gone from the castle. But the Demoiselle did not bring up the idea of the dresses again. Something in her changed toward Jehanne. She was more formal after that. A brisk, forced cheer in her smiles, a weighing look in her eyes when she thought Jehanne was not watching.

CHAPTER FIVE

On a cold, windy day in October Jean de Luxembourg stood in his aunt's parlor, watching the yellow leaves scutter across the grass. 'Bishop Cauchon has offered ten thousand gold crowns for her. I've accepted.'

The Demoiselle drew her head back like a snake. She looked at him. 'You can't do that, Jean.'

'I already have.' He held her gaze. 'You may not like me, Aunt, but the fact is, the girl is my prisoner. She was taken on my land, and it is up to me to handle her as I see fit.'

The Demoiselle stood up. 'They'll kill her.'

Luxembourg walked over to the dulcimer, which

lay on a stand near the fireplace. He ran a finger over the strings. 'Perhaps you would like to make a better offer?'

'You know I don't have that kind of money.'

Her nephew looked at her meaningfully. 'You would if you bought fewer dresses each month.'

The woman stared at him. 'How dare you?'

'I need the money, Aunt.'

'So you're sending the most astonishing woman France has ever seen to her death?'

'Cauchon says they plan to give her a full trial at Rouen.'

'Pff,' the Demoiselle said, waving a hand and blowing air out of one side of her mouth. 'Some trial that will be.'

'Be that as it may, the deal is done, and unless you want to pay ten thousand crowns for her, it will proceed as planned.'

The Demoiselle glanced at the fat black pearl on her hand. 'How can the King not pay?'

'Well, he won't.' The young man stood before the dulcimer, ran his finger back over the strings in the opposite direction, releasing a high, whimsical sound. He looked at his aunt. 'And neither, it seems, will you.'

CHAPTER SIX

Jehanne stood atop the wall of the high tower, walking slowly back and forth along the narrow edge with her arms held straight out. The sky behind her was heavy, plum-colored. The air reeked of rotting leaves.

330

The Demoiselle had allowed her access to the roof from the beginning, thinking to give the girl fresh air when she wanted it. 'I hate the idea of you all cooped up in there,' she'd said.

Jehanne stopped and peered cautiously down at the ground seventy feet below. The trees were blowing in the dark autumn wind. Brown leaves scuttled across the dead grass as if in search of cover.

The guard had told her that morning that the deal was finished; she had been sold to the English. Then later in the afternoon, she received worse news. The old flap-jowled servant who came to make her fire in the afternoon had said, 'They're going to kill everyone in Compiègne, you know. Every man, woman, and child over the age of seven. Burgundy's ordered his men to kill them all if they don't surrender by Saturday.' He shook his head, piled dry twigs atop the big logs. 'Poor fools are all there waiting on you. They think their precious Maid's going to come rescue them somehow.' He looked at Jehanne. Then yawned, revealing a horseshoe of brown teeth. 'Fat chance of that,' he said.

It was Compiègne that drove her up to the roof. The thought of all those people believing in her, waiting on her . . . For them she had climbed up on the roof's edge. For them she had walked forward into the air . . .

Not that I wanted to die, she thinks now. *It was never that I wanted to die.*

A long fall, yes. Sixty or seventy feet, she'd heard the doctor say later. After the guards had carried her inside. 'A bloody miracle she survived.' But she'd meant only to put herself in God's hands. She prayed that He would let her live and return to fight in Compiègne, if that was His will.

She'd believed He would save her. He had saved her so many times in the past. She could not believe that He would want her to stand by while thousands of innocent men and women and children were murdered. He had told her to save France, told her it was her holy mission. How could she not try to go to them, those people who had put their faith in her? How could she turn away from them in their hour of need?

I understand nothing, she thinks. *Nothing makes sense.*

The saints tried to warn her. After being silent for so long, they returned very suddenly, all three of them shouting at her on the rooftop that afternoon. *You must not!* Margaret said, her eyes blazing. *It is the gravest of sins to take your own life.*

I ignored them. I could not believe that He would have me stand by while all those people were murdered. I kept seeing their faces—the little girl Catherine I'd met the morning before I was captured with the auburn helmet of hair and the pink dimpled knees. How could He want me to stand by while she was killed, her throat cut or worse? If some wicked soldier got hold of her, she could go the way my sister did . . . they'd find only her small boot later in the woods, down by the riverbank. No, He would never want that.

Abruptly she stopped walking. She looked down from atop the great dark tower. The wind was blowing cold on her face. The sea of trees rustling wildly below. She crossed herself. *I fall into your hands, my love.*

CHAPTER SEVEN

Two guards stood on the drawbridge in the cold pink light of sunset, passing a bottle of wine back and forth. One of them went to spit off the side of the bridge, and it was then that he saw the girl, crumpled like a broken doll on the dry floor of the moat. 'Jesus,' he said. 'Robert, come here.'

Two guards run very quickly over the bridge through the autumn dusk. Over the stone bridge they go, across the lawn to the edge of the moat. 'Get a ladder,' says one.

'She can't be alive,' says the other man, peering down.

'I said get a ladder.'

Down at the bottom of the moat, the first guard crouched over the motionless figure, cracked mud branching out like a web around her. He touched Jehanne's throat, his face white as flour. 'She's got a pulse,' he said. He lifted the unconscious girl and carried her into the castle in the gathering twilight. Wondering as he walked about the creature in his arms—the little brown-skinned peasant who seemed to exist outside the rules of this world. 'Tough little thing,' he said as he laid her in a bed near the Demoiselle's chambers. 'Wish I was that tough,' said the other.

For three days she neither ate nor drank, simply lay still, watching the awe-struck circus around her. The women with their great hats and bright, astonished eyes, offering her broth, water, the doctor shaking his head, muttering, the guards defending themselves for letting her up on the roof alone. 'You said it was all right,' said one.

'You should have been with her,' snapped the Demoiselle.

'How could we know? Who'd be crazy enough to jump seventy feet?'

CHAPTER EIGHT

The duke of Alençon sat pale and drawn in the King's study, watching the rain sluice downhill through the streets of Chinon toward the flooded river. 'At this rate they're going to have to sail us out of here,' said Charles, with a smile.

Alençon did not smile back. His eyes were red and bloody. He looked as if he had not slept in years. 'They're going to sell her to Cauchon,' he said. 'Do you know that? He offered ten thousand gold crowns.'

'Christ, that's a bloody fortune.'

'You can't let this happen, Charles. You have to pay them. You have to get her back.'

'I don't have money like that to throw around. You know it as well as I do.'

'I know that you could raise it before dinnertime if you wanted to.'

'Not for her. She has no friends in this court any longer.'

'You'd stand by and let the English kill her, then? After all she's done for you?'

'She's become impossible,' said Charles. 'She stands in the way of France's freedom.'

'She is France's freedom.'

'Not anymore.'

Alençon looked at him. He was gripping the arm of his chair so tightly that his knuckles had turned gray. 'I beg you, Charles, as your oldest friend. Don't let them kill her. She is the life and soul of this country. You know she was sent by God as well as I do.'

The King sighed. 'It's been a long time since she's done anything God-like in my book.'

'Don't blame our losses on her.'

'Why not?'

'Because you gave her no money and no support—you sent her off to battle with a handful of men and no supplies. There's no way she could have won fighting like that. No one could.'

Charles made a face. Looked out at the gray curtains of rain. 'You act as if I haven't done anything for her. As if I didn't ennoble her and her entire family, as if I haven't relieved her entire village from paying taxes for the rest of their lives.'

'You owe her your life, Charles. You would not be king without her.'

'And I've repaid her handsomely for it.'

The Duke came and stood before him, his eyes very bright, his face shaking. 'So help me God, if you abandon her—'

The King looking at him very sharply now. 'If I abandon her what, Alençon?'

'You will burn in Hell for it, Charles.'

CHAPTER NINE

Not a single bone in Jehanne's body was broken. Not a muscle sprained. By the end of the week she was well enough to be moved, and so one freezing morning in late November, the chief negotiator for the English-controlled University of Paris, Bishop Pierre Cauchon, arrived at Beaurevoir Castle with an escort of six large soldiers. They bound Jehanne tightly with ropes and tied her to the back of a horse. Then they rode up through the cold north country toward the English-held city of Rouen.

The Demoiselle watched Jehanne's departure from a window high in her castle. The Demoiselle crossing herself, her face unreadable, as she watched them take the girl away.

CHAPTER TEN

In Arras Jehanne saw a painting of herself. The first she'd ever seen. They'd stopped for the night at one of the grand Burgundian castles along the way. *So many stops like that, so the Bishop could show off his prize.* After dinner, the Bishop and his hosts came and took her out of her cell. 'Something downstairs you should see,' the Bishop said, smiling at Jehanne with his thick brown lips as his men dragged her forward through the stinking straw. At first she was happy because she thought the room they were taking her to would have a fire where she could warm her hands, for her cell was very cold, the December wind whistling through the stones. *Like sleeping on a mountaintop.*

But she never noticed if there was a fire in the room, for she had caught sight of her portrait as soon as she entered. A tall, glowing oil portrait that had been painted by a Scotsman who'd seen her in Orléans. She was dressed in her shining white armor and kneeling on one knee before King Charles. Her dark hair was shiny and cropped short, and her eyes were radiant, as the crowds of richly dressed nobles all around her in court gazed on in awe.

Had she been alone, she would have looked for a while. Marveled at it, leaped at the chance to remember the strong, beautiful person she had been just a year earlier. The days when the saints sang in her heart. But she was not alone; there was a crowd of Burgundians around her, watching the filthy captive in chains to see what her reaction would be. 'Not so high and mighty now, are you?' one blonde woman said, her lips pressed into the left side of her face.

'Why would you think we'd want that inbred fool for a king?' another said. 'We're all much better off with the English.'

Jehanne did not look anymore at the picture. She knew if she looked, she would cry. She kept her eyes on the floor.

CHAPTER ELEVEN

At last, on Christmas Eve, they arrived in Rouen. There was snow on the ground and the rooftops by then, snowflakes falling lightly and steadily in the dark air, and Jehanne was shivering as they led her, still tied to the horse, through the great city. She saw people holding candles and singing in front of the cathedral in the town square, their faces glowing like golden plates in the candlelight. But

337

they stopped singing and came running when they saw the Bishop and his men with their torches, walking the famous prisoner toward the tower of Rouen. 'The Witch,' they cried. 'Look, the Witch of France!' And some of them hissed and shouted and threw snowballs at her, and a few fell to their knees, weeping, saying, 'God bless you, child.' But many more shouted 'Witch,' their faces black and twisted up with hatred.

That's the thing I don't understand, she thinks to herself now, alone in the cell. *The hatred*. A thick, bottomless thing. Enormous. Not like the hatred men had for their enemies or for greedy kings, but the hatred they had for child-rapists, child-killers. Ferocious, shrieking, pleasurable hatred. A thing that lit them up inside, spread its fire in their bellies. Their eyes shining as if they longed to see Jehanne flayed in public and then torn limb from limb, dragged through the streets, eaten by dogs. *They really think I'm a witch*, she thought, as she rode past those hating faces on her way to the tower at Rouen. *They cannot believe God would side against them, so they think I'm sent by Satan.*

And the churchmen, how they loathed her! But it was different with the churchmen. They had not hated her at the beginning of her trial. At the beginning, they had been curious, calm, composed. The Bishop had taken two months to prepare his case, and toward the end of February, they brought her to stand in the middle of the royal chapel at Rouen Castle with her wrists and ankles chained tightly, surrounded by the churchmen. Dozens of well-fed churchmen in their red robes and black robes, some with thick white hoods around their necks, others in small felt hats, all of them leaning

338

forward slightly, as if they were nearsighted, to get a better look at the Maid.

She had no defender, no lawyer or counsel to advise her. No one to explain to her how it all worked. There was only the Bishop and his examiners from the University of Paris—canon lawyers, doctors of theology, the Vice Inquisitor of Rouen—men of books and laws and theories, men who knew nothing of the holiness of the forest or the inner sunlight that rinses all through you, men the girl had never met before, come from all over England and Burgundy to see and hear about the famous Maid, to sit in judgment of her, and decide whether she was sent by God or the Devil. Whether she should live or die.

On January 3, 1431, the Duke of Bedford issued a letter in the name of King Henry VI, announcing the news of the trial.

It is well known how for some time a woman calling herself Jehanne the Maid, putting off the dress and habit of the female sex (which is contrary to divine law, abominable to God, condemned and prohibited by every law), has dressed and armed herself in the state and habit of man, has wrought and occasioned cruel murders, and it is said, to seduce and deceive simple people, has given them to understand that she was sent from God and that she had knowledge of His divine secrets, with many other dangerous dogmatizations most prejudicious and scandalous to our holy faith . . . And because she has been reputed, charged, and defamed by many people on the subject of superstitions, false dogmas, and

339

other crimes of divine treason.

The room where they tried her was shaped like a diamond, with the Bishop seated at one end, above everyone else, in a high chair in his big square red hat. In the beginning, they allowed the public in to watch. A sea of wide-eyed onlookers packed against one wall, desperate to catch a glimpse of the witch. And the hatred she saw in their eyes terrified Jehanne, made her want to run from the room, but she steadied herself. She wanted to make them understand how it had been for her. To make them feel it as she had. She planned to tell them about the day in her father's garden with the voice and the perfect joy and the cucumber plants, about Saint Michael pouring his light into her in the *bois chênu*, and about Saint Catherine and Saint Margaret smiling down on her like tender planets. She wanted to explain how she'd known it was Saint Michael from his voice—how his voice had melted her bones as if they were candles, how his voice had plucked a chord in the deepest canyon of her being. She wanted to say, 'I know I am sent by God the way you know your own child's cry in a great crowd of people. The way you know when someone you love has died, before anyone's told you. The way you know every hidden chamber in your own heart. That is how I know.' But she did not get a chance to say any of this because the Bishop had asked her first of all to make an oath that day that she could not make. And that had made the churchmen very angry.

They wanted Jehanne to swear on the Gospels that she would truthfully answer every question they asked. 'I do not know what you will ask me,' she answered. 'The revelations that have come to me from God, I have never told to anyone except Charles, my King. God has forbidden me to discuss them with anyone else.'

How the men stared at her when she said this. Stared as if their eyes would jump out of their heads. And she had felt them begin to hate her then. She could see it in their eyes. *How dare she? Who does she think she is?* 'I'm sorry, my lords,' she said finally, 'but even if you threaten to cut off my head, I will not tell you about my visions.'

The prosecutor, Jean d'Estivet, blinked, drew his head backward like a turtle and stared at her for several moments with his small black eyes. When at last he spoke, his lip was curled. 'For now, we'll start with something else, but I warn you, Maid, we will return to these visions of yours.'

CHAPTER TWELVE

They would not allow her to attend Mass. They would not allow her to receive confession. 'Please,' she said. 'I have never gone more than two days in my life without confessing.' To which Cauchon replied, 'Perhaps you should think about that the next time you refuse to cooperate with us.'

Every day the churchmen asked her to swear their impossible oath, and every day Jehanne refused. She could feel their hatred growing for her each time she refused, coming at her like a hot wind. And she felt it too as she answered their questions, all the questions she'd already answered in Poitiers. *Why do you call yourself the Maid? Why*

341

do you wear men's clothes, though the Bible forbids it? Did your voices tell you as a child to hate the Burgundians? Did they tell you to kill the Burgundians? Can you hear your voices right now?

Day after day Jehanne answered. *I call myself the Maid because I am a virgin. You may have me examined if you wish. I wear men's clothes because they were appropriate for my mission and because my council approved them. If I were in a wood right now, I would certainly hear the voices coming to me.* But it was clear to her that it was not really the battles she'd fought against the English and the Burgundians, or the boy's clothes, or even her voices that bothered Cauchon and his men. It was the fact that she would not submit to them. The fact that she insisted on keeping some things secret, inside herself, between her and God. That she would not kneel down at their feet and declare them more mighty than God. That she believed she was not subject to their laws. 'Do you say that you are in God's grace?' Master Beaupère asked one afternoon.

The room fell silent. Jehanne looked at him. 'If I am not, may God put me there; if I am, may God keep me there. I would be the most miserable person in the world if I knew that I was not in God's grace.'

*   *   *

By the end of the first month of the trial, the churchmen had begun to shout so loudly at Jehanne, to hammer her so hard from all sides with their questions, and to threaten her so violently that some in the audience had begun to pity the girl. Some cried out that she was being unfairly treated. Others complained that the clerks were writing down answers that were different from what Jehanne herself had said. And soon the courtroom was such a storm of fury and pity and confusion that the Bishop banned the public from the rest of the trial and moved the proceedings to Jehanne's cell.

Now their questions became more pointed. Everything began to circle back to the same place. Estivet asked: *If the Church Militant tells you that your revelations are illusions or diabolical things, will you defer to the Church?*

Jehanne answered: *I will defer to God, Whose Commandment I always do. In case the Church should prescribe the contrary, I should not refer to anyone in the world, but to God alone, Whose Commandment I always follow.*

Estivet asked: *Do you not then believe you are subject to the Church of God, which is on earth, that is to say to our Lord the Pope, to the Cardinals, the Archbishops, Bishops, and other prelates of the Church?*

Jehanne answered: *Yes, I believe myself to be subject to them, but God must be served first.*

Estivet asked: *Have you then command from your voices not to submit yourself to the Church Militant, which is on earth, not to its decision?*

Jehanne answered: *I answer nothing from my own head, what I answer is by command of my voices, they do not order me to disobey the Church, but God must be served first.*

Oh, the arrogance! The monstrous pride! It was more than they could bear—this mad peasant holding her head high as a queen and saying that

343

she knew more about God's will than they did, that she had received divine revelations from Him, and that such revelations, *such mad delusions!*, should take precedence over the holy laws of the Church!

The Devil must have sent her, they decided. That she was in the thrall of the supernatural was clear to all. But only the Devil could be behind such wickedness, such devious undermining of the Church. If the girl were truly sent by God, would she not have come to the Church as soon as she received her first 'revelation' at age twelve and asked for guidance? Shouldn't she have laid her visions out before her priest and asked him to decide if her visions were sent by the Almighty, instead of deciding for herself? Shouldn't she have shown more humility? More love for the Church? More deference to her elders? Should she have openly defied the Bible and dressed herself up as a man?

'It is time for sterner methods,' said Cauchon.

CHAPTER THIRTEEN

They took her down to the dungeon. Twelve men of God walking single file down the steep and winding tower staircase in their long red robes and their stiff hats, twelve white hands sliding down the smooth stone balustrade as they went, a tangible electricity among them as they moved closer to the thing that they most wished to do, and that which they also most feared to do. A thrill and a horror braided into one.

Inside the room they showed the girl their

instruments one at a time. The stretching rack. The pincers. The cat-o'-nine-tails. The brazier of red coals. The spiked Catherine Wheel. 'I'd rather not use these,' says Cauchon, shaking his head, his face like a troll's in the torchlight, long black lines on either side of his mouth, as if they've been carved with a knife. 'But I'm beginning to think it may be necessary.'

Jehanne smiling, radiant, defiant, Saint Margaret singing an answer in her ear: 'You can tear me limb from limb,' she says, 'and drive the soul from my body, but I won't say anything different from what I've already said.'

Somehow this stopped them. They took her back upstairs, decided that there was no point in torturing her, no point in trying to force her to repent through pain. 'Take her back to her cell,' Cauchon spat. He looked Jehanne in the eye. 'You will not win this,' he said. 'I see the Devil inside you and I am going to get Him out.'

CHAPTER FOURTEEN

So the trial dragged on. The shouting questions dragged on. Jehanne's voices came in and out—at times they grew loud, ferocious, shouted at her, told her that she was a sinner, a murderer. Other times they soothed her. *Take no care for your torment, my love*, Catherine said. *Then you will come into Paradise*. Jehanne grew thin and tired. Her voices grew harder to hear.

At times, in the deep of night, she dreamed of Gilles de Rais. 'How are you, Jehanne?'

She looked at him. Said nothing.

He sat on the bench outside the cell and pressed his face against the bars, gazing at her. 'My little twin. You look so sad, my little twin.'

'I'm not your twin. I'm nothing to do with you.'

He cocked his head. 'You believe that?'

'I know it.'

He smiled. 'You forget that I fought beside you, my love, that I've seen the bloodlust in your eyes. You say you fought for God, that you did not want to kill, that you mourned those who died at your command, but you lie to yourself, Jehanne, when you say such things. You dress up your wild hunger and call it a holy mission, you tie a white bonnet around your sharp-toothed heart and fancy yourself an angel, but I know otherwise, Jehanne. I know the deep caves inside you, that cave of ecstasy that you love so much and its opposite, the cave of rage that you refuse to acknowledge, though it directs your every step. I recognized them the first time I saw you. I looked into your eyes and I thought, *Ah, there she is. My secret sister.*'

'You're crazy.'

'You think there's such a thing as a good war, a justified war? You think there's such a thing as honest blood?'

'They were killing us. They were destroying France.'

'True. But nobody forced you to get involved, did they?'

Silence.

He smacked his forehead. 'Oh, I'm sorry, of course. God told you to get involved, God made you do it. Let me ask you this, Jehanne. What kind of a god would tell you that it's wrong to kill, and

346

then send you forth to do just that? To murder your fellow human beings—His own creations—in His holy name? Can you not see that such a god is a false god, a god who hates your innermost nature and wants to do nothing but set you at war with yourself, and that the only true one is he who sees your murderous heart for what it is and loves you for it, celebrates you as his own.'

'Get out of here. You're disgusting.'

'I speak the truth and you know it.'

'The Devil's truth is the only truth you speak.'

'The Devil's truth is the only truth there is.'

She turned away from him and faced the wall. The Baron continued speaking. 'We are one and the same, Jehanne, both holy freaks, driven to a life of extremes where the stakes are life and death every day. You think it's an accident that you're here in this prison, that they're going to burn you at the stake? You've been making your way here every day of your life. This is all you've ever wanted. To do a great deed, become a great saint.'

'I never wanted to become a saint.'

'Well, so you say. But your secret heart tells another story.'

'You can say whatever you want, it doesn't matter. I loved Him. I loved Him and I did as He asked me. I served Him with all my heart. That's all I know.'

'Yes, and look how He thanks you,' Rais said. 'Look at the splendor with which your King rewards you.' She noticed his hand moving in his lap. She saw the red flash of his cock, enormous, his hand fast, up and down.

'Get away from me,' she said. 'Get out. Right now.'

His voice changed, became high and pleading. 'Let me finish, Jehanne.'

'Get out now.'

He sighed deeply and dropped his hand. Then he stood up and walked away, the enormous member jutting before him. At the door he turned and faced her, smiling. 'You tell yourself pretty fairy tales, Jehanne.'

She awoke gasping, her hair wet, plastered to her face. Everything in the dark cell seemed wicked, the walls closing in, the ceiling lowering, filled with malevolent intent. She got out of bed and knelt on the floor, her hands clasped tight in front of her face. *Tell me it isn't true. Please tell me it isn't true*. She looked up at the ceiling. *Are you there? Please come,* she said. *I'm so afraid*.

CHAPTER FIFTEEN

At dusk they came to her cell and walked her out across the long-shadowed courtyard, her feet bare, chains scraping the stones as she went. A cold, raw wind at this hour. Wind blowing Jehanne's hair across her face, blowing the tops of the raw, budding trees and wrapping the churchmen's red robes around their legs like flags as they guided her through the high iron gates and into the walled cemetery of the Abbey Saint Ouen, where an enormous crowd stood chanting, 'Burn the witch! Burn the witch!' Their eyes wild with excitement as they stood, clapping their hats to their heads and turning their faces away from the wind, tears streaming down their cheeks.

348

Thousands of townspeople were packed in amidst the slanting rows of tombstones. At the end of the cemetery stood two high, freshly built wooden platforms: One was crowded with various official churchmen, bishops and cardinals, abbots, priors, and doctors of both law and theology. On the other stood a great wooden stake surrounded by a pile of firewood, and beside it stood Jehanne in her chains, her filthy boy's tunic and leggings, and the tall, gray-cheeked Maître Erard with a deep frown on his face, as if he had been forced to sip from a sewer.

Erard spoke for a time, shouting his sermon into the wind. 'The branch cannot bear fruit of itself, except that it abide in the vine.' Explaining that all Catholics must abide in the vine of the Church, planted by Christ himself, and telling the people of Rouen that they had been abused and misled by Charles, he who called himself their King, and by the infamous and dishonored woman who stood before them, a heretic and schismatic, an enemy of France. 'Those who deliberately deny and disregard the supremacy of God on Earth will not be tolerated by this court and will pay for their heresy with their lives.'

She won't submit. That's why she must be killed. Won't submit to the Church, won't let them judge her revelations, won't accept the Church as her authority, won't abide by its rules. 'God first be served,' she said, and this was the heart of it, the thing that drove them mad. The audacity. The gall. If a filthy peasant girl can talk to God, can receive divine wisdom, who needs the Church?

Impossible. It could not stand. 'For these reasons we declare you excommunicate and heretical, and pronounce that you shall be abandoned to secular justice, as a limb of Satan severed from the Church . . .'

Excommunicated. It's more than she can bear. The stake piled high with firewood, the executioner coming toward her in his cart, the crowd quivering, roaring in an ecstasy of horror and delight. 'God's sake, girl,' shouted a doctor from the platform. 'Do you want to be burned alive?'

'Hurry up, do it! Burn the bitch!' cried an Englishman. People were throwing stones, screaming. And Erard was next to her, watching her with furrowed brow. 'Submit now or you will end your life by fire,' he said. Her eyes on the firewood, imagining the red and yellow flames rising, licking at her feet . . . 'Wait,' she cried.

Wait.

CHAPTER SIXTEEN

So she took off her beloved boy's clothes. The tunic, the leggings, the woolen vest, the tall cracked boots. She folded them carefully, lovingly, and stacked them in a little pile at the foot of her bed. She looked at the rough brown dress the guards had brought to her. *The Bishop's dress*. She allowed them to shave her head—to rid her once and for all of the offensive boy's haircut that the Bishop referred to as part of her 'vain and wicked heresy.' What else did she agree to? What other lies did she agree to in her terror?

She didn't know. They'd handed her a long

350

piece of paper full of unknown words, told her to sign it, and she did. She was too afraid to ask that someone read it to her, and in truth, she did not care. Was so terrified of the fire, the idea of being burned alive, that she would have signed anything. Anything to live.

Later they told her. The paper said that it was all a lie. The voices, the revelations, the saints— none of it had come from God. Nothing. She'd promised never to bear arms again, never to wear male clothes again, and to submit completely to Church authority.

Once she'd signed the paper, Cauchon sentenced her to life imprisonment. 'Let her live on the bread of sorrow and the water of affliction so that she can weep for her sins and never commit such vile acts again.'

So she put on the brown dress. And with it came memories of another girl, a frightened girl who lived on a farm in the hills of Lorraine with her family, whose father beat her, and whose sister was murdered by the Goddons, a girl who could not ride a horse or carry a lance, or command an army, who had no idea how she would carry out the impossible mission she'd been given. She turned her face away from the memories. Turned her face to the wall.

Later her voices came to her. The voices waking her in the chill blackness, hissing in her ears. *Traitor*, they said. *Traitor, betrayer. Lying, greedy girl. You damn your soul to save your life.*

I'm sorry, she said. *Forgive me, I beg you.*

You lie for fear of fire. You betray the King of Heaven for fear of fire.

Forgive me, she said. *Please, I beg you. Forgive*

351

me.

He is displeased, child. He is most displeased.

She wept again. It seemed her tears would never stop. She said, *I'm sorry . . .*

The saints did not reply.

CHAPTER SEVENTEEN

That night Massieu did not come. She waited and waited, shivering in the corner of her cell, her dress pulled down over her knees and bare feet like a tent, her arms pulled inside the dress so she could warm them on her flesh. But he did not come. It was just the four guards now—Berwoit and the others. 'Where is he?' she says at last. 'Why isn't he here?'

'Your boyfriend?' says Berwoit, smiling. 'Your boyfriend's not coming tonight. The Bishop wants you to have some time alone. Think about what you've done.'

He's drunk. Already he's drunk. She can see it in his eyes. The wicked black glitter. 'Anyway, gives us a little more time together, don't it? Not quite fair, Massieu keeping you all to himself.'

Jehanne says nothing. Holds his stare. *Don't look away. Don't let him see you're scared.*

'I like your dress,' he says, opening the cell door, coming toward her. 'What do you think, boys? Big improvement, eh?'

'Still think she's got a dick under there,' says another.

'Oh no,' says Berwoit, standing above her now. Smiling terribly. 'I don't think so.'

352

CHAPTER EIGHTEEN

'What else about Paradise?' Jehanne had asked her mother one day in Domrémy, back when she was very young. They were sitting down by the river; Jehanne crouching in the cool green shallows, looking for minnows while her mother washed clothes. 'Tell me what it looks like.'

'Oh,' she said. 'It's very beautiful. Everything there is made of the finest sea pearls. All the houses and the streets and the churches and the buildings. A whole city made of pearls.'

'And it sits on a cloud?'

'Yes, on a pink cloud. And when the sun shines on it, the whole city lights up like the moon.'

'And God is with them all the time there?'

'Yes, God is there all the time.'

'And everyone is happy?'

'Everyone is happy.'

'And everyone is safe?'

'Everyone is safe.'

CHAPTER NINETEEN

At night she lies awake thinking. So much time to think, to doubt. A night in her mind like a maze of questions without end. *Was it not what You wanted? Did I not do as You wished? Did I misunderstand You, I who have loved You with all my heart, who have worked so hard to please You and be Your faithful servant? Is it possible I was wrong? Is it*

353

possible the voices were not Yours? I cannot believe it. I know it was You. But then why do You make me suffer this way? Why let them keep me like this, like an animal locked in a cage, beaten, mocked? Why let them murder me? Oh, please, don't let them murder me. Please, tell me if I have displeased You, if I have sinned in Your eyes, show me how, that I may learn from my sins and work to serve You better. Oh God, please don't let them kill me. I wanted nothing but to love You and do Your will. All I have ever wanted was to love You and do Your will.

Is it my pride You punish now? That I so loved the mink cape they gave me, the fine horses, was that my sin? I see that I loved them too much, I see it, and I see that I was full of bitter rage toward the English, that I was wrathful, vengeful, but was it not You who told me to raise the army and fight them? Was it not You who wrapped me so gently in Your golden light, who touched my cheek with such love and told me of my mission?

Is it possible I was deceived? Is it possible the Devil spoke in such honeyed tones, with such tenderness that I mistook him for You? Is it possible he cloaked himself in feathered robes and so enchanted his wicked face that he came to appear as light and love before me, singing so sweetly that I could only think him God? Did he throw a halo over his horns, lasso a cloud down from Heaven on which to stand? Is it possible?

But how could I feel such love and goodness, how could such joy, such perfect belief exist inside me, radiate through me like the sweetest sunlight, if it was not truth? Am I mad? Am I a fool? Has this all been a deranged hallucination, have I been nothing but the Devil's pawn, seduced and betrayed into believing

354

I did Your will? Do You wish instead that we give our bodies and our homes, our lives, to the English? Do You wish that they should continue to steal our land, burn our crops, murder us in cold blood? Is that, as the Bishop says, Your wish? I cannot believe it, Father. To believe it would be to call my own heart a liar, a poison flower, to call my faith a mere raving, my soul a mad cave for demons and fiends. How can I do that? How can I doubt the one true and beautiful thing in my life? The one thing that made me smile in darkness and strive to do good when those around me despaired and sank into lives of sin? How can I doubt You, whom I saw so clearly each morning when I walked out into the fields, when I heard the wind shaking and riffling the high trees, splattering light across the forest floor, when I splashed my face in the icy creek? How can I doubt what sang to me everywhere I turned, from the swaying daffodils to the great white cliff faces in the hills? How, when everything in me sang yes and wept with gratitude, how can this be a lie? How could I believe that this was not You?

I know it was You, and yet, in the darkest hours of the night, when I wake from my fevered sleep and find all the long knives of my mind turned inward, carving at me with questions far worse than those of the Bishop and his men, hissing such cruel doubts, such impossible questions: Does not the Lord say in His commandments to us, Thou shalt not kill, thou shalt honor the Sabbath day and keep it holy. *And did you not order the deaths of thousands of men, are you not directly responsible for the deaths of thousands of men? And did you not ride into battle on a Sunday? And did you not oversee the killing of one thousand men on the day I bade you to devote to*

355

Me? And in those dark hours, my heart is filled with such terror, and it seems to me that I am naught but a leech scraped from the bottommost floor of Hell, a blind, crazed banshee committing murder from sheerest bloodlust and veiling it in the white lilies of Jesus. In the night my knives turn against me, and it seems to me that I indeed deserve to burn for my sins and my pride and my blindness. But, oh God, then the morning comes. Every morning I wake and my heart brims anew with love for You and Your goodness and I remember how I felt in Your arms in the forest and how I knew it was You, my love, my Father, and how blessed I felt to have been given such a great and wondrous mission, and all the dark knives and foul Hell creatures of my night-mind shrivel before Your love, dissolve into dust and I know that they can do to me what they like for I am safe in Your arms, having sought only ever to do Your will and to love and honor You with all my heart.

CHAPTER TWENTY

In her last dream she goes up the dark tower stairs. They lead to her cell, the same tower cell she's been in all these months. The guards are there, but they're asleep, snoring. Carefully she picks up the sack at the bottom of the bed and takes out her boy's clothes. It's wonderful to see them, like seeing old friends. She hugs them before she puts them on. Presses her face into the rough cloth, inhales deeply. Then, on tiptoe, she goes to the door of the cell, and it's open, so she runs quickly downstairs. She runs to the market square, where a stake has been set up, and Christ is there, wearing an executioner's cloak and smiling at her. He reaches out his hand and helps her up onto the platform, and when she looks out, everyone she knows is in the audience. Thousands and thousands of people, her father and mother and Pierrelot, her cousin Durand, and Metz and Bertrand, also King Charles and Alençon and La Hire and the Bastard and Gilles de Rais. They are all crying out to her, 'Let us pray! Let us pray!' She doesn't understand what this means, so she looks at Christ, who is standing by with the torch, and she asks him, 'What are they waiting for?' 'They're waiting for you,' he says, smiling. 'Are you ready?' Jehanne says that she is, and he helps her up onto the stake, but as he does this, she becomes very frightened. 'I don't want to,' she says. 'I don't want to.' 'No one does,' says Christ as he touches the torch to the woodpile at her feet and the yellow flames leap up. A great admiring *Ah* goes up from the crowd, and suddenly everyone kneels down and bows their heads in prayer. They are very sad, many of them are weeping, but they're also very happy, ecstatic even. Suddenly Jehanne feels very lonely up on the stake, and the fire looks wicked and hateful to her. It's as if the flames are laughing at her. She looks through the smoke to see if she can see her mother, but she cannot see anyone she knows. Then she remembers that she can look up, and when she looks up, the whole sky is made of stained glass—a great sprawling glass mural of blues and greens and reds all glowing with sunlight, and she sees her whole life there in the glass, sees Michael and Catherine and Margaret standing tall in their golden light with their long robes and their sweet spoon faces, sees herself, the girl down among the cucumber plants, collecting the beetles in her father's garden, sees her village burning, the little hunchbacked house with the fine leaded windows, the church, the black horse, all in flames. She sees herself riding over the frozen yellow fields toward Chinon in her boy's clothes, sees herself kneeling before sad King Charles in his big velvet hat, sees herself in her armor, galloping over the fields with the ten thousand soldiers behind her and the violent, holy joy burning inside of her, and the fire is very hot and red beneath her, she can feel the soles of her feet burning, and suddenly she's terrified, she understands nothing. Nothing at all. 'Why?' she cries out to the sky. 'Why?'

At last God answers. He opens his enormous eyes in the sky, and says, *My love, did you not wish to be a saint?*

CHAPTER TWENTY-ONE

She wakes up very early, before dawn. She knows now what she must do. In the dark she creeps to the bag, lifts it onto the bed and opens it up. Inside lie her boy's clothes, the soft gray tunic and the snug brown leggings. In them the smell of the forest and of campfires, of horses and freedom. In the dark she puts them on, the gray linen tunic first, over her head, then the soft brown leggings, her fingers working quickly, expertly, as she laces them up and knots them at the waist. She slips her feet into the stiff, cracked brown boots and fastens her gray cape over her shoulder, smiling as the

358

familiar wooden button slips into the loop at her neck, for the clothes give her back her power. Her joy. They return her to herself. When she's dressed, she sits on her bed and leans her head back against the wall. She closes her eyes and takes a deep breath, in and out, preparing herself for the arrival of the guards. And she feels that she is home.

EPILOGUE I

They burned Jehanne's body three times. When at last it was reduced to ash, Massieu raked the pile of gray powder into a wooden box and dumped it into the river, as the Bishop had ordered, so that the townspeople could not keep any of it for relics. He turned the box over and hit the bottom of it with his hand. Weeping as he did this. Howling like a lost dog. Most of the ash fell into the river in a long gray curtain. But some was caught by the wind and blown upward towards the blue spring sky where it swirled a moment in the air before dissolving into the sunlight.

EPILOGUE II

Jehanne d'Arc's campaign definitively turned the tide of the Hundred Years' War, and in 1453 the French succeeded in winning their country back from the English.

In 1455 Jehanne's mother and her brothers petitioned the new pope, Callixtus III, to make an investigation into Jehanne's trial. On the findings of the investigation, an extensive nullification trial was held, and on July 7, 1456, Jehanne was found innocent. The court described her as a martyr and implicated the late Pierre Cauchon with heresy for convicting an innocent woman in pursuit of a secular vendetta.

In 1920 Jehanne d'Arc was recognized as a saint by the Catholic Church. She remains the patron saint of France, and of soldiers and prisoners, and an inspiration to people all over the world.

AUTHOR'S NOTE

Almost everyone who has read *The Maid* asks the same question: How much is true? The short answer: almost everything. Almost all of the characters are real people, and the book adheres closely to the established historical facts surrounding Joan of Arc's life.

Joan of Arc was an illiterate peasant girl who, in 1429 at the age of seventeen, rode across war-torn France and convinced King Charles VII to let her take charge of his army so she could kick the English out. She believed that she was on a mission from God (though many today dismiss her as schizophrenic), and that the Saints Michael, Catherine, and Margaret spoke to her and provided her with guidance.

The predictions that Joan makes in the book are all true: She did predict that the French would be defeated at the battle of Rouvray. She also predicted that she would raise the siege at Orléans and escort King Charles to be crowned in Reims. She knew that her time in power would be brief, telling Charles early on: 'Use me. I will last little more than a year. During that year let as much as possible be done.' On the day of the assault on Saint Loup, she did wake up at the Bouchers' house in Orléans shouting that the generals had begun fighting without her. The night before the attack on Les Tourelles, Joan did tell Father Pasquerel that she would be wounded in the coming fight, saying: 'Tomorrow the blood will flow from my body, above the breast.' Joan also

363

predicted that she would be captured by the English and Burgundians before midsummer in 1430.

Perhaps most spectacularly, Joan of Arc did jump from the roof of the tower at Beaurevoir (a distance estimated between sixty and seventy feet) and survived without so much as a sprained ankle.

The areas where I have taken novelistic license with Joan's life are as follows: Though Joan's sister, Catherine, did die in Domrémy around 1429, the cause of her death is unknown. Given the amount of Goddon-related violence in the area at the time, it seems plausible that Catherine died at their hands. Bertrand de Poulegny did not die during the attack on Les Tourelles, but does so here for dramatic purposes. And Bertrand's account of the Battle of Agincourt is a tale told round a campfire and therefore is subject to the sorts of embellishments that tend to take place in such tellings. It should not be taken as statement of fact.

The question of how much Joan actually fought in battle has been debated by historians for the last six hundred years. We know for certain that she was mounted on a warhorse and dressed in a suit of armor that the King had made especially for her, and that she carried Charles Martel's sword, which had been unearthed for her at the shrine to Saint Catherine in Fierbois. We also know that Joan was present on the front lines for most of the battles in which she was involved and that she was wounded three times in the process. At Augustins she stepped on a caltrop; at Les Tourelles she was shot in the neck with an arrow while she was climbing one of the scaling ladders (she later pulled the arrow out herself); and during the attack on Paris, she was shot with a crossbow bolt that split her armor and pierced her thigh. Although Joan claimed that she did not use her sword—or kill anyone—this seems unlikely given her active role in the field.

Finally there is the question of whether or not Joan was raped in prison. Historians are divided on this point. What we know is that throughout her trial, Joan insisted on remaining in her boy's clothes—stating that they protected her from the guards and others who regularly attempted to sexually assault her. When Joan finally took off her boy's clothes after her abjuration and replaced them with a woman's dress, she was left completely vulnerable to the guards' assaults for three days. We also know that Bedford had it made clear that Joan's trial must result in her death sentence, and that when it looked like her abjuration would save her from this fate, he was furious. At this point, the English stepped in. Suddenly, the courtyard around Joan's prison tower filled up with ax-wielding English guards who refused to let any of the clergymen in to see her. Jean Beaupère, Nicolas Midi, Jean Massieu and Guillaume Manchon all attempted to visit Joan during this period, and all were turned away. At Joan's nullification trial in 1456, Manchon testified that when he entered the courtyard 'about 500 Englishmen surrounded them, roughing them up and calling them traitors, saying that they behaved badly during the trial. Only with great difficulty and fear were they able to escape.' The Dominican priest Martin Ladvenu testified that in Joan's final confession (on the morning of her execution), she said she had been violently assaulted by an English nobleman who attempted to rape her during this time.

Of course, no one will ever really know what happened in the tower over the course of those three days, but we do know that Joan—wearing nothing but a dress, chained up and guarded by five English-sympathizing guards, with no clergymen in attendance—was completely vulnerable; anyone who wanted to rape her could have. Which leaves us with the final question: If Joan was in fact raped in prison, why would she not just have admitted as much to Ladvenu? Here, we must remember two things: The first is her fierce and enormous pride—a pride which would undoubtedly have made an admission of rape seem like an admission of defeat. The second is the great importance that Joan had placed on her virginity (she called herself 'the Maid,' after all) and how inextricably the notion of her virginity was bound up with her sense of specialness and mystical power and self. If the Maid was no longer a maid, then who was she?

As her admirer, I can only offer my humble opinion that, virgin or not, she remains the most extraordinary woman who ever lived.

ACKNOWLEDGMENTS

More books have been written about Joan of Arc than any other woman in history, and I have plundered many, many of them for information and inspiration, but I am particularly indebted to Willard Trask's compilation and translation of testimonies from Joan's condemnation trials, *Joan of Arc: In Her Own Words*; to Larissa Juliet Taylor's biography, *The Virgin Warrior*; and to Vita Sackville-West's biography, *Saint Joan of Arc*. Other books that were helpful or invaluable were: *Joan of Arc: Her Story* by Régine Pernoud and Marie-Véronique Clin, revised and translated by Jeremy duQuesnay Adams; *Joan of Arc* by Régine Pernoud; *The Varieties of Religious Experience* by William James; *The Interior Castle* by St. Teresa of Avila; *The Structures of Everyday Life* by Fernand Braudel; *Life in a Medieval Castle* by Joseph and Frances Gies; *A World Lit Only By Fire* by William Manchester; *A Distant Mirror* by Barbara W. Tuchman; *The Medieval Village* by G. G. Coulton; *Medieval Civilization, 400–1500* by Jacques Le Goff; *Ramon Lull's Book of Knighthood and Chivalry*, translated by William Caxton, rendered into modern English by Brian R. Price; *Chivalry* by Maurice Keen; *The Hundred Years War* by Desmond Seward; *War Is a Force That Gives Us Meaning* by Chris Hedges; *Dispatches* by Michael Herr; *War in the Middle Ages* by Philippe Contamine; *The Art of War in the Middle Ages* by C. W. C. Oman; *Blood Red, Sister Rose* by Thomas Keneally; *The Life of Joan of Arc* by Anatole

France; *Saint Joan* by George Bernard Shaw; *A Brotherhood of Tyrants: Manic Depression and Absolute Power* by D. Jablow Hershman and Julian Lieb, M.D.; *An Unquiet Mind* by Kay Redfield Jamison; and *The Black Baron: The Strange Life of Gilles de Rais* by Tennille Dix. I am grateful to the following websites: Saint Joan of Arc Center (www.stjoan-center.com), International Joan of Arc Society (www.smu.edu/ijas/), Joan of Arc—Maid of Heaven: All About Joan of Arc (www.maidofheaven.com), myArmoury.com: A Resource for Historic Arms and Armour Collectors (www.myarmoury.com), Catholic Online (www.catholic.org), The Original Catholic Encyclopedia (oce.catholic.com), and Wikipedia (www.wikipedia.org). I also owe a great debt of gratitude to Carl Theodor Dreyer's magnificent film *The Passion of Joan of Arc* and to Andrei Tarkovsky's awe-inspiring *Andrei Rublev*, which emboldened me to begin this journey, and kept me swimming when there was no land in sight.

I want to thank Neil Ryan and Phebe Thorne for their enormous generosity in providing me with the haven of Canfield Island, where I finished this book. I'm also grateful to Cathy Baptista and everybody at the Narraganssett Inn on Block Island, along with Joe and Liza Szarejko at the Getaway by The Falls, in Woodstock, New York, for providing me with magical, affordable places to hole up along the way. Celerie Kemble and Boykin Curry, Elizabeth and William Stewart, and Amanda and Christo Brooks saved the day by so generously opening their homes to me when the money ran out!

Profound thanks to the amazing Eric Simonoff,

who believed in this project when it was just a glimmer in my eye, and helped me bring it to life in ways both tiny and enormous. Thank you, Eric. Similarly, I want to thank my brilliant editors, Andrea Schulz at Houghton Mifflin Harcourt, and Helen Garnons-Williams at Bloomsbury UK; their patience, faith, and insight continue to be a source of wonder to me. I'm indebted to Jim Leonard, Mark Jarman, and Deborah Eisenberg, who've inspired and encouraged me as a writer since the beginning. Mark Gimein, John Stephens, and Lorin Stein gave me the great gift of reading various drafts of this book at crucial junctures, and showing me how to make it better. Robin Bellinger made the book leaner, stronger, and clearer. David Hough was the best copyeditor and fact-checker anyone could hope for. Dr. Ilene Reeman kept me sane throughout. Till Osterland created a world in which the seed of this book could germinate and flourish, and supported me in countless ways throughout.

I want to thank Carrie, Christo, Coco, and Zachy Brooks for their boundless love and encouragement. Thanks to my dad and to Little Carrie, for loving this project way back when it was just a tiny spark of an idea, and for their enthusiasm and encouragement throughout. Thanks to AK, Celerie, Fully, Berly, Christina, Alissa, and Nena, my dearest friends, who cheered me on, even when they didn't know what state I was in. And eternal thanks to my beloved Benjamin for supporting and nurturing and discussing and championing every single page of this novel—and for feeding me pasta ai rapini when I did not have the strength to cook, and making me laugh whenever it seemed like the sky was falling.

Most of all, thanks go to Piki and William, my amazing parents, for their incredible love and support throughout. This book would not exist without them.